When I Choose

by

Kathryn Long

This is a work of fiction. Names, characters, places, and incidents are either the product of the author's imagination or are used fictitiously, and any resemblance to actual persons living or dead, business establishments, events, or locales, is entirely coincidental.

When I Choose

COPYRIGHT © 2020 by Kathryn Long

Cover Art by *Rae Monet, Inc. Design*

The Wild Rose Press, Inc.
PO Box 708
Adams Basin, NY 14410-0708
Visit us at www.thewildrosepress.com

Publishing History
First Mainstream General Edition, 2020
Print ISBN 978-1-5092-3030-3
Digital ISBN 978-1-5092-3031-0

Published in the United States of America

"Ha. I'm a long way from thirty. Besides, hooking a guy and landing a marriage are not at the top of my to-do list." Camellia stepped toward the closet. A sudden queasiness rippled through her stomach and she wasn't feeling hungry any longer.

"Oh, I'll agree to a certain extent. Careers are essential for either sex. Gotta make a living, but I hope for marriage and a family someday. Don't you?" Freesia's eyebrows puckered into a frown.

"Maybe." Camellia lifted her bag out of the closet and straightened. She caught the concern on Freesia's face. Pausing for a moment, she fished out her keys. "Of course, I think about those things. I imagine every woman does, but the situation doesn't require a time table. Not nowadays. I do know one thing." She slid her finger playfully along the bridge of Freesia's nose. "If and when I decide to get married, you'll be my maid of honor."

"Nice." Freesia's grin spread from ear to ear. "Maybe I'll be your matron of honor, if I beat you to the altar."

Camellia shrugged. "I could take your words as a challenge, but I won't. Because I don't care. Thirty, forty, or whenever, I'll wait until the time feels right. You'll be wiser to think the same." She squeezed Freesia's shoulder. "Now, I'm off. I have tons of errands to run and things to do at my shop." *My shop.* Those words sounded pleasing. Despite the tragic news of Gloria's death, she grew more confident about her decision, her shop, and her fashion line. The idea was becoming her own possible reality.

Praise for Kathryn Long and...

A DEADLY DEED GROWS:

"An exciting and satisfying read with a cast of memorable characters, an interesting setting, plenty of twists and turns, and all of the loose ends tied up as they should be."

~Cherie Jung, Over My Dead Body
—A Mystery Magazine

~*~

"Kathryn Long pens an emotional mystery with this suspense-filled adventure... If you like your mysteries surrounded with complex emotions, this is the one to read."

~Night Owl Romance Books

Dedication

First, to all the authors of women's fiction
whose stories touch me, ones that evoke emotions
to make me laugh, to cry, and leave me spent.

~~

To my family—
my husband, my son, and my daughters,
who've given me the heart to take this journey.
I love you all.

~~

To my editor and mentor, Leanne Morgena.
We will take this journey together and make *WHEN I
CHOOSE* the best story it can be.
Thank you.

~~

To my partners in all things written,
our creative group of six authors.
We give each other the support, the strength,
and the courage to move forward and never quit,
no matter how discouraged we might become.
You've certainly done that for me.
It's a great ride, ladies!

Chapter 1

My life is over. Camellia Holiday flinched as if tiny shards of glass stabbed her eyes. *My. Life. Is. Over.* If she repeated these words into the next millennium, who'd care? In truth, no one gave a crap. Not the media. Not the gossipmongers. Surely, not the competition. They all wanted one thing—a piece of her spirit. Vultures pecking at her body left her shredded and torn.

"Miss Holiday? Miss Holiday? How do you respond to the recent allegations? Did you help Gloria V steal those designs from Eva Stine, Calvin's latest haute couture phenom?"

She had taken a detour through side alleys to get home. Gray fog with the drizzle of rain drenched the New York skyline. Most transients hailed taxis or traveled the subway on such a day, but not Camellia. Unfortunately, avoiding media hadn't worked. The reporter cornered her outside her apartment entrance. Since yesterday's explosion on social media and the evening news report on *Fashion Nightly*, her phone hadn't stopped ringing. She cringed at the slightest noise and chewed her nails to the nub. Nothing gave her peace. A gust of wind rearranged her shoulder-length mane. She yanked at one stray curl and tucked it behind her ear. A smile forced its way through gritted teeth. "I have nothing to say. Why don't you ask Gloria? I'm

1

sure she has plenty of comments to dish."

With one swift move, she orchestrated a slight shove to the reporter's shoulder as she pivoted on her heel to face the building. After jamming her key into the lock, she stepped inside and leaned against the closed door. Relief rushed throughout her. Fewer than twenty-four hours had passed. Crying throughout the night left her empty and exhausted until she became a puddle of emotion. How could her life go so wrong? New York City was a fashion designer's dream, but her dream had been shot to pieces in one brief moment. Even worse, she was only twenty-two.

Vibration resonated through her bag, and Camellia ignored it. Hiking her skirt, she sprinted up the stairs then into her apartment. "Damn you, Gloria. Damn you to hell." She muttered the words before dropping her bag and coat onto the sofa. The buzzing resumed. "Oh, for the love of Pete." She snatched the bag and rummaged through it to retrieve the phone. With a scowl in place, she geared up to lash out at whoever wanted another shot at her. A quick glance at the screen dissolved the agitation swelling inside. With a quick finger swipe, she brought the phone to her ear. "Hey, Squirt."

"Cammie! Sweet sister of mine. What have you been up to?"

"As you've probably heard, nothing good. How are you, Sia?" Camellia warmed to hear the familiar southern drawl, even if the person who possessed it was, at times, one mean hellcat. She pictured her youngest sister with her unruly red hair and freckled skin. Her forehead would scrunch together in a roll of wrinkles while she concentrated on how to rescue

Camellia. Despite the depressing reality of her situation, Freesia remained her cheerleader and lifted her spirits.

"Oh, I've been my usual self, full of spit and vinegar, as you might imagine." Freesia laughed.

Camellia smiled hearing the rich and robust sound as she played with the fringe of her sweater. "I guess you've heard the rumors about my scandalous behavior?"

"Rubbish. All of it. All the gazillion comments are pure hogwash. What do those people from *Fashion Nightly* think they're doing by spreading such rumors? Why, if I were you, I'd hire the best lawyer and sue their asses for slander."

Camellia snorted. "You would. But I'm not you. Gloria won't stand up for me. She's the sort to take me down with her. We'll both be ruined. The only difference is she's got a fat bank account. And mine? Oh, let me think. Last bank statement showed I'm up to three hundred dollars and some change. Barely pays my monthly utilities in this place." The reality truly hit her. She settled on the sofa and dropped her chin.

"Come home, then."

Freesia's voice softened, and Camellia's heart ached. "Home? Yeah, great idea. Come running home with my tail between my legs, ashamed and defeated. Doesn't get much better." She quipped through the tears as she sank deeper in the sofa.

"Cam. Sweetie, don't cry."

"I'm not crying." Camellia hiccupped. Her chest tightened as worry enveloped her.

"Yes, you are. That hiccup proves it. Besides, I need you. Dahlia and Zinnie need you. We sisters are a team and should stay together. Before you argue, let me finish. Your dream has always been New York and a shiny fashion career, but you can create your designs from any place. Right? Why not in Serenity?"

Camellia remained quiet. Serenity. Home. The tiny barrier island off the South Carolina coast was a safe distance from the trend makers and moguls of the fashion industry. Since yesterday, she'd played out the scenario in her head many times. *Safe*. As if the word left a sour taste on her tongue, she wrinkled her nose. "Sia, coming home does sound tempting, but running away from my problems isn't the answer."

"Oh, hell. It's not running away. You're taking a break to rest up and regenerate. Simple, right? Remember when I returned home from California?"

A smile curved her lips. "You were a total mess. But with the sisters' help, we pulled you out of the rut."

"Exactly. So, come home. We want you with us. I speak for Dahlia and Zinnie, too."

Camellia glanced around the apartment with the slick, modern décor. She'd worked so hard to find the perfect details, like the Picasso print hanging above the fireplace mantel. She'd spent a month's salary on it. Moisture blurred her eyes, and she squeezed them shut. Her lease wasn't up until September, but she knew someone who'd love to sublease. Admittedly, the mechanics of packing up and returning to Serenity was the easy part. If only her emotions cooperated, as well. "I'll think about it. Besides, I'd need time to arrange things here, if I do leave."

"Good. Look, I have to get moving. I have an early shift at the club and rehearsal with the band afterward. Stay strong, big sister."

In silence, Camellia stared at the phone. No place was far enough away to erase the mess she'd fallen into. By the end of the week, the European and Asian fashion news circuits would broadcast the scandal. She had to face the truth. Her career as a designer was over.

Gloria V had her team of lawyers, but Camellia doubted even they could save her boss from this debacle. The fashion grapevine echoed every salacious detail. Eva Stine possessed physical evidence—evidence enough to brand Gloria and her company with the words "thief" and "fraud" written in scarlet letters across her chest. Gloria was finished. So were Camellia and Emily, her apprentices. Camellia propped her legs on the coffee table. Emily came from a well-respected and rich Boston family. She'd find another way to survive, thank goodness.

"Could life suck any worse?" Camellia groaned and hugged the sofa cushion. *Come home.* Freesia's words echoed in her head.

For distraction, she switched on the television. Romantic comedies always lifted her mood. Images blurred on the screen as she clicked the remote button with rapid staccato punches. In a few seconds, she paused and registered the identity of a particular photo, her photo. The smiling face mocked her and churned her insides. The remote dropped to the floor, landing with a thud.

"Fashion icon Gloria V has been charged with forgery and theft. Her assistants, Camellia Holiday and Emily Van Louver, have yet to be included in these accusations. At present, Gloria V isn't talking. Her lawyers will issue a statement tomorrow morning."

Camellia nearly missed the reporter's words. Her

photo displayed on the screen paralyzed every one of her senses. Now, people had a face to go along with the name. She was toast. In the next second, she grabbed it and pressed the numbers. "Hello, Em. How are you holding up?"

"It's unbelievable. The nerve of that woman. Just wait. You'll be getting the call next, asking when you can come into the shop and help pack the merchandise. That total self-serving, spoiled bitch thinks she's entitled. How can such a creature always manage?"

Camellia gripped the phone. "Manage what?"

"To fall into shit and come up smelling like roses?" Emily laughed until she snorted.

"Are you having a mental breakdown, Em?" Here, Camellia believed she was the one who'd crumble and fall apart.

"No, of course not. As hard as I try, I can't see the humor in the situation, sad as it seems. I'll be fine. The family is giving me a loan, and my dad has called in a huge favor, which most likely will turn into a job opportunity. It's not fashion but a magazine about fashion. Ironic, right? Anyway, I figure my second-best choice for a career will do." Emily's voice trailed off.

Before she blurted out her question, Camellia bit down on her lower lip. "Would you still want my apartment? My lease doesn't expire until September, but I'm sure the landlord won't mind subletting it, especially if you stay longer." Her mouth dried. She honestly considered packing up and leaving New York for good. The decision took all of five minutes. What did her grandmother used to say? Hasty climbers have sudden falls. "Of course, if you aren't interested any longer…"

"No. I mean, I love your apartment. You know how much I do. Plus, I'd bet your rent is cheaper than mine, which is a bonus."

The plan was set in motion. Camellia's stomach flip-flopped. "Great. It's settled."

"Wait. Where are you going?" Emily asked.

"Home. I'm heading home to Serenity," Camellia announced, her tone subdued. She prayed the decision was the right one.

****

Camellia stifled a yawn and shifted in her seat. She was exhausted after driving for hours. Slowly, she turned onto the causeway. The trailer tires thudded as the car traveled over the speedbump. She winced. Her belongings rumbled in a thump-thump as they shifted. Only one more mile remained, and she'd land in the heart of Serenity. Home.

Despite all her objections to Freesia and to herself, Camellia welcomed the soothing calm sweeping over her when saying the word *home* and picturing images of their house on Rosewood Lane, the pier, the shops along Divinity Boulevard, and the ocean. She powered down the window and took a deep breath, drowning her senses with the fresh smell of salt air. Along the shoreline, she spotted sea oats waving pale white fronds in the breeze and specks of pinkish coral gaillardia flowers sprouting in the sand.

Home. Nearly two years had passed since she'd taken off on her adventure in the Big Apple without a single backward glance at her life in Serenity. A heavy weight settled on her heart as she recalled the moment that filled her with adrenaline, hope, and excitement. Now, the dream had all but vanished. Other emotions took their place. The blow to her self-esteem upended her.

As the car and trailer cleared the causeway, the green welcome sign came into view. Turquoise letters with a curly cue font announced, "Welcome to Serenity—population small but growing." Camellia released a tiny chuckle. No one bothered to count or question the latest tally until a new face showed up in town.

Of course, since the barrier island was one of the few accessible by car, plenty of tourists flocked to Serenity. Locals recognized them in one glance: the clothes, the cameras, the constant lathering with sunscreen, and kids yelling and arguing over their choices to swim in the ocean or visit Serenity's wildlife marina. Those signs said it all.

But a new resident set down roots, maybe opened his or her own business, rented, or purchased a house. By the end of the first week, everyone knew. Friendly residents delivered welcome-to-Serenity gifts along with conversation and coffee to learn all about the newcomer. The downside was everybody knew everybody. No chance to hide any details about one's life, personal or otherwise. New York was to the other extreme. After moving there, Camellia found anonymity a relief. Ironically, the monstrous city found another way to devour her, scandal and all.

Camellia passed by the boat dock, Sunset Bay, and the assigned slip with the family vessel floating in the water. *Lady Serenity* wasn't much bigger than a dingy, but it handled the ocean waves, as long as the winds didn't kick into a stormy gust. A sudden spark of excitement lifted her spirits. Recently, she'd been missing that feeling. Her mind filled with a to-do list—cruising around the barrier, maybe a visit to Dolphin Island, lunching on fresh crab at Emile's—all those things she hadn't done since her last visit more than a year ago.

She glanced out at the wide expansive view of ocean water. Her gaze settled to the far right and a spot on the shore. In a frenzied windmill motion, someone standing on the boardwalk waved his arms. Camellia slowed her car and squinted to make out details. In the next second, she stuck a hand out of the window and waved back at Ben Walters, owner of Catch of the Day, a seafood business. Her sisters must've announced her homecoming, maybe only to a couple people, but a couple was all it took. She'd bet her last nickel before pulling into the drive on Rosewood Lane most of Serenity would know Camellia Holiday was home. The lump grew and lodged in her throat. Good or bad, she couldn't turn back.

****

"*Eeee*! I'm so happy to see my big sis." Freesia clapped while jumping up and down. A few seconds later, she settled both feet on the floor. "Where are my manners? Give me those." She snatched the luggage from Camellia's hands then hollered over her shoulder. "Dahlia, Zinnie! Come down here. *Now*. Cam is home."

Camellia chuckled and shook her head. "I'm relieved to see you haven't changed any, Sia. Enthusiastic and determined." She leaned in to give her a squeeze.

The surroundings of home prompted a mix of emotions. The flavorful scents of food cooking wafted through the air, and family portraits decorated the foyer and hall. Those captured moments of childhood brought tears to her eyes. She quickly swiped them away.

"How about you tell our big sister?" Freesia whispered with an eyebrow wiggle.

"Still on her bad side, huh?"

"Let's just say when Dahlia gets the look on her face, you know the one where her unibrow forms and her lips curl? Well, that look is for me and me alone. I want to crawl under the bed or slink out the back door before she throws a lecture my way." Freesia sighed and set the luggage by the bottom step.

Camellia relaxed and squeezed her hand. "You've got me. I'm here, now. Please don't worry." She filled with warmth as Freesia brightened the room with her smile.

"You always come to my defense. One of the many things I love about you." She twisted to face the stairs. "Dahlia! Zinnie! What in all the heavens is taking you so long?"

The thump and plop of feet thundering down the steps brought Dahlia and Zinnia into view. She bit down on her lip to keep the tears from returning. Wise decision or not, at this moment she felt better than she had in months. In an instant, the sisters were teamed together in a tangle of hugs.

"About time you returned home. We've missed you." Zinnia choked on her words as she wiped her eyes with a hanky and dabbed at the sweat on her ample cheeks and neck.

Camellia tugged on one of Zinnia's thick blonde curls. "I love what you're doing with your hair. And those eyes of yours. Are you wearing contacts? No? Lord. Could they be any greener? You look absolutely gorgeous." Zinnia had put on a few more pounds since they'd last seen each other, which, Camellia suspected, meant she'd been sampling more of her bake goods than normal. No doubt, she'd be trying diet number one-hundred-and-something.

She tipped her chin and sniffed. "Is that brisket I smell? I swear, eating one of your meals has been on my mind for too long."

Zinnia chuckled. "I made it especially for you."

Dahlia leaned closer to give Camellia a brief hug. "I see you're in one piece, at least. Welcome home."

Camellia shrugged. "Takes more than an earth-shattering scandal to destroy a Holiday sister, right?"

"Uh, huh. If you say so." Zinnia flipped her hand. "Those New York types sure know how to sharpen their fangs and attack. Truth is, from the stories you've shared, I never trusted Gloria Vulture. She's the worst."

Despite the tightness in her chest and stomach upsetting her, Camellia laughed. "Gloria V isn't much of a lady, true enough. But vulture might be overstating her abilities. I imagine she won't fight her way out of this one."

Crossing her arms, Dahlia stepped back. Her gaze narrowed as she studied Camellia. "How about you?"

Camellia tensed and shifted her feet. "Meaning?" Her experience with Dahlia left no doubt as to what she implied. All of them were aware.

Freesia targeted Dahlia with a cool gaze. "No need to go there."

"Well, don't you think we should ask?" Dahlia straightened her shoulders. "Clear the questionable air?"

"Fine. She's right." Camellia waved an arm. "No,

Dahlia. I didn't have anything to do with whatever unscrupulous action my boss dug her claws into this time. However, guilt by association is obviously as damaging." She sighed. "New York and I are no longer on the same team."

Silence took over the room. Zinnia shuffled her feet while Freesia tapped fingers against one thigh.

With a sudden grin, Freesia then tilted her head. "Oh, who cares? Right? You can start over, here in Serenity. We don't need those snobby New York fashion people to say what your designs can do for themselves."

Camellia clenched her fists. She didn't blink or break away from Dahlia's judgmental scowl. Two years away gave her a stronger sense of independence. She didn't miss Dahlia's motherly attitude, nor would she cower.

"We can start tomorrow. I know the perfect place you can rent. Bobby McCree took his business to Norfolk and partnered with his cousin. Cam, it's the right size to showcase your designs, with a big picture window and plenty of room for a desk." Freesia shifted her gaze from one sister and back to the other. "Oh, for Saint Christopher's sake. Would you two stop? I swear. What's the point of this staring contest? Cam says she had nothing to do with the mess her boss created. Let it go, Dahlia."

Camellia shrugged and switched her focus to Freesia. "No matter. Maybe I'll give the realtor a call first thing in the morning. Thanks, Squirt." She gently pinched Freesia's cheek.

"Since that issue is settled, how about lunch? I think the oven timer buzzed a few seconds ago." Zinnia hurried down the hall to the kitchen, leaving the others to follow.

"Good. I'm starved. Seems forever since breakfast." Camellia wrapped an arm around Freesia's shoulders and pulled her close as they walked down the hall. A moment later, the patter of Dahlia's footsteps caught up to them.

"She's been a grump all week," Freesia whispered in Camellia's ear. "I think the August bash for the mayor gives her a tizzy fit. *Huge* event, you know. She's worried because too many things are going wrong."

"I can hear you." Dahlia stepped closer. "I'm sorry, Cam. I *am* glad you're home. How you ever managed to put up with Gloria for two years is beyond me."

"She wasn't always this bad." Camellia pulled out a chair to sit at the table along with the others while Zinnia set plates of brisket and glasses of sweet tea in front of them. "I noticed the change a few months back. She'd become irritable, short-tempered, and clumsy."

"Odd combination to throw clumsy into the mix." Dahlia sipped from her glass of tea.

"I'm talking about clumsy designs, like a five-year-old child created them. After several efforts bombed, she stopped altogether. She'd sit and stare at the artist pad for hours without once putting pencil to paper." Camellia shook her head as she bit into a tender morsel of brisket. The warm aroma of garlic potatoes and buttered beans teased her senses and her appetite. "The work she created last year with those designs was impeccable. Then months of nothing until several weeks ago. As if overnight, she transformed, like the old Gloria awoke. She turned out one design after another. Emily and I agreed. Her transformation was a miracle, if you believe in that sort of thing."

"You never once suspected something was odd about the situation?" Zinnia shoved a generous bite of brisket into her mouth.

"Honestly, no. Call it my naïve respect and admiration for Gloria, but I wasn't alone. She had a reputation as a true goddess of fashion and one of the top designers in the world. Someone like her didn't need to steal another's designs. Or at least it's what I believed." Camellia's voice trailed off into silence. She stared at her half-eaten meal and suddenly grew queasy at the scent of garlic. With one finger, she slid the plate out of reach before glancing up. "A real sucker, aren't I?"

Dahlia slid her hand across the table and folded her fingers over Camellia's wrist. "Nothing wrong with having faith in people. The world would be far better, if more trust and less cynicism existed. However, when you see the signs, you can't ignore them."

"She displayed no signs. At least, none I noticed," Camellia argued. After spending so much time with her, she should have seen something, but Gloria was stoic and hard to read. She grabbed her glass and gulped down the sweet tea.

Dahlia withdrew her hand. "How about the upsurge in designs? Did you ask her about them?"

"No one questioned Gloria V. Not in my world." She dropped her chin. "My former world, that is."

"Well, I'd have suspected something fishy." Water trickled from the spigot as Dahlia rinsed off her plate.

"Only because you are the skeptic of the family," Freesia retorted with a wink.

"Arguing about signs and whether I could've noticed them doesn't matter." Camellia pushed away from the table and stood. "I strongly believe she's about to go down in flames. No place left for me in New York. Not anymore. You know, I'm exhausted from the drive down here. I think I'll lie down for a bit."

"Of course. If you want to freshen up, I hung fresh towels in the bathroom." Zinnia turned. "Sia, why don't you help Cam with her luggage? Dahlia and I will bring in whatever's left in the car. We can unpack the trailer later this evening."

Camellia curved an eyebrow upward. Zinnia taking charge was a new and refreshing twist. Dahlia needed someone besides Freesia to put her authoritative manner in check once in a while. "Thank you. I'm sure I won't need much rest. Plenty of time for me to help you prepare supper."

Zinnia patted her shoulder. "Poppycock. You've been through enough today."

Camellia grinned at Zinnia's choice of words but gave her head a firm shake. "I need to keep busy. Busy is a good thing." Within minutes, Camellia was in her old bedroom, alone. She sat on the edge of the bed, her arms braced behind her while she leaned back and stared around. The cheery, bluish green wallpaper with the seashell design still remained. In fact, everything appeared the same, right down to the tiniest details. Her watercolors of the ocean hung on the wall, next to the fashion images of her idols, including Gloria V.

She scowled at her mentor's design. The bitter taste of betrayal curdled in her throat. In the next second, she sprang off the bed and crossed the room. She snatched the picture frame off the wall and tossed it into the wastebasket. The gesture didn't help much, but the bitter taste was gone.

A strong breeze fluttered the curtain and blew it inward to tickle her arm. She stepped to the window and peered out. Buds burst on the loblolly shrubs, and the Yaupon evergreens topped twelve feet high. Camellia smiled. Years ago, their mother planted the Yaupons near the border of the property and often warned her daughters to never eat the toxic red berries. However, she insisted the Yaupon leaves were for the Cherokee Indians, in case they needed to make the "Black Drink" for their purification ceremonies. One of the many tales she shared at night, and quite a departure from the standard fairytale or bedtime story.

Camellia crossed her arms and swayed back and forth as a convoluted mix of relief, fear, and happiness filled her with emotion. Closing her eyes, she listened to the whoosh of leaves blowing in the wind, and far off, the faint ring of a bell buoy echoed across the ocean water. Home. If only home didn't include Noah. Suddenly feeling hot, she threw back the covers. The last time they were together brought her nothing but sadness and hurt. Why expect this time to be any different? Yes, Noah could be trouble if she didn't keep him out of her life.

Chapter 2

"You should let her sleep. She must be exhausted," Zinnia whispered.

"Too much sleep leaves the door open to depression." Dahlia tugged at the bedcover.

Camellia's eyes popped open before she smacked away her sister's hand. "Aren't you overreacting a bit? I swear, Dahlia. Your constant worry and concern will give you ulcers."

"Someone has to do the worrying in this family. Otherwise, everything we've built will go from sugar to shit." The bedcover and sheets snapped as Dahlia gave them a final pull. "Supper will be on the table shortly. You have time enough to wash up. See you in fifteen."

Camellia waited until Dahlia disappeared from the room. "What's gotten into her? Seriously, Zinnie, she's more than a little stressed."

Zinnia twisted the apron in her hands. "Maybe family issues are worse than you realize. More than Sia realizes."

"Oh, lord." Camellia sank her head into the pillow for a moment, and she stared up at the ceiling. Her mind mulled over a dozen questions. She lifted her head and steadied her gaze on Zinnia. "Tell me. Is Holiday Events and Catering going under?"

"Not yet." Zinnia sat next to her. She dropped her shoulders and wagged her head. "But I won't lie. We're getting there. We lost two major accounts last month. They were regulars who'd host three or four parties a year. Such good money, too."

Camellia dropped her jaw. "Where'd they go? Or did they have their fill of cake and fun?"

"Sad to say, a major chain opened a new party planning branch in Claysville. Too close for competition if you think about it. They have a great deal more to offer than we do, and at a cheaper cost." Zinnia sighed. "Going under is only a matter of time."

"Like hell it is."

Camellia gasped and sat up.

Freesia stood in the doorway with her fists resting on either hip.

Camellia's brow raised. "Then what's your plan to save the day? Hmm?"

The expression on Freesia's face was comical, like a chipmunk with her cheeks puffed out. Within seconds, Camellia threw back her head to laugh and couldn't stop. Tears welled up and spilled onto her cheeks. Her emotions had been wound so tightly the past couple days. A belly laugh was the release she needed. Taking a deep breath, she calmed herself.

Freesia screwed up her face. "I don't see what's funny. I can think of something. Give me a day or two."

"Or three, maybe four." Camellia bit down on her lower lip.

"Or dozens more." Zinnia giggled.

"Enough. Stop, you two. I'm dead serious. If what Zinnie says is true, we need to put our brains together and figure out a plan."

"Oh, now it's *we* instead of *you*. Slick move, right, Zinnie?" Camellia jabbed her in the side and winked.

"Yeah, why should *we* help? *You* had the plan all figured out." Zinnia smiled.

"Oh, for…" Freesia grabbed a throw pillow off the chair and pitched it at them. "I'm done talking. Dahlia sent me up to tell Zinnie the oven timer buzzed." She spun on her heel and marched out of the bedroom.

Camellia shrugged. "You think we laid it on a bit too thick?"

"Nah." Zinnia waited a second before wobbling her hand back and forth, and then grinned. "Maybe a little much, but she'll be fine. How about we get some of my chicken pot pie? I'm starving."

They raced to see who'd get through the bedroom doorway first. The childish behavior reminded her of old times. Camellia squealed as she slipped past Zinnia and raced down the stairs. As soon as she entered the kitchen, she skidded to halt. Her breath hitched before she drew in a huge gulp of air.

"Hey there, Cam. Been a while."

"Noah. How've you been?" Camellia stepped to the counter and grabbed a plate. She scooped up a generous portion of pot pie and plopped it on the dish. Not trusting her reaction, she kept her gaze downcast, refusing to look at him. He stuffed both hands in his pockets and leaned against the wall. "Oh, I've kept busy."

Camellia nodded and took a seat. The silence soon became uncomfortable, which was worse than making conversation.

"I called Noah and invited him over. Figured seeing an old friend might be a nice surprise." Freesia stumbled over her explanation and ended with a wavering smile.

Old beau, you mean. Camellia stabbed her fork into the pot pie. "Well, I'm certainly surprised." She gave Freesia a scowl and filled her mouth with a bite of food to stop any harsh words from escaping.

Noah grabbed a chair next to Camellia. "You seem well, considering."

His expression was full of innocence. Camellia stopped chewing as she digested the comment slowly, one word at a time. Without thinking, she gulped down a large bite of chicken and gagged as it caught in her throat. She grabbed for her water glass and guzzled the contents. "Considering? Considering what?"

Noah drew back. He shifted his gaze to Freesia and back again to Camellia. "I meant... Well, you've had such a rough few days and all."

"How did you know about my rough few days?" Camellia face-palmed Freesia when she opened her mouth to speak.

"Why, the story was on the evening news. I imagine everyone who watches television or listens to the radio knows about the Gloria V scandal."

"Don't forget the newspaper." Zinnia added the words.

Camellia shot her a nasty glare. "I see." She stood and traveled to the cupboard. "Do we have any bourbon in the house?" Her career was tarnished by one catastrophic failure, which was bad enough. Noah, her ex fiancé, standing here to point it out, only made her more miserable and embarrassed.

"Cam, do you think drinking is wise to—Oh, okay. Never mind." Freesia covered her mouth.

Dahlia set a glass on the counter and the bottle next to it. "Here. Take the whole bottle. Perfect answer to your problems, right? Drown them in booze. Make them all go away. All you'll have is a retched hangover in the morning." She crossed her arms. Her mouth formed a rigid line.

Camellia ignored the judgmental comment and poured her glass half full. She took a sip, and then twisted around to lean her back against the counter and face Noah. "Seems you know all about me, but I know so little about what's going on in your life these days. Doesn't seem quite fair, does it?"

Noah cleared his throat. "I guess you're right. I've opened up another store since last year. Down in Wilmington. Everybody needs bath fixtures, so business is good. Dad was proud to receive the Businessmen of America award last month. Had a nice ceremony for him in Raleigh. Yeah…some year." He lowered his head and stared at his shoes.

Camellia tipped her glass and finished the brandy. The burn in her stomach warmed more than her body. Her temper fumed. "Must be nice. Standing in my kitchen, serving up pity for poor me in my miserable state of affairs."

"Cam," Dahlia murmured while grabbing for her hand.

Camellia waved her away. "But you know what, Noah Burke? I don't give a shit. So, get the hell out. God's honest truth, I can't stand the sight of your smug and righteous face."

"Camellia Ann Holiday, you apologize this instant. Dishing out rude behavior is certainly not how we treat a guest," Dahlia snapped.

"He's not my guest. I didn't invite him." Once again, she glared at Freesia. "Thanks, but no thanks."

With long strides she moved to the back door and escaped outside. She braced herself against the wall and sank to her knees. Her shoulders heaved as she sobbed. Whatever gave Freesia the idea she'd want to see Noah? He was the one serious relationship she'd had. In fact, they'd come close to making it permanent, very close. At least before she became the classic runaway.

Her rash behavior wasn't entirely her fault. He claimed he was meeting a business associate. Yet, one meeting grew to several times a week for months. On business. Sure. For good reason, Camellia never found trust an easy companion. When she spotted Noah and a very attractive woman through the window having lunch at Serenity's Cozy Eatery, she crumbled. Insecurity wormed its way inside, leaving her to doubt every word Noah spoke and every action he took.

The woman turned out to be Trina Averaux, one of the most conniving, manipulative human beings Camellia had ever known. Competitive enough to cross the line of ethical behavior. Of course, she knew her well. They'd been college roommates. Fate played a hand and an unfair one. She failed to let the issue go, so she let Noah go.

Noah coming here to remind her of all those feelings and memories when she was so vulnerable wasn't fair. But how could she blame Freesia? Camellia never told her what really happened. She'd never told anyone. Her story was much more innocent; she and Noah decided the time wasn't right to make such a commitment. Surprisingly, Noah played along with the story. Maybe he loved her enough to keep quiet. Or maybe he was glad to get rid of her and didn't care what story she concocted.

In any case, a month later, she'd headed for New York to pursue her dream. Looking back, she questioned whether leaving town honestly was her dream or an excuse to run away. Her action from the past no longer mattered. The dream, fake or real, was gone. The idea of starting over, even in Serenity, exhausted her.

Her legs cramped, and Camellia slowly rose to stand. She approached the rear property line to stretch. A strong breeze swayed the branches of the Yaupons. She fingered the leathery, dark green leaves of the nearest tree. Berries peppered the evergreen with specs of deep red, while blossoms lay on the ground, announcing spring was over and summer arrived.

The change of seasons reminded Camellia she had time. Each day brought new promises. She'd move past this roadblock in her life and not dwell on mistakes, mistakes like Noah Burke. Trina Averaux could have him, sorry asshole that he was. Someone much better was out there for her. With a prayer and a promise, she might find him someday. She gave her chin a firm nod before pivoting on her heel. With deliberate, long strides, she marched back to the house.

"Nobody or nothing puts down a Holiday sister. That's a promise *I* will keep." Cam forced a smile, shook her shoulders, and threw open the kitchen door. "What's for dessert?"

****

"I swear, you must be possessed. Or...does schizophrenia run in our family?" Freesia's gaze shifted from Camellia to Zinnia.

"Oh, stop. I've heard enough." Camellia smacked Freesia's arm lightly. "Sia, I'm not sick or possessed. I

23

am tired of moping, though. You were right. I can start over, right here in Serenity. While I'm on a roll, thank you for inviting Noah. Your gesture helped."

Freesia scowled. "It did? But I thought… You sure you're not ill? Maybe running a fever? Let me check your forehead." She extended a hand.

Camellia waved it away. "What I mean is seeing Noah reminded me not to live in the past. I won't sink into a depression over bad business already done and over with, especially when I had nothing to do with the Gloria V scandal." *Or the romance collision with Noah.* Camellia threw the towel on the counter and smiled. "Nope. This girl is moving onward and upward."

"Well, thank the heavens." Zinnia sighed and rested her elbows on the counter. "I'll be honest you had me worried."

Camellia ruffled her hair. "Well, not any longer, Zinnie. Now, I could definitely eat another piece of cobbler." She opened the freezer and pulled out a container of ice cream. "A la mode. Even better."

Zinnia and Freesia laughed. Warmth spread through Camellia's heart as she heard the familiar sound—a part of her past she welcomed. Scooping up the huge bowl of cobbler and ice cream, she joined them round the table. According to Freesia, Dahlia remained outside, removing baggage from the trailer and trunk of Camellia's car.

"She walked Noah to the front door, hollered she might as well kill two birds with one stone and fetch your belongings." Freesia took a long sip of sweet tea. "Of course, she invited us to join her."

Camellia nodded. "Yet, here we sit." She scowled at the bowl as she scooped the rest of her dessert. She hardly enjoyed the sweet and tart tastes of fruit and ice cream, and she knew why. "I can't sit here and not help carry in my own luggage."

Sia groaned. "Okay, but I can hear her now. 'You're doing it wrong. Pick up that box and carry it this way. Don't set the suitcase on that table. You don't know what germs that baggage carries. Oh, let me do it myself.' Her rants are so predictable."

Camellia wagged a finger. "Where's your sisterly love? Besides, we can handle a little bossiness. We should at least offer to help." She stood and carried the bowl to the sink.

"She's right, Sia," Zinnia said. "Besides, Dahlia's had a rough day. The poor woman carries too much on her shoulders."

"Why do you take her side? Every single time." Freesia shoved her chair against the table.

"I don't know what you mean." Zinnia's cheeks puffed out. "I take your side and Cam's. I take everyone's side."

Everyone's but your own, Camellia thought. The kitchen rooster clock chimed eight times. "Let's get moving, ladies. Daylight's growing thin." She grasped both her sisters' hands and steered them down the hall to the front.

When they reached the foyer, Camellia sighed. A quick count proved Dahlia had retrieved every package, box, and bag from the car trunk and back seat. "I'm sorry, Dahlia. We should've helped, but we can haul my stuff upstairs to my room. Except for this bag and that one." She pointed twice. "You'll find gifts inside." She grinned, and a warm glow filled her heart. She had missed these three, more than she realized, until this moment. Sisters, her sisters, were like therapy. Their love healed her in ways no one else could.

Freesia squealed, jumping up and down while clapping her hands. "Please tell me the gifts have designer labels from a certain establishment you no longer work for. Or maybe swag from your trip to the Milan fashion show?"

Camellia gave her a double eye roll. "Maybe one or two from Milan. I never dared to take anything from Gloria in the past and especially not now." She cast a vacant stare and a bitter smile surfaced. After clearing her exit plan with the NYC investigators to make sure she wasn't under suspicion, she'd left town. Of course, the man in charge did ask for her cell phone number, her home address, and a promise to notify their office if she moved or traveled elsewhere. She got the picture.

Dahlia handed Camellia her garment bag. She gave each of her sisters a curt smile. "The rest is up to you three. I'm pooped."

Camellia leaned in to smother her with a hug and kiss. "Thanks, Dahlie. I love you."

"Not a problem, but you know better than to call me Dahlie. You all love your nicknames, but I'll keep Dahlia the way it's always been."

"I remember the first school year after we moved here. Do you? I was in sixth grade, Dahlia in ninth. Cam, weren't you in third? Oh, and Squirt had started kindergarten." A glaze covered Zinnia's unblinking expression.

"Yeah, the pernicious Miss Pearl. An evil sourpuss who despised me." Freesia snorted.

"Only because you told the class our mom was a witch who grew herbs and flowers to make potions."

Zinnia nudged Camellia in her side and winked.

"I remember. You claimed Mom named us after flowers so we'd have magic powers to battle evil forces." Camellia rubbed a spot of ice cream off of Freesia's blouse. "Oh, Sia. Your imagination has always been priceless."

Freesia huffed. "Well, what did she expect from a five-year-old? We all have wild stories at that age."

Zinnia shook her head and shrugged. "Not me. Always told the truth. How about you Dahlia? Camellia?"

Both shook their heads.

Camellia grinned at the irritation etched across their baby sister's face as she pulled back her shoulders. Freesia meant feisty and brave. Gwen Holiday certainly knew what name to use. Although, how she'd figured out what flower matched each when her babies were days old was a mystery.

"I think we should let Sia off the hook and get these upstairs." Dahlia hefted the nearest bag in her arms.

"I thought you were pooped." Zinnia pressed her lips into a fine line.

"I am, but most of these were easy, like this one. The bag is full of toilet paper. Light as a feather. Why on earth bring toilet paper on your trip, Cam? Afraid the rest stop bathrooms might run out?" Dahlia didn't crack a smile.

Camellia narrowed her eyes. "You're serious? Okay, I had lots to move out of the apartment. Seemed a waste to throw away toilet paper."

"Why didn't you leave it for Emily? Isn't she leasing your place?" Freesia pulled her hair into a

27

ponytail, and then stooped to gather two boxes in her arms.

"The plan fell through. Seems Daddy Van Louver had other ideas and a better offer. Would you believe she's moving to Paris? She landed a job writing articles on fashion for *La Bonne Vue*. A gift from the family and all tied up with a pretty pink bow. Plus, Emily found someone else to sublet my apartment, which is a relief."

"How lucky for you." Zinnia spoke in breathy spurts as she trailed Camellia, lugging a suitcase up the stairs.

"Yeah, and the renter turns out to be Detective Ryan. You know the one who leads the investigation into the Gloria scandal? When he spoke to Emily and heard about the situation, well, one question led to another, and now he's the new tenant," Camellia said.

"No wonder you didn't want to leave anything behind." Freesia set the boxes on the bedroom floor.

"What do you mean?" Camellia puckered her eyebrows.

"Detectives are the biggest snoops." Freesia shrugged. "What if he found something to suggest you're involved with Gloria's crime?"

"Like toilet paper?" Zinnia blinked at Freesia.

A full minute of silence passed while Freesia scowled at each of them.

Steps grew louder, and then Dahlia entered the bedroom. "What's going on? Why are you all so quiet?"

Camellia sat on the bed before she let the air escape her lungs. She laughed until tears blurred her vision.

Zinnia sat next to her and joined in, alternating giggles and snorts.

Meanwhile, Freesia stood with arms crossed and her foot tapping.

"What is this? Pick on Sia day? You know very well what I mean. Of course, not toilet paper. But other things like…" Freesia released a sigh.

Zinnia drew in a long breath to stop her fit of giggles. "Like toothpaste? Or maybe the salt and pepper shakers. Those items are especially incriminating. I hope you remembered to bring them home, too, Cam."

"Oh, absolutely." Camellia nodded and erupted once more.

"You two are certifiable. I'll be back when you can control yourselves." Dahlia pivoted on her heel and marched out of the room.

Camellia leaned close to Zinnia's ear. "She's wound up tighter than an eight-day clock."

Zinnia patted her hand and sighed. "I know. I know." She lifted off the bed and crossed the room. "Time to bring up more boxes of your incriminating evidence."

"Yes, indeed." Camellia sprang to her feet and trotted to the door.

Freesia released a lengthy groan and followed.

Box after box after bag after suitcase cluttered her room. Though she was exhausted, Camellia spent the evening unpacking. With a weary gaze, she stared at several unopened boxes, including one with work-related items. She shoved them all into the closet, too tired to continue.

Instead, she crossed the room and threw open the window. Fresh air and the scent of salt, seaweed, and summer flowers wafted into the room, carried by the evening breeze. She breathed deeply in an attempt to clear her mind. However, fatigue muddled her brain and drowned her spirits. Tomorrow, she might think more clearly, devise a plan, and take action. Tonight, she needed rest and no more thoughts about work or Noah.

Switching on the television, she scanned through the channels searching for some boring program to lull her to sleep. She stopped when Gloria's face covered the screen. Reporters surrounded her on the courthouse steps. Wording at the bottom of the screen included Camellia's and Emily's names, identified as associates of the fallen designer icon.

Camellia mumbled, clicked off the power button, and closed her eyes. "I'm never getting away from this nightmare, am I?"

Chapter 3

"This place is perfect! Right?" Freesia clasped her hands together. A smile stretched across her face. "And I found it."

Camellia chuckled. "Yes, you did, Squirt. If the rent is something I can afford, you're right. This place will be perfect." She eyed the building with the peeling exterior. The owner hadn't kept up with a yearly paint job. Salt water and sunlight had damaged the structure. The weathered surface with its cracks, peels, and bubbles looked an eyesore. Stepping closer, she leaned forward until her nose touched the window. To see inside, she shaded her eyes from the sun. Relief eased her worries. The walls showed bright and shiny, the color of seaweed. The floors were polished and swept clean. Bobby McCree took pride in his business.

Freesia glanced at her watch. "Mr. Samson is late. As usual."

Camellia nodded. Samuel Samson was the town realtor. He'd started late in the business, after he retired as the high school principal. Too much commotion and noise pushed him out, he claimed. Everyone else figured sleeping in late was the real excuse for retiring. No matter. He still arrived late for morning appointments, including this one. "He's only ten minutes overdue. I'm sure he'll be here soon."

While shifting her gaze from one end of the street

to the other, Freesia scowled. "Says the optimist." She rubbed her arms briskly. "Cool air is coming from the north. I bet we're in for stormy weather this afternoon."

Camellia glanced up to study the sky. The wispy feathers of white had thickened and darkened to ominous gray, blocking out the sunlight. At least oppressive New York skyscrapers weren't blocking the view. "Looks like it."

"Oh, good. There he is." Freesia's brow wrinkled. "He has company. Oh boy. What if somebody else is interested in renting? Mr. Samson promised no others had inquired."

"Good morning, ladies." Sam's voice boomed loud enough to hear a block away. "This is my nephew, Weston Murphy. He's come to stay for the summer before heading north. Weston, these are two of the four Holiday sisters, Freesia and Camellia. The family runs a catering and event service. Fine cook, your sister Zinnia. Nobody can top her chicken fricassee. I can attest to it." He patted his generous middle and laughed.

A crooked smile spread across Weston's face. "Freesia, Camellia, Zinnia. I'd bet my last cent the fourth sister is Azalea? Petunia? Gardenia? No?" He laughed.

Camellia frowned and shook her head. "Actually, her name is Dahlia. Our mother is a horticulturist and herbalist. She's infatuated with flowers." She steadied her gaze on Weston Murphy. He was slim but fit, extremely tall, and carried himself well. Thick tufts of blond hair swept across his forehead when the wind gusted. His eyes were a deep, blueish green. He stared, unblinking.

"I suppose each name was chosen carefully,

symbolic meanings and all." His grin widened.

"Well, interesting as this conversation about flowers might be, how about we go inside to take a peek?" Freesia nodded at Sam. "I find the air a bit chilly out here."

"Why, of course. Where are my manners? Weston asked to come along. He's interested in local architecture. He's been traveling through the south, studying the antebellum dwellings up this way and the Spanish colonials in Florida." Sam unlocked the door.

They stepped inside.

Camellia gave one last glance at the exterior walls before following. "I can't imagine this building is exactly an architect's dream."

Weston laughed. "True enough, the structure is not antebellum. However, I can say it has a more interesting background."

Camellia lifted her brows. "Oh? How?" She wiped a finger along the window ledge. No cracked paint or other telltale signs of wear showed on the inside, at least.

"Steven Simms, a nineteenth-century architect, designed many buildings in his home town of Philly. People in South Carolina commissioned him to design plans for a new church. While visiting, he fell in love with the area and built a vacation home on the coast. You're standing in it." Weston smiled, and then tipped his chin toward the ceiling. "Exquisite detail."

Freesia dusted off a chair McCree left behind and sat. "Shouldn't this place be registered and protected as one of those historical sites, then?"

"Most folks wouldn't find the issue that important. Only architect geeks like myself do." Weston traced a hand along the chair railing.

Camellia tore away her attention from Weston and gazed at Samuel Samson. "Hmm. Well, what *we* are interested in is how much the owner wants for monthly rent."

"Yes, of course you are. Let me show you the building owner's offer." Samson pulled a folded document from his pocket and flipped through pages until he tapped a finger on the last one. He smiled. "I think you'll be very pleased." He extended his arm until the paper came into Camellia's view.

Her breath caught. She couldn't touch a studio apartment in Washington Heights for less than fifteen-hundred a month, and she considered that price cheap. "Really? I mean, the rent sounds very reasonable, and—you've got yourself a deal, Mr. Sampson." She blushed with enthusiasm.

"Wonderful. My assistant Agnes will type up a rental agreement to sign, and I'll have it delivered to your home by this afternoon or evening at the latest. You can drop it off the next time you're out my way. Congratulations, Miss Holiday. Here's to a long and prosperous business venture." Samuel shook Camellia's hand.

"Thank you. I hope it will be, too." A hiccup escaped, along with her words. She quickly covered her mouth. "Sorry." Her stomach fluttered. Nerves threatened to destroy all of her enthusiasm.

Freesia flickered a frown, and at once, she grabbed Camellia's arm. "All right, then. Thanks, Mr. Samson. We won't take up any more of your time. Besides, we've got lots to do. Lots and lots. Nice meeting you, Weston." She bobbed her head and rambled on while leading Camellia out the door.

"What's the big hurry?" Camellia yanked away her arm once they landed on the sidewalk.

"You hiccupped, which is what you do when you cry or when you're nervous. You weren't crying, so…" Freesia raised both arms, palms facing up. "I was afraid you'd panic and change your mind and tell him to forget the deal. Seriously, Cam. You let your nerves and insecurity get the best of you." She wagged a finger. "Not a very healthy attitude, if you're making a go of this."

"I'm thinking reasonably. I do want my plan to work, but it has to be right." Camellia hugged her handbag against her waist.

"So predictable. Camellia. The flower of perfection and reason. Mom sure got that part right. I wonder how she always knew."

Camellia smiled. "You mean like Dahlia, meaning someone with strength and values."

"Zinnia, always the loving, affectionate sister believing in the goodness of others." Freesia sighed. "I miss Mom. I know California is far, but I wish she'd come home to visit."

"She and Robert are happily married and still going through their honeymoon stage, I imagine." Camellia's heart warmed, knowing how Gwen had been given this second chance.

"Dad must be very proud of her. Right?" Freesia's eyes glistened. She stepped away from Camellia and wiped a hand across her face.

"Extremely proud. Of all of us." Camellia pulled Freesia close again. "Let's go do some shopping. I have lots to buy if I'm opening a boutique."

They traveled north toward the main retail district. Though smaller than most all the barrier islands nearby, Serenity offered quite a few stores to cover residents' needs—a gas station, grocery store, two clothing shops, drug store, hardware store, bakery and, of course, Holiday Events and Catering to name a few. Camellia's future store was located a block south of the main drag. The upside? Cheaper rent. With an online website, word of mouth, and news fliers posted throughout town, the business should do well.

Freesia stood alongside Camellia at the corner, waiting for traffic to clear. "You'll have to order a desk and chair from Maxine's on the mainland, but I'll bet you can find everything else here in town."

"I need a couple of mannequins for the display window. Maybe I'll make the trip to Charleston. Explore Maxine's and order my purchases from there." Camellia mused over what her place needed and pictured the results. A tingle of excitement lightened her mood. Let her nerves be damned.

Freesia squealed and gripped her sister's arm. "Ooo, I want to come. We can make a day of it. Eat lunch at Salvatori's, and for dessert, we can stop at the park and order ice cream from the vendor."

Camellia laughed. "Of course, we should go to Charleston to eat and forget about the shopping I need to do."

"You know what I mean." Freesia scolded but her smile remained.

They crossed the street and proceeded into the next block until they arrived at Browne's Hardware. Within twenty minutes, Camellia ordered enough supplies to complete all the do-it-yourself projects, which covered the decorative aspects of her store. "Please have everything delivered to this address." She handed a slip of paper to the clerk before she and Freesia left the store.

"Now where?" Freesia glanced farther down the street, and her eyes brightened "I've been dying to visit this new boutique that opened a couple months ago. I hear lots of exciting buzz about it, but I've been avoiding the place. I'm saving my money, you know."

Camellia tilted her head. "Why go, then?"

"Because I need to shop for a new dress." She latched onto Camellia's arm and tugged.

They hurried across the intersection as the light turned amber. Another few hundred yards and Freesia skidded to a stop. Her arm fanned out toward the display window. "A la Chic. Isn't that a gorgeous name?"

A clapboard exterior painted coral gave the building a tropical feel. The flamingo-shaped sign above the door welcomed visitors. Camellia studied the mannequins draped in trendy fashion. She recognized the European couture and gave an appraising nod. "Pretty highbrow for Serenity. Business has been working well for the owner?" She glanced at her sister.

Freesia shrugged. "As good as it gets. I've seen plenty of folks come into the club wearing la Chic's clothing. Fashion editor Ina Perot even toots a horn or two in the weekly gazette about the shop."

"I guess hope exists for me after all." Camellia took a step toward the door. Curiosity about her competition livened her pace. "Let's have a look."

They headed for the cashier's counter.

"I'm anxious to see if the latest shipment of dresses

came in." Freesia tapped the bell. Within seconds, the clip of heels coming from the rear grew loud.

"Good morning, ladies. How can I help you?" The woman froze as she rounded the corner. Her lips creased into a thin line.

"Trina Averaux." Camellia spoke, but her voice was flat. Like receiving a punch to the stomach, she struggled for air. Here was a replay of one more miserable memory from the past. "I'm surprised you still live here. As I recall, you were hellbent on getting out of Serenity and seeking your fame in Paris, or was it London?" She cursed under her breath at the catty side forcing its way to the surface.

Trina smirked while her gaze shifted up and down, giving Camellia the once-over. "Seems to me, as *I* recall, you voiced the same comment. In my case, I actually made a success of my career. You, on other hand…"

Freesia grasped Camellia's wrist and squeezed. "Ladies. Let's call a truce to bickering over old times, shall we? Trina, I hear you've received a new line of dresses recently. I'd love to take a peek. A big party is coming soon, and I want to shine like a star."

"You mean the mayor's gala? Isn't your family business handling the affair? I hear Dahlia is having nothing but troubles getting things organized. Such a shame. Tell her I'd be glad to help out in any way I can. I have a marketing degree, you know." Trina rattled on as she led them toward the rear of the shop.

Camellia scowled at Freesia and spoke under her breath. "You failed to mention Trina is the owner."

Leaning closer, Freesia lowered her voice to whisper. "I didn't think that detail was such a big deal.

Besides, aren't you over your college days' drama? Your school girl tiff with Trina is so yesterday's news."

Camellia cringed but held her tongue. If she only knew. Coming home sure had its downside with unpleasant reunions. First Noah, and now Trina. Could her discomfort get any worse? With Trina, her former dorm room buddy and best friend, the past kept creeping back into the present. Rivalry to win first place in the Charleston Fashion Charity event during their sophomore year, along with Trina's dirty tricks, started the rift and ended the friendship. Fast forward to after graduation, and the cutthroat game continued when her rival took over marketing for such local businesses as Burke Bathroom Fixtures.

A sour taste coated her mouth, being reminded of how the relationship with Noah Burke became more than professional. Though she'd kept the story about Noah and Trina from her sisters, she knew Dahlia was suspicious. Not much remained hidden from her. Still, Dahlia never dared to bring up the topic. That can of ugly worms should stay sealed forever.

"Cam?" Freesia nudged her in the side and tipped her head to where Trina stood waiting.

"These are the latest imports from London." Trina's chin tilted upward and her shoulders straightened. "On this rack, you'll find my designs."

A smirk inched its way across Camellia's face. Proud Trina, flaunting herself, as always. She took deliberate steps over to Trina's creations and flipped through the rack of a dozen or more dresses. She finished within a minute or two. Spinning to face Trina, she smiled. "Very nice. I guess we'll be rivals, once again. Like old times." A smug, satisfying sensation warmed her insides at Trina's frown. "Oh, didn't you hear? I'm opening my own shop down the street. I plan to carry a few things from various designers, including my friends from the New York circuit. But I plan to have most of the shop filled with my own designs as quickly as I can."

Freesia leaned against Camellia's shoulder. "Cam, stop."

Trina wiped a stray curl from her face. "Seems I missed that particular bit of gossip. Or maybe your news is too insignificant for people to talk about." She lifted her chin to stare at Freesia. "Well, I'll leave you to glance over the merchandise. If you have any questions, I'll be up front at the register." Her heels clicked across the floor, faster and louder.

Camellia chuckled before releasing a loud sigh. "Giving her that bit of information felt so good."

"I swear. You're acting childish. What's with you two? I know Noah cheating with her of all people still riles you, but let it go, Cammie. Please." Freesia stuck to the London designer rack and pushed aside dresses until she reached a shimmery, emerald green sleeveless frock. She plucked the hanger off the rod and draped the dress over one arm.

"Okay. Dahlia told you. That's great. Just great. You know, I'm over the past. In fact, I don't give a hoot if you'd like to dig through Trina's designs." Camellia fanned her face with one hand. The heat wasn't the only thing raising her temperature. She scowled at the designer rack. "Although I don't give her much for originality."

Freesia groaned. "Yeah, I can see you're so over your beef with Trina. As for Dahlia, she said nothing. I figured out the story all on my own. Of course, the way your thorns bristle every time Trina's name is mentioned sure helped." She marched off to the dressing room.

"You're one to talk about forgiving and forgetting. You know, I'll wait outside, if you don't mind. Get some fresh air. It's too stuffy in here." Camellia called out, louder than she needed. Taking long strides, she passed by Trina without so much as a brief glance or good-bye.

A crisp breeze filtered through the air, bringing fresh scents of seaweed and salt water. Camellia breathed deeply, several times until she relaxed. Out of habit, she patted her pockets, searching for a pack of cigarettes. She'd quit over six months ago, but old habits didn't fade from her mind as easily. Spotting a bench next to the sidewalk, she crossed over to it and sat, facing away from the shop. The view of the ocean calmed her even more.

Returning to Serenity was like visiting a therapist by digging up old issues and confronting them, possibly resolving her insecurities to make her stronger. Otherwise, moving here might end up like, how did the expression go? Jumping from the frying pan into the fire. Leaning forward, she gripped the edge of the bench. To keep from getting burned required her to build a ton of strength and courage. She figured that much. The question remaining was, could she?

Chapter 4

Camellia checked her watch and sighed. Freesia was known to stretch her time in a dressing room to unreasonable lengths, twirling in front of the mirror to see every angle, primping, pinning up her hair, trying on pumps, and maybe some jewelry—all to get the full effect. But this wait was unbearably long. After another time check, Camellia stood. She spun and took quick steps toward the store, only to bump straight into a pedestrian.

"Oh. I'm sorry." A sudden gust of wind tousled her hair. She brushed away the unruly curls, and then stifled a gasp.

"Why if it isn't one of the flower ladies. Camellia, right?" Weston laughed. His eyes glinted as he gazed at her.

They sparked with intensity, enough to make Camellia squirm. "Mr. Murphy." She backed away.

"Oh, please. Weston sounds much better. Only students call me Mr. Murphy, and my pastor. Never could get on a first-name basis with the man."

"You're a teacher? You told me architect." She struggled to find an answer for her uneasiness. He was friendly, not in a creepy way, but totally natural—like they'd known each other for years.

"Both. I teach a few evening classes in architecture at the university when I can." Weston smacked the envelope he held against his thigh. "I was on my way to your place, but you saved me the trip." He held out the envelope.

"What's this?" Camellia opened the flap to peer inside.

"The rental agreement. I offered to deliver it. Uncle Samuel is a busy man."

"Thanks." Camellia managed a smile. "I'll read through and sign it then stop by the realty office tomorrow." She glanced toward the shop and spotted Trina peeking out the window. An impulsive gesture caused her to link an arm through Weston's. She directed him toward the bench and motioned for him to sit, and then edged closer. She widened her smile.

As she pressed her nose against the glass, Trina's jaw dropped open.

"How are you finding Serenity?"

"I like the peaceful quality." He nodded. "Though I haven't found much time to enjoy things like boating or fishing, yet."

"We have a boat. It's small. Not much bigger than a dingy, but perfect for a leisurely ride around the island. When you have a day open, I'd be glad to take you out." As soon as the invitation escaped her lips, Camellia clamped her mouth shut. What was she thinking? Damn Trina Averaux. Running into her fueled all this competitive drive. At once, a flood of panic sent her back pedaling. "But I'm sure you have better things to do. Besides, I have a full plate myself. A business to get up and running, belongings to unpack, so much…"

Weston rested a hand on her arm.

She stopped the babbling of excuses.

He chuckled. "I understand. Maybe later. After we've conveniently run into each other a few more times, spending a day or evening with me won't seem as frightening."

His eyes crinkled at the corners. Camellia blushed more from anger than embarrassment. What a presumptuous ass. She stood and gave him a curt nod. "I'll be sure to let you know, if the day comes." Her words snapped out at a hurried clip. Taking a wide path around him, she headed for Trina's shop.

"I'll be waiting patiently," Weston called out.

Camellia grabbed hold of the door and threw it open. A deep, throaty laugh followed his remark. She growled under her breath but erased any signs of her sour mood as she stepped inside to face Trina. A forced smile surfaced. "Such a nice guy. He's an architect— educated, beautiful hair, and dreamy eyes. But I'm sure you noticed. You with your face glued to the window." She left Trina speechless and marched to the dressing room to find Freesia.

"Mom's emerald necklace will go perfect with the dress. I can't wait to show her. Do you think she and Robert will return before the gala?" Freesia rattled on as they exited the shop and headed south toward home.

"Hmm?" Camellia shifted to glimpse Freesia's questioning stare.

"What's wrong with you? I don't believe you've heard a word I've said. Something's got your mind stuck in another world." Freesia poked at Camellia's handbag. "What's this envelope? You didn't have it earlier."

Camellia glanced down. "Oh. That's the rental agreement to sign."

"Yeah? How did it end up in your bag?" Freesia stopped at the next crossing and pressed the button to prompt the walking signal.

"While you were taking an eternity in the dressing room, I ran into Weston Murphy," Camellia said.

"Weston." Freesia's wrinkled forehead and frown melted into a smile. She wagged her finger then touched Camellia's shoulder. "I think he's interested in you."

The heat of annoyance spread inside. She batted away Freesia's hand. "Oh, for—what gives your over-imaginative mind that crazy idea?"

"Ah, see? You feel the same way! I knew you would." Freesia jumped up and down, and then stopped to tip her head up to the sky. "I am good, aren't I, Daddy?"

Camellia gritted her teeth. "You don't know any such thing. Why are you talking to the sky and calling out to Daddy? Maybe you're the one with a fever." She trailed her fingers across Freesia's face.

"Stop." Freesia shoved away her hand. "I always talk to him. This way gives me comfort whenever I'm missing him. You understand?" Her lips quivered.

Her sister's voice lowered to a soft whisper. Camellia slowly nodded. "I don't blame you. However, you are wrong about Weston. I don't have any interest in him or any other man. Not at this point in my life." Images of Weston and their encounter framed her mind. The way he spoke and what he said echoed in her ears. "Weston Murphy is a friendly person. I'm sure he's that way with everyone."

"But…"

"Don't. No romance is brewing. Not for me. If you

want romance, Squirt, I suggest you go looking for your own." She tousled Freesia's hair and laughed, though Weston's suggestion they should keep meeting until she felt comfortable spending time with him made her all the more uneasy and anxious of what to expect.

Freesia studied her with narrowed eyes.

Camellia winked. She threw back her head to stare up at the clouds. "Glad to hear you're doing well, Daddy. Let's talk sometime soon."

Freesia rolled her eyes. "Nice. Make fun, but he's listening. I'm sure of it."

"You think? Let's say I believe you and leave it at that." Camellia tweaked her sister's nose and grinned.

A break of thunder rumbled across the sky. A few seconds later, the first drops pattered the sidewalk. Freesia's brow puckered. "Now, you've done it."

"Done what?" Camellia asked, turning her head side to side and behind her.

"You've made him angry enough to send the rain. We'll be drenched before we cover another block."

"Oh, okay. The rain is my fault, huh? Well, if I have that kind of power, wait until you see what I do to you." Camellia wiggled her fingers at Freesia. "Bruuhahaha."

"You're insane," Freesia shouted above the next boom of thunder. A streak of lightning followed, and she squealed. She jogged down the sidewalk and ducked under the canopy of Browne's Hardware, back to where they'd started their morning shopping.

Camellia joined her. They stepped inside and waited out the brief storm until the sky broke free of clouds, and sunlight glistened and sparkled on the wet pavement. Within minutes, they were home where

Camellia claimed an excuse to find solace in her bedroom. She needed time to think, set her mind on the right path, her preferred path, and the plan shouldn't include romance.

****

"I don't think you should tell her."

"Well, you don't get the final say. We vote. Majority rules."

"At least wait until after supper. No point in ruining her appetite."

Camellia lifted her head off the pillow and stretched. She squinted at the clock and moaned. Sunset bathed the room in a golden hue. She raised her back to sit then strained to hear more of the conversation going on past the door.

"Think about food much? Seriously, Zinnie. Putting off the news isn't fair."

Camellia cupped both hands around her mouth. "I can hear you." In the next second, she sniffed and scrunched her nose. "Is something burning?"

"Oh, my gosh. The apple pie," Zinnia screeched. Soon, the pounding of footsteps faded.

Freesia cleared her throat and knocked on the door. "May I come in?"

"Seriously?" Camellia laughed.

"I was being polite." Freesia entered the room and dodged the pillow flying at her head. "We have to talk."

Camellia recognized the stern set of her mouth and the slight tip of her chin. Freesia never wore that face. Too serious. Too Dahlia. "Where's big sis? Shouldn't she be giving me this talk…whatever this talk is?"

"You think I can't handle serious? I can." Freesia sniffed and settled next to Camellia on the bed. "We've

47

been watching the television news." She twisted the bedspread into a tight knot. "No way to ease into the subject, I guess."

Camellia scowled. "Ease into what?"

"Gloria V is dead."

Camellia gasped, but couldn't take in enough air to calm her. "Dead? No, she can't be dead. Oh, my god. Was it murder? Please don't tell me she was murdered." She clenched her hands to stop them from shaking. "I mean she had enemies, lord knows. Oh, wow. I can't believe she's dead." Speaking chafed her throat. She grabbed her glass off the nightstand and sipped at the water. "Dead?"

"No! I mean, yes, she's dead, but no, not murdered. Murder would make this situation so much worse." Freesia worked to untangle the knotted bedspread.

"That's a relief." After her next thought, Camellia's shoulders stiffened. "Wait. The story has been on the news? Oh, lord, whatever happened to her has to be bad if it's on the news." She grabbed for the remote.

Freesia beat her to it. "Maybe you should take a moment. Let it sink in, you know?" Freesia's jaw muscles tightened as she gripped the remote and clutched it to her chest.

"Sia. *Now*." Camellia snapped her fingers then pointed at the television.

Freesia sighed and flipped through the channels until the local news covered the screen.

When Gloria's photo appeared, Camellia gasped.

"Authorities won't release certain details, but we do know Miss Volteri dined alone at Salvatori's in Charleston when she dropped to the floor. EMTs attempted to revive her, but witnesses say she never came to. Her personal assistant explained Volteri planned to visit a former employee about a confidential matter. However, as we now know, Gloria won't be making that rendezvous."

"You don't think she meant to see you?" Freesia asked. "Oh, my." She sank back onto the bed.

Camellia grabbed the remote and flipped to another channel. *Entertainment Nightly.* Her attention riveted to the screen as the show's host spoke.

"Such a tragic blow to the fashion world, isn't it, Marlene? Some of us can't help speculating how the scandal involving Gloria and the theft of Eva Stine's designs might have affected this famous designer. Of course, only her closest… Just one moment, folks." He broke off the conversation with his co-host to accept a sheet of paper, and after a brief glance, he looked at the camera. "Our sources tell *Entertainment Nightly* the confidential rendezvous Gloria Volteri planned was to Serenity to meet with her former employee, Camellia Holiday."

"Oh, my," Freesia groaned.

"Yeah. Oh, my." Camellia echoed the words. The screen grew fuzzy for a second. Forcing air into her lungs, she then rolled her shoulders and neck. Her mind wandered through the possibilities. Why did Gloria want to speak with her? Did Emily know? She grabbed her phone off the nightstand. "I need to call Em."

Freesia laid a hand over Camellia's. "Easy. She might not know about her death yet."

"Oh, she knows. Trust me. Everyone who has anything to do with fashion probably heard about Gloria's death before the news stations." Camellia punched in the number.

"Is she even in New York? Wasn't she taking the job in Paris?" Freesia sat on the settee next to the window.

"Not until the end of the week." Camellia paced the room and waited while the phone rang, but the call quickly went to voicemail. She gripped the phone tighter. "Hey, Em. It's me. I'm sure you've heard about Gloria. Give me a call as soon as you get this message. Love you."

Both she and Freesia stared at the television anchors, who now discussed the latest Hollywood gossip.

"Reporters will be calling." Freesia nodded.

"I'm sure they will. Until the coroner in Charleston rules her death due to natural causes, add the authorities to the list."

Freesia gasped, popping up from her seat and pacing the floor. "You honestly think they'd suspect foul play?"

"Why not? Assuming the worst is how law enforcement works."

"Yeah, but…" Freesia's shoulders dropped. "This catastrophe is not the homecoming I envisioned."

"This *life* isn't the one I envisioned." Camellia walked across the room and lifted the window sheers to view the backyard. Gloria had been her employer, but she'd never thought of her as a friend. Nor did she favor her with compliments. However, now, Camellia's heart filled with sympathy and regret. Such an unfair tragedy. True enough, the fashion guru faced a dismal future, perhaps a time in jail, but not this crappy ending.

A knock at her bedroom door carried her back to

reality.

Dahlia entered, carrying in a tray with a decanter and three glasses. She stood rigidly, her face pinched to deepen the worry lines.

Camellia felt all the worse. What had she brought on her sisters? Trouble followed her home all the way from New York. When would it stop?

"I made iced tea, but I thought you'd prefer some refreshment with a kick to it." She set down the tray on the dresser top. After pouring a generous portion of wine, she handed Camellia the first glass. "Now, what's your plan to handle this nightmare?"

At her choice of the word nightmare, Camellia frowned. She steadied her gaze as she sipped. She paused for a moment while resting the glass in her lap, and then she shrugged. "I can't answer that question when I don't know all the details. You do realize I have no clue why Gloria wanted to see me, right?" The unfurling skepticism on Dahlia's face implied otherwise, or at least hinted at uncertainty.

"Having a plan is always wise, Cam. That's all I'm suggesting. You said yourself. Gloria never wasted time discussing trivial matters. Business always came first. Why should her trip to see you involve anything else?" Dahlia handed another glass to Freesia. After filling her own, she sat at the end of the bed. "Besides, reporters will have questions. You should prepare what you'll say."

"That's just the thing." Camellia massaged her forehead. "I don't have anything to say. Other than admitting I have no idea why she wanted to see me."

"Okay, but they'll ask you about the scandal, suggesting your relationship with Gloria must have changed afterward, and wonder if you were involved with Gloria's crime."

Dahlia's voice softened as if to lessen the blow of her words. Camellia bit down on her lip to stop from crying. She pictured the New York scenario all over again with the reporter hounding her, shoving the mic in her face, right outside her apartment. "I've had plenty of practice fighting off nosy reporters." She strolled over to the dresser and poured another glass.

Dahlia nibbled on her fingernail for a moment then nodded. "We could stall them, if you need time. We'll tell anyone who calls the house you're visiting friends in Raleigh or something equally convincing."

Camellia lifted her brow, and her heartbeat quickened. Dahlia offering to lie for her was a rarity. She never told anything but the truth, no matter how much the message hurt. "I might as well deal with it rather than put off the inevitable. In the meantime, let's make our way to the kitchen. I smell apple pie, and I do believe Zinnie prepared her fried chicken and hush puppies." She planted an "I'm-happy-but-faking-it" smile on her face and waved an arm in a wide arc to motion them into the hall. Her one hope? Emily would shed some light on Gloria's intentions. As she told Dahlia, she hadn't a clue why her former boss had traveled all this way south to see her.

****

"I swear. You should have seen him. All googly-eyed and practically salivating at the sight of Cam." Freesia threw back her head and howled with laughter.

"He did no such thing." Camellia fanned her face with a napkin. They gathered on the screened porch to eat their dessert. The air had grown wet and sticky with evening dew.

"Aw, look. She's blushing." Freesia pointed at Camellia.

"Am not. This heat is stifling." Camellia scowled and fanned her napkin faster.

"You New York City types. Can't tolerate the heat." Zinnia teased and poked at Camellia's side.

"You mean the heat of embarrassment. Why don't you admit the truth, Cam? Weston Murphy is a hottie, and you wouldn't mind finding out what he's like in bed." Freesia winked.

Dahlia's face reddened as she pointed her fork. "Freesia Holiday, you stop, right now."

Camellia rolled her tongue across the roof of her mouth. She set down her plate. "Why don't we talk about your love life, Sia? Get any lately? I mean, all those groupies who come into the bar, salivating over you while you sing your pretty little heart out on stage. Must be hundreds who want to take you home and…"

"Enough. Both of you." Dahlia pounded the chair arm with the flat of one hand. She stood and gathered the plates, stacking them with a clatter. "The likes of talking about romps in bed. You two should be ashamed."

Camellia smiled and leaned toward Freesia to whisper. "I know somebody who's definitely not getting any."

Freesia threw back her head and laughed until tears pooled in her eyes.

"Fine. I'm returning to the study and work on some accounts. You all have your fun and talk about whatever pleases you. I won't be sticking around to listen." Dahlia arranged the plates on a tray along with the silverware and glasses. "Oh and, Sia, it's your turn to clean up the kitchen." Without looking back, she stepped inside the house.

"She seriously needs to get laid," Freesia said while Camellia and Zinnia nodded. "Now, back to Weston Murphy."

Camellia smacked Freesia's arm. "We're done. I have no interest in him or any man at the moment. I've got enough on my plate."

"She does." Zinnia picked at the crumbs of her dessert. "We do, too. The August gala for Mayor Buell is a little over a month away. If Dahlia can't sugar-talk the owner of our venue, we're sunk."

Camellia tensed. She fought jumping to any disturbing conclusion. Her emotional state couldn't handle any more challenges. "Why? What's going on?"

"A personal issue with the mayor may put a snag in the deal." Zinnia nodded.

"I did hear people talking at the bar. Something about the mayor's brother-in-law Teddy causing trouble." Freesia shoved her plate to the side.

Zinnia leaned closer and wiggled her brows. "Well, the story I heard at Willa's Hair Gallery is Vincent hasn't been exactly on the straight-and-narrow path with his wife."

"I'm not sold." Freesia wagged her head. "Rumors don't always turn out to be the truth, you know."

"Wait a minute. What you're saying is Florence's brother Teddy has a stick up his butt because he thinks Vincent is cheating on his sister?" Camellia grinned. "Sure is good to be home among the crazies."

"That story is nothing but gossip, Cam. Teddy agreed to reserve us the hall for the gala several months ago. We signed the papers. He reneged on the deal, telling Dahlia last month's storm damaged the building, and he needs time to get the repairs done. August third might find them still working on it." Freesia shot Zinnia a warning stare.

Camellia tossed each of them a glance, starting with Zinnia. "I don't get it. Why don't you believe Sia's story?" Turning to Freesia, she added, "And how did you come by your information?"

"At the club. Vince comes by every week, along with a few of his business associates. They shoot the bull, and I've overheard things while tending bar." Freesia shrugged. "I could write a book or two on town gossip. Bars and booze always make for loose lips."

Camellia aimed her gaze at Zinnia with a questioning stare.

"Gossip in a beauty parlor's the same thing. Enough said." Zinnia waved a hand. "Truth told, my version of events has been the major topic of conversation for several months, including the showdown between Vincent and Teddy."

Camellia groaned. "Stop. I don't need to hear any more. I need time to re-acclimate to small town life where, everybody knows everybody and news moves too fast. I've been away longer than I thought." She stood and stretched. "I'm going upstairs to finish unpacking. Maybe call Emily again. Afterward? Sleep. Then tomorrow, who knows? I do have a business to plan. If you all need me, try putting off waking me until noon, unless one of those reporters calls. I'll need to deal with that problem. Night."

Not waiting for a response, she hurried to get inside the house then tiptoed through the kitchen.

Desperate to avoid another face-to-face moment with Dahlia, Camellia leaped up the stairs, taking them two at a time. Despite her light-hearted façade, she couldn't shake the feeling of impending doom. Something bad, worse than Gloria's death, was coming her way. Ridiculous or not, the sense of unpleasantness left a chill in her bones. If she were the superstitious type, Camellia bet a visit to a fortune teller would give her nothing but bad news.

She opened one of the boxes and pulled out several picture frames and bric-a-brac to decorate the bedroom. Giving her mind a brief rest from all thoughts of Gloria, she pictured something more pleasant, like an image of Weston Murphy and his engaging smile. She moaned. "Not you. I can't think about you." She set a framed photo on her desk and smiled at the faces of her sisters and parents. The shot was taken a few months before their dad's passing. They stood on the deck of *Lady Serenity*. Camellia remembered a joyful time, all of them happy and naïve, unaware of the destructive storm soon to crash into their lives. With her fingertips, she lightly stroked the photo while tears wet her cheeks. She closed her eyes. His laughter echoed, the deep, husky tone belonging to their dad. Oh, how she missed him. He would know what advice to give her. He'd understand what she was going through.

Chapter 5

Surprisingly enough, no reporters called the house that evening or the next morning. At least Dahlia told Camellia as much. One side of her argued she shouldn't be annoyed with her sister, if she smudged the truth. However, being treated like she was some frail and easily broken patient who needed to be protected from the world was not an easy pill to swallow.

Strangely, Gloria's death didn't affect her the way she'd expected. Even though Gloria was never the type to allow someone to get close, they'd worked side by side, sometimes fifty to sixty hours a week for almost two years. That sort of relationship with Gloria should mean something and touch her in some way. But it didn't. Maybe the scandal debacle soured her attitude. Now, the only reaction she had left was a growing curiosity about why Gloria wanted to speak with her.

She eyed the nightstand where her phone rested. If she called Emily again, she'd most likely get her voicemail. Impatience left her edgy and desperate. She grabbed the phone. After five rings, the tone clicked. "Em?"

"What a funny coincidence. I was about to call you." Emily laughed. "So, what's up with you? Let me guess. You're screaming with boredom in that sleepy little town and want to fly to Paris. Trust me. Parisian life is everything you've dreamed about and more."

Camellia frowned. Maybe news hadn't travelled overseas yet. "Ah, no. Being home is great. I'm fitting comfortably into the easygoing Southern lifestyle. I guess you haven't heard the news?"

"What news? I was up all Sunday night flying to Paris since *La Bonne Vue* wanted me to start ASAP. Anyway, I slept most of Monday, and I'm still feeling major jetlag. Let me guess." Emily snorted. "Gloria called to ask you for a favor, I'll bet. She's certainly got plenty of audacity, doesn't she?"

"Em." A tremoring fear weakened Camellia's legs. She collapsed in the chair. "Gloria is dead."

"You're kidding, right? People like her never die. Their mean attitude keeps them alive forever."

Emily's laugh switched to a nervous twitter.

"I'm not. Kidding, that is. For now, the story is she had a heart attack, but the Charleston authorities are investigating." Camellia's throat grew thick and choked off her words. Somehow, the situation became morbidly real.

"Heart attack?" Emily squeaked. "Wait. You said Charleston authorities."

"Yes. Here's where the situation gets weird, and I hoped you might have an answer."

"An answer about what?"

Camellia fussed with a loose string hanging from her sweater. "According to the news report, Gloria was in Charleston having dinner when the incident occurred. Stephanie told authorities Gloria traveled south to visit a former employee, and according to the news report, that person turned out to be me. Strange, right?"

"You. Why in the world would she visit you?" Emily asked.

"I was hoping you could shed some light on why." Camellia sighed. The opportunity to satiate her curiosity and find answers vanished.

"Seriously, I haven't a clue. All she wanted the day the scandal news broke was to ask me to come to the store and help clean. Remember?"

"Yeah." Camellia raked fingers through her hair as she raced to think of what else to ask. "Did she mention anything that day? Talk about me? Any detail you can recall?"

"Nothing, other than complaining about Eva being a snot-nosed upstart who didn't have an honest bone in her body and how the truth always comes out in the end." Emily cleared her throat. "Why do you think she wanted to see you?"

"I don't know, which really bothers me." Camellia stood once more and paced the room. "But I'm determined to find out and not let it ruin my mood. Even from the grave, she's giving me grief."

"Which I'd guess has nothing to do with feeling badly about her death."

Camellia took a deep breath then released it slowly. "No. I'd have to say not at all. How terrible can I be?"

"I think you're acting honest and reasonable. She was ready to take us down with her. You know it's true, Cam. Don't feel a bit sorry. She drove us hard, taking every ounce of our energy. Never once did she give us any credit for our work. We were the ones who helped with the designs and kept the business afloat while she struggled with her creative dry spell. Right? You know I'm right," Emily argued.

"Yeah, but she's dead. What if...never mind. I'm letting my imagination run wild." Camellia raked a hand through her hair. "How's Paris and the job? I can only imagine."

Emily laughed. "My life's so much better. I've been here only a couple of days, and already I want to kiss the stars and thank the gods of fate for giving me such an opportunity. And my dad, of course. I'll owe him for the rest of my life. Trust me. Look, I have to scoot. It's evening here, and I have a business dinner to attend. You okay? I can call later if you need me."

Camellia detected the worried tone in her voice. "I'm fine. Crossing my heart as we speak. I'll keep you posted. If this situation turns out to be something big, which in Gloria's case it usually does, I'm sure someone, maybe several detectives, reporters or nosey bodies, will come by or call. Everyone will want to know what I know, which is nothing." She rubbed her hand up and down her thigh. "How ironic. The Gloria V drama continues beyond the grave."

"Obviously. Love you, and we'll talk soon." Emily ended the call.

Despite Emily's encouraging words and her own determined agenda, Camellia couldn't shake the ominous feeling of impending doom. She'd talked to Emily and got no answers. Shifting in her seat, she stared out the window and at the distant Yaupon trees. At once, she jumped to her feet. "Stephanie."

A quick search of her nightstand drawer produced the ledger in which she'd recorded all of her personal appointments, client meetings, design deadlines, and contact info. She had a strong mistrust of modern technology. Her phone, as with any personal device, might break or be stolen, records hacked, and valuable information revealed to the world. Choosing good old paper and pen proved the safer route. As it was, she deleted most of her work contact numbers from her phone. The ledger had them all, and that contact info was what she needed now.

"Stephanie Tumler. Stephanie Tumler." She slid her finger down the page. "Ah. Here it is." She tapped the entry and quickly punched in the numbers on her phone. Each additional ring deflated her expectations. Ready to leave yet another voicemail, she opened her mouth.

"Hello?"

As she recognized the high-pitched squeak of Gloria's personal assistant, Camellia smiled. "Hi Stephanie. It's me, Camellia."

"Well, well. I should've known you'd be calling."

The pitch squeaked higher and Stephanie's words puzzled her. "I was shocked to hear about Gloria. I had no idea she'd come to Charleston," Camellia started.

"Or that she planned to pay you a visit? Come on, Camellia. I don't believe you for a second. I suppose you'll beg me to change my story. Well, forget it. I never liked your attitude, not the way you talked to me, or the disrespectful way you treated Gloria. You've got something to hide. I can feel it. I told that detective from Charleston as much," Stephanie snapped.

"What?" Camellia's heart raced, upon hearing the accusation. "Where does this attitude come from? I've always been nice to you. As far as Gloria is concerned, she didn't exactly bring out the warm and fuzzy in people. I did my job. She was my employer, and our relationship was professional. Despite what you might think, I'm truly sorry she's dead, and I don't appreciate your implication." The tirade, fueled by anger and indignation, left her breathless.

"Her visit to you, of all people? It made no sense. After Gloria told me her plans, I persuaded her to explain why. She refused. Not once have you defended Gloria since those vultures accused her of stealing. Not one word. You'd sooner throw her under the bus."

A venomous tone layered Stephanie's words. Camellia winced. Gloria's assistant was either insane or enveloped in grief over losing her boss and, most likely, her paycheck. "You amaze me, Stephanie. I don't know what to say, other than you're dead wrong." Camellia ended the call and tossed her phone on the bed. If anything, Gloria treated Stephanie worse than she did her and Emily. Why defend her?

"Hey, you intend to hole up in there all day?" Zinnia's words muffled through the bedroom door. "I've got fresh baked biscuits and Aunt Sarah's famous vegetable soup ready to serve. Why don't you come on down?"

Camellia glanced at her watch and cringed. The hands pointed at noon. Where had the morning gone? "I'm sorry, Zinnie." She threw open the door. "I've been talking to Emily and Stephanie. Time sort of flew by without me noticing." She shrugged.

Zinnia nodded. "Who's Stephanie? And did Emily answer your questions?"

"Stephanie is, *was,* Gloria's personal assistant. As for answering my questions, Emily did not." She slumped against the doorjamb.

"Well, I'm sure you'll figure it out. Or maybe you won't. Does it matter?" Zinnia's forehead creased.

"I guess not. Especially hard to come up with any new ideas on an empty stomach." Camellia winked, slipped her arm through Zinnia's, and led them down the stairs. "Did you make the soup, or did Aunt Sarah deliver? Either way, it will be yum." If nothing else, she was good at deception. Nobody at the kitchen table would have a clue how concerned she was. She refused to let her problem become *their* problem, too. Such a burden wasn't fair to put on any of her sisters.

Reaching the kitchen, Camellia grabbed a bowl and spoon from the cupboard.

Freesia sat at the table, dipping a biscuit into her soup while Dahlia's head bent over a stack of papers, her lunch left untouched.

Zinnia wagged a finger. "You insult me, Dee Holiday. I spent all morning preparing this soup."

Dahlia slid her glasses to the tip of her nose and leveled Zinnia with a frown. "Don't call me Dee. I plan to eat, so stop nagging. Anyway, the soup's too hot." She pointed at Camellia. "Did you talk to Emily?"

"I did." Camellia dipped a biscuit in her soup. "She hasn't a clue what was in Gloria's head. But I'm not interested in discussing it any longer. Not until I have to. I've got more urgent business, like eating this soup." She winked at Freesia.

"Of course. Typical." Dahlia shook her head.

"Will you put a cork in it?" Freesia dropped her spoon with a clatter.

Dahlia held up both hands. "Far be it from me to interfere."

"Ha! You always interfere, but not this time. Cam won't let you. Right, Cammie?" Freesia lifted her chin and smiled.

Dahlia crumpled one sheet of paper into a ball and tossed it at Freesia. The target hit its mark and landed in her soup.

Freesia squealed. She plucked the ball out of the bowl before pitching it back to Dahlia then grabbed a napkin to dab at a spot where soup splattered on her blouse. After a moment, she turned her attention to Camellia. "Well? Are you putting up with her bossiness? Or do I have to intervene?"

Camellia opened her mouth to speak, but the doorbell rang.

"Saved by the bell." Zinnia giggled then munched on a buttered biscuit.

"I'll get it." Camellia shot out of her seat and sprinted to the door, relieved to escape being put in the middle of another Freesia and Dahlia squabble.

She opened the door, and a grin curved her lips. "Weston Murphy. What a surprise."

He tipped his hand and returned the smile. "Good afternoon, Miss Holiday. Not meaning to intrude. I had some free time, so I stopped by to pick up the rental agreement and save you a trip into town."

Camellia stared. Those lips were full and sensuous. His eyes sparked like blueish-green fire with intensity enough to melt her reserve, which she struggled to maintain. She swore off men in her life for now. The declaration was turning out to be a constant mantra since she returned home only two days ago. She let out a long sigh, her shoulders heaving. "I totally forgot. Though you needn't have come all this way."

"You mean all this way as in three blocks?" He laughed. "It's no problem. Besides, Uncle Samuel was growing anxious and worried you'd change your mind."

With the wave of her arm, Camellia motioned for Weston to come inside. "I don't know why. Once I make up my mind to something it sticks. I want to rent the building. I *need* to."

Weston chuckled as he stepped to the side of Camellia. "You make it sound like a life-and-death situation."

"In a way, it is." She shrugged. "Come on back to the kitchen and meet the rest of the family." After making introductions, she left Weston with her sisters. "Let me run upstairs to fetch the agreement." Returning with the signed papers, she found everyone at the table.

Weston sat at the center with all three women circled around him. Their chins rested in their hands while he talked.

Camellia cleared her throat, which made Weston pause.

"I was telling your sisters the story about the building you're renting." Leaning back in his chair, he took a long draw on a glass of iced tea.

"I swear, Cam. I didn't realize what a rich history this town has." Zinnia pointed a finger. "You be sure to take good care of your building."

"Okay." Camellia grinned in amusement. She approached Weston and laid the agreement on the table. She set her mouth in a straight line and forced a serious tone. "Here you go. All signed. Although, maybe Samuel should add a clause about the historical value and how any renters should take care not to damage the structure. We certainly wouldn't want to upset you or the historical society." A grin forced its way to the surface.

"But, Cam. Did you realize President Lincoln stayed in it once? I wouldn't be surprised if Weston got the state to declare the place a historical monument."

Zinnia gestured with a thumbs-up and firm nod.

"Exactly what I suggested. Weston says a murder occurred back at the turn of last century. Some famous vaudeville actor killed his lover and tossed her into the ocean." Freesia shivered. "Guaranteed to give you the willies when you're all alone in the evening."

Camellia ignored the warning and fixed her attention on Dahlia who'd kept quiet. "What's your opinion of all this talk, Dahlia?"

Dahlia slowly nodded. "I think from a business standpoint, you'll have an advantage. Maybe the whole town will. If any of the story turns out to be true, that is." She narrowed her gaze at Weston.

"Oh, it's true. I've found documentation. Plenty of it. In fact, I've written an article for the university journal which explains everything and will be published later in the year." He finished his tea, and then folded the rental agreement and tucked it in his pocket. After a brief nod at each woman, he settled his gaze on Camellia. "When you come into town, stop by Uncle Samuel's office. He has the keys to your building."

"Sure. I'll be around by three or four, unless something comes up." Camellia shifted her gaze to the others for an instant then to Weston. "Thanks for stopping. Why don't I walk you to the door?" Somehow, her sisters watching and listening rattled her nerves.

"Perhaps you'd let me take you to supper, and afterward, you can show me around town?" he suggested as they stood in the foyer.

"Huh, I count this meeting as only our third. You said it would take several before I'd feel comfortable enough to spend an evening with you," Camellia teased.

His easy-going manner made her relax. She could handle it. Right? Getting together for supper would be a casual meal between new friends and nothing serious.

"It's just supper, Camellia," he said.

"Cam. Please call me Cam." Her heart fluttered. That sort of reaction teased her resolve. She gripped the door handle. The metal felt cool in her hand. With a gradual ease, she steadied her breathing. "Yes, all right. Just supper." She nodded before moving aside for him to step out the door.

"Later, then." He smiled and waved over his shoulder as he jogged toward the drive. "I look forward to our date."

Camellia closed the door and scowled. "Our date." What was wrong with her? From what she gathered, Weston was a gentleman. He was pleasant on the eyes and possessed a sense of humor. If she could convince herself he was totally harmless to her emotional state, the situation would be perfect. She groaned.

"Cam? Are you okay?" Freesia leaned close.

The warm air from Freesia's breath tickled her ear. Camellia splayed her fingers to cover her chest as she gasped and twirled. "Well, I was until you startled me."

She poked a finger. "Hmm. Seems to me it's Weston Murphy who has you out of sorts."

Camellia laughed and poked back. "Never will a man, especially someone I recently met, get to me that way."

"You're sounding like Dahlia. Better watch it, or you'll be inching up to thirty with no ring on your finger."

"Ha. I'm a long way from thirty. Besides, hooking a guy and landing a marriage are not at the top of my to-do list." Camellia stepped toward the closet. A sudden queasiness rippled through her stomach and she wasn't feeling hungry any longer.

"Oh, I'll agree to a certain extent. Careers are essential for either sex. Gotta make a living, but I hope for marriage and a family someday. Don't you?" Freesia's eyebrows puckered into a frown.

"Maybe." Camellia lifted her bag out of the closet and straightened. She caught the concern on Freesia's face. Pausing for a moment, she fished out her keys. "Of course, I think about those things. I imagine every woman does, but the situation doesn't require a time table. Not nowadays. I do know one thing." She slid her finger playfully along the bridge of Freesia's nose. "If and when I decide to get married, you'll be my maid of honor."

"Nice." Freesia's grin spread from ear to ear. "Maybe I'll be your matron of honor, if I beat you to the altar."

Camellia shrugged. "I could take your words as a challenge, but I won't. Because I don't care. Thirty, forty, or whenever, I'll wait until the time feels right. You'll be wiser to think the same." She squeezed Freesia's shoulder. "Now, I'm off. I have tons of errands to run and things to do at my shop." *My shop.* Those words sounded pleasing. Despite the tragic news of Gloria's death, she grew more confident about her decision, her shop, and her fashion line. The idea was becoming her own possible reality.

She jogged down the front walk. Sunlight sparkled and the brisk breeze of ocean air tickled her nose as Camellia drew in a long breath. With a brief glance at her car, she passed by and took a path across the street leading to the shoreline walk. The barrier island's mild summer weather renewed her energy. She looked forward to the afternoon's agenda. Despite the heavy load of busy work, she'd throw a little personal interlude into the mix.

"First stop, Office Supply and Copy. Gotta get these fliers printed, pronto." Making a mental check of her to-do list, she blocked out all other noises and nearly missed the phone buzzing and ringing in her bag. She stopped to check the name on the screen. "Hey, Dahlia. I was hoping Sia mentioned I left the house."

"She did, but we got a call a couple minutes ago. Clifton Jones, a reporter from Charleston, was asking for you." She sighed. "The media was bound to reach out, Cam."

Her bubble of enthusiasm deflated a bit. "Yes, I know. I suppose he needs a comment or two for his paper."

"Not exactly. Mr. Jones wants to come to Serenity tomorrow morning. He hopes you'll agree to a television interview. He's a reporter for Charleston's local news, not the paper."

Camellia let go of her purse strap. The bag landed on the sidewalk with a thump. "Oh, lord. Please tell me you said no. I can't handle TV publicity. Not after the New York scandal."

"I told him. None of us should be dealing with attention of that sort."

Dahlia's voice carried a reprimanding tone. Camellia winced. She blamed her for bringing trouble home. Wasn't dealing with her own guilt bad enough? "I'm sorry." She sniffed and took a deep breath. "Did Mr. Jones leave a number? I'll call him right this minute. You shouldn't have to run interference."

"No, Cam. You don't want to call. Doing so will only make things worse. One word will lead to another. He's a reporter. He'll twist everything you have to say and turn your words into some awful admission of guilt. We've been through this sort of situation with Daddy. You were young at the time, but I remember it clearly. I won't have this family dragged through the mud again."

Dahlia's tone and words pierced her like tiny daggers. The time wasn't right to argue, not when she was in Mother Mode. "Fine, but I don't need to be reminded of Daddy's situation. Mom went through it worse than anyone. As kids, we loved him unconditionally, but his affair damaged all of us. I do remember that much. Look, I have to go. When I get home this evening, we'll talk. Okay?" Camellia choked out the last few words. She snatched her bag off the ground and shoved her phone inside. The media wouldn't stop calling. She'd need to face the Gloria V issue eventually. Hiding and avoidance were a coward's actions. She released a shaky breath and, with determined steps, she made it across the next two blocks in short time.

Chapter 6

How one totally unrelated incident conjured up the hurt from another time was ironic. Maybe hurt was nonexclusive. Camellia powerwalked along the beach and glanced at the line of docked vessels. Ben Walters shouted hello as he pulled the day's catch onto his boat. Without stopping, she waved and steered toward the main drag. Hurt was a timeless emotion, without regard to where it happened or whom it touched—each new hurt reminding one of all the others. However, Gwen Holiday tunneled through the hurt and formed a new alliance with Joseph Holiday. 'Til death do us part and all that comes with marriage remained her credo. She kept the family together. They carried on despite the one hiccup on life's path to interrupt it.

Of course, Joseph dearly paid the price. His liaison with a Charleston socialite made front-page news. No wonder the husband threatened Joseph with a tire iron during the Biltmore spring charity event for orphaned children. Fortunately, the family luxury sedan's front bumper became the victim rather than Joseph's head.

Joseph relocated the family to Serenity, despite Gwen's worry that running away wouldn't solve anything. Still, Joseph made a promise to a higher power to turn around his life. They began attending services at Faith Assembly of God. From that day forward until his death, the family never missed a

Sunday. The next few years proved an uphill battle with almost three hundred services of spiritual guidance.

In the months following her husband's death, Gwen explored her own path with Eastern spiritualism and the tenets of Buddha before veering back to uniform Christianity and a non-denominational church, which she seldom attended, especially after marrying Robert Hench. New Age philosophy of worship was her current spiritual attraction.

As she reached her destination, Camellia slowed her pace, hefted her bag on her shoulder, and sighed. Gwen's perseverance gave her hope. Her strength glowed like a beacon. Camellia had reason to think she could turn her life around, to be brave, and to remain optimistic because she was a Holiday. Her mother's blood ran through her veins.

The bell hanging above the door tinkled as she opened the entrance to Office Supply and Copy. The clerk behind the counter, a ruddy-faced teen with spikey, bleach-tipped hair, smiled.

"Can I help you, ma'am?"

"I surely hope so. I need five hundred copies of this flier by six this evening. Is that possible?" Camellia eyed the clerk with a critical stare. He was a boy, sixteen or maybe eighteen, wearing bleached jean cutoffs and oversized T-shirt. Fingers on one hand thumped in time to a song playing on a radio nearby. He was so very young and probably with questionable experience, but Generation Z's aptitude with technology should never be underestimated.

"I think I can handle it." A lopsided smirk covered his face. Taking the flier, he chomped on his gum and popped a bubble as he examined it. "You want color?

Color print costs fifteen cents per. Adding cardstock brings it to twenty cents. Or black print on regular copy will get you the cheapest price. Ten cents per." He waited, chomping and popping his gum.

"I think color on regular paper will be fine." Camellia added her contact info and signature to the order form as she pursed her lips to hide an amused grin. "You live around here?"

"Yes, ma'am." He nodded. "What about you?"

"My sisters and I do. Been nearly fifteen years, come to think of it. I'm Camellia Holiday." She paused a few seconds to see if he'd offer his name in return. "You have family in Serenity, then? Maybe I know them."

He shrugged. "My name's Remy. Remy Averaux. Moved to this pissant town after my dad passed away. So, I'm stuck living with an aunt I never set eyes on before this summer."

Shocked by his openness and to learn he was an Averaux, Camellia swallowed hard. "Sorry to hear that, Remy." Uncomfortable, she steered the conversation in another direction. "You must be cousins with Trina."

Remy nodded. "Sucks, but yes, I am. However, we have a comfortable arrangement. Whenever we share the same space, I stay clear of her, and she doesn't get in my shit."

"I see." Offering her own snarky opinion would probably be immature, though Trina deserved it. Instead, Camellia rummaged through her bag to find a packet of breath mints. Popping one in her mouth, she then extended the packet to Remy who shook his head.

"It's almost two o'clock. Your order should be ready by five. We close at six-thirty." Remy wiped a palm across one pant leg before extending his arm.

Camellia hesitated, surprised by his gesture, but then shook his hand.

"Glad to meet you, Miss Holiday. See you in a few hours." Remy smiled before turning. The pounding of hurried footsteps fainted as he disappeared to the rear of the store.

"Huh. Well, Serenity is a small town, after all." Camellia stepped outside and to the sidewalk. In one way or another, Trina Averaux's name popped up too often. Now, another Averaux had come to Serenity. Remy's dad and Trina's had to be brothers.

Though she'd just met him, Camellia liked Remy, and not only because they had mutual feelings about Trina. Maybe she pitied him more than anything. Poor kid didn't have a dad and now lived with people he didn't much care for in a place he called a pissant town. Camellia smiled. Most residents of Serenity would argue the point six ways to Sunday.

In less than an hour Camellia covered the next several stops. She'd ordered more than enough supplies, at least what she located on the island. She'd wait to buy the rest after she and Freesia traveled to the mainland.

Only one task remained. She glanced down at her watch and tapped her foot. With a quick touch of a button she phoned Sampson Realty. "Good afternoon, Mr. Sampson. I was wondering if I could stop by to get those keys?"

"Why certainly, Miss Holiday." His voice boomed across the phone.

"Great. I'll be there in five minutes." She started to hang up but then added, "Oh, and I don't suppose your nephew is there?" Her heartbeat raced to match the mounting anxiety. She ventured into dangerous territory and tempted fate.

"He sure is. Tells me you two are going out to supper." He paused. "I'm grateful he's found a friend. I was beginning to think he'd get bored and run off back to Charleston or New York before we had some real family time. I thank you for giving him a reason to stay."

A flush spread across her cheeks. "Offering a dose of Serenity hospitality is what folks around here do, right? Tell Weston I've made reservations at Shoreline Bar and Grill." She ended the call before Samuel spoke another word. Removing her sunglasses, she pinched her finger and thumb to massage both eyelids. Why not enjoy a fun time, relaxing and a welcomed escape with a new friend?

In a short while, Camellia faced Samson's Realty. She stood outside the door with her feet cemented in place. Through the plate glass window, she spotted Weston and his uncle.

Samuel spoke, and Weston threw back his head and laughed.

A full, rich laugh, the sound of which penetrated the thick glass, eased her somehow. She climbed the steps and passed through the doorway.

"Why, Miss Holiday. How are you this beautiful afternoon?"

Samuel bellowed in a sweet tone full of energy. "Wonderful, and you?" She glimpsed at Weston before shifting back to Samuel.

"As ornery as ever." He slapped his knee. "Darn my scattered brain. I forgot to fish the keys out of the drawer. Weston, you keep our guest company while I fetch them. Tell her more about those ghosts. Ah, no, wait. Never mind about the ghosts. She might change her mind about renting the place." He winked at Camellia before sauntering down the aisle.

"Ghosts, huh? Wasn't the story you told my sisters about murder?" Camellia was amused at Weston's reddened cheeks.

"The ghost *is* the murder victim. Or so I've heard. I haven't substantiated that detail, yet," He cleared his throat. "You see, Uncle Samuel does enjoy a little embellishment in my stories. He doesn't care whether or not the particulars are true, only that they're interesting." Weston skirted around the desk to sit.

"Ah, well, whatever makes him happy." Camellia set her bag on a chair. Crossing her arms, she stepped over to the window and peered out at the gulf. Soft sunlight filtered through the glass and warmed her skin. After a moment of silence between them, she twisted her head in his direction.

"You didn't need to make the reservations. I'd have gladly done it." Weston laced his fingers together, put both hands behind his head, and leaned back in the chair.

"I realize, but I do know the area businesses. Me making the reservation made things easier, don't you think?"

"Uh-uh." He smiled. Bringing one hand forward, he pointed a finger. "You want control."

"What?" Camellia stiffened while her chin tipped upward. "I don't know what you mean."

Laughing, he stood and circled the desk to stand within inches of her. "You want control, like with our date. You want to call the shots so you won't feel…what? Insecure? Threatened? Do you feel threatened by me, Camellia Holiday?"

He uttered the last words in a soft whisper, his breath tickling her face. Her heart beat triple-time. "I don't feel anything of the kind. I took care of the reservation, which makes things easier on you. Right?" Camellia blinked and took a couple steps backward.

"Easier, hmm?" He moved forward until his lips touched her ear. "Are you afraid I might complicate your life and make it more confusing?"

Camellia circled and took long strides to the other side of the room. Pivoting on one heel, she faced him. "Maybe this evening was a bad idea. I don't know what men do where you come from, but around here they certainly don't make such bold comments to a lady after meeting, let's see, less than twenty-four hours ago." The distance between them gave her courage. Before she could add more words, Samuel returned. While she glared at Weston, Camellia gritted her teeth, and her stomach churned. She couldn't hide the anger and irritation on her face fast enough.

Samuel shifted his gaze between them. A half-hearted smile formed as he dangled the chain. "Found the keys."

"Good." Camellia held out a hand, keeping her back to Weston. "Do you still want to go to supper? I'm game." She turned on her heel and smirked. "If you can behave yourself, that is."

Weston rubbed a finger across his upper lip and chuckled. "Well, I can't promise, but I will certainly do my best. If I so much as utter one inappropriate or unkind comment, say the word. I'll leave and never bother you again."

"Oh, don't worry. I'll make sure." Camellia tossed her bag over her shoulder and took long, determined strides toward the door. "Thank you again, Mr. Samson."

"You two have a good afternoon." Samuel waved.

"You believe we'll have a good afternoon?" Weston asked as he caught up.

"What I believe or do doesn't matter. The success of the evening is entirely in your hands." As she came to recognize Weston's type, Camellia regained her confidence. She had dated men like him. Boastful, overbearing at times, thinking they were all women dreamed of or wanted. If not for his geeky sincerity, and his honest enthusiasm for history and architecture, Camellia might find Weston totally boring. At least she'd spend time with him to see if they could be friends. She picked up her pace and Weston fell in beside her. The evening promised to be interesting.

****

"I have to admit, your choice proved better than mine." Weston shoved his plate to the side and took a sip of his beer.

Camellia had enough time to tour the town and make a quick stop to pick up the flier order before heading to the Shoreline Restaurant. The ambiance was perfect with candlelit tables, the mellow tone of soft jazz music, and dimmed lighting, but not too dim to send an overly romantic message to Weston. She had to set boundaries because they were friends and she was a southern lady, after all. "Oh? You had a choice?" She laughed. "I'm kidding. Where would we have gone?"

"Some place ten or so miles up the coast? I believe

the name is Delmonte's Delight." He shrugged.

"Oh, my." Camellia choked on ice-cold mint julip. "They serve food all right. But they also provide entertainment of a certain sort." She wrinkled her nose.

"You mean if I give a big enough tip, the offer of a lap dance is my reward?" Weston wiggled his eyebrows and nodded.

Her lips narrowed until he bellowed with laughter. "Why you—you knew about Delmonte's."

"Uncle Samuel claims they serve the best ribs in the state." He grinned.

"Oh, I'm sure what got his attention were the ribs." Camellia scoffed. She drained the rest of her drink and set the glass to the side.

"Criticize all you want. From what I hear the owner clears more profit than any restaurant around."

"I'm sure he does. Plenty besides your uncle take a particular interest beyond the food." Camellia softened and let a smile form. "Like yourself."

Weston held up both hands. "Oh, no. I'll pass. Besides, from your reaction I'd guess you don't approve."

"Why does my opinion matter?" Camellia picked up her napkin and dabbed at the ring of sweat left by her glass. She glanced up at him. "We hardly know each other, and here you are talking about topics like the risqué activities at Delmonte's. I can't imagine what will come out of your mouth next."

Weston flashed a smile. "Makes my company all the more appealing, doesn't it?"

"Maybe, though I'm still deciding." Camellia relaxed. She had to be honest. The past couple of hours with him were the most fun she'd had in weeks. "How long do you think you'll stay in Serenity?"

Weston took a sip of his drink. "I'm in no hurry to leave. My classes won't start until fall, which leaves plenty of time for me to explore the area. Charleston has loads of historical sites."

"Hmm. Charleston. I love its southern charm. Just so happens, I attended UNC."

Weston smiled. "You are the tour guide of all tour guides, Miss Holiday. I'm flattered you'd want to share your knowledge."

"Who said I was offering *my* services?" She practically choked on the laugh struggling to escape and bit down on her lip to control it.

Weston clutched his chest and moaned. "My heart is sorely damaged, not to mention my expectations." In the next second, he grinned.

Camellia wagged her finger. "Serves you right."

"Ah, the payback. All right then whoever you have in mind, I'm sure the choice will be perfect. As long as the guide you choose is a she, say around twenty something? Long legs, killer smile, and she must have a sexy voice. That way, I'll hang on her every word, you understand." He rested his elbow on the table and cupped his chin with one palm as he stared, unblinking.

"You're incorrigible, you know?" Camellia smiled and tossed her napkin at his face.

"I do my best." He stood then stepped over to Camellia and pulled out her chair. "I'll help you with those packages and walk you home."

"Such a gentleman. But you needn't bother. Plenty of daylight's left, and I have a short distance to go."

"A Southern man does not let a lady walk home alone, not after they've shared a meal together, and let's not forget the pleasant conversation." He cradled shopping bags in one arm.

Camellia opened her mouth, but seeing the firm, stubborn set to his jaw, she remained quiet. They walked out into the cool evening air. The sunset sky shimmered with streaks of purple, pink, and orange. Switchgrass with its purple blooms swayed in the breeze. Trails of smoke from the beach announced clam bakes while the musky, burnt smell stung her nostrils. "Let's take the walkway along the beach."

"Sure. If you have time, take me to your slip. I'd love to see the family boat." Weston hefted the packages, switching them from one arm to the other.

Camellia laughed. "I think the quicker we get home, the better the chance those purchases will survive. Unless you'd like me to carry a bag to lighten your load."

"Ha. I'm good. Besides, you're taking a stab at my masculinity." Weston drew his eyebrows together, and his lips curved into a pout.

The expression didn't work because the twinkle in his eyes brightened. Camellia shook her head in an exaggerated gesture. "Stop. No shame in admitting you're not up to the task. I certainly won't think less of you. Well, maybe I will a little, but not a big deal."

Weston juggled the packages to one arm and pointed with the other. "To the boat, woman. Or else."

Camellia tossed her hair and chuckled. "Have things your way. However, let me warn you. She's docked clear at the other end of the reef. I'd say the walk is about two miles, maybe more." She bit down on her lip, waiting for his reaction and expecting disappointment or shock. Instead, he shrugged with an expression of total indifference.

"Lead the way."

She grunted and stepped ahead. Male pride. What men did to impress a woman was something she'd never understand.

****

Sweat beaded on Weston's forehead and darkened the underarms of his shirt. He set the packages next to the front door and heaved with a groan. "Thank you for a wonderful evening."

"Thank you for the entertaining company." Camellia smiled.

"Entertaining, huh? Well, I guess entertaining is somewhat appealing. Anyway, I'll take the compliment. I hope whatever is in the one bag didn't break when I tripped on the boardwalk."

She noted his flushed cheeks. "Could happen to anybody. Warped and weathered boards are a hazard. Maybe you'd like to come inside for a cool drink. Don't know about you, but I'm parched."

Weston shook his head. "A bottle of water to go would be nice. Uncle Samuel wants me to help move some furniture this evening, and I'm late."

"Sure. One water coming up." Camellia rushed inside with her purchases, dropped them on the sofa, and jogged back to the kitchen. One successful evening didn't mean everything. She liked him and enjoyed his company, which was a start. Yes, she vowed no romance in her life for the moment. But a friend, a male friend, was a relationship she could manage. Decisions on anything more complicated could wait. "Here you go." Camellia handed him the bottle.

"Thanks." He chugged half of the contents then

tipped the bottle toward her and smiled. "Been a pleasure spending time with you. I look forward to the boat ride."

She swiped away the loose strands of hair tickling her cheeks. "I can't promise how soon. I have lots to do." Not to mention other complications occupied her time. She refused to share her soap opera drama with Weston and give him reason to make fun of her, or worse, scare him off.

"Just holler when." He pivoted on one heel to turn but paused. "Oh, before I go, I'd like to do one more thing."

Before she had time to stop him, Weston pulled her close. The woodsy scent of his cologne was intoxicating. As his lips touched hers, she closed her eyes. Though brief and gentle, the kiss somehow sparked her insides. In seconds, she drew back and gasped. Reason battled with her emotions. How nervy could he get? They'd only met yesterday. For sure, he'd made one bold move.

"If the offer stands and the timing is right, perhaps we can ride over to Charleston together. I'd really love for you to be my guide and not the long-legged lady with the sexy voice I so flippantly requested." His chest heaved in and out as his finger traced the line of her jaw.

The hope on his face fired with intent. She jerked away. "I'll check my schedule and speak with Sia." Camellia's voice was unsteady. How could she deny liking the kiss? She wanted to, but the words refused to come out. Instead, her emotional and rational parts fought to determine what made sense. One thing was obvious. She'd had enough for one day.

Weston shrugged. "Whatever you say. Good evening, Miss Camellia." He whistled while jogging to the end of the drive.

After he disappeared across the street and down the block, Camellia turned and twisted the front doorknob. "What a complicated man he is. He kisses me and asks me to sightsee with him then acts like he doesn't care whether or not I agree. How's a woman supposed to know what he feels?"

Chapter 7

"Men certainly are a complicated bunch, aren't they?"

"Good grief." As she stepped into the foyer, Camellia pressed one hand to her chest. "I'd nearly forgotten how everyone in this family sneaks around. You nearly gave me a coronary."

"Sorry." Zinnia chuckled. "I didn't mean to eavesdrop. I heard your voice and came to find you. You have company waiting. Everyone's in the kitchen."

Camellia slumped her shoulders. "Please don't tell me a reporter has come calling. I can't deal with probing questions right now. I'm exhausted, and I'd rather go up to my room and relax before bedtime."

"Noah is here." Zinnia waved an arm toward the kitchen.

An acidy taste soured her throat. She grimaced. "Oh, well, I can't deal with him, either. Good night." Camellia grabbed her packages off the parlor sofa and took the stairs.

Zinnia leaned over the railing. "Cam, don't be rude. He's made a trip here to speak with you. I think he wants to apologize for what he said the other day. You know how upset you were."

As she turned to face Zinnia, Camellia tightened her hold on the packages. Her sister's pouty mouth and doe eyes squashed any argument. "Fine. Though I can't

85

imagine any kind words coming out of his mouth." She dropped the bags, filled with her purchases, to the floor and cringed at the clinking of broken glass. "I can't believe you're suggesting an apology rattles around somewhere in that calloused brain of his."

"Gripe all you want. I believe he's sincere and wants to make amends." Zinnia led the way back to the kitchen.

Camellia lagged far behind, her arms crossed. "How dare he show up uninvited?" A body should be given time to prepare, or in this case, armor herself with plenty of witty comments and comebacks.

Zinnia stopped and pivoted on one heel. "Why are you being so difficult?"

"Because I…" She clenched her jaw.

Zinnia's brow rose. "You were going to add 'because you broke up', which, as I recall, you managed amicably. You're still friends, aren't you? Or have your big-city ways put a snoot in your snout?"

"Oh, for the love of Pete, Zinnie. Of course not." She waved at her. "Move along. Let's get this awkward moment over with so I can escape to the quiet of my room."

"You are a pain in the patootie sometimes. Now, straighten that mussy hair. I'm guessing a make-out session with Weston is to blame. Shameful girl." Zinnia giggled.

"Mind your Ps and Qs, sister." Camellia had no intention of the forgive-and-forget approach. Like Trina, Noah didn't deserve such kindness.

They entered the kitchen, and Camellia stiffened at the sight of Noah leaning against the sink counter.

"Why good evening, Cam. How great to see you,

again." Noah strode the length of the room in seconds, gripped both her hands, and squeezed.

Camellia wrenched free of his grasp. His approach and touch were invasive and aggressive. "Wish I could stick around to chat, but I've had a long day." She forced a yawn and patted her mouth.

"Maybe your date with Weston had something to do with you being so exhausted. How was he, by the way? The man certainly seems like a charmer," Freesia said.

Camellia took in the Cheshire grin that spread across Freesia's face and ran her tongue along her upper lip. The sweet taste of Weston's kiss lingered. "The evening was fine. We ate at the Shoreline and then walked home."

"Oh, he walked you home, did he? What a gentleman. Don't you agree it's a very gentlemanly act, Noah?" Freesia batted her eyelashes.

Camellia groaned. The well-intended tone and words of innocence rankled with sarcasm. "Maybe we should let Noah explain why he stopped by instead of talking about Weston. Okay?"

Freesia tipped her head to one side. "Yes, why did you stop by, Noah?"

"I'd like a word with Camellia." He glimpsed at each of them. "In private?"

Camellia crossed her arms. "Whatever you have to say, go ahead. I have no secrets."

He cleared his throat. "About us breaking off the engagement?"

Camellia fidgeted with the buttons on her shirt. He wouldn't dare mention his fling with Trina, would he? And if he did, why should she care? Dahlia and Freesia already knew, and most likely Zinnia did, too. She rubbed the back of her neck and the touch of her skin was uncomfortably warm. "We have nothing to talk about. Our breakup was a *mutual* decision. We've both moved on, haven't we? Live and let live, is what I say." She bit her tongue on such a colossal lie.

"You're upset with me. I can tell." He turned his back to Freesia and Zinnia and leaned closer. "We haven't moved on, not in my opinion. We need to clear the air."

"Maybe we should leave." Zinnia gave Freesia a furtive glimpse.

"No way. Go, if you want. I'm staying." Freesia's grin stretched wider. She slid her chair closer to the table.

Camellia groaned. She grabbed Noah's hand and tugged. "We're heading outside to the porch. Go find your gossip elsewhere."

"You're absolutely no fun," Freesia called out as they exited the kitchen.

"Sia hasn't changed a bit." Noah chuckled and took a seat in the wicker settee.

As she walked to the far corner, Camellia stood and, with a defiant glare, raised her chin. "What do you want, Noah? The way I see things, we covered everything thoroughly two years ago." She studied his face. The creased lines across his forehead had deepened. Worry lines, most likely. The vivid blue of his pupils had faded to a dull hue. She lifted her gaze to his hair, once thick and jet black was now peppered with gray. How did someone age that much in such a brief time? Maybe someone who carried around a ton of guilt. She brushed off the faint hint of emerging satisfaction.

With a heave of his shoulders, Noah sighed. "I know you were, *are,* angry with me. I'm not sure why since I explained everything."

"You had an affair." She punctuated each word with venom, bristling at his phony display of innocence.

Noah raked fingers through his hair. "We've covered this subject, haven't we? I didn't have an affair. Trina wanted to, true enough, but I didn't, *couldn't,* be unfaithful to you."

He pleaded with his eyes, and Camellia ignored him. "I wish I could believe you, Noah. Trina usually gets what she wants. Besides, even if you're telling me the truth, you can't erase the reason I left." She uncrossed her arms and spoke with a softer tone. "I lost trust in you. Without trust, no relationship can survive. So, I had to leave you, right? Besides, I've moved on, and you have, too."

"Have you? Have you really moved on, Cam?" As he smiled, his cheekbones lifted. "You're angry. Any feelings about me, good or bad, prove you still care."

Camellia snorted. "Hogwash. Plenty of couples break up and still have some regard for each other. In my case, I might be angry." She held up a finger when he opcncd his mouth. "Λ part of me might be angry, but I have no other feelings for you. I don't care one way or the other what you do with your life. Seeing you the other day reminded me of why."

"Wow. You're spouting some harsh words." He scratched the line of his jaw with one hand. "Not at all like you."

"But I'm telling you the truth. You asked for honesty. Well, you got it." She took long strides toward the back entrance. "Now, if we're done, I'd like to get some sleep."

"I'm not giving up on you. I still love you, Camellia." His voice cracked.

Camellia froze. As his declaration registered, her heartbeat quickened. He *loved* her? All at once, her insides exploding, she twirled. "How dare you say those words? You love me? Well, I sure as hell don't love you."

She marched inside and slammed the door. Throwing the bolt, she locked him outside. He could leave through the backyard. She didn't want to see his face. She turned on her heel and leaned against the wall. The pain she'd worked hard to escape flooded her heart. How dare he make her feel the hurt again? She hated him for everything between them—for being the kind, generous soul she fell in love with, for making her want to spend the rest of her life with him, and for breaking her heart and destroying her trust in people. Most of all, she loathed the reminder of how she was broken and flawed.

"You all right?"

Camellia blinked away tears to see Dahlia. "I'll be fine." She sniffed. Dahlia was the last person she wanted to show how weak she'd become. Besides, this bump in her road was temporary. Everyone had their lows, those depressed moments when everything seemed bleak, but she always powered through those difficulties.

Dahlia tipped her head and wagged a finger. "You don't look fine." She filled the tea kettle, set it on the burner, and flipped on the switch. Steam soon trailed from the spout. "Maybe a bit of Chamomile tea with honey will help calm you."

"I am calm. I'm fine. You don't need to fuss over me." Camellia shook her shoulders and ruffled her hair.

"Sit." Dahlia pointed to the chair.

Her tone was sure and authoritative and made Camellia close her mouth as she saw no point in arguing. She slowly pulled out the chair and sat. Leaning over the table, she cradled her chin in both hands. "I know you know." Her voice dwindled to a faint whisper.

"I do." Dahlia sat next to her and placed a hand on her shoulder. "I knew the moment it happened, why you broke off things with Noah, and why you left. I knew everything."

Camellia leveled her gaze with Dahlia's. Her oldest sister was hard on all of them, but never cruel. In the end, they expected the truth from her and nothing less. "You never said a word. Why?" She tasted the hint of bitterness. Being ignored stung worse than her sister's harsh words, like she'd been cheated because Dahlia refused to console her and denied any advice.

"The idea crossed my mind once or twice to persuade you to stay and argue that maybe you were wrong about Noah, but you weren't ready to hear those words." She shook her head. The kettle whistled, and she stood to fix the tea. She gave Camellia one cup, while she held the other, and settled into her seat.

Camellia sipped. The warm brew with its honey sweetness calmed her. "You're absolutely right. I never wanted to hear I was wrong about him and about leaving."

"What about now?" Dahlia studied her, unblinking.

"He wants to put everything back together; as if he

could." Camellia scoffed. "Like I'm Humpty Dumpty, broken into pieces, but nobody can."

Dahlia sniffed with a shake of her head. "Don't be silly. You're not broken. You're strong, like all of us. You had your heart broken, and you've survived. Noah made you cry because he reminded you of it." She patted Camellia's hand. "You're human, Cam. We all hurt once in a while, and we heal. Life goes that way."

"How'd you get to be so smart? Hmm?"

Dahlia straightened and tipped her chin. "Good genes from our parents. Mom's wisdom and Dad's business savvy. You can't beat those qualities."

"See? You're helping me after all. A couple years after the fact, but your words delivered the perfect sentiment. Thank you." Camellia squeezed Dahlia's arm then finished her tea. "I should get some sleep. I imagine tomorrow will be no less busy than today. I have tons of stuff to do before opening the shop."

"Let us know what we can do to help. Of course, this August venue for the mayor has me needing a third arm to get things done, but I might have a spare moment or two. Also, Zinnie has time. She won't start on the catering details until the week before. Sia is another story." Dahlia waved an arm and whistled. "That girl flits and flutters around so fast, going here and there, I certainly can't keep track."

"She does, doesn't she? Her personality reminds me of Mom. A bit flighty but always thinking or planning her next adventure."

"Sounds about right. Go get your rest. I still have paperwork to finish." Dahlia carried the cups and saucers to the sink.

Camellia paced toward the doorway then paused.

She frowned and her voice quivered. "He told me he still loves me."

Dahlia turned off the spigot and set the final dish in the drain tray. "Of course, he does. I knew that, too. Good night, Cam."

"Good night." A question lingered, but she let the thought pass. Wanting to know taunted her from time to time. Whether her sisters believed the same as Camellia piqued her curiosity. Why did none of them have a man in their lives?

****

After a restful night, Camellia threw open her bedroom window and breathed in the outside air. The neighbor's lawnmower hummed, and children squealed and laughed while playing hopscotch on the driveway pavement. She stared for a moment, smiling, then walked to her closet. She dressed in grubby clothes, ready for a day of cleaning and tidying her new work environment. Hard, physical activity was the distraction she needed. If she got lucky, no reporters, no men, and definitely no haunting memories from the past would interrupt her agenda.

Ringing pierced the air, and she gave her phone a weary glance. Why run the risk of ruining a pleasant morning? She sighed and snatched it off the dresser. A frown surfaced since she didn't recognize the number, though the area code was local. "Hello?"

"Miss Holiday? Camellia Holiday?" A gruff voice sounded.

"This is she." Camellia sat on the edge of her bed.

"Detective Hulsey of the Charleston City Police Department. Do you have a moment to talk?"

Her heartbeat quickened. "Of course. What can I

do for you, Detective?"

"I wonder if we might schedule a meeting, possibly within the next couple of days? I have questions about a former colleague of yours, Gloria Volteri."

Clenching her hand, she dug fingernails into her palm hard enough to pinch and make creases. "Yes, but if you're hoping to get answers about why Gloria planned to visit me, I have nothing to tell you. I have no clue. We didn't end on the best of terms. The fashion scandal, you know." She clamped her mouth shut. Spiked nerves turned her into a blathering fool. She was totally in the dark without any idea how she fit into this final dramatic act of Gloria's life.

"Still, I'm sure you could share other details about Miss Volteri. Can we set up a time to meet? Trust me. You have nothing to worry about. I'm merely following procedure."

She scowled. Didn't they always say not to worry? "How about tomorrow afternoon? Where would you like to meet?"

"I'll come to your house, say about two? I have your address."

His voice remained monotone but in a fast clip. Camellia's mind worked as quickly. "I'd rather meet at my store in town, if you don't mind. I'm in the middle of getting the place ready to open." Actually, she had miles to go before reaching that goal. Her motive was more personal. She didn't want her sisters involved or exposed to any of this trouble. "Otherwise, this meeting will have to wait. I'm very busy."

"Okay. Then give me the address and I'll meet you there. I won't take long. After a few questions, I'll be on my way."

As soon as the call ended, Camellia released her tight grip on the phone. No plausible reason explained why he needed to speak with her. She shifted. No doubt, Stephanie's information might've led the authorities to Serenity and to her, but why? Whether Gloria died of natural causes didn't make any difference.

Camellia stood and paced the room then plopped on the chair next to the window. She faced the mirror and studied her reflection. Lines of worry and exhaustion had aged her. "All right, Camellia Holiday, you've done enough moping. Time to get to work." She smacked her thighs then sprang up from the chair. Grabbing her belongings, she marched out of the bedroom and took the stairs two at a time, nearly colliding with Freesia as she landed in the foyer.

"Whoa! What fire got you running so fast?" Freesia held up both arms and widened her eyes.

"Ha. The only fire is the one inside me. I'm anxious to get my place in order. You want to hit the road and travel to Charleston later this week? I need those supplies."

Freesia nodded. "I have work and the band to keep me tied up today and tomorrow. Rico wrote a couple of new tunes we need to learn, and I'm working a double. How about Friday?"

"Friday's good. See you later." Camellia waved good-bye and stepped outside. After tossing her purse and bag of cleaning supplies onto the backseat, she slipped into her car. Within minutes, she raced down Divinity Boulevard. Though early, many shop owners had started their day—some sweeping the walkways in front of their shops, others inside straightening merchandise on the shelves. Camellia smiled and straightened her shoulders. To be a part of this community of merchants was nice.

She inched alongside the curb in front of her shop and killed the engine. Getting out of the car, she twisted to face the road and stilled. Someone sat on the bench shaded by a tree. Camellia made out the features of a woman. Curly hair touched her shoulders. With her arm extended, she tapped ashes from a cigarette onto the pavement then stood. A tiny gasp bubbled from Camellia's lips.

Trina crossed the road and walked straight toward Camellia, swaying her hips while stiletto heels clicked on the hard concrete. "I hope you don't mind. I had to come and see your shop. Curious, you know."

A heavy dose of sarcasm froze Trina's lips in a rigid line. Camellia hugged the large bag of cleaning supplies to her chest. Heat flushed her cheeks and made her sweat. Trina's designer dress. She recognized the make and the snug form with simple but flattering lines created by Bouchra Girardi. Camellia wanted to sink through the pavement and disappear. When she put them on this morning, her stained shirt and sweat pants with a hole in one knee had felt so comfortable.

Trina stepped closer.

She shifted her gaze up and down in a flash of disapproval, though the movement was barely detectable. Camellia stepped away to distance herself from both Trina and the familiar behavior her nemesis used to demean her. Some things never changed.

"I hope you don't mind." She nodded toward the door.

Camellia shifted the heavy bag in her arms.

"Nothing to see but an empty room with a couple of chairs the previous tenant left behind." She stepped backward and widened her legs in a stubborn stance to block the doorway.

Trina lifted her shoulders and shrugged. "Maybe later, then. I do have a busy schedule this morning. I'm meeting with a representative from Elle Laurante who's interested in a couple of my designs."

Camellia sucked air between tight lips. A thousand wisecracks raced to state the obvious. No way in hell would Elle Laurante want anything Trina Averaux designed. Who was she kidding? Especially someone who knew her, once roomed with her, took classes together, *and* shared a man with her. Camellia's stomach churned.

"You have a good day. Enjoy cleaning and tidying your little shop." A sneer curled her lips. She pivoted on her heel to leave, swaying her hips while she clip-clopped down the sidewalk.

"Lord help me," Camellia groaned and dropped her bag. She twisted the key in the lock to open the shop. How could she possibly forget the irritating, narcissistic, self-righteous snob who stole her fiancé? The woman who seized every opportunity to compete with Camellia, her once best friend in college? She wanted to forget, but she couldn't. Trina was making sure of it.

Camellia tossed the bag in a corner and dropped into the closest chair. She rested her elbows on her knees and cradled her chin in opened palms. Staring out the window with its scene of waves cresting and rolling onto shore calmed her. A speed boat bounced across the water with a skier trailing by several yards. That person was having fun. Something she wished to be doing instead of cleaning.

Fueled by unspent anger, she sprang out of the chair and balled her hands into fists. "Who does she think she is? Flaunting her ass in that cute designer dress, spouting off about Elle Laurante, and dismissing my shop by calling the place little? The nerve." Camellia grabbed the bag and picked out the cleaner and a rag. She sprayed the windows and rubbed with brisk strokes. Cleaning was therapy and never felt so good. She rubbed and sprayed and scrubbed some more.

When she finished the window, a huge sixteen by ten-foot pane of glass, Camellia stood several feet back and admired the clear shine. "Not bad." She smiled and nodded.

Before turning away, she spotted a familiar figure cross the sidewalk and stop to peer inside the shop. She scowled and rummaged through her bag for more supplies, ignoring his presence.

Noah walked inside. "Morning, Cam. Figured I'd drop by to see your place." He shoved both hands in his pockets and glanced around. "Nice."

Camellia couldn't avoid him, not while he stood only feet away. She raised her arms. "Why are you here, Noah?"

"I told you. I wanted to come by to see your place." His smile wavered.

"Seriously?" She'd taken enough for one morning. People she didn't want in her life refused to get the message. "You didn't hear a word I said last night, did you? Go away, Noah. Now. Please." She pointed toward the door.

"Aw, come on. Don't be rude. That kind of behavior isn't like you." Instead of moving to the door, he sat in the chair.

"How do you know what I'm like? Maybe I've changed." She turned to ignore him once more and busied herself with polishing the chair rail. At this point, she didn't care if he was inches away. She clamped her mouth shut, refusing to say another word.

After five minutes of a one-way conversation, Noah heaved a sigh and left.

As always, he was stubborn and annoying. Camellia waited until the door clicked shut before turning to face the front. She scowled at his retreating form. In the next instant, she threw the sopping rag at the window, smearing the surface with suds. "Damn you, Noah Burke."

****

Cleaning the place took the better part of the day before she finished. The walls and window trim wore a fresh coat of paint. The floor's wood planking shined and smelled of O'Toole's oil soap. Camellia nodded and rested her fists on her hips. Sweat dribbled down the middle of her back and chest and soaked her shirt, leaving dark patches stuck to her skin. She plucked open the front and blew air to cool herself.

"My word, surely you are a sight for this man's eyes." Weston stepped into the shop with a smile and a wink.

Camellia scowled. "I'm not giving you a peep show. I believe you know where to go for one of those." This day was certainly hers for visitors. At least, this guy didn't rile her temper. Much.

Weston laughed. "I apologize. You seem to bring

out the mischief in me."

"I can't imagine why." Camellia smoothed back damp curls of hair then waved an arm toward the chair. "Sit."

"Yes, ma'am." Turning around the chair, he straddled his legs on either side and rested his arms and chin on the back while he stared. "You've been working hard. Why don't you take a break? I'll treat you to supper. Of course, Delmonte's is out of the question. Seeing as you enjoy control, I'll even let you choose, again."

Camellia's cheeks puffed out with an impulse to defend herself. She nearly took the bait. Instead, she wagged a finger. "Not snagging me this time. I'm learning your game, Mr. Murphy. Besides, I think a supper date two nights in a row might give people reason to gossip."

He got up and stepped closer, inches away from her face. "Then we go someplace where most folks who dine at the Shoreline Grill won't be. New faces. No gossip. You see where I'm going, don't you?"

He spoke in a husky tone. *Yeah, where exactly are you going, Weston Murphy?* She struggled not to break eye contact, a sure sign of her discomfort. He was dangerous, exciting, attractive, adventurous, and oh so sexy. Yep. Dangerous. How could she remain simply friends?

She swallowed hard. "Sure. I mean, I do see, but no. I have plans with my sisters this evening. Besides, I want to get to bed early because tomorrow is another busy day. So, you can see I have no time." She cursed herself for rambling.

Shrugging, he backed away. Rolling his head side

to side, he examined the room. "Nice job sprucing up. All you need is stuff to fill the space." He turned and smiled. "Maybe you'll have time tomorrow? Seriously, I'd love to spend another evening with you. I enjoy your company, Camellia Holiday."

Once again, her heartbeat fell out of rhythm. Why did he have to be so damned appealing? No romance. No. Romance. She repeated the words in her head but struggled to agree with them. "Maybe tomorrow. I'll be here all day, except I have an appointment in the afternoon with…with someone which shouldn't take long."

"Setting up shop does take a lot of doing, I'd imagine. I'll stop by, say around four?" His brow lifted.

"I didn't exactly say yes." She gripped the hem of her shirt. As sweat trickled down the small of her back, she shivered.

"I know. You said maybe. However…" He paused to approach once more and stood close. "I have this irresistible charm the ladies can't seem to ignore. I turn maybes into yeses." He lifted her hand and kissed it. "Until tomorrow."

Camellia stared at her hand, and then at Weston as he exited the shop. "What just happened?" She blindly grabbed for the chair and sat. Resisting him wouldn't be easy. He'd made his intentions perfectly clear. She rubbed her arms to erase the sudden chill. Not easy at all.

Chapter 8

"This song is for all you guys. Make sure you give your ladies a good reason to stay around." As she broke into a Tracy Chapman tune, Freesia smiled her sexy grin at the audience. Fingers tapped the sides of her thigh to keep rhythm while lead guitarist Tony played a riff on his guitar.

Camellia, Dahlia, and Zinnia sat at a table near the stage.

Zinnia placed two fingers in her mouth and blew a shrill whistle.

"Seriously, Zinnia." Dahlia wagged her head and scowled.

"Oh, lighten up, Dahlia." Camellia grinned. "Freesia loves the attention. Not to mention, this kind of support is good for the band's morale."

"Beats getting booed and hissed at, doesn't it?" Zinnia winked and stood from the table. "Think I'll take a spin on the dance floor. Care to join me?" After a moment, she frowned. No? Fine. See ya later."

"I suppose you're right." Dahlia relaxed her shoulders a bit and motioned to the server. "Got some good news today, as well as some bad, which might be why I'm in a flustered mood."

"Oh? How so?" Camellia shouted over the band's guitars and drums drowning out the room. At this point, her ears were ringing.

Dahlia leaned closer. "We have an okay from Teddy Layard on the venue. Seems someone has been hustling to get the repairs done on the hall. The place should be ready a week before the mayor's gala, which means plenty of time to bring in the furniture and decorate."

Camellia waited while Dahlia took a sip of her beer. "And the bad news?"

Dahlia dabbed at her lips with a napkin. "Teddy wants a ten percent increase on the rental. We don't have the spare change to cover it, not before payment from the mayor."

"Why not ask Mayor Buell for an advance? I'm sure if you explain the circumstances, he'll cooperate." Camellia popped a handful of peanuts in her mouth.

"I don't believe he will. You see, all of the money comes out of his wife's pocket. Vincent doesn't have any dollars to his name." Dahlia groaned and took several swigs from her mug.

Camellia leaned back in her chair. "So, there might be truth to the rumor. Florence suspects or knows her husband has cheated."

"She's hell-bent on punishing him? Yes, I've heard. Sad to say, the rumor might be fact, which means we're up that creek without a paddle." Dahlia pursed her lips.

"You mean because Teddy Layard is cheap and he tends to squeeze a quarter so tight the eagle screams?" Camellia laughed. "Isn't that saying one of Dad's?"

Dahlia grinned. "Along with many other words of southern wisdom. But yes, I'd suspect Teddy figured this opportunity was as good an excuse as any to make a buck."

"What do we do, then?" Camellia scrunched her eyebrows.

"I'll talk to Florence. Woman to woman. Try appealing to her decent side and make her understand punishing Vincent will punish us and our business."

"Seeing as we haven't done her any harm," Camellia reasoned along with her sister. "I think she'll listen." She refused to voice the hint of doubt bubbling to the surface.

"I hope. Anyway, we've got a venue, whether we can afford to pay or not." Dahlia leaned back as the server set another round of drinks on the table, along with bowls of salsa and chips. "If I must get down and dirty, I will. I can play Vincent against Teddy then let them spar to settle the matter."

"Could get ugly." Camellia dipped a chip into salsa, popped it into her mouth and chewed slowly. Her sister's tenacity was impressive.

"Serves them right. The cheap ass and the adulterer," Dahlia grumbled.

"What are you two gossiping about, all secretive and such?" Freesia squatted between them.

Camellia had been so involved in Dahlia's conversation that she didn't notice the music stopped. "Business."

"Yep. Business." Dahlia clucked her tongue then sipped her drink.

"Huh." Freesia frowned and shifted her gaze from one sister to the other. "Fine. You don't want to share? I don't want to know. Probably boring, anyway." She plucked a chip from the bowl. "Speaking of *not* boring, I spotted Noah over by the bar."

"So?" Camellia scowled. One day's run-in with

him was more than enough.

"Well, guess who's sitting next to him, all chatty and cozy like?" Freesia wiggled her brows.

"Sia, don't play games." Camellia didn't glance at the bar, though she exercised extreme effort not to turn around.

"Weston Murphy. How's that man for not boring? Right? Figured you should know, Cammie." Freesia winked, and then sprinted toward the stage.

"What's going on?" Dahlia gave Camellia a sideway glance just as Zinnia returned to the table.

"Yeah, what's up?" Zinnia blotted at the sweat on her cheeks with a napkin. "Did I miss some juicy gossip?"

"It's totally nothing." Camellia wrinkled her nose. She wiggled in her chair to shift more toward the stage with her back to the bar. "Besides, I couldn't care less what they do, and I don't have time to bother with Sia's taunts and teases."

"Hmm," Dahlia and Zinnia said at once.

"Hmm what?" Camellia's raised voice hinted at her agitation.

"Oh, maybe you sound like somebody who does care. We're talking about Noah, right?" Dahlia frowned. "Or has Weston made an impression you can't ignore?"

Camellia glowered at both of them. "Nobody's made an impression. I've told you, or maybe you haven't been listening, I don't have time for romance."

"You never told me." Dahlia lifted her brows. "Did she mention anything of the kind to you, Zinnie?"

"I can't recall." Zinnia shook her head.

"Why are you getting so defensive?" Dahlia leaned

back in her chair.

"I'm not. Geesh. How ridiculous. Can we drop it?" Exasperation flooded over her. Very likely, after reminding herself many times how romance was off the table, she'd confused who she might or might not have told. Camellia sighed. At this point, she didn't know her head from a hole in the ground—another of Dad's homespun words of wisdom.

For the rest of the evening, Dahlia didn't have much to say. Even though unintentional, Camellia had nipped at her feelings. In any case, the music and the drinks kept them all occupied. As the time drew closer to leave the club, Camellia relaxed, figuring she escaped any awkward moments with Noah or Weston.

"Good evening, ladies. I must say you all look divine." Trina stood next to their table.

Her voice dripped with its usual sarcasm. Camellia braced her shoulders as she gave Trina a once-over. She wore a tight, sequined halter top, skinny jeans, and her signature footwear, stiletto heels which fit the look. Her hair was teased to the ceiling. Long dangly earrings with diamond studs swung while she bobbed her head. All suited for nightclubs like The Darby or Avenue in New York, maybe. Not in Chico's Club Serenity. Not that she'd ever get into places like those New York exclusives.

"Hello, Trina," Dahlia answered with a jab to Camellia's side underneath the table.

Camellia stretched her lips into what might pass for a smile. "Uh, yeah. Nice outfit."

"I'm surprised you're not at the bar playing referee, Cam." Trina tipped her head in that direction. "Your ears should be burning with all the talk about you. I'd put a stop to that nonsense before a barroom brawl explodes."

"What do you—I mean, how ridiculous," Camellia sputtered.

"Oh, I can assure you it's all systems go. Those two men don't know when to quit. I'd be surprised if either is left standing on two legs by the time Chico closes up the place. Well, as the French say, *à tout à l'heure.* I'm off to visit a tall hunk of a man standing over by the door. Hey there, sweetie. Don't you move," Trina hollered and pushed through the crowd.

Camellia couldn't resist laughing, and both sisters joined her. "I swear, she is one piece of work."

"Amen." Zinnia pointed behind Camellia. "Although, when two men are interested in the same woman, in this case you, and they're all chummy while they talk and drink, I'd say you've got a ticking time bomb."

Camellia let out a mournful groan. "They're not cave men, Zinnie. Just two grown men sharing conversation and drinks. I doubt a problem exists. Trina enjoys creating drama, and needling me gives her added satisfaction." With a weary gaze, she studied Noah and Weston. Their body movements indicated no sign of tension or heated fireworks ready to explode. She squirmed in her chair. "I'm heading to the ladies' room." She rose and worked her way through the crowd of tables to the opposite end of the club, relieved the path didn't take her past the bar.

She glanced at her watch. A full hour remained until closing, and they had to wait until then to give Freesia a ride since her car was in the shop. Camellia prayed for luck. No Weston and definitely no Noah confrontations this evening, especially not the two of them together. Picturing that image made her shudder.

Peeking out of the restroom doorway, she spotted Noah. He turned the corner and was traveling in her direction. At once, she hopped back inside and slammed the door. She gave a young girl coming out of a stall an uneasy glance then stood at the sink and washed her hands. She hummed the Happy Birthday song more than once, which took up a minute or so, more than enough time for Noah to disappear into the men's room. She scrambled to the door and opened to take another look. Her breath expelled in a long sigh of relief. With no sign of him, she exited and hurried down the hallway. Circling a couple making out in the middle of the aisle, she crashed into someone with a resounding thud. "Oh, I'm sorry. I didn't see." She raised her chin to stare directly into Noah's face. Her shoulders collapsed. So much for dodging the unwanted.

"I thought you walked this way. But then you disappeared, and I figured you'd gone to visit the little girl's room." Noah smiled, though one corner of his mouth twitched.

The nervous tic. The sign he'd grown unsure of his actions. Camellia knew it well. She set her mouth in a determined scowl. *Strike while the moment is yours. Hit him while he's vulnerable.* All those bits of advice crossed her mind. She jabbed his chest with one finger. "Noah, how often will you make me repeat myself? I don't want to talk with you. Not now. Maybe not ever." She skirted around him, but his hand stopped her.

"Can't we start over? Seriously, Camellia. With so much history between us, we can't chuck everything we had without trying again. In my opinion, our relationship was solid and worth fighting for." He steadied his gaze on her.

She twisted her arm but couldn't escape his tight grip. "Our relationship *was*. Past tense. However, you were there. You know what happened. Sometimes, only one experience is needed to test a person's love. Mine wasn't strong enough to trust you. You should get on with your life. Find someone new. Now, I'm going back to sit with my sisters and enjoy the rest of the evening. Good-bye, Noah." She yanked her arm out of his grasp and marched away, leaving him speechless.

Her hands shook, her legs wobbled, and her blood boiled, but Camellia reached the table.

"Okay, what's wrong? You look and act like you're ready to pop a blood vessel," Dahlia said.

As she gripped the chair and sat, Camellia shook her head. "The usual mess. How about another round of drinks?" She motioned to the server.

"I noticed Noah walking in your direction." Dahlia studied Camellia's face.

"He can walk where he pleases." Camellia shrugged. "We'll take another round of beers," she announced as the server approached.

"Judging by the scowl you're giving me, he must've said something to upset you." Dahlia leaned across the table to tap the server's arm. "We need more chips and salsa, too. Thanks."

"He can say what he pleases and go where he chooses which is no matter to me. Can we drop it? I'm done talking," Camellia argued, hoping to give Dahlia the warning not to cross any line.

"Say, Zinnie. Did you order those rolls for the

Thompson reception? We have no time to make them from scratch, you know," Dahlia said.

Camellia relaxed. Noah wouldn't dare return for round two. As for Weston? She glanced at the bar to find no sign of him. Relieved or disappointed, she wasn't sure. How pathetic. When would she make up her mind? They were friends. Friendship was all she wanted. Right?

"Well, if it isn't my favorite tour guide."

She looked up to greet him with a smile. Heat rose inside as her heart hiccupped. Okay. Confess, Camellia Holiday. You like him, and more than a little. Remembering that kiss brought a flush to her skin. How right it felt. How *good*. She cleared her throat and said, "Favorite is an awfully strong adjective. Besides, one experience hardly counts for evaluation."

Weston widened his grin. "Oh, I'd say it's enough. We already have a date for the second tour. I have confidence in you."

Camellia squirmed in her seat. His dogged determination was becoming quite the habit. "We'll see." She turned to Dahlia and Zinnia. "I promised Weston a tour of Charleston, when and *if* I find the time."

"What a fantastic idea." Freesia sneaked up behind Camellia and squeezed her arm. "Because I was about to tell you I can't get away this Friday for our little shopping spree. I worried you'd be disappointed, but here I don't need to feel badly since you can go with Weston."

Leave it to Freesia. Camellia blushed and wanted to run out of the building. However, she gripped the sides of her chair.

"Such a lucky thing. Right, Dahlia? Zinnie?" Freesia bobbed her head.

Camellia scowled at each of them, saving the biggest scowl for Weston. "Yeah, lucky thing. I guess it's settled. Can you go Friday?" She spoke through gritted teeth.

"I do believe I can clear my schedule. Although a shopping spree sounds far from my comfort zone." As he frowned, Weston's brows knitted together.

Camellia wanted to laugh. Now, who was uncomfortable? Served him right, putting her on the spot in front of her sisters. "Don't be afraid. I promise we'll only visit a dozen or so stores, which won't take more than half the day." Seeing his eyes widen and jaw drop, she nearly burst.

Freesia winked at Camellia. "She's kidding, of course. Cam hates shopping. *So* not the typical female. Nothing like me at all. She visits most of those stores for my sake. I am the true shopaholic."

"Do you have to ruin all my fun?" Camellia griped. "I planned to let him squirm for a while longer."

"Gee. I might have to re-evaluate my assessment of your guide skills, Miss Holiday." Weston relaxed back into his playful, teasing mode.

"I warned you." Camellia winked and waited for him to say his good-byes, but when he remained, she looked at Freesia. "You done for the night? I'd like to get home."

"Because she has a busy day tomorrow, you know." Weston widened his lips to grin at Camellia.

Camellia sighed. At least he didn't mention their supper date for tomorrow, which wasn't something she'd agreed to, yet. "Good night, Weston." When he bid everyone good evening and departed for the exit, she sighed with relief.

"Wow. Awesome," Freesia exclaimed. "I love playing matchmaker."

"Seriously?" Camellia pinched her lips. She refused to let herself be goaded into another edgy exchange of words. Not with Freesia. She stood and grabbed her bag strap off the chair. "Let's go. I'm drained and need sleep."

"What? No protest about how you're not interested in romance? I am truly surprised." Freesia laughed, wrapped her arms around Camellia, and squeezed. "I love you, Cammie. Count on me to watch out for you."

The club chatter had dwindled to a few laughs and shouts of good-bye as people filed outside. Camellia cleared a path around the tables to exit the bar. Her sisters gabbed and giggled while she remained quiet. A replay of the conversation with Weston captured her mind. She might have asked what he and Noah discussed. But how would her curiosity make her look? Like she cared what they found to talk about? "Nope. Not going in that direction." She smacked the door with the flat of her hand and exited the building. Fresh air. A couple of deep breaths and the tension rolled off her shoulders. She wiggled her fingers to loosen her tight grip on her bag.

The lot remained crowded with cars. She scanned the rows, groaned in frustration, and then pressed the remote until her car lights blinked. Third row near the light post, right where she intended to park so she'd remember, but her preoccupation with Weston and how she felt about him consumed all her thoughts. She pictured home and bed. The idea put her in a better mood. As they neared the car, Camellia slowed and raised a palm behind her to signal her sisters.

A girlish giggle sounded from the next row. "You are such a cutie. Can I take you home and keep you? Ooo, yummy." Trina and the tall, hunky guy she had mooned over pawed each other while their lips locked.

Camellia groaned. The picture rivaled any steamy romance book cover.

"Does she ever stop?" Zinnia whispered over Camellia's shoulder. "Men are like the flavor of the month club with her."

"More like flavor of the week. None of them last a month." Camellia glared at the couple. In the next instant, she curled her mouth into a satisfying grin. She lifted one arm and pressed the alarm button on the car remote. Loud beeping erupted.

Trina screamed.

The tall hunky guy ran behind a car and out of sight. He hissed and motioned for Trina to do the same. "I can't let my wife see me." He whined loud enough for anyone nearby to hear.

Camellia and her sisters, even Dahlia, laughed. Camellia was close to tears.

Freesia jumped up and down.

Zinnia and Dahlia clutched their sides and leaned against the rear bumper to keep from falling.

Once she caught her breath, Camellia's words tumbled out. "I can't imagine, but I think Trina saved my evening. Yep. Definitely a memorable moment."

Camellia and her sisters made their final steps to the car. As she drove through the lot, Camellia laid on the horn.

"Just you wait, Holiday sisters." Shrill and loud,

Trina spewed her words. "I'll get you." She pummeled her make-out date with her designer Gucci bag, extra-large size.

Camellia grinned. "Definitely a memorable moment."

Chapter 9

The irritating, incessant buzz of the alarm penetrated her ears. Camellia snatched the clock off the nightstand and tossed it across the bedroom. Her head threatened to implode. She threw the covers over her head.

"Not so fast, Princess Camellia. You have much to do this morning. Or so you told me last night." Zinnia rushed into the room and ripped back the covers to expose her sister's face. "Ugh." She shuddered. "Maybe the world isn't ready for that look." She threw the sheet over Camellia's head and laughed.

"Ha. Funny girl makes a joke." Camellia peeked out then inched to a sitting position. A scowl pulled her brows together. She glowered at the mirror and her bed hair which stood out in a tangled mess.

"Beyond a doubt, you don't manage well from a night out. A healthy breakfast and a few cups of java should cure you. I think you'll be fine. Come on. Chop, chop." Zinnia clapped her hands and marched toward the doorway. She threw a glance over her shoulder and nodded at the floor. "Guess you need to add an alarm clock to your shopping list." She tisk-tisked on her way down the stairs.

Camellia stuck out her tongue before dropping her head to cradle it in both hands. "She's right. I don't manage well. Look what all work and no play has done,

Camellia Holiday." Put the blame on Gloria V, the work horse. Camellia lay back on the bed once more. She'd be meeting with Detective Hulsey this afternoon. Having no hint as to why he wanted to talk accelerated her anxiety into maximum drive. How would she look to him? Twitching eyes, fidgety hands, and sweaty brow conveyed she was guilty of something.

Camellia bounced out of bed and slipped on her clothes. "I'm certainly not lying around and fretting about it. No sir. I'll finish cleaning my store, and this evening I'll go out for a relaxing, enjoyable supper with a very nice man. Yep."

Crossing the room, she stopped at the mirror and shuddered. With a few quick brush strokes, she tamed the bed hair then marched down the stairs with deliberate steps, as if charging into battle, which is exactly what it felt like. Entering the hallway, she slowed the pace and lightened her steps. No point in alarming Zinnia, or especially Dahlia, who could read any sign without Camellia saying a word. Yeah, she loved home and family but missed her privacy sometimes.

"Good morning." Dahlia sat at the table with her hands folded tightly around a coffee mug.

Camellia frowned. "You seem, ah, cheery?"

"Why shouldn't I?" At once, Dahlia's smiling lips tightened into a grimace.

Camellia scratched behind one ear and glanced at Zinnia who gave her head a quick, understated shake. She returned her attention to Dahlia. "Of course, you should. Don't mind me. I'm still groggy from last night's outing."

"Amateur." Freesia entered the kitchen. "I'd say

New York softened your bones. We've got to do something to put the southern back in you, don't we, sisters?" She looked to Dahlia and Zinnia with a wide-eyed stare.

"I'm fine. Stop fussing." Camellia snatched the coffee pot off the counter, poured, and then scooped eggs onto a plate. She scrambled to think of a topic that kept the conversation away from where Freesia steered it. "Trina in the parking lot." She wagged her head and laughed. "How funny was that sight? I'd have given anything to snap a picture of her and the hunky, married guy cowering behind the car." She sat at the table with her breakfast and cradled the hot mug in her hands to warm the awkward chill inside her. "Maybe next time, because I'm sure one will happen, right?"

"Speaking of hunky guys." Freesia scooted a chair closer to Camellia and winked. "Weston Murphy is pretty hunky, don't you agree?"

Camellia sipped her coffee then slowly set the mug in front of her. "I'm not talking about him, Sia. Or about Noah. Please, let the issue be. Okay?"

"Fine. You're absolutely no fun, Cammie. But I'll stop, like you asked." Freesia patted her hand. "Hey, Dahlia? Tony wants to know if we still need a band for the mayor's venue. He has friends looking for work."

"Today, I can barely promise food, flowers, and chairs for the guests. Until I see a check in my hands from the mayor, Holiday Events and Catering's assets are frozen, which means contracting a band is not in the works." Dahlia stabbed at a piece of fruit.

Freesia leaned against the chair and stared at Dahlia in silence. Her gaze circled the table, landing on Camellia then Zinnia. "Is it that bad? Business, I mean?

I sort of suspected, but being busy at the club, I put any of those thoughts out of my mind." She grew quiet and chewed on a fingernail.

Dahlia leaned across the table. "You keep working at Chico's and singing with the band. We might need the income before long."

Freesia's mouth dropped open. "Please tell me you're kidding."

Dahlia waved a hand. "I doubt matters get to that point. You keep saving for college classes, and let me worry about the family business. We've been in worse situations, right?"

"Right." Freesia sniffed. She rose from the chair and nodded. "I should go. Early practice this morning. You all have a great day, and I'll see you at suppertime."

Camellia knitted her brows and studied Freesia as she jogged down the hallway. "I do believe that conversation is the most serious I've ever witnessed come out of Sia's mouth. You know?"

"Serious as a Sunday sermon." Zinnia agreed then smiled while holding up the basket. "Who wants more biscuits?"

Camellia grew silent. She shifted the untouched eggs from one side of the plate to the other. Thoughts of the future pummeled her brain. If the family business, which had been running for over a decade, couldn't make a go of it, what hope did she have for her simple designer shop?

****

Morning swept by in a flurry while Camellia cleaned. She took one break to eat lunch and call Maxine's Office Supply. Once Maxine reassured her

118

the store had everything she needed and agreed to put the order on hold, Camellia brightened. She grinned while images of Weston with a sour face formed a picture in her head. She'd show him the historic sites around Charleston, as promised—*after* a full tour of the city's businesses to complete her shopping list.

A glance at the clock made her nerves shift upward a few notches. The time approached for Detective Hulsey to arrive. As if on cue, the door chime tinkled and in walked a stocky but muscular male, dressed in a tailored, navy-blue suit. He wore dark sunglasses, which he removed once the door closed behind him, revealing an intense, yet indistinct, expression.

"Good afternoon. What can I do for you?" Camellia greeted, not wanting to assume the obvious.

He tipped his head and extended a hand. "Detective Bill Hulsey. If I found the right place, you must be Camellia Holiday." A smile surfaced, which feathered the corners of his eyes with tiny lines.

Camellia returned the smile. "Pleasure to meet you." Of course, this meeting was hardly pleasurable, but she shoved those thoughts to the back of her mind. "Won't you sit? I'm sorry. I haven't yet furnished the place with comfortable chairs. They are on my shopping list, though." A nervous hiccup erupted, and she quickly covered her mouth.

"Not a problem. I won't take up too much of your time." He settled into a wooden, folding chair and fished out a small notepad and pen from his pocket.

Good grief. He needed to take notes? She sat across from him and fussed with where to place her hands until they fell into her lap. "Such a shame about Gloria. Dying from a heart attack is so sudden, isn't it?"

Detective Hulsey glanced up from his notepad and steadied his gaze on Camellia. "Why do you say a heart attack? Nothing has been verified by the coroner."

Camellia ran her tongue along the roof of her mouth. "Hmm. The television news carried the story and, well, you know." She shrugged.

He smiled. "The media always jumps to conclusions, doesn't it? Only in this case, the story will probably turn out true. Until we hear from the coroner, her death remains under investigation."

Camellia patted her thighs with both hands. "Why did you need to speak with me?" She held her breath for several beats.

"Miss Volteri's assistant claims her boss planned to visit you in Charleston," he started.

"I told you. *If* she intended to see me, I haven't the slightest idea why." Camellia suppressed the urge to explain how she and Gloria hadn't parted on the nicest of terms. Hulsey might get the idea she wanted the woman dead. He might even add her to his list of suspects. She gripped the edge of the chair. Somehow, she needed to get a hold of herself.

Hulsey tapped the end of his pen on the notepad and remained quiet. In the next instant, he smiled. "I need to confess something, Miss Holiday. I've been told to keep this detail quiet, but maybe you should know. Heck, even the media isn't aware, nor is anyone else outside the precinct. Miss Tumler explained the reason her boss planned to visit you was…"

The shop door flew open.

Camellia startled and clutched her throat with one hand while Remy, the spikey-haired boy, entered. His signature smirk crossed his face. Piled in his hands was a stack of papers.

"Remy." Camellia gave the detective an apologetic smile. "What brings you here?"

"Sorry to barge in, but maybe you could use more fliers? In fact, maybe I can put some up for you. You know, like around town?" He shrugged but shifted his gaze back and forth from Camellia to Detective Hulsey.

"Why, how very generous of you, Remy. Why don't you leave some with me and put up the rest?"

"Sure thing. That'd be great. I have the afternoon and evening off. I'm bored out of my skull, and this job will help." He sneaked another glance at the detective.

Camellia frowned at Remy.

He swallowed hard, and his Adam's apple shifted. "Everything okay with you, Miss Holiday?" Remy shuffled his feet.

"Sure, it is, Remy." She pointed at Hulsey. "We were in the middle of a private conversation. If you don't mind?"

"Oh, yeah. I'll see you later." Remy skipped backward a few steps then stormed out of the shop as quickly as he'd come.

Hulsey chuckled. "Interesting kid. Now, where was I? Oh, Miss Tumler's comment, which comes from someone I know next to nothing about, not her or her credibility. NYPD wants to follow up, and since I'm here…" He shrugged.

"I get it. No problem." Camellia smoothed the edges of her shirt.

"All right, then. Seems the personal assistant claims Gloria wanted to speak with you about a selection of dresses that went missing from her shop after the scandal broke. NYPD took everything in stock as evidence, but the records supposedly didn't match. A dozen or so of, let's see…" Hulsey raised the notepad to study it for a moment. "Christine Dio dresses?"

Camellia pressed her lips to stifle the laugh. "I haven't a clue where the dresses are. I certainly don't have them." At once, she stiffened her shoulders and gave a firm shake of her head. "Understand. All those dresses have special labels in them, specially made as a collaborative creation between Gloria and the Dior designer to model at the next major fashion event. The designs are unique. No one could sell them without being caught eventually. Doing so would be like passing counterfeit money or marked bills and way too easy to track." Camellia clutched the sides of her chair until her knuckles ached. What was Stephanie up to?

Detective Hulsey's brow wrinkled. "If that's the case, why not remove the labels and then sell them?"

"Because at some point, anyone who knows fashion would recognize them." Camellia's voice grew louder. She waited several heartbeats before trying again. "To get away with such a crime is impossible. Unless someone planned to hide the designs and never wear or sell or give them away, which is insane."

Detective Hulsey shrugged. "Well, I'm sure NYPD will come up with answers. Those problems aren't mine. But the case of Gloria Volteri's death is. At least until we hear from the coroner." He stood and offered her a hand to shake. "It's been a pleasure. Good luck with your new business. Going to design your own clothes, I take it?"

"Some. Other designs will have to fill the racks, until I can create more of my own. Building my line takes time." She formed a rigid smile. Allowing Hulsey to see how unsettled she was wouldn't be wise.

"I'll be in touch if I have any further questions. But I'm sure everything will turn out fine." He tipped his hand and strode toward the door.

"How long will the coroner's report take?" Camellia chewed her bottom lip.

"Don't like to speculate about such things, but when the news comes, I'll phone you. In the meantime, try not to worry. The case seems cut and dry. I'm just going through procedure." He stopped at the doorway then spun on his heel. "One more thing, about Gloria's other assistant. Emily Van Louver? Do you know where I can reach her?"

Camellia blinked. "Ah, yeah. I have her number. She's overseas, working in Paris, but I'm sure you can get a hold of her. Why?" She retraced her steps to behind the desk and fished her phone out of her bag.

"Me being thorough. Investigative procedure, like I said." He smiled and wrote the number displayed on Camellia's phone in his notepad.

Camellia resisted the urge to wipe the sweat trickling down her underarms. Emily wasn't the type of person to take the dresses. She was neither stupid nor greedy.

"You have a good afternoon, Miss Holiday." Hulsey tipped the notepad in her direction and then stepped outside.

Camellia watched from the window until he got in his car and drove away. Her muscles refused to relax, and her hands shook. Whatever was going on, she had no answers. Stephanie behaved like a vindictive, bitter, crazy person whose one agenda drove her to lash out and hurt Camellia. But why? Jealousy? She sensed as much from their phone conversation. What were her words? Something about never liking Camellia's attitude and suspecting she had something to hide? Camellia's knees weakened, and she collapsed into the chair. "Unbelievable." She swiped at the tears stinging her eyes.

"What's unbelievable?"

Camellia twisted her head to face the doorway and Weston. He leaned against the door frame, smiling that lazy smile, until he saw her face.

"Hey, what's wrong?" He rushed over and knelt. Grabbing both her hands, he squeezed.

The intense worry reflected in his expression wasn't lost on Camellia. Her heart quickened at the touch of his hands on hers. "It's nothing, really. Just one of those days that runs out of control and causes all sorts of trouble." She glanced at the clock. "You're early."

"I am. Truth is, I couldn't stand another minute cooped up in Uncle Samuel's tiny house. Starting our evening a bit early seemed a pleasant alternative." He leaned closer. "You sure there's nothing I can do? I'm a fairly good listener. Ask any of my three sisters. They taught me well."

Camellia drew an unsteady breath and smiled. "Three, huh? I can't imagine you had much choice, being outnumbered and all."

"Hardly. I have three brothers, too, which should've given us the upper hand, but you know how powerful women can be."

Surprised by his admission, Camellia let go of a deep belly laugh. She carried on for a minute or more until all her energy was spent, but her spirits lightened at the much-needed release. "I do know." She wiggled her hands free of his. His touch consumed and electrified her. If she pulled him close enough to smell his cologne again... She cleared her throat. "Thank you."

"My pleasure." Weston stood and took a few steps back. "I suggest now might be a good time to leave and go to supper early. Maybe have a couple drinks to calm the nerves and brighten the mood. What do you say?"

"I say yes." Exiting the building and steering toward his car, Camellia held onto her smile. She left behind all those ugly thoughts about Stephanie and the untimely death of Gloria. No more sad times. She'd had enough of sad. The remainder of her day would be filled with fun.

****

The dim lighting of Southern Belle Tavern enhanced the romantic atmosphere. Conch shell candles decorated the table and filtered the air with the aroma of sandalwood.

"I must say your taste in restaurants has greatly improved." Camellia sipped wine and savored the sweet, crisp taste. She peered at Weston over the edge of her goblet. He'd been the perfect gentleman, though something seemed off. She couldn't quite put a finger on the reason. He wasn't transparent like most of the men she'd dated. The overplayed scenario was more like, "let's get this meal over with and move on to the bedroom for steamy sex."

Of course, Noah had been different. He was a true gentleman in every sense. Or at least, she believed he was until his relationship with Trina waved a red flag in her face. Nope. They were mostly all the same. Weston

125

might be harder to figure out, but did she expect to find him any different? A sigh escaped her lips. Was she jaded, or what?

"Is the meal to your satisfaction? Uncle Samuel recommended the place. He claimed the lobster bisque is the best in town. And he assured me no unsavory entertainment would be present." Weston dabbed his mouth with a napkin.

Camellia shook her head. "You are a funny guy, Weston Murphy. One minute you're all full of jokes and teasing barbs. The next, you behave like you stepped out of a nineteenth century southern plantation, spewing proper manners and etiquette, not to mention using words like unsavory. And yes, the lobster bisque is delicious, creamy, and the perfect blend of mushrooms and onion. The rice could use a tad more of garlic seasoning, though." She curled her lips into an impish grin.

Weston gleamed with amusement. "I'll make a note to add your comments when I post my review on the restaurant's website." He scratched the side of jaw. "You know, truth be told, I have quite a story to explain why I speak this way."

Camellia frowned. "You admit you imitate a southern antebellum gentleman's way of talking?"

"Not exactly." Weston leaned over the table. "I don't like to brag, but my family is old money. Part of Carolina's first settlers, far back in the 1700s. My great grandma is still alive, one-hundred-fifteen on her next birthday, which means her grandfather lived during the Civil War. She's got a mind as sharp as a tack, my great grandma, that is. The stories she tells." Weston whistled. "I've written them down and plan to have them published sooner or later."

Camellia waited to digest what he said. If he was making a point, he was failing miserably. "I'm not sure where you're going with this story."

"Right. I'm taking a detour when a straight road is ahead. What I mean is since I've grown up listening to southern formality from most all my elders, quite a bit of their mannerisms has stuck with me and become a habit. Especially when I'm nervous. Like now." He sat straight and grew silent.

The intense blue and hint of green in his eyes shone brightly. Camellia's breath hitched, and the sudden urge to wander inside them, even drown there, hit her. She tipped her head and smiled. "I think I like you, Weston Murphy. Maybe now, your nerves can settle a bit, and thanks for sharing your story. I hope one day to meet your grandma. She sounds like an interesting person."

"She is. I'd love for you to meet her. Meet all my family, in fact." At once, he grinned and snapped his fingers. "Why not tomorrow?"

Camellia scrunched her forehead. "Didn't you say you live up north?"

"I do. Originally from Charleston, but I moved to New York three years ago. When NYU offered me a teaching position, I couldn't refuse. Especially for the income." He chuckled. "A poor architect has to feed and clothe himself, doesn't he?"

Camellia frowned and wagged a finger. "You played me. I should be asking you for the tour of Charleston."

Weston bowed his head. "I apologize. I'll admit my method was underhanded. I like spending time with you, no matter what excuses I have to make. I hope you'll forgive this poor, starving architect."

His droopy eyes and pouty mouth gave him a sad and remorseful look. Camellia remained silent for a minute or more. His confession was harmless, but she'd let him squirm with guilt, all the same. "I forgive you. This time. You know, I'm surprised. Don't architects make good money?" She slid her plate to the side and settled an elbow on the table. One palm cradled her chin. "Don't tell me you're one of those men who's joined a crusade against the establishment and capitalism."

Weston threw back his head and laughed. "Hardly. I haven't found an employer I feel is a comfortable fit in every way, and offering a decent salary is only one component."

Camellia stared, unblinking and with eyes narrowed.

"Okay, I might be a little of what you think. As rebel against society's ways, I won't compromise my values and be a part of tearing down the old to build the new. Some people call those deals progress. I call their attitude a desecration of history."

The fire in his words animated his tone.

"Well. I didn't expect such enthusiasm." Camellia twirled a ringlet of her hair while she considered his confession. Instead of getting closer to figuring him out, she understood even less. He was truly a complicated man, carefree, easy-going, but tinged with deeply meaningful intent. Penetrating those layers of personality would be like peeling an onion.

He shrugged. "I hope I don't disappoint your enterprising ambition. I admire what you aim to accomplish. I have goals, too. I'm selfish and want everything my way. No compromise."

Camellia scratched her cheek. "No. I understand. Sometimes I wish I'd done things differently. My life in New York with Gloria, for instance, could've used some forethought." She wanted to forget. Life without compromise sounded nice. However, as long as she let personal crap like her reaction to Noah's fling get in the way, foolish decisions would happen. Running off to New York on a whim was a big one.

"Always room for a do-over. I admit, I'm not perfect." Weston waved a hand in an exaggerated gesture. "I know. I know. Difficult to believe, but I'm not. I made dumb decisions in my young and foolish years, but no time like the present to straighten out my act."

"Boy, you sure know how to spin a story, don't you? Weston Murphy, you should have taken up sales or become a preacher. You're a natural at slinging bull," Camellia teased.

"Not bull. Just straight-up facts. My gut tells me you'll pull through and be back on top in no time." He chewed on his lower lip then sighed. "You've got energy, imagination, and moral character."

"Guess we all can use some improvement." Camellia broke away from his gaze to scan the restaurant. Southern Belle Tavern was the trendy hot spot along the Carolina coast. According to Freesia, many celebrities and politicians frequented the place. No wonder, with the excellent cuisine, plush atmosphere, and mellow music, it was easy enough to lull her into a state of romantic complacency.

She gazed around her then paused at a view of the

Kathryn Long

front entrance. She flicked her gaze back to Weston. The quickening of her heartbeat triggered light-headedness. "Say. Maybe we can skip dessert and go for a walk along the beach. My insides are about to burst with all those generous portions. What do you think?"

"Well, if you insist. Let me finish this beer and get the server's attention to bring the check. Sound good?" Weston took a swig from his mug.

Camellia tapped a foot against the chair leg. "Sure. Anytime." Failing to resist, she peeked once again at the front table. She was right. Noah sat with a woman whose back faced this way. Not Trina, whose flaming red, bouffant hairstyle was an obvious giveaway. No, this woman was a brunette with thick luscious curls. Seeing Noah turn in her direction, Camellia quickly lowered her head. She picked at a smudge of red sauce that dropped on her lap.

"You seem nervous. Is something wrong?" Weston finished his drink and set the mug to the side.

"No! I mean, no, of course not. Though this wine seems particularly strong." She let go of a nervous laugh. "My head is swimming. Do you think we could leave now?" Camellia struggled to focus on Weston. However, her mind was losing the battle with her emotions. Her reaction was stupid. She didn't care if Noah saw her out with Weston. Why give a hoot about who he took to supper? She slumped back in her chair. Except she didn't trust him. What if he said or did something to embarrass her in front of Weston? She forced her lips into a smile. "I'll be fine after a good night's sleep. Too much going on in my life, I guess."

"I'm sorry. I've been insensitive. I should've

realized. I mean, after all you've been through in the past." As their server drew near, Weston waved an arm to grab his attention.

"Wait." Camellia straightened in her seat. "What exactly are you referring to? The all I've been through part." Her heart pounded, slamming against her chest. She glared at Weston whose face reddened. "You know." As she gasped in a raspy breath, she failed to keep her emotions from exploding. Squinting, she leaned closer. "He told you about us, didn't he? Last night at the club. That little shit. When I—what else did the two of you talk about?" She dug her nails into the palms of her hands. "Did you compare notes on how I kiss? Or maybe Noah shared stories of our past relationship, and you listened. He certainly can tell a great story. I bet you sat at the bar, soaking up every detail." The taste of bisque soured in her stomach. "God, Weston, you invaded my privacy, and probably enjoyed the fact. Do you know how cheap you've made me feel?" Not caring whether Noah spotted her, Camellia rose from her chair. Maybe she was being irrational, spinning over the top and into a full blowout of rage. She didn't care. "I can get myself home. Bill me for my meal. I don't want anything from you."

"Camellia, wait. I didn't, we didn't talk about you that way." He grabbed hold of her arm.

But she jerked away. "Don't," she snapped. "Just leave me alone, will you?" Camellia marched off toward the exit. As she approached Noah's table, she lifted her chin. The urge to punch him overwhelmed her, but she chose option number two. She circled to face his date, who was beautiful, which made the situation all the worse. "Watch this one, sweetie. He likes to kiss and tell all. And I do mean all." She glared at Noah. "Asshole."

She couldn't travel fast enough to reach outside. Landing on the exit steps, she quivered, took an unsteady deep breath, and another, and finally relaxed until a hand rested on her shoulder. She gasped and twirled. "Oh, my lord. You nearly caused me heart failure. What are you doing here?"

"I planned to meet a friend at the restaurant after my shift but looks like I got stood up. Question is, why are you out here and alone? Where's Weston?" Freesia rubbed her arms. "Gotten a bit cool out, hasn't it?"

Camellia eyed the skimpy camisole and skinny shorts and scowled. "Maybe you should wear more clothing. Who were you supposed to meet, anyway? You look like a paid escort."

"Camellia Holiday! I do not. My outfit is perfectly suitable attire when—oh, never mind. You're avoiding my question." Freesia tapped her heel in double time.

A smile spread across Camellia's face, despite her sour mood. "Aren't you touchy? Well, I ended the date early, which wasn't going the way I liked."

Freesia dropped her shoulders. "Oh, Cam. He seems like such a nice guy. How could you give up on him already?"

The pouty expression on her face was priceless. Camellia's smile grew. "NOYB, like your explanation of the vanishing date."

She planted her fists on her hips. "Well, just so happens I spoke to Weston a minute ago. Yes, I did. I recognize that face of yours. So, don't go spewing any of your reprimands. He says you refused to give him a chance to explain." She wagged a finger. "I do believe you're being paranoid. Why don't you go back inside and listen to what he has to say? And while you're at it, maybe throw in an apology to Noah. He was minding his own business, having dinner with a beautiful lady, whom I strongly believe has been scared away, permanently. Thanks to you." Freesia stopped and took in air.

Camellia had her chance to throw in a few words. "How in the world did you…? Never mind. I don't want to know details about your sneaking around. As for Noah, he doesn't deserve an apology. Or Weston." She smacked her thigh. "Not after what they did. I'm done with them. Period. I should've listened to myself and stuck with my plan. No romance until I get my career on track. Or maybe never." She glowered at Freesia, daring her to argue.

Freesia grimaced. "Fine. Die an old spinster. I'm through saving your ass. This is me being done with you." She spit on the ground and rubbed the toe of her heel back and forth over the spot.

Camellia lifted a brow. "Not too dramatic, are you? Look, Sia. I am beyond exhausted. I've had a trying day." She chose not to mention any details, like about her visit from Detective Hulsey. Freesia might not worry, but she'd most likely run and blab to their sisters who would fret and fuss.

Freesia scowled. "Anything I can do to help?"

The restaurant door flew open.

Camellia tensed until she spotted a couple holding hands step outside. "You leaving soon? Maybe you could give me a ride home." She fixed her gaze on the exit door.

"No time like the present. I have an early rehearsal

tomorrow morning and need the shuteye. Let's get a move on." She clasped Camellia's hand and led her through the rows to reach her car.

As Camellia opened the door to get inside, she heard someone shout. She twisted to face the building.

Weston had exited the restaurant. Both hands cupped his mouth while he called her name.

Without waiting another second, she slid into the passenger seat. "Quick. Let's get out of here before he sees us."

Freesia sighed. "Whatever you say." She turned over the engine and backed out of the parking space. Instead of heading toward the road, she steered toward the building.

Camellia's chest tightened. She gripped the dashboard. "What are you doing?"

"If you didn't notice, someone's blocked the far end of this row. I have to circle to the next and find a clear path." Freesia tapped the steering wheel and hummed a tune.

With her lips pressed flat, she stared. She didn't miss the nervous clip of Freesia's words to go along with her actions. "Uh huh. Sure." Bringing both arms together, she hugged her chest. "I'm not speaking to him, so don't bother to stop."

"You're stubborn and incorrigible, you know?" Freesia stepped on the gas pedal.

Camellia moaned and grumbled under her breath. By now, Weston waved his arms and jogged toward the car. "Keep going. I need time to think before I speak to him again."

"Seriously, I don't understand you. New York sure did a number on your emotional stability." Freesia exited onto the road and drove south toward Serenity.

Maybe Freesia was right. She certainly didn't feel like herself. But why would she? After all that happened, including her suspected involvement in Gloria's scandal of stolen designer dresses and her breakup with Noah, she could add Weston to the traumatic turmoil. Life experiences changed a person. No wonder she'd become paranoid and insecure. For now, she needed time to heal by retreating into her personal space, at least for a while. She sighed while leaning against the headrest. Running away again was a matter of opinion, and personal space couldn't build a wall to keep her problems from pushing their way inside. She'd have to face them sooner or later.

Chapter 10

Camellia recoiled, clutching her stomach. Bad seafood, bad company, and overall a bad evening. "Why does everything I touch turn into a crappy mess?"

"Maybe because you have evil demons running around inside you, determined to make you miserable." Zinnia swiped Camellia's hair from her face.

"Ha. Funny. Not." Camellia spit a few times into the toilet then leaned back. "Okay. Enough. Nothing's coming up. I'm going back to bed."

"Won't you be getting a late start on your trip to Charleston?" Zinnia followed Camellia to the bedroom.

"Not going today." Camellia sniffed her shirt and gagged. She tugged at the sleeves and slipped the stinky garment over her head then dropped it.

"Oh. Well. I see." Zinnia bent to pick up Camellia's clothes off the floor and placed them in the hamper.

"No, you don't. So, stop pretending and being nauseously nice." Her voice sounded muffled through the covers she'd pulled over her head.

"Nauseously. Really? Fine. I won't." Zinnia snapped before marching toward the door. "I will say this much. Sure as I'm standing here, your problem is you've spent more time in that bed since you've been home than anywhere else. Stop with your pity parties and get on with your life."

"I'm not having a pity party." She smashed the pillow to the sides of her head. "I'm adjusting."

The morning passed and dipped into afternoon before Camellia hauled herself out of bed. She plodded to the bathroom once more, dragging her feet, and slouching her shoulders. Twinges of stomach cramps lingered, but the pounding headache and urge to upchuck last evening's meal were no longer a threat. If only she could empty her mind the same way. Weston Murphy occupied her thoughts. To be fair, she hadn't given him a chance to explain or defend himself. That call was on her. Guilt weighed as heavily as the king crab and cranberry rice churning in her stomach. She hadn't decided what to do next, but she would, eventually.

With a certain amount of effort, she put on a clean shirt and pair of jeans. After taking a quick peek in the mirror then running a comb through her hair, she shuddered. Still not satisfied, she dabbed blush on each cheek and added passion pink gloss to her lips before heading downstairs. Eventually had to be now, or she'd lose all her nerve. "I'm going out." She shouted to no one in particular and grabbed for the doorknob but stopped when Dahlia popped her head through the library doorway.

"Where? Will you be home by suppertime?"

"Uh." Camellia chewed on her lip and frowned. "I'm not sure, but either way I'll call you." Before Dahlia responded, she stepped outside.

The air thickened and grew heavy, carried on a warm breeze from the ocean. The mugginess wrapped around her, like a comforting hug. She drew a deep breath to fill her lungs. The smell of damp earth and salt water reminded her of childhood. An image of her mother in the garden, picking herbs, delivered a warm smile to her face. Gwen tilted her head. *You should get over yourself. Let others inside. Weston is a good man. So is Noah, in his own way. Enjoy life, Cammie. It's what we all do.*

Camellia gasped. She hesitated but then extended one arm and waved back and forth. Air…only air and nothing more. She hurried to fish her phone out of the bag then punched a number on speed dial and waited.

"Cammie, dear. How nice to hear from you," Gwen greeted her.

"Hi, Mom. I-I'm relieved to hear your voice." Her hand shook, and she gripped the phone tighter to steady it.

"How funny. Why are you relieved? Oh, my. Is something wrong? Is Sia okay?"

As Gwen's pitch rose, Camellia gripped the phone tighter. "No. Everything's fine. I-I wanted to hear your voice, is all. I had sort of a weird dreamlike moment, and you were talking to me." She paused. She must sound like a crazy dimwit but couldn't take back her words. Might as well dive in all the way and spill the rest. "You were telling me to lighten up and let people into my life so I can enjoy it. Or something like that." Her words trailed off into silence. Gwen didn't answer right away. "Mom?"

"Well, of course, you should enjoy life. Try accepting people for who they are. Once you get started, you'll find each time easier. We all have faults, Camellia, and some are worse than others."

"I know, but I can't get past my doubts about

certain people."

"You'll have to decide what to accept and who to trust but try not to be too harsh. Otherwise, you'll end up with no one. That life, baby girl, is a lonely one. Would you like me to send you one of my herbal mixes to help? I have just the thing to brighten your day."

Camellia widened her eyes. The last time she tried one of her mother's concoctions, she laughed and cried for most of the week. She didn't plan on repeating that kind of emotional experience. One herb or flower at a time wasn't bad, but a mix? No way. "I'm fine, Mom." She paused to laugh. "I'm saying those words too often, aren't I? Anyway, we're all excited about you and Robert coming to visit over the Fourth. We have a grand party planned, well, more like a cookout, but all our friends will be there. You'll love getting together with everyone."

"I'm sure we will. Or at least, I will." Gwen chuckled. "Robert and his California roots will surely feel out of place, but he acclimates well. Oh, dear, I should go. I have yoga class and my Umanki religious service afterward. Although, I'm thinking of returning to Buddhism. Buddhists are much more spiritual."

Camellia laughed. Only in her world. "Okay, Mom. Tell Robert I said hi. Enjoy your day."

"I always do. Oh, one more bit of advice? Go apologize to the young man. He meant no harm. He cares about you. I'm sure all that nonsense about New York will go away soon."

Camellia dropped her jaw. Before she recovered or thought of a response, she heard the click as Gwen ended the call. "Well, I never." Her comments baffled Camellia, but somehow, through all the craziness of her dream, one thought became clear. She needed to find Weston and make peace, tell him how much she liked him and how she wanted to spend time with him. Though at present, a serious relationship was out of the question. If he was willing to be patient, maybe what they had could turn into more later. Or the time could come sooner. She exhaled. At this pace, she'd never make up her mind.

She crossed Divinity and walked along the beach. Words of apology swirled in her head. Which ones gave her the best shot at saying what she needed to say? She stared at the sandy path to help her concentrate. She had the right message, or at least she thought she did. The perfect apology, she hoped. "Lord love a duck. I'm screwed if this plan doesn't work."

"Cam?'

She snapped her head to look forward and gasped. Noah approached with a grin, stretching ear to ear. Drat. Even if today was hers to make amends, an apology to this man wouldn't come as easily. In her heart she didn't believe he deserved one. Later, she might change her mind. "Noah, I really don't have time."

"Look, Cam. I'm sorry. I've been such a heel. I know you probably can't forgive me, but can we at least talk civil to one another?"

That response was unexpected. Camellia scratched behind one ear before she nodded. "Okay, fine, but can we talk later? I have someplace to be."

With an arm extended, he stopped her. His forehead creased. "Wait. You mean you forgive me? Or you mean, that is, what do you mean?"

Camellia sighed. "I mean, okay. I'll be civil, if

you'll be civil. But I can't give you any more, at least for now." Most likely forever. The feelings for him had been tainted with images of Trina. How was she supposed to get those out of her head?

"Fair enough. Maybe soon we can, you know… Heck, I can wait. I'm a very patient man." He held out his arms. "How about we hug? Call the gesture an agreement to being civil. Please? I could really use one."

His face and those puppy dog eyes made Camellia wanted to scream at him and cry for him at the same time. "Yeah, a hug's okay." She held up a finger to warn him. "Only one."

He leaned toward her and wrapped his arms around her waist.

His body was warm and cozy. Camellia found herself relaxing. Her emotions were spent. She was tired and only wanted her life to be as rosy as Gwen's. Was that request too much to ask?

"Cam, I still love you. I'll always love you," Noah whispered in her ear.

She struggled to back away, but he quickly kissed her lips. For whatever insane reason or uncontrollable thought possessed her, she didn't resist. She leaned closer and let the warmth of his touch wash over her. Not a single molecule in her body told her being with Noah was right, yet she didn't fight him.

"Well, I see you two have made up. Congratulations."

As she recognized Weston's voice, Camellia's breath hitched. With full force, she shoved Noah away. "Weston. I was on my way to see you. But…"

"But life took another turn. Is that your

141

explanation?" Weston's jaw worked back and forth as his muscles tightened. "Well, I'll leave you both to getting reacquainted. Have a good life."

"Wait!" Camellia trudged through the sand to catch up.

Noah stepped right behind her and grabbed her arm. "Cam, don't go."

She landed a punch to his chest. "Leave me alone. "Haven't you caused me enough trouble and misery? Go away, Noah Burke." Her chin trembled and pulse raced as she kicked at the sand. Weston was too far ahead and, from the looks of his gait, in no mood for the sight of her. She didn't blame him. What was wrong with her? The idea she might still have feelings for Noah curdled her stomach.

Camellia left Noah and ran across Divinity Boulevard to her shop. Like most times, work promised to distract her, along with loud music. She sniffed and wiped the tears dry. *Here's to you and your pleasant life, Gwen. May Buddha be with you.*

****

The afternoon passed quickly. Though unexpected, Camellia accomplished a ton of work. She'd taken a short break to return home for her car, having left some of her work in the backseat. The design papers scattered across the table. She stood back, hands on hips, and smiled. "My career is what I should be focused on. Right?" She answered herself with a firm nod. The bell tinkled, and Camellia turned toward the front to find Remy. "Hey there. How are you?"

He shrugged without a word. Shoving both hands in his pockets, he turned his head back and forth from one end of the shop to the other before he paused to stare at Camellia.

His unruly red hair stuck out in all directions and looked stiff, like he'd sprayed on a whole container of hair product. Faded jeans, a worn T-shirt with the words *Punk Rules* across the chest, and leather sandals completed his look. "You want a soda? I have some in my cooler."

"Nah. I'm good." He glanced once more around the shop. "Any chance you need help around here? I mean, the office copy and supply store cut back my hours. I could use a second job. I mean, if you'd want to hire me?" He scratched his neck and bit down on his lip as he stared then quickly lowered his head.

"I see." Camellia sat in one of the chairs and motioned for Remy to sit in the other. She waited, until he appeared settled and comfortable. "I can't pay you much, at least not until I start selling the merchandise. Maybe in a week or two?" If only her guess turned out to be the case, she'd be pleased and grateful.

Remy nodded. "Awesome. I just need to make some cash to, well, cash for any future emergencies, if you get my meaning."

Camellia frowned. "Not sure I do. Anyway, how about you start today? If you're free, that is. I need help unpacking those supplies. UPS delivered them an hour ago. Seems Maxine has a heart after all." She chuckled. When she'd called earlier to let her know she postponing her trip to Charleston due to a personal crisis, Maxine suggested one-day express shipping for some of the smaller items. Free of charge. Camellia was grateful.

"Sure, I got plenty of free time." Remy grinned and grabbed a box cutter off the table.

Camellia returned to studying her designs. They'd need a little tweaking, but she'd come up with some of her best work. While working for Gloria V, she never had much time or freedom to be personally creative. This experience was liberating.

"What are those papers?" Remy nodded at the table while removing containers of paper clips and sticky notes from a box.

"Oh, I'm working on my own designs. One day, I hope the shop will be filled with them." Camellia sketched more lines on the paper.

"Cool. Good luck with all your stuff." He resumed unpacking and sorting supplies.

"Yeah, super cool," Camellia mumbled. With luck and a bit of Gwen's faith thrown in, maybe the rest of the world would come around and think the same.

Another hour slipped by, and Camellia suggested they take a break. "I'm thirsty. How about you?" She pulled two cans out of her cooler and handed him one.

They each sipped their soda while chatting about school and the night life of Serenity, or lack of, according to Remy.

"This place moves as slow as a turtle on race day. And quiet? Don't get me started. I mean, I love the ocean and all, but the sound of waves crashing gets old fast," Remy griped.

"Have you been over to Chico's Club Serenity? They've got entertainment. My sister's band plays most evenings, and lots of folks come, all ages of folks, including yours." Camellia stretched her legs and rested both feet on one of the boxes.

"Yeah but not my thing." He pointed to his shirt. "Unless they've got You Blew It or some other band like Fall Out Boys playing."

Camellia laughed. "Not a chance. Country, blues, and southern rock are all Chico and folks in Serenity allow. I guess you'd have to travel to the mainland to find what you like, right?"

"Guess so." Remy glanced up at the ceiling before he rested his attention on Camellia once more. "You got to give your place a name. How about Camellia's Cave?"

She smiled. "Sounds ominous. You're right though. I do need a name." She tapped her foot against the chair leg. "I like your suggestion. Camellia's Cave sounds both ominous and mysterious. With a name like that one, shoppers might be curious enough to come inside."

Remy nodded. "Awesome."

Camellia opened her mouth to respond, but the bell tinkled again.

Dahlia entered. She glanced, for a second, at Remy before turning to Camellia.

Taking a quick glance at her watch, Camellia groaned. "Oh, Dahlia. I'm sorry. I completely forgot about calling. Forgive me?" She frowned, all at once noticing the ashen hue of her sister's face. "Dahlia? What's wrong?" Her heart skipped.

Dahlia leaned against the door frame and took a breath or two before answering. "Noah. He's been in a car accident. It's bad, Cam. Real bad."

Uncertainty tightened her throat. She gripped the soda can until the aluminum crushed. She glanced at Remy. "You should go, Remy."

He nodded. "You want me to finish stocking? I can lock up afterward."

Camellia shook her head. Queasiness churned her stomach. "Tomorrow is soon enough. Go on home. Please?"

"Sure, boss." The door slammed as Remy left.

Dahlia stepped closer and touched Camellia's arm. "I don't know many details, but his mother called the house to tell me. Noah was driving home a few hours ago and called to let her know he'd stop by. She says he sounded upset. Anyway, he's at Saint Margaret's Hospital in Charleston. We should leave now."

Too shocked to say a word, Camellia nodded. Especially when the one thought coming to mind was how the accident happened right after she'd encountered him on the beach and yelled at him to go away. If he was upset, she was the cause.

Chapter 11

The surgeon attached his pen to the clipboard, nodded, and then walked out as an orderly rolled a cart into the room to deliver towels and sundry supplies.

Camellia clenched her hand with a tissue wadded inside. She dabbed her eyes, but the tears kept coming. Her heart ached. Only three hours had passed, but the time dragged as she and Noah's mom waited to learn the surgery had gone well. She stood near the doorway and listened to Noah breathe, studied the monitor, and waited. Guilt overwhelmed her. She'd put him here.

An arm wrapped around her shoulder and squeezed. Bethany Burke leaned against Camellia. "He is such a good man. Why did this tragedy happen? He's a careful driver and never had a ticket or caused an accident. Why?" One hand covered her mouth while she shook her head.

Camellia flushed, her chin quivering. As she took a deep, painful breath, she wiped her eyes again. "I don't know, Mrs. Burke. I just…" She should stop talking. Her words were empty. She was a horrible person, and she lied to Noah's mother. "Excuse me. I need to use the restroom." Ignoring her weakened knees, she ran out of the room and down the hall, right past Dahlia who sat in the waiting room.

"Cam, where are you going?" Dahlia quickly caught up.

"I want to be alone, Dahlia. Please." Camellia pushed open the restroom door and hurried into the closest empty stall.

"I'm not leaving you alone, sweetie. You're hurting. I can see it plain as day. You still care for Noah. Please come out so we can talk."

Camellia placed both hands between her thighs and squeezed to stop the trembling. If wishes were real, and she could zap herself out of this stall, she'd disappear to someplace peaceful to sort out her thoughts, rearrange her life, and do something right. She straightened her shoulders, released her hands, and stood. Taking a deep breath, she left the stall. Life shouldn't work this way.

"Better?" Dahlia nodded while stroking her sister's back.

"In truth? No, but staying in here won't help me improve." Camellia's voice fell flat. Hiding her thoughts didn't matter any longer. "I caused his accident, Dahlia. He crashed because of me, and now he's lying in that bed, broken and unconscious and— oh, lord. What have I done?" When the sobs erupted, she couldn't keep her body from quaking.

"Hey." Dahlia's forehead creased. She wrapped both arms around Camellia. "You did no such thing. Nobody, not even you, has such power. Silly goof." She chuckled and sniffed at the same time.

"You can't know because you don't know what happened. I argued with Noah this afternoon. I yelled at him to go away and leave me alone, which he did. He d-did." The sobs grew into blathering, interrupted by a succession of hiccups, and then more blathering.

Dahlia leaned away. She gripped Camellia's upper arms and shook. "Stop that talk this instant. You. Did.

Nothing. Wrong. You hear me? Nothing."

She practically growled with that tone. Camellia jerked her arms out of the tight grasp. "You can't wish away the facts like they were nothing. My heart and my brain tell me his accident is all my fault. If we, if *I,* hadn't argued with him, he wouldn't have left that way and been upset over my words when he drove his car and, and then end up in a hospital. Don't you see?" She rambled and released the words in a raspy tone strained with emotion.

"What I see is my sister broken and sad over a close friend who's badly injured. I think you need to reconsider the facts. We all have arguments, Cam. What you're describing is a human reaction to emotion, and saying you are the cause of Noah's accident is illogical. In fact, we aren't sure what happened. We don't know what the witnesses and officer on the scene had to say. Why don't you calm down and wait until we get the complete story? Hmm?" She lifted her eyebrows.

Camellia sucked in air and forced her heartbeat to grow steady. "Sure. I can manage." She said the words but doubted they carried much weight. In truth, she suffered the guilt but kept those thoughts to herself. With her emotions spent, she didn't have the energy to fight another round with Dahlia.

"Good. Now, would you like me to drive you home? Maybe you need some rest," Dahlia suggested.

"No. I'm staying." Camellia set her jaw firmly. "I need to, Dahlia, but you should go home. I'll be fine." She hugged Dahlia good-bye before directing her steps to Noah's room.

"Oh, you didn't leave." Mrs. Burke smiled and

squeezed Camellia's hand. Curly wisps of hair covered her forehead and cheeks, and sweat beaded on her forehead. "I hoped you'd stay. Noah thinks highly of you, dear. When he opens his eyes, seeing your face would be nice." Her lips pressed together, though her chin quivered.

Camellia stepped next to her and patted her shoulder. "He'll be fine, Mrs. Burke. He will. You'll see."

"Thank you, child, and please call me Bethany." She sniffed while squeezing Camellia's hand.

An urgent impulse prompted Camellia's words. "I'll stay with Noah, if you'd like to go home and get some proper rest? I'll call you immediately if he wakes up, okay?"

"Bless you." She touched Camellia's cheek. You've a kind soul. I am exhausted. At my age, very little is needed to do me in, I guess. A couple hours to rest and I'll be fine. The doctor says all we can do is wait. He needs rest, is all." She glanced at Noah. In a few seconds, she stood, and as she aimed toward the exit, her steps faltered. "I'll return before long. I promise."

Camellia dragged a chair over next to the bed. She sat and, with light fingers, touched Noah's hand. "Well, seems like we've come full circle, haven't we, Noah Burke?" She studied him from head to toe. The years had deepened the fine wrinkles on his face. She remembered the…loved those eyes. If only he'd open them now.

A hard lump lodged in her throat. No matter how often she swallowed, it didn't dissolve. She suppressed the urge to cry again, afraid he'd awaken and hear. She wanted to forgive him, but not because of the guilt consuming her now. If she got past the feeling, if she erased the guilt, what was left? What then? With that kiss, he'd stirred something inside her. She'd buried and wanted to forget those emotions. The realization scared and confused her at once.

She blinked against heavy eyelids. The day had been too long and more than she could handle. Leaning against the chair, she released Noah's hand and let her thoughts drift into unpleasant places. What if Noah never forgave her? What if she couldn't forgive herself?

****

"Camellia?"

With a gasp, she straightened in her seat and blinked to find Noah staring at her. He smiled for a second but then his forehead wrinkled as he scanned the room. "You're in the hospital." She paused to take a deep breath. "You were in a car accident, Noah."

He spent a moment in silence before he spoke. "I remember. I was crossing the intersection of Divinity and Orange Road. I had a lot on my mind." He gazed at Camellia for a brief moment. "I thought the light was green, but a car on my left rushed straight at me. I swerved, but the vehicle clipped my back side. My car started rolling, and I…" He cradled his head in both hands and rocked back and forth. A moan rattled his breath.

Camellia shot out of her chair and grabbed one of his arms. "Come on, now. You're fine. You'll be okay." She swallowed the sob forcing its way up to her mouth. He blamed her. How could he not? Thickness in her throat labored her breathing. "Noah, please. Try and stay calm."

Noah lifted his head. His jaw muscles tightened while his eyes grew wider. "I can't move my back. Why can't I move, Cam?"

"Well, you dislocated two of your vertebrae and…"

"My spine? You're telling me I'm paralyzed?" He shouted while gripping the sides of his bedrail.

"Will you let me finish? The vertebrae were dislodged but not broken or fractured. The doctors performed emergency surgery. You're wearing a brace to keep your back stabilized. Understand? You're not paralyzed." Saying those words aloud gave her as much reassurance as she hoped they'd give him.

"Thank god." He relaxed. His head rested against the pillow. "How long before I can get off this contraption and walk again?"

Camellia shook her head. "You should let the doctors talk to you. I can't explain everything like they will. I'm going out to the lobby and calling your mom. I promised. I'll stop at the nurse's station. They can page your doctor. You'll be fine." She squeezed his arm then hurried out of the room before he protested. She needed to get away before losing control. Her nerves were shattered and her emotions out of whack. Blurting out the wrong thing, like what she wasn't ready to say, couldn't happen. Not yet. Once she crossed that line, she couldn't turn around. She refused to run away a second time. Somehow, she must find a way to forgive him.

After the call, Camellia deliberated over whether to return to the room or wait for Bethany Burke to arrive. More fear churned her insides and froze her ability to act. Panicked? Yes, obviously. Worried she was making a mistake? Most definitely. However, she responded this way most of the time—indecisive and running from her problems. Not much had changed.

"Are you Noah Burke's wife?"

Camellia looked up to see a nurse who cradled a clipboard in her arm. "Pardon?"

"Are you his wife? I need these forms filled out, if you don't mind?" She extended the clipboard.

"Oh." Camellia blinked and then shook her head. "No, I'm a friend. A close friend. His mother should be arriving soon. I think she's the one to ask. Excuse me." She took long strides away from the nurse and toward Noah's room to let him know Bethany was on her way. When she drew close to the door, she heard the clear sound of the doctor's voice. Holding back, she remained hidden outside the room.

"The brace will remain on until I'm sure the vertebrae are stabilized. We wouldn't want to do further damage and need another surgery. Right?"

"But for how long? I have a family business to run. I can't do it from a wheelchair," Noah protested.

"Perhaps another family member can help?"

"My mom is too old, and my dad is bed-ridden. I don't have any siblings. I'm all I've got."

The strain in Noah's voice nearly caused Camellia to weep. She stepped into the room and nodded at the doctor. "I'm sure we'll figure something out, and in the meantime, I'll help you as much as I can, Noah. At home or with the business—whatever you need, I'll help. Don't you worry." She forced a smile. Her heart ached. No matter how many times anyone, even Dahlia, argued, they couldn't sway her thinking. She might as well have been the driver who crashed into Noah. He lay in that bed because of her. The emotional fight inside landed at the finish line, and only one winner remained standing. Guilt.

Noah waved an arm. "You don't have to, Cam. This problem isn't yours."

"But I want to." She nodded at him and the doctor.

The doctor tapped the clipboard with his pen then nodded. "Good. Problem's solved. You'll spend a few more days here, and then I'll sign the release papers if everything checks out. Have a good day, Mr. Burke. You're a lucky man. A crash like that one? Most don't come out alive."

His words sent an earthquake of shock through her core. She waited to speak until the doctor left the room. "Some bedside manner, right?"

"Well, I'm sure he sees too much and can't afford to get emotional and all." Noah's lips trembled.

Seeing the fear in his expression, Camellia shivered. "Your doctor seems nice."

"As long as he knows what the hell he's doing, I don't give a shit how nice he is," Noah snapped.

She lifted her chin and shook a finger. "Noah Burke. Since when did you start swearing?"

"I don't. Sorry." He splayed out his hands in front of him. "This whole situation is a heck of a lot to take in."

Through blurred vision, she focused on details of the room, the bed, the monitor, the IV drip—anywhere but on him. "I'm sorry. You're a good man, and lord knows you didn't deserve...." She drew in air and straightened her shoulders. With a deliberate swipe of one hand, she cleared her eyes. "But the accident happened. We're, you and I, will get through this challenge one day at a time. Understand?"

In silence Noah nodded. His chest heaved with quick, rabbit-like moves but finally slowed. After a moment, he turned to stare at the window. "Thank you," he whispered.

Camellia wasn't certain, but she took his words as acceptance. If only she'd accept what happened as easily. At the sound of footsteps, she shifted her gaze to find Bethany Burke standing in the doorway. The poor woman looked miserable. Dark shadows underlined her eyes, and her shoulders drooped.

Hands covered her mouth, and she gasped. "My poor boy. Oh, my Noah." She hurried forward and leaned over the bed to kiss his cheek. "Your father and I were afraid. So afraid. But you're okay. You hear me? You're okay." She rambled on and on.

Noah squeezed her arm. "Mother. Mother, stop. You're right. I'm fine. You can stop worrying." Noah smiled. "Would you please let go of my shoulder? It's a bit sore."

"Oh, I'm sorry, dear. I didn't think. Your father, he's frustrated at not being able to come, but he sends his love." She patted him gently. After a brief pause, she turned to Camellia. "Thank you for calling me and for staying with my son. You're a good person."

Oh, boy. Camellia didn't know if she wanted to flee from the hospital or shout her confession to Bethany that she was responsible. She'd caused Noah's suffering. However, she did neither. She wrung her hands before finally shoving them in her pockets. "You're more than welcome. I should go. It's after midnight, and I'm exhausted. How about I come by in the morning?"

"I look forward to seeing your beautiful face, Miss Holiday." Noah winked.

At hearing the flattering quip, Camellia smiled. He must be feeling more like himself, which gave her confidence. Everything would be all right. She said her good-byes and left the room. Maybe the time she'd given herself to think about her choice helped. Whatever the explanation, she was relieved and not complacent. For once, she'd made a decision and wouldn't change her mind. No second thoughts, no running away. This affirmation was her being responsible.

Pushing open the exit door, she sighed and wove through the rows of cars. Backing out of her parking spot, she caught sight of a police cruiser.

The officer exited the vehicle then glanced her way.

"Benny." She waved an arm out the window.

At once, he returned the gesture before jogging over.

Camellia smiled. "Good evening, or should I say good morning, Officer Collins? I see you're working the graveyard shift." She chuckled, remembering how they'd attended school together since third grade. Benny was the one usually covered in paint or clay by the end of class. "Wow, sure has been a while." She moved her gaze up and down. His hair, once carrot-top red, had darkened to brown, and his tall frame was attractively fit.

"I know. Good to see you, Cammie. Yeah, night shift sucks, but Captain calls the shots." He shrugged. "Question is, why in blazes are you here this time of night and not all cozy in your bed?" His eyebrows wiggled.

"Stop. You're such a tease. Always have been." Camellia's smile collapsed after a brief moment. Her lips formed a straight line. "I was visiting Noah Burke. He's been in a car accident."

"I know." Benny nodded. "News traveled through the police grapevine. You know, I have guard duty at the hospital. Maybe I'll stop in to visit. Think he'll be up?"

"His mother is with him. When I left the two of them, he was wide awake. I'm sure he'd enjoy seeing you." Camellia chewed on her upper lip. "I don't suppose you know what happened? The accident, I mean?"

He straightened and crossed his arms. "I do. A car T-boned Noah's. The other driver is okay. He claims the light was green for him. Police still need to investigate. I can't tell you anything else."

"Hmm. All right, I should go. You have a good evening and take care. Great talking to you, Benny." She powered up the window and continued driving out of the parking lot. Sleep deprivation starved her brain. She could handle no more thoughts about guilt, commitment, or duty. Tomorrow, she'd deal with all those grownup problems.

Her eyelids hung heavy, until Camellia could barely focus on the road. Lowering the window, she breathed in the cooler night air. She approached her driveway and made a slow turn. Turning off the engine, she rested her head on the steering wheel for a minute then straightened to stare out the windshield. The time approached one in the morning, but another car sat in the drive, a familiar one. "Not tonight. I can't see you tonight." She gripped the wheel. Dragging herself to the door, she found it unlocked. She tiptoed inside and crossed the foyer to the steps, only wishing to escape to her room.

"There you are! I thought I heard a car pull in the drive." Freesia rushed toward her.

Camellia dropped her bag to the floor. She pursed her lips. "I'm tired, Sia. I'm going to bed."

"Not just yet. Weston is here. He's been waiting to see you." Freesia's eyes widened. "You won't be so mean as to ignore him, will you?"

Camellia raised her hands, palms up, and shrugged. "I can and I will, because the hour is way too late. Goodnight." She grabbed the railing and took another step.

"Cam, please wait." Weston now stood next to Freesia.

Camellia stiffened. Despite her fatigue, she managed a firm voice. "Weston, I have nothing to say to you. Nothing I want to hear from you. Not tonight."

"Please, let me apologize." He reached for her arm then hesitated. "I made a mistake. I'm sorry. Sometimes what you see isn't what's real. After earlier today, I'm sure you understand. I came to offer my condolences and anything I can do to help you. Can't we call a truce? I didn't talk about you to Noah. Believe me. I know what happened between you two on the beach was not what it appeared to be. Right?"

The flickering eyes and tightened jaw hinted at his desperation. "Listen. I jumped to conclusions just as you did. However, you were wrong." She sucked in air as her heart beat in overtime. "What you saw with me kissing Noah is something, the most real something

I've had in a long while. Thanks for offering your help, but if you'll excuse me, I'm tired and want to crawl into bed." She pivoted on her heel to face the stairs. As soon as the words slipped from her mouth, she knew the comment was impulsive. She wasn't sure about Noah, not really. Why did Weston provoke her to say such things?

"Cammie, please don't." Freesia touched her wrist. "You're making a big mistake."

"I'm not." She whipped her head sideways to face Weston. "Honestly, if you want to help me, leave me alone."

"But you don't love Noah. Give Weston a chance," Freesia whispered.

Camellia pressed her lips together for a moment but failed to dampen the heat fueling her anger. She nodded at Weston. "If you're so concerned about him, Sia, why don't you date him? There. Another problem solved. I'm on a roll today, aren't I?" As she continued up the stairs, a bitter laugh escaped. What was the expression? If life gives you lemons, make lemonade. How appropriate was that? She entered her bedroom and slammed the door. If only she could block out her problems for a few hours. Two men and three sisters all demanded she listen to them and to believe the choices she made weren't as good as theirs. Well, she'd show them. Camellia Holiday wasn't such a pushover.

Chapter 12

If days were minutes, this month would have been the perfect example. Camellia juggled her time between working at Camellia's Cave, designing, ordering, and attending to other business during the day. With Noah home from the hospital, she spent her evenings with him, helping with both personal and professional tasks. She was stretched thin, lacked energy, and had lost too much weight. She had no time to think about what she'd done. The unexpected part? She grew closer to Noah. His touch, his smile, and the deep timber of his voice triggered old memories. Happy, pleasurable ones colored her feelings and dissolved the miserable ones. She couldn't guess how her attitude was possible, but the change happened.

The evening breeze delivered a summer storm, which died out in minutes. The air remained balmy yet cooler. She sat on Noah's deck, sipping iced tea spiked with bourbon while he slept in his wheelchair. As he snored, his lips quivered. Every so often, his eyelids fluttered and twitched.

All at once, he jerked and popped open his eyes. "Cam?"

She touched his arm gently. "I'm right here."

He drew a breath, long and trembling. "I had a bad dream."

She nodded. "You were mumbling in your sleep.

What was the dream about?"

"You were in the car with me. You know, on that day? And you lay on the road, bleeding. I was desperate to wake you. I screamed your name and kept screaming." Noah gripped the wheelchair and swiveled to face the other way.

"Oh, Noah." She stood and circled to face him. "None of those things are real. See?" She held up both arms and twirled. "I'm perfectly fine. Now, how about that ice cream? We have chocolate fudge and butter pecan and who knows what else. Your mother stopped by and stocked the freezer this morning." She raised her chin and waited.

"Butter pecan sounds good." He wheeled toward her and wrapped his fingers around her hand. "Thanks for being so kind to me. I know I'm not deserving, but I do appreciate the gesture."

"Silly goof. Of course, you deserve kindness. Why don't you wheel into the kitchen, and we'll pig out on dessert?" She strained to sound joyful. The day at the shop had been horrific. Tons of orders rushed in, and Detective Hulsey called again. The CPD coroner confirmed Gloria died of natural causes, but the detective found no explanation as to why the fallen fashion mogul wanted to see Camellia. So, she remained in the dark. One more brick added to her pile of emotional baggage. If not for Remy's help, she'd have a total meltdown.

"I hear from my mom your shop is gaining quite the reputation. One week open and you're already showing the competition who's the boss." Noah steered the wheelchair inside. "Before long, you'll need to hire an assistant."

Camellia smiled. She liked the way he never directly mentioned Trina, who had to be spitting nails by now. At least, the news from Remy implied as much.

Every evening at the supper table, Trina swore up and down if pushed too far she'd find a way to destroy Camellia. Remy enjoyed his cousin's misery.

"Well, I've put a ton of work into my business. Being rewarded is a nice feeling, and I already hired someone three weeks ago. I thought I mentioned that news, but maybe not. Life has been crazy since, well, you know. Anyway, I hired Remy Averaux. You know him?" She tensed, waiting for his response. Taking her time, she filled two bowls with ice cream and carried them to the table.

Noah scowled and bit down on his lip. "Ah, yeah. I do. Trina's cousin. I'd say you've hired yourself some serious trouble. You should've asked me before making that move."

Camellia scowled. "He's a nice boy and a hard worker. Why would you say such a thing? Trouble how?" She set the bowls on the table and stabbed the mounds of ice cream with spoons. Since that conversation when he and Camellia first met, Remy hadn't said anything more about his parents, and she'd never asked about them, considering how uncomfortable the topic would make him.

Noah swallowed a spoonful of ice cream. "Remy's an orphan. His mom died when he was a little tike. Cancer, I was told. After his dad passed, Remy lived in foster care for a while. He had a few run-ins with the authorities before Laverne finally agreed to take him in. He's a real charity case."

Charity case? No wonder Remy hated living with Laverne and Trina. Poor, typical orphan relative not welcomed into the house. He was a real-life version of Cinderella. "I heard about the father dying, but what happened?"

Noah dropped the spoon and leaned back in his chair. "Here's where the story gets ugly and probably left scars the boy can't shake. After his wife died, his dad fell into a serious depression. For years, he drank most every day, so the boy became the responsible one. Then, this past Christmas, I guess the dad had enough. He put a gun in his mouth and ended it. The boy found him the next morning."

Camellia blinked against blurred vision. With wobbly legs she collapsed into a chair. "Poor Remy." She drew in a deep breath. "Well, in that case, I'm really glad I hired him. He needs friends, not to be outcast or shunned."

"Camellia." Noah reached for her hand.

"Nope. Not arguing with you because it's my decision. Change of topic. Please?"

"Fine. Next week is your Fourth of July family celebration. I bet you're excited to see your mom." Noah scraped the sides of his bowl.

"I am. Get-togethers are far and few between." She recalled the phone conversation with Gwen, the day of Noah's accident. Live your life, she advised her daughter. Camellia eyed Noah as he devoured his dessert. She was living her life and enjoying it. Right? She finished the last bite while walking to the counter then shoved the bowl in the dishwasher.

Grabbing her bag off the counter, she then approached the table. "I should go. I have an early delivery tomorrow, and some designer friends of mine are meeting me for brunch. Busy, busy day, as usual." She bent over to kiss Noah's cheek.

He placed his hands on her shoulders and drew her closer. Their lips connected.

His passion caused a slight ripple in her stomach. They weren't earth-shattering tremors or sparks of fire found in juicy romance novels, but these feelings were real. Ripples were good, satisfying in their own way. Besides, passion grew in a relationship.

"Don't go," he whispered.

She struggled to put distance between them, but he resisted. "Noah, I can't."

"Please? I need you lying next to me. You know, in case?" His forehead touched hers.

The ache inside was strong and threatened to break her in two. "Tell you what. I'll stay until you fall asleep." She lifted the prescription bottle off the shelf and popped the lid to shake out one pill. "Take this. You'll sleep better."

"Cam, I'm hurting and need you tonight. A pill won't stop the nightmares." His jaw set in a taut line.

"Fine. I'll set my alarm for tomorrow a few minutes early. But take the pill, Noah. Dr. Hamachi knows what's best."

He dropped his shoulders and nodded with a sigh.

At least she'd conquered one battle. With one finger, she swiped a curl from his face. Here was her do-over, sitting right in front of her. Her chance at a serious, life-long relationship. Damned if she would blow it.

****

In the morning, Camellia stayed until Noah was fed

and back in his wheelchair. Her mind reeled with concern, more anxious than him for the day he'd be back on his feet. The doctor warned a few weeks would pass before he could progress to a walker or cane. The brace had to stay on longer, maybe three or more months, depending on his healing progress.

Shameful to admit how seeing the evidence of his accident flamed her guilt and convoluted her feelings. She dreamed of the day when everything would return to the way life used to be—when the wheelchair and brace were gone and Noah walked again. Only then would she know if her love was real. Only then would she find peace in her decision.

Most everyone accepted her life with Noah. Even Dahlia seemed satisfied. At least, she never once commented otherwise. But not Freesia. If any person made Camellia have doubts, her little sister managed with a vengeance. Two or three times a week, she'd get the cold stare and the disapproving shake of her head. Most hurtful were Freesia's lectures. She'd say Camellia was throwing away her life because of a stupid accident, which had nothing to do with her.

She got as far as the kitchen doorway when Noah called out for her to wait. "I'm late for work." Yet, she paused to hear what he wanted. She always did.

"Why don't you move in with me? I know our reconciliation is less than a month old, but really, we've been a couple for years, Cam. We should think about a stronger commitment. Living together is a start." His voice trembled.

Slowly, she turned to face him. The flushed tone of his cheeks and bright eyes grew prominent. The opportunity to avoid any more Freesia lectures or scathing stares over the supper table proved tempting and weakened Camellia's reserve. She swiped her tongue to moisten her lips. "I'll think about it, but I really, really have to go."

She hurried to escape before he'd say more. She was vulnerable. He'd taken advantage of her weakness. She flushed with anger over his suggestion to move, which made her feel guilty, and that feeling angered her even more. His love for her was genuine. She had to believe it was. He wanted what was best for their relationship. Still, she needed time. This move was too soon. As she got into the car, the image of Noah in the wheelchair flashed in her head. Yeah. Moving in together was a huge step.

After checking her watch, she cursed at the time. Pressing on the gas pedal, she sped across town to her shop. She promised to meet Adelaide and Monique after this morning's delivery. Camellia's Cave had been in business for a week. The dresses her colleagues promised on opening day hadn't arrived, but they assured her they'd bring them today. Who was she to argue about the arranged time? They were doing her a huge favor.

"Call Remy." She waited several rings. Her hands displayed white knuckles as they gripped the steering wheel. How could she avoid behaving differently around him after learning about his dad's tragic death? She'd pretend like nothing changed, but that attitude would prove difficult. Suddenly losing her nerve, she extended a finger to end the call.

"Hey, boss lady. What time is it?" Remy answered with a sleepy yawn.

"It's a quarter after seven," she said in a quaky, but

upbeat, voice.

"Seven?" he squeaked. "I never get up earlier than ten."

"Well, today starts a new page in your life. I need you. Take the spare key, go to the shop, and unlock the back door. The delivery guys will be arriving in fifteen minutes." As a sports coupe swerved to pull in front of her, she cursed and slammed on the brake pedal.

"Not cool. I need serious sleep or the ugly comes out."

"You should go to bed earlier and not three or four in the morning. Now, Mister Ugly, if you want to keep this job, do as I said and wait for the delivery." Camellia enunciated each word, leaving no room for arguments but prayed her words didn't sound too harsh. "I'll be there as soon as I can."

"Sure thing. You're the boss." Remy drawled in a yawn.

"That I am." She sighed, tossed the phone back on the seat, and continued her drive home. After a quick shower and change of clothes, she'd be on her way to the shop. She had to impress her colleagues. Wearing one of her own designs might do the trick. No way was she letting them think of her as a has-been in the fashion world. Stephanie gave it her best shot, but loyal friends were bound to stamp out those rumors and lies about her. "Lump it, Stephanie Tumler."

Freesia met her at the front door. "Well, good morning, sunshine. Out late partying? No. Wait." She raised her brow and pointed a finger. "You don't party. You play nursemaid and secretary to somebody you don't love." She blocked the doorway.

One of Freesia's now-familiar sneers covered her

face. "Not now, Sia. I'm in a hurry." Camellia tapped her foot while she crossed her arms. "I mean it."

Freesia stood for several seconds but then shifted to the side. "Be my guest. Funny how that is. More and more you seem to be a guest in this house since you spend most of your time at Mr. Wonderful's prison. Surprised you continue to call this home."

"Maybe not for long," she mumbled and traveled toward the stairs.

"What did you say?" Freesia asked.

"Nothing." Camellia wanted to get upstairs and take a shower. She was too tired to engage in a sparring match. Tired and frayed nerves sparked like livewire, but she forced her stern face into something more pleasant. "Sia, I don't want to argue with you. All right? But you have to let me make my own decisions. I'm an adult and deserve respect, no matter how much you disagree."

Freesia's brow knitted as she clenched her hands. "I know, but I care about you too much to stand by and say nothing. I'll try not to argue any more, but I won't share in your warped idea of happiness. I can't respect a lie." She threw open the front door and stepped out of sight.

"Give her time."

Camellia gasped. "Zinnie. Lord, you scared me."

"I mean it. Give her time. Sia will come around."

"Sweetie, I appreciate your opinion, but I believe you're wrong. All the time in the world won't make her change. She's stubborn, like Mom."

"She loves like her, too. So strong and fierce, she'd die to protect you. No matter how much she disagrees, she'll never stop loving you. Remember that." Zinnia nodded and walked toward the kitchen. After a few steps, she paused. "If you truly love him and he loves you the same, maybe it's all that matters. Have a great day, Cam."

Camellia stared after her before rushing to her bedroom. Zinnia, the loyal peacemaker, and Freesia, the brave, feisty one. She loved them both, but she had to live her life the way she saw fit. Whichever way her story ended, the choice must be hers, not anyone else's.

****

When she pulled around back to park, Camellia found the service doors to the shop open.

Remy helped the delivery man carry in the last of the boxes.

She beeped the horn and waved before getting out of the vehicle. Dashing around front, she entered the shop and dropped her belongings on the nearest chair.

The place lacked some finishing touches. The walls remained mostly bare, and her counter unit hadn't arrived yet. Impatience filled her, despite knowing by next week everything would fall into place, which included racks hung with Adelaide and Monique's designs. A glance at her watch told her she had forty minutes before their arranged meeting. To reach the restaurant took ten minutes.

"All done, boss lady." Remy strode to the front, dusted off his jeans, and grinned. "Huge delivery. I think your countertop unit arrived."

"Great. Any little detail to brighten my day." Camellia grabbed a pair of gloves and a smock from the shelf before heading to the storage room. Not one speck of dust would smudge her dress. She needed to shine today.

Three crates towered on the floor, and each was big enough to contain the unit parts. She reached for a crowbar.

Remy grabbed it from her hand. "You don't want to dirty your outfit. Looks kind of fancy. Besides, don't you have a brunch thing to get to soon?" He broke loose one side of the crate.

"I do. Thanks, Remy." Camellia stood close with her arms crossed. Once the last piece of wood fell to the floor, she relaxed. The countertop. "Okay, the other two must be the side boards. Go ahead and open them while I grab some cleaner."

"I'll take care of that, too. Why don't you go on ahead to the restaurant?"

"Remy, I don't pay you enough. Thanks, again." Camellia smiled and slipped off the gloves and smock.

"No, you probably don't. We can talk about a raise later."

In the awkward moment of silence which followed, Camellia chewed on her lip.

Remy lifted his shoulders. "Worth a try, right?"

Camellia studied his face. Sweat on his brow made his freckles glisten, and his hair stuck out in tufts. She easily forgot he was almost a grown man at seventeen. "We'll see. After another week, it might be possible."

"Wow. Cool. I was joking, but cool." He smiled wide enough to split his face in two.

"I'll be back this afternoon. If anyone stops by, tell them to come around later. Or if a customer is interested in a particular item…"

"I know. Put it on hold in the storage room. I got the drill, Cam." With a downturned smile, Remy groaned.

As she rushed to the door, Camellia called out over her shoulder. "Sorry. Force of habit. You're the best, and I shouldn't forget how quickly you learn." She had enough time to stop at the gift shop and buy a couple of souvenirs. Her friends might enjoy the cheesy gesture or laugh at it. Either way, an icebreaker couldn't hurt. Oddly enough, she was nervous. She didn't know what to expect or what they'd have to say. Anticipation of the unknown made her stomach cringe.

****

For the tenth time, Camellia checked her watch. Five minutes wasn't late. They'd walk through the door any second now or call to cancel. She frowned at her phone resting on the table.

"Cam Holiday. How great to see you." Adelaide rushed over, weaving among the tables and clip-clopping on five-inch heels. She leaned in to give her a hug.

Camellia broke from her reverie and relaxed her shoulders. She appraised Adelaide's milky-white complexion, her short-bobbed blonde hair, and her frilly tangerine dress to match her heels. In contrast, Monique wore a tailored black and white suit and flats. "You made it. And you both look fantastic."

With a casual gesture, Monique air-kissed her cheek.

"The traffic in Charleston is brutal, don't you think?" Adelaide scooted in her chair to sit on the opposite side of the table.

Monique slid her chair sideways, much closer to Camellia, and stroked her sleeve. "How absolutely adorable. Is this dress one of yours?"

Camellia eased her breath to answer. "It is." Their

meeting was pleasant and not what she expected.

"Well, I love it. Don't you, Addie?" Monique tossed her wavy black hair over one shoulder.

Adelaide nodded. "You are a creative genius. I'm jealous."

"Nonsense. You both are so much better. I'm a newbie and still learning the ropes. But I truly am glad you like it." Camellia smiled with her gaze lowered. A warm blush covered her face.

"Three icons of fashion design. That's who we are. Cheers." Monique raised her water goblet to salute.

"Maybe something stronger to celebrate?" Camellia motioned to the server and ordered a bottle of wine. She surveyed the two of them, careful not to be obvious and show disappointment at their empty hands.

"Cam, you don't have to worry. The dresses are in the car." Adelaide flipped her manicured fingers and laughed. "Just like you, though. Haven't changed any."

"Wouldn't you be worried, if you experienced what I have in the past few weeks?" Camellia was quick to defend herself but instantly regretted her words. This behavior wasn't the way to show confidence. In a matter of five minutes, she botched up the meeting.

"You poor thing. Truly, I don't know how you handle it. All those rumors. I absolutely despise Stephanie Tumler." Monique's lips pursed as she clipped her words.

"Please don't tell me she's still wagging her tongue." Camellia took a generous sip of her wine. The tart, dry flavor tingled her mouth. Why was Gloria's assistant insanely vindictive? She needed to find a way to stop her.

"No one who knows you, or knows her for that matter, believes a word of it. From what I hear, even the police think she's a whack job." Adelaide tipped her glass then nodded at Monique who quickly agreed.

Camellia groaned. The Gloria V fiasco was a living nightmare with multiple episodes. At this rate, she'd never dig out from underneath the whole mess. "Have the police found those missing dresses?"

"*Nada*. Maybe Stephanie stole them. You know, her way of setting you up?" Adelaide poured more wine into her empty glass.

"Ooo. You're right, Addie. She's the type to do such a horrible thing and frame Cam. Such an extremist." Monique puckered her mouth.

Camellia remained quiet while her friends discussed the possible framing scenario. She tossed and filtered through ideas of what to do about it, if any explanation worked. She had her doubts. To believe Stephanie stole the dresses to hurt Camellia and that the police might catch her seemed a long distance from reality.

"Oh, my lord. I forgot the biggest news." Monique twisted her shoulders and squeezed Camellia's arm.

"You won't believe this one." Adelaide rolled her eyes and smirked.

"Let me tell her, Addie." Monique faced Camellia. "Mind you, this news is strictly on the Q.T. from Addie's cousin who works for the NYPD. So, please don't pass it along. Promise?"

Camellia struggled to swallow the huge lump of tension suffocating her and took a generous sip of water. Could the news coming from the NYPD that needed to be kept quiet involve the Gloria V scandal?

"Perfect. Just so happens Eva is suing the estate for damages to her career. Can you believe that news?" Monique puckered her eyebrows along with her lips. "The woman is dead, and Eva wants to reach into the grave to get her revenge."

"She has a strong case. Isn't that what your *lawyer* said when you told her?" Adelaide winked at Camellia.

Camellia's mood relaxed. She raised a hand to cover a grin, and coughed. "Um, excuse me. Tickle in my throat."

Adelaide laughed until her eyes watered. "You are such a blabbermouth whore. When will you ever learn a secret means don't tell anyone?"

Straightening her back, Monique tilted her chin skyward. "My lawyer isn't just anyone. Whatever I discuss with her is confidential. As for Cam, she has a right to know."

"Telling me doesn't matter." Camellia drummed fingernails against her wine glass. "I doubt Gloria's estate amounts to much. She always spouted off how the design business was draining her dry."

"True, but then why did Eva bother? Seems likely she knows something we all don't." Monique sipped at her wine and flipped through the menu pages.

"Well, I'm glad I have your back. Without friends like you defending me, I'd give up." She hiccupped, her vision blurring. She blinked several times to clear her vision and hide the emotional overload.

"You know we're here for you. Every stab at your reputation meets with our evil eye and a quick defense." Adelaide punched the air with a pointed finger.

Camellia snorted. "Good to hear. Okay, let's eat. I'm starving. After we're done, I want to take a peek at those dresses you brought." She squirmed in her seat, and then cupped her chin in one hand. "I'm so excited. You know I'm totally indebted to you."

"We do, and we are just as grateful. Getting our designs this far south should open a new market of buyers." Monique covered Camellia's hand with her own. "We're ready to do the same for you back in New York. We'll spread the word about your creations, or whatever it takes. Promise."

She was a sinking ship, yet here were two people ready to grab hold of her before she drowned. Camellia sighed. In the past, when she was in New York, guessing who was genuinely honest and not scheming to cheat or destroy her was difficult. What did people say? When you're down on your luck, you'll know who your real friends are. Well, two of them sat here at the table, which meant more than any words she could deliver. "Thank you. To both of you," she whispered.

The meal of crab cakes and rice was as delicious as the conversation. Camellia forgot how much she enjoyed talking fashion to like-minded people. Too bad the frequent buzzing of her phone threatened to ruin the moment, vibrating against her thigh enough to irritate her. She glanced at it the first time. Noah's name lit the screen. He left a text message asking when she planned on getting home. No big emergency. Nothing crucial. Each time afterward, she ignored it.

"Are you sure you don't want to answer?" Adelaide frowned.

"Nope." Camellia gave them a lukewarm smile. "He, that is, the call can wait."

"Ah, boyfriend problems? I totally get it." She waved an arm. "When they want you, you're supposed to come running, but when we do, it's a totally different story. So immature and selfish, don't you think?"

If you only knew, Camellia thought. Her chest tightened under the weight of her anxious mood. Even when apart, he'd ruin a relaxing meal with friends. The next time the phone buzzed, she fumbled in her bag to press the power off button.

Despite her effort to ignore the interruption, a tiny hint of guilt lingered. What if the call was important? What if he really needed her? She swallowed the last bite of crab cake and set down her fork. A constant battle in her mind and heart threatened to take over, and she was torn between duty and self-preservation. Then add love, or what she believed was love, to muddy the waters.

Dahlia made personal sacrifices, one after another. At nearly thirty, she had no love life and practically no social life. Camellia didn't want to go there. Noah was her shot at a genuine, long-lasting relationship. He had faults, but so did everyone. Were his any worse? She was being selfish. Nothing more.

"Thanks for a wonderful time. I guess we should be heading back to Charleston," Adelaide announced. "Our room at the hotel will be available by now, and I'm dying for a cool shower." She fanned her face. "How can you stand this heat?"

"Oh, come on. New York gets hot, and you know it," Camellia teased.

"It's true. Addie likes to complain. Don't you, Addie?" Monique threw her New York colleague a grin. "Come on, Cam. Let's get those dresses out of the car. I can't wait for you to see them."

Camellia followed them outside. Together, they

laid the dresses clothed in bags, all two dozen of them, in her backseat.

Adelaide clapped her hands. "Go on. Take a peek."

Camellia screwed up her face then laughed. "You know me so well." Ripping open the zippers, she viewed one dress after another. She gasped. "They're beautiful." She smothered her friends with hugs and kisses. "Thanks, again. I'll let you know how they're selling."

"When you're ready for us to do our thing, give us a call. Good luck. We love you, Cammie Pie." Monique blew her a couple of kisses before sliding into the passenger side.

Camellia waited until the convertible was out of sight. She climbed into her own car and took a moment to study the dresses in more detail. They were truly beautiful with sleek, stylish lines and intricate stitching. "Let's hope you can give me temporary life support until I finish my own designs." Sighing, she rummaged through her bag to find the phone. She speed-dialed Noah and waited, tapping her fingers on the steering wheel, until she heard the click. "Hi, Noah. Is everything okay?"

"Camellia, I need you. I—I don't feel well."

She stiffened. A mix of guilt and worry surged through her as she sped down the road.

Chapter 13

The drive took twenty minutes, and another ten passed while Camellia sat in the driveway to calm herself. With shoulders braced, she stepped through the doorway and placed her bag on the foyer table. Their conversation had been short, though each word carried enough weight to squash her cheerful mood like a bug. Fear switched to frustration when she suspected no emergency existed. He'd admitted as much when she pushed for the truth.

Yet, sadly enough, here she was, ready to forgive and forget. No doubt, Noah had a strong hold on her. She couldn't escape or deny how she grew to love him again, which made his behavior and her effort to be supportive such a struggle. Or maybe nothing he did could stop her from loving him. Oh, she didn't *like* him after the issue with Trina, but like and love were two entirely different emotions. No matter how long it took, she'd have to work on the liking part.

"Cam? Is that you?" Noah called from the kitchen.

"Yeah. I'm home." As soon as the words escaped her lips, she regretted them. Even though Noah invited her to stay, this place wasn't home. Suddenly, Freesia's comment came to mind. Her sister's words rang true. Camellia had become a guest in the Holiday household. Pausing in the foyer, she struggled for air. Where did she belong, then? "Maybe nowhere." Swiping a loose curl from her face, she hurried down the hall to the kitchen.

"I missed you. You've been gone twelve hours." Noah sat close to the window with his hands folded in his lap.

Camellia ignored the whine in his voice. Obviously, he expected she'd react like she always did. Console him, entertain him, and cater to his every need—the routine grew tiring. "I've been gone fewer than ten, and I do have a business to run, you know."

He puckered his brows and sighed. "I guess being apart makes it feel like an eternity, but you're here now. How was your day? Make lots of money?"

Camellia shrugged. She circled her arms around his back to fluff the pillow and straighten his shirt collar. "A couple of sales. I got a late start this morning, thanks to you. Still, I kept the brunch date with my friends from New York. Didn't spend much time at the shop."

"Oh, I forgot. Alice and Maurine, right?"

"Adelaide and Monique." Camellia hitched her breath and gave the pillow an extra hard punch before stepping away. "Anyway, I got the dresses they promised to deliver. Their work is impeccable. Those items should draw the customers and increase sales."

"Good. Otherwise, this little endeavor of yours is a waste of time."

While her insides simmered, Camellia blinked. "I enjoy my career, Noah, no matter what. As Sia puts it in her cornball way, fashion is my passion."

His lips pruned. "Cute words, but not a testament to business savvy, are they? Speaking of Sia, has she come around any? About you and me, I mean."

"Maybe a little." Camellia refused to ruin the day by opening that can of worms for debate. She could predict where the conversation would end. Noah would insist she live with him. He'd offer the perfect solution to solve all her problems, like arguing with Sia, for instance. Perfect. Avoidance as a solution. She swallowed to wash away the bitter taste in her mouth. Hadn't she been running away from every difficult or uncomfortable situation all her life?

"Great. Say, what if we invite her over one evening for supper?" Noah slapped the arm of his wheelchair and widened his mouth into a grin. "When she sees how happy we are together, she won't be able to deny it. Don't you agree?"

Why did she hesitate? Camellia poured a glass of iced tea and sat at the table. "I don't think the idea is a wise one. Once Sia forms an opinion, it sticks." She ticked off her fingers. "No wining, dining, or sweet talk will change her mind. I know my sister."

"I know her, too. Remember? We all grew up together. I believe an invitation is worth a shot." He wheeled to the table and cupped her hand in his. "How about tomorrow evening? Or later in the week? Come on, Cam. Let's do it."

His face softened along with his voice—as did her resolve. "Fine. I'll ask, but don't get too hopeful."

"That's my girl. I knew you'd agree." He smiled. "Heck, before long, we'll be picking out his and her towels for the master bath. I can't wait for you to move in. Can you?"

"Sure." She slipped her hand out from underneath his. "Maybe we can discuss it more after the mayor's gala? Everybody is scrambling to get event details wrapped up. I can't throw a wrench into the works by taking time to move out. You've hit me at a bad time, you understand." She didn't miss the tell-tale signs, the droopy face, and slouchy shoulders.

"You're right. I'm impatient, I guess. After the gala sounds perfect." Noah wheeled to the refrigerator and grabbed a bottle of wine.

Camellia frowned. The bottle, the same one she'd fetched from the wine cellar this morning to chill, was nearly empty. "Keeping busy today?"

As he emptied the bottle into a goblet, Noah shrugged. "Not much. I finished processing the orders. We're all caught up until the next round comes. Mom stopped by for a bit. She's leaving for a week to visit Aunt Lorrie in Memphis."

A hint of worry seeped inside and Camellia tensed. The image of Noah with his arms flailing while he demanded attention overwhelmed her. "Nice. You hungry? I can fix a sandwich to go with that wine, if you like." She skirted the sensitive issue because the direct approach never worked. Besides, he knew when to stop.

"I'm good. Already finished off the leftover quiche pie." He patted his expanding belly.

Wheelchair life was not the formula for staying fit. "Perfect. I'm going upstairs to change. Be back in a few minutes." When the doorbell rang, Camellia paced toward the foyer. A quick peek through the front window made her freeze but not quickly enough, because he saw her face. She struggled to maintain her composure, feeling both fearful and excited. Of course, she couldn't avoid answering, right? After swiping the loose strands of hair off her forehead and smoothing her dress, she opened the door. "Hi, Weston. What a surprise." She didn't know if she wanted to cry, laugh, or shout, but her emotions definitely filled her to the brim.

Weston's chin dimpled, and, as he smiled, warmth brightened his eyes. "I know I'm probably not welcome." He stepped closer.

He came within inches of her face, and she leaned back, afraid of how his closeness made her feel. "No, I suppose not. Why are you here, Weston?"

He extended an envelope.

"What's this?"

"Uncle Samuel found an extra key to the shop. Maybe you can use it." He nodded.

"Well, thank you, but I already made a spare to give to Remy." She hesitated. "You could've left it with my sisters, though."

Weston took a deep breath. "Yes. I could have." He stared while his jaw worked back and forth. "Cam, I can't give up that easily. Not when you mean so much to me." He seized her hand. "Don't you understand? I'd never hurt you. I wouldn't, not to anyone I like. And I…like you so much."

His voice softened to a whisper with those last words. Camellia slid out of his grasp and stepped farther back into the foyer. "It's fine. I'm over it. Now, if you'll excuse me, Noah is waiting."

Weston nodded. His arms hung loosely at his sides. "Sure. Can't keep Noah waiting." He took a step down from the porch but all at once stopped. "I hope we can still be friends. I don't have many."

"I can't imagine why not. You're friendly enough. You certainly have the gift of gab, right? Good evening,

Weston." She closed the door before he said another word, before she'd cave and invite him in, because doing so was tempting. Her thoughts raced with tidbits of conversations she'd had with him. He was funny, full of wit, and very comfortable to be around, which was a lethal combination to resist. She failed to think straight or be rational about her reactions to him. All those heart-pounding emotions threatened to drive her to reckless lengths, and she didn't need that sort of turmoil at the moment.

"Cam? Who was at the door?" Noah wheeled out to the foyer and rested a few feet behind her.

Camellia shoved a stubborn lock of hair behind her ear. "Weston Murphy. He stopped by to drop off a spare key to the shop." The statement was close to the whole truth or as close as she wanted to admit to Noah.

The muscles in his neck twitched. "I see. Why did he feel the need to come all the way to our home? Why not leave it with your sisters?"

Her heartbeat quickened, and she folded her arms tightly across her chest. "I don't know, and I certainly don't care." She marched toward the stairs. "I'll go up and change now. Unless you have more questions?"

He wheeled closer. "I trust you, Cam, but I don't trust him. You should keep your distance. He makes you angry and upset. I can see it happen."

Tightness weighed heavily on her chest. She took a deep breath. "Of course, you're right. I'll avoid him as best I can."

"Wonderful." Noah grinned, and his body relaxed. "Go change, and I'll fix you a nightcap, since I seem to have drunk all the wine." He chuckled.

Camellia pinched her lips together. Of course, he

did. "Thanks. Meet you in the parlor in a few minutes?" She waited for him to nod and then ran upstairs. The lump in her throat was hard to swallow. He was right. When Weston was around, she did get angry and frustrated and excited. Then why did she feel this cloud of misery settle around her, choking and constricting her very existence? "Because he makes you angry, frustrated, and excited. That's why." She grumbled while she ripped off her dress and threw it on the bed in a crumbled bunch.

While slipping into jeans and a T-shirt, she forced thoughts of Weston out of her head and planned her next move with the shop. Tomorrow, she'd place a few of Adelaide's and Monique's dresses in the window display and maybe have Remy make a sign. *Latest trendy fashions from New York.* She ran a brush through her hair and then twirled in front of the mirror. Tomorrow. Something she looked forward to.

She stepped toward the bedroom door but paused when her phone buzzed. A message from Dahlia, requesting a meeting about last-minute changes to the July Fourth family get-together, made Camellia smile. She skimmed her fingers across the keys to answer. Tomorrow evening for supper. Of course, Noah wouldn't be happy. At the same time, he'd refuse to come along if she invited him. However, she'd try. She always tried.

She entered the parlor and arched an eyebrow at Noah who smiled ear to ear with two drinks in his hands. "Yum. Chocolate martinis. Are we celebrating something?"

"Absolutely. We're celebrating us." He reached behind him to grab a plate from the table. "Here's some brie and those water biscuits you crave. I figured you must be starving."

Camellia massaged the back of her neck. "Why are you so good to me when I don't deserve it?"

With his face flushed he leaned forward. "Oh, but you do. You deserve to be pampered and loved, which is exactly what I plan to do for the rest of our lives. Now, eat and drink, and let's enjoy the rest of our evening."

After a few sips, Camellia forgot all about Weston. She even laughed at Noah's jokes. As she listened to stories from their childhood, she smiled and her heart warmed. Everything about the evening was perfect. All of it seemed natural. Things would fall into place. She stiffened as queasiness roiled her insides. They had to.

****

At a quarter to eight, Camellia backed out of the drive and headed for town. As light glared through the windshield, she flipped down the visor and donned her sunglasses. Despite Noah's insistence she stay longer and talk, she needed time alone. Not to mention, a ton of things remained to finish before opening the shop. The traffic on the road was sparse, which was another plus. Remy wouldn't arrive for another hour or so, depending on how much sleep he had. She had plenty of alone time to think, and mostly about Weston. Though brief, the encounter with him last evening left her emotions in a tailspin, which reminded her of the convoluted mess she didn't want to face. She *loved* Noah but hadn't regained the "like" part since their breakup. She *liked* Weston, but… "I don't love him. I barely know him," she argued aloud and slammed a hand against the steering wheel. "Not going anywhere with this argument, am I?"

Before getting any deeper into her relationship with Noah, she was determined to figure out why Weston affected her so much, or better yet, how to stop. In the meantime, she had plenty to keep her mind occupied—the shop, the Fourth of July bash, and the Mayor's gala.

Camellia steered into the side alley and parking area behind the shop. Remy's bicycle was chained to the post, but, after scanning the area, she found no sign of Remy. She glanced at her watch and frowned. Where was he? As if to answer her question, Remy ambled around the corner.

He stuffed his hands deep into his pockets. He shuffled across the parking lot, and then stopped to kick at the gravel. When he raised his head, the scowl on his face softened. He smiled and waved.

Camellia killed the engine and got out of the car. She waved back. "What are you doing here this early? Did you take my advice and get to bed on time?" As she approached him, she winked.

"Nah. Too much noise at home. Figured I'd come here to wait for you," Remy said with an unwavering stare at Camellia.

She chewed on her bottom lip and avoided questioning him further. Camellia unlocked the service door and led the way inside. Something wasn't right, but she didn't press him with more questions. "Why don't you get on the phone and order us some breakfast from next door? Unless you've already eaten?" She studied his face.

Remy shrugged. "No. You want the usual? Bagel with egg, cheese, and bacon?"

"Yep, and get whatever you want. I'm paying. Oh,

get me a large coffee this time and with lots of sugar." Before leaving Noah's, she'd skipped coffee and barely touched her eggs and toast. He never stopped chattering about future plans. All that talk gave her yet another headache, and she'd had too many of those. Here was her chance to relax and have a quiet meal with Remy. Maybe after a few bites of bagel, he'd open up about what really made him leave the house in such a hurry.

"Sure thing." Remy stepped to the front of the shop.

Camellia looked around the storage room. In a way, she was relieved to have his company to occupy her otherwise-preoccupied mind. During her drive to work, she'd had enough troubling thoughts about Noah and Weston. Nothing was solved, but concentrating on business always lifted her mood.

After finding hangers for the dresses Adelaide and Monique delivered, Camellia carried them to the front. "These hangers will work," she announced to Remy after he finished the call. "How about you take the empty rack and place it near the front window? I'll put the new dresses there, which will have to do until the mannequins arrive later this week."

"Sure thing. Right after I run next door for our food. Anita's shorthanded this morning and has no one to deliver." He shuffled his feet.

Camellia handed him the cash. "Don't take too long." She didn't miss the gleam in Remy's eyes whenever he returned from the coffee shop. Anita had left her mark on Remy. Of course, she was five years older. She and Camellia graduated from high school together. Obviously, the infallibility of infatuation was never to be discouraged, no matter the odds. Camellia chuckled while Remy jogged out the door.

She examined the dress rack for a minute, and then stirred into action. Dragging it across the floor, she stopped before the display window. This spot caught the sunlight but not too much. Deciding to examine the display from the outside, she opened the door and stepped onto the sidewalk. At that moment, she caught sight of Remy, his hands full of bagged breakfast bagels and coffee.

He stood next to a car idling in the road.

Camellia recognized Trina's car and scowled at the unwelcomed sight.

Remy hunched over.

He appeared far from happy about the subject of their conversation.

Trina pointed her finger at him.

Remy kept shaking his head. In the next moment, he leaned away from the vehicle and turned toward the shop.

Not wanting to appear like a nosy body, Camellia hurried inside.

"Here's breakfast. Sorry it took me. Anita had a line of customers." Remy placed the bags on the counter before handing Camellia her coffee.

Why was he hiding the truth? Camellia frowned. Whatever happened, Trina left her mark. Remy dragged into the store with a scowl planted on his face, acting gloomier than ever. "Umm, smells fantastic, and I'm starved. Why don't we sit and enjoy breakfast?"

Twenty minutes passed, and they'd emptied their plates *and* their conversation. Camellia took the last few sips of coffee. "Remy, is something wrong? Something you'd care to talk about? I'm certainly a good listener."

Remy balled up his bagel wrapper and lobbed it into the waste can. "Nope. My life's totally cool. I have a job, and school will start soon. One more year before graduation, and then I'm off, ready to be a man and doing man things. Right?" He wore a stiff and awkward smile.

Camellia snorted. "If you say so. Growing up isn't all it should be. Plenty of troubles and heartache come along with the job."

"Plenty when you're a kid, too," Remy mumbled. He stood and explored the shop until he noticed the dress rack. "I could've moved it. You should've waited."

"No problem. I need to keep busy." Weren't they a pair? His sarcastic, gloomy remarks prompted her to take a more positive approach to life, unlike what this display of mood killer offered. An idea brightened her attitude. "Say, you should come with me and my sisters to watch Sia play at the club tonight. We're stopping by after our supper get-together. You know, I bet I can get her band to play some tunes you'd like. How about it?" She bounced out of her chair. "Oh, snap. I'm on a roll. You should come have supper with us, too. Make a full evening. Call your aunt and let her know you'll be spending the evening with us. I'll drop you off home afterward. Sound good?" She held her breath. If her hunch was right, he'd jump at the chance to escape home and whatever bugged him.

Remy twisted his mouth into a scowl. "I don't know. She might not like the idea. Aunt Laverne is weird in that way."

"Let me handle your aunt Laverne. I'll call for you.

I can be polite. If she objects, I won't take no for an answer. I also can be extremely persuasive." Whether the mood was genuine or not, Camellia remained upbeat. Remy needed it.

He sighed. "Fine, but I warn you, she's no pushover."

Camellia lifted from the chair, tossed her breakfast trash in the waste can, and then held up her hand in a salute. "Consider me warned."

****

"You are such a sweetheart. Isn't he, ladies?" Freesia laughed at Remy's comment.

Camellia sniffed the aroma of fresh-brewed coffee as it wafted through the kitchen.

Zinnia cleared empty dessert plates off the table. She eyed Remy. "You'd like a another helping, wouldn't you?"

Remy smiled and nodded. "Please."

Camellia warmed with pleasure. As the evening progressed, Remy acted relaxed and got on so well with everyone. His behavior was a true transformation from this morning.

He'd been right about Aunt Laverne. She put up a fight, but, despite all the protests, charm wore her down and won her over.

The puzzling question which floated around in Camellia's brain was why be such a bore about Remy's social life? Counting the ten hours at the copy store, the boy worked thirty-plus hours a week. All work and no play made Remy a very dull and moody person, and she was determined to change the situation. She'd spent a half-hour on the phone, approaching exhaustion to maintain her charming but affirmative self. Laverne caving was a true victory.

Remy blushed at Freesia's compliment and dug into his extra-large slice of rhubarb pie.

"We should get started on our business talk," Dahlia suggested. "Still plenty to do before the Fourth. Sia, did you finish the guest list like I asked?"

Freesia nodded. "I did, but with a few last-minute changes." She scratched her upper lip and cleared her throat. She steadied her gaze on Camellia. "One of them being Weston Murphy. I asked him to come as my date."

Camellia stiffened.

Freesia glared.

Everyone around the table remained quiet, even Remy who stopped moving, his fork in midair with his last bite of pie poised near his lips.

Camellia suppressed all the protests aching to explode from her mouth. No way. Not one word. Freesia expected as much, ready to pounce on any objections. The possibility of various verbal lashes knocked around in Camellia's head. *You don't want him. So, why can't I take a shot? Why should you care whether he's my date?* She shuddered and clamped her lips.

"How nice of you, Sia. He's such a pleasant man," Zinnia said, her voice quaking a bit.

Freesia stood and carried her plate to the sink. "We get along so well. He seemed the perfect choice." She tilted her head and looked at Camellia. "Besides, I'm tired of attending these family things alone. Alone is not fun."

Rather than lash out to accuse Freesia of using Weston just to teach Camellia a lesson, she took another approach. "Since we're expanding the list, I'd like to invite Remy and his family, including Trina. Despite our differences in the past, I think it's time for me to take the high road and make amends." She locked gazes with Freesia's and didn't blink, not even when Remy's fork clattered onto his plate.

"Well, you're certainly gracious, Cam." Dahlia sipped her coffee then set the cup in its saucer.

Her voice was calm but her face scowled with usual skepticism. Camellia wasn't fooled.

"Are you crazy?" Freesia raised her voice before adding an aside to Remy. "No offense, sweetie, but your cousin is a vindictive little b—"

"Mom, you're here." Zinnia ran toward the doorway and embraced Gwen and Robert.

Gwen shifted her gaze from Camellia to Freesia and back again then dropped her handbag on the chair. "Okay. What did we just walk in on? I can sense when my girls are unhappy." She gave each of them a squeeze.

Camellia gave her mother a quick appraisal. Her tall, thin frame towered over all of the sisters except Dahlia. Those blue eyes didn't seem quite as bright, and her blonde hair was touched with gray, but the yoga classes kept her figure in great shape. "It's nothing, Mom." Camellia's voice muffled into Gwen's shoulder. The familiar scent of her mother's perfume somehow comforted her.

"Yeah, we were discussing the guest list. Cam wants to invite Trina and her family." Freesia nodded at Remy and patted his shoulder. "By the way, this is Remy, Trina's cousin. He's visiting for a spell."

Gwen frowned at Camellia. "Trina Averaux. Isn't

she your nemesis? Including her will be like poking a hornet's nest with the evening full of biting, stinging remarks." She glanced at Remy. "No offense, young man, and I'm glad to meet you."

Camellia didn't know who she was sorrier for—herself or Remy. With his slouched posture and puckered frown, he seemed as miserable as she felt. "No. I want to bury the proverbial hatchet, Mom. Everything's fine." Of course, everything was far from fine. A moan shuddered through her. She cursed herself for blurting out such a dumb suggestion. She blamed Weston. If he didn't get under her skin by sending her emotions into a frenzied turmoil, maybe she'd think and act normal, not like some crazed, jealous b-word, as Freesia termed it.

Gwen brightened with a full smile. "Maybe you need one of my herbal solutions. I have the perfect thing to calm the nerves. I'll bring some tea mixes this evening. I need to stop by the garden first."

"None for me," Camellia and Freesia both blurted out simultaneously.

Seeing each other's face, they burst out laughing.

"Well, looks like it won't be necessary after all, dear," Robert interjected. "They seem to be getting along fine."

His smile deepened the creases at the corners of his eyes. Camellia admired the tall, ruggedly handsome man her mother chose as a mate.

Gwen chuckled with a head shake. "You're absolutely right. Now, is there any rhubarb pie left? The meal on the plane was disgusting with all of that prepackaged garbage. I couldn't eat a bite."

"I made two, knowing you'd like some." Zinnia

grinned with her pie spatula in one hand and ice cream scooper in the other. "A la mode?"

"I'll take another slice with two scoops," Remy announced, making everyone laugh.

The mood in the room quickly lightened.

"Don't get too full. We need you out on the dance floor tonight." Freesia winked.

Remy scowled with arms crossed over his chest. "I don't dance."

"Nonsense. Everybody dances." Gwen poked Robert in the side. "Well, most everybody."

Robert wrapped an arm around Gwen and squeezed. "I slow dance, but not with those crazy, fast moves you young folks call dancing."

"No matter who goes or stays, we should leave in a half hour. I need to warm up with the band or the other members will threaten to kick me out." Freesia grabbed the sheet of paper off the table and shoved it at Dahlia. "Here's the list of guests. If you have any questions, let me know tomorrow. I have to run upstairs and get ready."

"But we haven't finished our discussion." Dahlia shrugged then glanced around the table. "Well, you heard her. I guess it's time to get ready for our evening out."

"Are you and Robert coming with us, Mom?" Camellia asked.

"We wouldn't miss a family occasion. Life's too short to let opportunities slip by." Pulling the dessert plate close, Gwen licked her lips. "Especially when I get the chance to enjoy one of Zinnie's pies."

Camellia glanced at her family and Remy. She thought about Noah and her second chance, about

Weston and her questionable feelings for him, and about Trina who rattled her confidence. She obsessed over Gloria's undoing and how the fiasco ruined careers, hers and Emily's, but she shouldn't. Sure, some of her opportunities had been cut short or burned to ashes, but not all. She had plenty for which to be grateful. Yes, she had to agree. Life was too short to ignore the wonderful things in it. If only she could avoid worrying about the moments to come.

Chapter 14

The evening geared up to be fun and entertaining, and Camellia nearly forgot her problems, at least most of them. This morning, after she explained how she was spending her evening, Noah pouted like a baby. Fortunately, she'd most likely not hear the beep of any texts to emphasize his disappointment. Chico's was packed and loud, which also made phone conversation impossible, unless she stepped outside.

"Come on, you guys. What y'all waiting for? Get up and dance." Freesia shouted from the stage. She held her arms above her head and clapped. "This song is for a dear friend. Remy Averaux, the dance floor's calling you!"

Remy slouched in his seat and groaned. "Did she really just say my name?"

"She did. Now, why don't you follow me?" Gwen wrapped her fingers around Remy's hand. "We certainly can show these slugs how it's done." She leaned closer and pointed at Robert. "Besides, this guy sometimes slows me down. I need a little outlet once in a while. What do you say?"

Camellia laughed at the varying shades of red coloring Remy's face. Still, he was a good sport and let Gwen lead him onto the dance floor.

"Well, well. If it isn't the Holiday bunch. Did you decide to ditch your frumpy, uppity attitude and come party with us plain folk?"

At the sound of Trina's sing-song voice whining next to her ear, Camellia cringed with an irritation that clouded her upbeat mood. "Did you hear something, Zinnie? Sounds like a bug, maybe a mosquito buzzing around?" She tilted her head, pretending to listen, and then gave it a shake before turning to face her nemesis. "Nope. No mosquito. Trina, how's tricks? No pun intended, of course." So much for making amends.

Trina gritted her teeth. "None taken, I'm sure. I was in the neighborhood and dropped by to check on my dear cousin. Where is Remy, by the way?"

"On the dance floor with Gwen." Dahlia pointed. "Why don't you join them?"

Camellia grinned. Score one for Dahlia. "Yeah, shoo. Go away. We were having such a good time until a few seconds ago."

"Talk about rude, though I should remember you're the one I'm dealing with, right?" Trina stomped off but not in the direction of the dance floor. She climbed on a bar stool and shouted at the bartender to bring her a whisky sour.

Camellia smacked the table with the flat of her hand. "Ooo. That was too much fun."

"What happened to burying the hatchet?"

Zinnia's expression crumpled into a puzzled frown. "Tomorrow will be soon enough. Tonight, I'm having a grand time with no emotional baggage like guilt to ruin it." Camellia drained the last of her drink and motioned to the server to deliver another.

"Don't have too much fun. Remember your hangover from the last time?" Zinnia handed her a napkin. "You have a spot on your blouse."

197

"I do remember, and I won't relive that misery. I promise. One more drink and I'll quit." Camellia blotted the wet spot then crisscrossed her chest. She had too much to do before Saturday's party to end up a morning-after heap of misery. Finishing the new outfit she'd designed and planned to wear for the event was only one item on her to-do list but majorly important. Though she extended the olive branch with her invitation to Trina and company, Camellia couldn't squash every competitive gene inside her. Too much, too soon. She was only human, flaws and all.

Zinnia jerked her head toward the bar. "Uh-oh. She's finished her drink and headed for the dance floor. You think we should worry about Mom's safety?"

As her gaze followed Trina's beeline path toward Remy and Gwen, Camellia tensed. Trina wasn't smiling. In fact, the scowl and gritted teeth implied she was ready to do battle with someone or anyone who challenged her. "Mom can handle her, but be ready to dive in, just in case."

Tony turned the amp's switch to dial up the volume, and the band kicked in with a faster tune. Drums thumped and guitar strings squealed.

Camellia couldn't hear the conversation transpiring on the dance floor, but the visuals were totally enlightening. Arms flailed and nose-to-nose moments between Trina and Gwen didn't imply nice. A queasy sense of dread seeped in. Matters were digressing fast as a torpedo dive.

Dahlia stood.

Camellia and Zinnia followed.

Within seconds, Freesia jumped off the stage. No doubt, she'd reach Trina and Gwen first. Not the safest scenario, but stopping Freesia was impossible. Heaving a sigh, Camellia led the way toward the dance floor with Zinnia and Dahlia close behind. She fought through the thick crowd, getting elbowed by dancers whose arms moved to the music beat, and had to stop a few feet away from the action.

By now, Trina poked Gwen in the chest while waving her other arm.

Remy skirted around Trina to step in between them.

Poor Remy. No wonder he was so miserable. He was surrounded by controlling, temperamental women, which included Laverne, Trina, and all the Holiday ladies. Only Robert provided male camaraderie. Camellia glanced behind her. "Where is Robert?

Zinnia squeezed Camellia's arm. "Look. He's pulling Gwen off the dance floor."

"Ah, not good. Sia is shoving Trina." Dahlia groaned and shook her head. "We have to stop them, or somebody will end up with a black eye, and it won't be our baby sister."

Camellia grunted in agreement. Freesia was the scrappy one among them. She was all girly, but, in a pinch, she fought like a man.

"Oh, boy." Zinnia squealed and stood on her tiptoes. "Look who's jumped in to join them."

Laverne in her camouflage jacket and army boots, reminiscent of her service days, marched into the scuffle and yanked on Trina's arm.

Trina spun like a top to face her mother. She dropped her jaw and cowered.

"No daughter of mine should cat fight like some lowlife bar tramp." Despite the noisy bar, Laverne's commanding bark silenced all nearby conversation. She pointed at the exit door. "Now, go home before you embarrass yourself any further."

Lifting her brow, Camellia gazed at the mother-daughter duo. Who's embarrassing *whom*? She stepped aside to avoid a collision with Trina and Laverne as they barreled through the crowd. No doubt, the entertainment for the evening achieved new heights. She loved the show, but it was over. She nudged Zinnia and, weaving through the lingering gawkers, retraced her steps.

Soon, Gwen, Robert, and Remy returned and took their places at the table.

At the same moment, Freesia dusted off her jeans and hopped back onto the stage for another song.

Once they were all back together and seated, Zinnia turned to Remy. "You were awfully brave to step between your cousin and Sia. Not wise but definitely brave."

Remy shrugged. "I'm used to women fighting all the time. Least ways, in the Averaux house it's nothing strange."

A tiny thread of doubt wormed its way inside, and Camellia tensed. What was going on in the Averaux home? The urge to blurt out an invitation to stay at the Holiday house was tempting.

"You can always come and stay at our place for a few days if you need a break. I'm sure Dahlia and Freesia…" Zinnia paused for a second then heaved her shoulders as she glanced at Camellia. "And Camellia won't mind. We have plenty of bedrooms."

Remy rolled back his shoulders and lifted his chin. "Nah. I can handle women."

Camellia covered her mouth to stifle a laugh. "Well, if you change your mind, you know where we live." She gave his shoulder a pat then sipped more of her drink. She perused the bar and dance floor but found no sign of Trina or Laverne. Score one for the Holidays and Remy, which left one issue to resolve. Why was Trina determined to get to Remy this evening? "Hey, Mom? What did Trina have to say before you two wanted to scuffle?"

Gwen wrinkled her nose. "We weren't going to scuffle, as you put it. I simply told her she was rude and whatever she had to say to Remy could wait until after the dance."

"What was all the arm waving about, then?" Dahlia asked. "You two acted like a couple of crazy wrestling contestants."

"Or maybe lady mud wrestlers." Zinnia giggled.

Dahlia rolled her eyes. "Do you see mud on the dance floor, Zinnie?"

"Oh, right." Zinnia chomped on a tortilla chip.

"I understand what the confrontation looked like, Robert, but you didn't need to come rescue me." Gwen patted his arm. "I had everything under control."

"From my view of things, I don't believe you did." Robert shook his head. "That woman is insane."

"Did Trina say why she wanted to speak with Remy?" Camellia refused to let the matter go. Somehow, that detail seemed important.

"Drop it, will you? Like he says, Trina's insane and a real loony tune. She probably was drunk, and, and— oh, forget it." Remy shot out of his chair and marched across the room toward the exit.

Camellia hitched her breath and stood.

Gwen caught her arm. "Leave him be. The boy obviously needs time alone. You pestering him with questions won't help."

Camellia settled in her seat. Remy was troubled. Trina or Laverne had to be the cause. Her gut told her the ordeal involved more than a silly teenage problem. "Fine. I'll talk with him later."

Gwen frowned but said nothing more.

Freesia tapped her thighs and stomped her feet while she belted out, "What's Your Name?" by Lynyrd Skynyrd.

All thoughts about Trina and the ugly incident were soon forgotten by the time Remy returned to his seat. However, Camellia kept her eye on him, the worry holding strong.

****

As the ocean breeze traveled inland, the evening air cooled. During the ride to Laverne's, Camellia remained quiet, keeping her promise to Gwen to give Remy time.

After powering down the window, Remy planted his chin on the ledge. Once the car stopped in front of his house, he jogged up the drive without saying goodbye.

Dahlia rested her hands on the steering wheel. "You've done what you could. Why not leave the boy alone?"

Zinnia rode home with Gwen and Robert while Freesia stayed at the club.

For the past twenty minutes, while her mind raced, Camellia orchestrated a nervous tap dance on the floor mat. "He's hiding something. I can't stop wondering what's troubling him, and I'm worried."

"You heard Mom. Trina babbled about nothing." Dahlia steered the car onto the road. "Besides, since when did Remy Averaux become your responsibility? You're his employer, not his guardian. That job belongs to Laverne."

"You're right, but that's the problem. Laverne." Camellia snorted. "Add Trina to the equation and wow. Some household he lives in."

"Stop. Don't you have enough to worry about?" Dahlia pointed at Camellia's phone as the screen flashed.

Camellia groaned then shoved the device deep inside her bag. He'd sent four messages in the past twenty minutes. His silence was too good to last the entire evening. "I can handle Noah. Besides, he's a grown man."

"Is he? Really? He sure doesn't act like one." Dahlia gripped the steering wheel and turned into the drive.

Camellia pressed her lips tightly together. She had no words to argue the point. Noah acted more and more like a needy child. She traced a finger along the outline of her phone, making her realize she hadn't removed her hand from the bag. If she was the one in a wheelchair and not able to walk, would she act less needy than Noah? The doubts in her mind crumbled her resolve. This evening was supposed to be hers—a night of fun, a night to be carefree and independent.

"You plan to sit in my car all night, or are you coming inside?" Dahlia stood in the drive with her bag clutched to her chest.

Guilt creeped inside and replaced the buoyant mood from earlier this evening. Camellia glanced at her car parked next to Dahlia's. "I think I'm spending the night at Noah's. Let Zinnie know I'll be back in the morning to help her in the kitchen. Okay?" Before her sister barked a single word of protest, Camellia popped out of the car and into her own. At the next corner, she pulled to the side of the road and stopped. With phone in hand, she gave Noah a call.

"I miss you."

He spoke with a strain to his voice. Camellia choked on the urge to cry. She bit her lip instead. "I miss you, too. Be home in a few minutes." She laid the phone on the seat and steered back onto Divinity Boulevard. In a strange way—maybe in a damaged way, which was frightening when she thought about it—she needed him as much as he needed her. If someone asked, she couldn't completely explain why. He was familiar ground and a huge part of her past. That part, along with all its flaws, she understood. The question was, could those positives be enough to hold her to him forever?

****

When Camellia woke the next morning, the romantic, love-filled mood from the night before had soured—one that might have been caused by the alcohol or maybe fatigue and stress. She stared at Noah across the breakfast table. His smile and eyes shined in a way she couldn't match with her own. Of course, maybe her current mood had more to do with the anticipation of the reaction she was about to receive.

"Sorry, I might have forgotten to mention it, but I promised to help Zinnie this morning with the food preparation for the party." Camellia walked to the sink and opened the dishwasher door. She stiffened at the sound of his long-winded sigh.

"I was hoping we could spend a lazy morning out on the patio. The sun is shining, and a cool breeze is coming from the ocean. The view is perfect. Why don't you stay a bit longer?"

She bit her tongue and waited. Once she turned to face him, her smile was in place. "I'd love to, but Zinnie needs me."

He clenched the arms of his chair. "I need you, too, dammit. When do I count, Cam? Your excuse is always one of your sisters, or the store, or that punk kid who works for you."

She trembled with anger and smacked one fist against her hip. "Noah, you're not being fair. You know I love you, and I do spend time with you."

"Do you? Lately, I have to wonder." Noah wheeled out of the kitchen.

His move was her cue to follow. He expected as much. She chewed on her lip. "I'm not giving into your pouty mood, Noah."

He stopped and wheeled around. "I'm not pouting. I'm being honest. You are first in my life. I think of you this way each day and every hour. Why can't you do the same?"

His voice softened and matched his loosened posture. She opened her mouth to speak but found no words. This situation frightened and confused her. They were back to square one. "Family is just as important, and I keep my promises." She sighed. "Look, we'll talk later. Zinnie is expecting me."

"Fine. You always say later, don't you?" Noah grumbled under his breath.

Camellia sidled sideways past him.

He caught her hand. "I'm thinking about staying home on the Fourth."

Glaring, she tugged her arm. "Why ever would you stay home?" In truth, she didn't need an answer. She had a strong hunch this comment was one more ploy to gain her sympathy.

He shrugged but kept his grip on her hand. "I don't want people to stare and feel sorry for me. That kind of attention hurts too much."

Camellia didn't believe what she was hearing. She wanted to tell him and to point out the irony. Noah was all about gaining pity and attention, which he proved every day. "Nonsense. Of course, you'll come. I'll stick by you and make sure no one bothers you." She wiggled her hand out of his grasp. "Now, I need to get going. We can talk more this evening." Gripping her bag, she rushed out of the house, as if being near him a second longer would suffocate her.

****

Mid-morning sunlight peeked through the window. Camellia adjusted the shade then turned to Zinnia. Heat from the oven flushed her cheeks. The sweet aroma of fresh-baked bread and rolls permeated the air. She inhaled and sighed.

Zinnia shook her head and pounded her fist into dough. "I don't understand. You love him, but you don't like him. He annoys you with his needy, whiny act, but you feel sorry for him. Sounds pretty mixed-up to me."

Camellia sprinkled more flour on the counter. "Sorry. I'm venting. We need time to adjust is all. Maybe I'm complaining because the change has been huge." And boy, was it ever. One day she despised the very sight of him. The next, she practically lived with him.

"What about the liking part? How can you be with someone you don't like?" Zinnia molded the dough with her hands and placed the loaf into a pan. "Your significant other should be a best friend as well as the one you love."

Camellia raised an eyebrow. "*Redbook*?"

She winked. "*Lady's Home Journal.* Would you pass me the flour?"

"I'm working on the friends' part. Your article should have also mentioned relationships take extreme effort and lots of time." Camellia's mood stabilized, even if it wasn't bubbly and bright.

Zinnia snorted. "Too much work isn't exactly ideal or healthy. We need joy in our lives and laughter and, well, the part that takes place in the boudoir. Those moments should happen most of all." She wiggled her brows.

"Stop." Camellia poked her arm. "We have that part. Trust me. Like I said, we're adjusting. Once Noah is back on his feet, he'll be himself again. Everything will be fine."

Zinnia wiped off her flour-dusted hands with a dishtowel. "Remember when you and Noah first started dating? You'd come home talking nonstop about love and bouncing off the walls with all that excitement. 'I found the one, Zinnie' you said. That person was you the first couple of months." She tipped her chin. "You know I'm right."

She stared out the window in silence while recalling those moments and the happiness he'd given her. "You think this relationship with Noah is all temporary, but it isn't."

Zinnia tossed the dishtowel into the sink. "You're missing the point, which doesn't surprise me since you're blinded and all."

Camellia frowned. "Then make your point. Enlighten me."

"Well, let me start with the time Noah refused to go with you when you got the award for USC's fashion designer of the year. He had more important business to attend to, as I recall." She tapped a finger on her chin. "Hmm, let me think. Wasn't it his night with the guys to play poker?"

Camellia cleared her throat.

At once, Zinnia held up a hand. "Eh, eh. I'm not finished. What about the day you returned home from a class trip to New York and told us about this wonderful opportunity to study design at the University of Paris? Remember his reaction? 'Cam, why do you need to go? We already have plans to stay at my family's beach house in Cape Cod. You can't disappoint Mother.'" She rolled her eyes. "That part was rich."

Zinnia layered her tone with syrupy sarcasm. Camellia ran her tongue across dry lips. Her heartbeat pounded as she scrambled to find an answer. "Seriously, Zinnie. He's changing, and when he's walking again, he'll be even better."

Zinnia gently took hold of Camellia's shoulders. "No, he hasn't and won't. Be better, that is. You know why? Noah is too selfish to change. He's always been. I guess you never noticed until…"

"You mean his affair with Trina. Does everybody know?" Camellia shook her head and backed out of Zinnia's grasp to remove the tray of rolls from the oven. Anger sparked and heated her face. "Lately, I'm having doubts as to whether it really happened. Back then, I was insanely insecure and quick to imagine most anything. Seriously, all Noah and I need is time to work on what we have." She squeezed her sister's hand and sighed. "Zinnie, I can't convince you you're wrong about him. You've made up your mind." Without possessing any energy of conviction, she released her words in a whispered tone.

She resisted the possibility Zinnia was right. Truth told, pride and fear of failure were her weaknesses, but she had to win this time. If they worked out a few kinks and got over this rough patch, their relationship would be better than ever. She had every confidence in a positive outcome.

"Right. Taking more time is certainly one way of putting off what you should do." Zinnia held up both arms. "Still, I'm not saying another word. Nope. Your life is your business."

Camellia poked her chest with one finger. "Damn straight it's my life and my decision. You'll see. Noah and I will be fine. Subject closed. Now, what do you want to bake next?" She prayed Zinnia meant what she said. By coming this morning, she hoped to avoid conversation about Noah. When Zinnia had asked how things were going, she caved and opened up about what bugged her. Not everything because some details were too personal, too embarrassing, and too frightening.

Lowering her head to stare at the counter, she picked at dough stuck to the board. How could she admit that lately she experienced panic attacks? When the walls of Noah's bedroom shifted inward, closing tighter and tighter until they squished her flat, and then *poof,* she'd disappear. If that image wasn't metaphorical, she didn't know what was. More and more often, she felt suffocated, which posed another sign of anxiety. If only he'd stop mentioning the moving-in-together scenario. That suggestion certainly didn't calm her nerves. Yet, here she was, defending him and their relationship at every turn.

"Why, it smells absolutely yummy in here. Maybe I should sample the goods to make sure they taste okay?" Freesia stepped up to the counter and reached for a roll.

Zinnia smacked her hand.

"Ouch!" Freesia scowled. "Greedy grump. Where were you when Mom taught us to share?"

"Plenty of time to share when we get to the reunion. Now, back off or else." Zinnia waved her spatula.

"Fine. I'll settle for a slice of leftover cold pizza." Freesia grumbled then, turning to Camellia, she moaned. "Ooo, where's my head? I'm supposed to tell you Detective Hulsey has been calling you. He says your phone keeps going to voicemail. Don't you ever check those?"

"Shoot." Camellia snatched her handbag. Last night, after she'd received numerous texts from Noah, she'd set her phone to mute. This morning's craziness made her forget. She glared at the bubble next to the voicemail icon which numbered to five in the past few hours. "Okay, maybe I should answer him. Be right back, Zinnie."

Alone in the foyer, she listened to the messages. They were brief, asking her to return his calls. She pressed the callback key and waited. Chances were the message was nothing important. Still, her heart raced hard enough to burst.

"You've reached the number of Detective Hulsey. Please leave your name and number, and I'll get back to you as soon as possible." Camellia waited for the beep. After saying a few words, she pressed the End button. She heaved a sigh and returned to the kitchen. Within a few feet of the doorway, she heard Freesia and Zinnia arguing. Stepping closer, she peered around the corner.

"I refuse to let her immature actions stop me. If I want to, I will." Freesia lifted her chin.

Zinnia waved an arm. "Please. You're doing it to spite her."

"I want to get through that thick brain of hers. She doesn't love Noah. Not the way you should love the person you plan to marry." Freesia slammed the refrigerator door. "I won't give up, not until she sees what everyone else sees. Or at least I do. I don't know what you're thinking."

"Now who's the immature one? We all love and care about her, but some of us know there's a point when we stop interfering. You can't force your ideas on Cam." Zinnia planted her fist on one hip.

Camellia stepped into the kitchen. As the high-pitched voices of her sisters resounded, she clenched her jaw, yet managed to speak. "Having a warm and wonderful chat, I hear. Do me a favor. Talk about the weather instead? Or maybe chat how summer has been unseasonably warm. Discuss anything, but I don't want to be your topic of the day, or any other day." As tears welled and blurred her sight, she cursed under her breath. She hated showing them how they got to her. As she took a deep breath, she couldn't keep her body from trembling. Straightening her shoulders, she pried her lips into a smile. "Now, let's finish baking before the kitchen gets any hotter."

The shift to awkward silence left Camellia feeling worse than ever. What happened to the comforting refuge of home? The place you go to when you needed the support of family and familiar surroundings was missing. For a nanosecond, she questioned whether staying in New York would have been healthier. In her most vivid imagination of the future, life couldn't change as drastically as it actually had.

Camellia faced the sink and listened as Freesia's steps grew faint. In seconds, the front door slammed, leaving behind an echo of emptiness.

"She didn't mean…I didn't…I'm so sorry, Cam." Zinnia blurted her words then wrapped a tight hold around Camellia's shoulders.

"It's okay." Camellia nodded, her chin brushing the top of Zinnia's head now buried in her chest. "I know you both mean well, but I'm not a child. Maybe sometimes I'm immature like Sia claims but still not a child. All grownup, that's me."

"Got it." Zinnia dropped her arms and sniffed. "I know I promised before, but this time I mean what I say. I won't interfere unless you ask."

"Deal." Camellia smiled and swung sideways to bump her hip. "Say, let's bake some of those spectacular sugar cookies. You know, the ones Mom loves so much?"

"You mean with walnuts and chocolate drizzle? Sure, why not. Maybe Mom will stop pestering us with all those herbal potions if we feed her enough sugar, right?" Zinnia laughed.

Camellia wiggled her eyebrows. "Exactly what I thought. Devious minds think alike, don't they?" Smiling and humming a tune, she lifted a couple of mixing bowls from the cupboard. The moment, filled with a cozy goodness, warmed her. She doubted the feeling would last.

Chapter 15

Camellia wheeled Noah into the backyard. The Fourth of July party was in full swing as the noisy background of chattering voices and mellow tone of bluesy music filled her with comfortable warmth. The peace of home and family and friends was part of the reason why she returned to Serenity and hoped to find. Finally, she felt like she had.

Pink, orange, and blue crepe lanterns hung from tree branches to give the early evening sky a rainbow glow of colors. "Isn't this scene absolutely gorgeous, Noah? My sisters sure know how to throw a party," Camellia exclaimed.

"Let's not forget your contribution. I sure haven't. All those hours you spent with them preparing this extravaganza." Noah hunched in his seat.

She recognized the sour tone in his voice but ignored it. Nothing would ruin her evening, not even Noah and his complaints. "Ooo, I see Leann. We haven't talked since I returned home." She stepped into the crowd but not before glancing at Noah.

He frowned and gripped the arms of his wheelchair while remaining silent.

"But I'll catch her later. Would you like something to eat? We can park ourselves there under the shade tree, and I'll fix us a couple plates. What do you say?"

"Sure." Noah shrugged. "Why not?" His lips

flattened into a smile.

The expression wasn't genuine, and Camellia knew it. Jaw clenched, she shoved the wheelchair forward into the crowd, bumping and bouncing over the uneven spots in her yard, not bothering to avoid them.

"Hey, slow down. I'm about to lose my teeth." He glared over his shoulder.

"Sorry," she mumbled and slowed her pace. As they neared one of the tables situated under a huge ash tree, she spotted them.

Weston and Sia walked out from the house, hand and hand.

Camellia drew in a sharp breath, and her heart paused several beats. She brought the wheelchair to a halt.

"What's wrong? Why'd you stop? There's the shade, and that table is empty." Noah pointed.

"Ah, yeah. Sorry." She said it again but froze in her spot.

Weston lowered his head and planted a kiss on Sia's cheek.

Seriously? Since when had things gone that far with them? A rush of heat surged through her. With steam, she'd look like a kettle on a hot burner ready to pop its cork.

"Cam, it's hotter than Hades. Let's get to the shade. All right?" Noah's hands smacked the arms of his wheelchair.

"Oh, don't be so pushy." She snapped and shoved the chair with such a jolt, Noah's head jerked forward. "Sorry." Good grief. How many times would she apologize? How many times had she said the word in the past several weeks?

"Watch it. I swear I don't know who's grumpier about being here. You or me." He maneuvered the chair closer to the table. Resting both forearms on its surface, he tilted his chin. "I know why I'd rather be someplace, anyplace, other than here. What's your reason? This day is all you've talked about for weeks."

Camellia shrugged but refused to comment. She was too angry to explain or defend herself.

"Honestly, some days I question whether I know you, Camellia Holiday. Good thing I still love you." He winked. "I'll take a plate of Zinnie's fried chicken and potato salad, if you're ready to get food."

His shift in mood eased the tension in her body. She glanced across the yard but found no sign of Weston and Sia. Thank goodness. She didn't need any more visuals. She swung her attention to Noah once more. "One plate of chicken and potato salad coming up." She patted his hand and left the table.

Leann swerved into Camellia's path and nudged her shoulder. "Why, Camellia Holiday. Been ages since I set eyes on you. How you doing?" She released a soft whistle. "You look fantastic, by the way."

"Thanks. You do, too." Up close, she studied Leann in more detail—her shiny, thick hair, bright eyes, and a smile stretching ear to ear. In fact, Camellia swore she glowed. With a loud gasp, she pointed at Leann's middle.

"Yep. Two months along, which means a winter baby, but I'm happy. Serenity is quiet and boring in January and February. A little one will keep me plenty busy." She laughed.

Grinning, Camellia squeezed her hand. "How wonderful, Leann, but when did you get married?"

"Last fall. Marriage was bound to happen. David is such a sweetheart. He proposed on my birthday. Here, I expected a surprise bash to celebrate the big twenty-one." She shifted her weight from one leg to the other and chuckled. "He gave me a surprise all right."

"Well, you both deserve this happiness. I'm sorry I missed the event." She squeezed Leann's arm. "Promise you'll invite me to the baby shower?"

"I sure will, but let's not wait until then to get together. How about a double date? Heaven knows, after the baby comes, David and I won't have as much free time. You, Noah, David, and me. We'll go someplace special." She raised her brow and nodded. "From what I hear, your business and relationship with Noah are doing well, which make a perfect reason to celebrate. I know. How about Southern Belle Tavern? I remember you love their cuisine."

Camellia's smile faded, and a rumble of discomfort shimmied through her. Of course, she had to suggest Southern Belle Tavern. Avoiding reminders about Weston was next to near impossible. "I'll give you a call later on this week. Okay? Right now, I should scoot. Noah's starving and begging for Zinnie's chicken. Later?" She talked and walked in reverse until her backside bumped into the food table. Leann gave her a puzzled frown until another guest interrupted and engaged her in conversation. Camellia clutched her stomach to calm herself.

"You feel okay?" Zinnia asked.

Camellia turned. "Great. Just great. I'll take two plates of your chicken and potato salad, add a side of green beans on one of them. And I don't want to talk about it, so don't ask." She held up a finger to punctuate the warning.

"Two plates coming up...minus the questions." Zinnia saluted then dished out generous servings. She nodded. "Now, stop frowning and go enjoy your food."

"We will." Camellia marched off, determined not to let anyone stop her this time. Trina, Laverne, and Remy stood across the yard, but she focused on only one person. Noah.

"Ah, I swear, your sister should win a contest with this chicken." Noah held the plate to his nose and took a sniff.

"She's earned a first-place blue ribbon at the county fair." Camellia nodded.

"When? I wasn't aware." He frowned then bit into his chicken.

The crunching of crispy coating while he chewed irritated Camellia. She paused to think before pointing a finger. "It happened three summers ago. Everyone but you rode along to Charleston. I think you had a business thing. Or maybe a golf date with your buddies."

"Come on. Everyone went?" He rolled his eyes. "A bit of an exaggeration, isn't it? Besides, I'm sure whatever I had to do was important. I'm certainly supportive of everything your family accomplishes." He waved an arm.

"Right." She chomped on a bite of garlic-flavored potato salad, leaving the rest of her comment unspoken. Zinnia's words rushed back. *He's always been this way. Why should he change now?*

"Let's not argue about the past." He patted her hand. "I'll be sure to congratulate Zinnie, first chance I get."

She snorted. "Oh, I'm sure she'll appreciate it, three years after the fact." Was he so clueless? Maybe the accident and being in a wheelchair for weeks affected his behavior. She couldn't have been that naïve when she fell in love with him. What happened to those qualities she admired, the sweet things which made her smile, and the endearing words? Why couldn't she remember any of those? She needed something to spark her interest again.

"Better late than never." He sat straighter in his chair.

His voice was cheerful and positive. Camellia sighed at the futility of making him understand. "Yep. More chicken and potato salad?" she suggested, provoked by the sudden urge to exercise the tension and grouchy mood out of her. She was overreacting, letting her anger get the best of her. With all the chaotic episodes that happened in the past few weeks, her behavior made sense. Her emotions were like livewire, ready to ignite.

Noah leaned back in his chair and patted his stomach. "I'm stuffed, but dessert would be nice. I'm sure the choices are plentiful, knowing your sister."

"Hello, sweetheart. I haven't had a moment until now to come around and chat." Gwen approached the table and leaned over to plant a kiss on Camellia's cheek. She straightened then glanced at Noah. "Hello, Noah. Nice to see you."

Was Camellia mistaken? She hid a grin. When she greeted Noah, Gwen's voice had stiffened like a robot's. She looked around. "Hi, Mom. Where's Robert? You two are like Siamese twins."

Gwen waved a hand. "Oh, he's jamming with the

band."

"Seriously?" Camellia laughed. "Good for him. I didn't realize he played an instrument."

Gwen sighed. "He does but not very well. Still, whatever keeps him happy, I support. Like every couple should do."

This time, Camellia caught the critical glance Gwen gave Noah. Had Zinnia been blabbing, maybe about what she'd told her sister in confidence? Camellia blushed with the heat of embarrassment.

"Have you gotten the chance to speak with Sia? She's been looking for you." Gwen gently touched her arm.

"I'm sure she has," Camellia muttered.

"Anyway, I should let you two get back to your meal." Gwen swiveled on her heel to face Noah then pursed her lips. "Do you feel okay, Noah? You haven't said a word."

She'd played enough being glib and sarcastic. *Time to rescue the poor man.* "Mom, I think our constant chatter hasn't left any room for him to comment." Camellia wanted to add more when she spotted Weston and Freesia.

They zigzagged through the crowd, stopping to have a brief chat with some folks then continued to head this way.

When Weston squeezed Freesia tighter and held her close, too close, Camellia's breath hitched

Gwen glanced in the same direction then settled her gaze on Camellia. She leaned close. "Are you all right? Something seems off, and I don't mean with Noah. You want to talk about it?"

She tensed. All attempts to hide her mood failed.

Truth be told, this was a bad day, and she'd had more than her share of them in the past several weeks. When would things get better? Nodding, she faced Gwen.

"Good. Let's go inside. Plenty of privacy there," Gwen wrapped her arm around Camellia's shoulders.

"You're leaving? But what about dessert? Cam?" Noah protested with a pout.

Gwen swung around. "Grow up, Noah Burke. For once, think about someone other than yourself."

Camellia didn't know whether to laugh or cry, or maybe she'd let go with a bit of both. Her emotions surged. She'd been dropped into the middle of a regular soap opera. Who loves who? Who's jealous of who? Worse yet, who despised who?

She followed Gwen. From the corner of her eye, she spotted Weston and Freesia who approached and sat at the table next to Noah.

Noah's jaw dropped and his eyes widened.

Camellia laughed and hiccupped uncontrollably then gasped for air.

"Oh, my Lord. You are a mess. Come inside and we'll get you a cup of tea." Gwen stepped through the kitchen doorway, ahead of Camellia.

"Regular tea, Mom. No concoctions."

She shrugged. "Have it your way. I aim to please. Now, sit." She pointed to a chair.

Camellia did as she was told. Grabbing a napkin, she dabbed at her eyes. "I'm not myself. I feel like a broken faucet you can't turn off, and I'm crying so much it hurts."

Gwen set the cup of tea in front of her. "You're right. Falling apart is not like you, but then again, we're talking about love."

She rattled the cup in its saucer. "Love? I'm thinking my circumstances are more about me caught in the middle of a scandal and being associated with a police investigation. No, wait. Let's make that two investigations—one concerning an untimely death and the other about stolen property. I've had to start over with my career, or what's left of it, by opening my own business." She threw up her arms. "Who knows if it will fly? Then Noah's accident happened. Need I go on? Seeing love through that mess is a struggle."

Gwen arched a brow. "Hmm. Well, then what's with the painful strain on your face like you were about to break into a million pieces when you spotted Weston with Sia?"

Camellia's mouth opened, but the words stuck in her throat. Caught in the act, she had no defense. She didn't want to talk about Weston, not even with her own mother. She gulped the rest of her tea and extended the cup. "More, please?"

Without saying another word, Gwen flipped the switch under the tea kettle.

At least someone knew how to take a hint. Camellia appreciated her silence. Too bad Freesia hadn't inherited the skill of restraint from Gwen.

"You know, Robert and I will celebrate our third anniversary next month. Time rushes by so quickly, at least at my age it does." She traced the outline of the placemat and smiled.

Camellia studied Gwen. The crinkly laugh lines showed a happy face, one content with life, though she hadn't always been that way. Her eyes, a striking cornflower blue, were a bit faded in color but hadn't lost their spark. "Do you think of Dad very often?"

The kettle whistled. Gwen added another teabag and poured water into Camellia's cup. "I do almost every day. He was such a good man. I loved him like no other. Yes, I see the look in your eyes, and I know. We all suffered during that time, but can you honestly measure a life based on one incident?"

"Well, things like murder, abuse, and other unforgiveable acts destroy your theory."

"You know what I mean. Anyway, I forgave him, and it's not nice to speak ill of the dead. After he passed, I vowed to never let another man in my life. As you know, I kept that promise for many years. Until I met Robert." Gwen clutched her cup with both hands.

Her voice sounded almost wistful but in a happy way. A strong hunch nagged her. Gwen wasn't simply making conversation. She had a point to her story. She always had a point. Telling little anecdotes was her way of offering advice, like taking the scenic route on a drive when the straight shot was faster. Faster was not as entertaining, though. "You truly are head-over-heels in love with him, aren't you?" Camellia set her empty cup to the side and rested both elbows on the table.

"More than I ever thought possible. Love's odd that way. You might not expect it, never see it coming, or you fight the notion, thinking you know better, but then the attraction hits you like a force of nature." Gwen sipped her tea. "No amount of reasoning can talk you out of that feeling. You're sucked in from head to toe. Sometimes, your heart knows what's best."

Camellia slowly nodded. "I'm sure a message is in there somewhere. Maybe in a day or two, I'll understand it."

She patted Camellia's arm. "I'm sure you will.

Love conquers all, as folks say. Do you love Noah?"

While searching for an answer that made sense, Camellia hesitated. "I'm leaning that way. Funny, but I think the car accident was fate bringing us back together. That accident convinced me I'd been petty, insecure, and unfairly suspicious of Noah's faith in our relationship. True, he's not perfect, but who is?" She shrugged off her lingering doubt and strived for a glass-is-half-full mentality. "Certainly not me. We'll be fine together. We're going through a rough patch. So, please don't worry. As for Weston, he is, *was*, a momentary attraction. I don't feel anything for him, not that way. I wish Sia and him every happiness." Camellia stood. The confession made her uneasy, and she prayed Gwen would let the matter go. "I'm going back to the party. Will you join me?"

With her lips drawn into a thin line, Gwen nodded. All at once, she lifted from her chair and wrapped her arms around Camellia. "Always remember, I love you."

"I love you, too." She forced a smile she didn't feel. The pep talk she'd reeled off had a boatload of holes, and Gwen probably suspected as much. She was her mother, and mothers could tell when their children were lying. Her head pounded. She had a strong urge to spill all the details she'd left out, the part about her struggle with feelings for Weston, and the confusion she'd been experiencing, but she couldn't. She wouldn't confess to one more failure, especially this one. The admission was too humiliating.

Stepping off the porch, Camellia picked up speed to cross the lawn, anxious to be with Noah and start proving he was the right choice, and hopefully the perfect choice. She'd try harder, be more understanding, and more patient. One way or another, she'd make their relationship work.

Weston extended both arms. "Whoa. Slow down, lady. No need for a collision."

Camellia jerked out of reach before he touched her. Thank goodness Freesia was nowhere in sight. Somehow, dealing with both of them overwhelmed her. "Sorry." She stepped aside, her heart racing.

Weston dropped his arms and smiled. "No harm done. How you doing? Don't get to see you much nowadays."

"Not bad, and you?" The words spilled out but sounded stiff and void of any emotion.

"Good." Without speaking, he worked his jaw while his feet shuffled from side to side.

The fidgety gesture made Camellia laugh. "Well, now everybody's good. I guess we can all go home happy. See you around, Weston."

"Cam." Weston caught her arm.

She flinched at the touch as her heartbeat quickened. She pictured herself running away as far as possible from the intense closeness Weston created. He stepped within inches, close enough to smell the sweetness of his breath. Warmth radiated off him. She fanned herself with one hand. "I need to go to get back to—Noah."

"Nonsense. Why don't you two visit a spell? I'll bring Noah his dessert and keep him company." Gwen stepped between them.

Camellia winced. She'd forgotten about Gwen. "I'd rather not. I mean, we can talk later, Weston. Noah needs me." As she left Weston behind, Camellia hurried down the steps, soon being swallowed by the crowd.

Once, she turned and gave him a brief glance. A frown furrowed his brow, and Gwen had one to match. She'd hear about the incident later, no doubt, and receive a full-blown "mom lecture" when that happened. She steered toward Noah and sat. Within a minute or two, she evened her breathing. "Did I miss anything?"

"How about dessert? You missed that part and so did I." Noah slumped in his chair. "Oh, but the wonderful conversation I had with Weston and Sia was a real blast. You know, they make a great couple, acting all bubbly and talkative. Man, are they ever chatty. Occasionally, I interjected a word or two before one of them hijacked the conversation, blabbering on about Lord knows what nonsense. A real fun time, it was." He turned his chair away.

Camellia winced. "Sorry. I haven't been the best date, have I? Let me get us some dessert. Sweets always make up for unpleasant moments, don't they?" She popped up from her seat and stepped away from the table before he made another comment.

"There you are! I've been trying to speak with you all evening." Freesia approached. "We need to talk. Zinnie told me what you said, and I want to clear up what you're thinking."

Camellia stiffened. "I don't have time, Sia. Why don't you get back to your date? Weston is waiting, I'm sure." She grabbed two plates and filled them with goodies. She couldn't face her. What if she lost her temper and shouted words she could never take back?

"You don't understand. Let me explain the thing with Weston." Freesia tugged at her sleeve.

"The thing with Weston is none of my concern. Later, Sia." Camellia twirled and marched off to her table.

"But Weston is. Cam, please." Freesia caught up and grabbed her arm with a hard jerk, causing plates of cookies, brownies, and pie to fall on the ground. "Oh, sorry. Let me get you another plate."

"Forget it." Camellia snapped her words and twisted her arm out of Freesia's grip. "Don't do anything for me. I can't handle what you have to say. Not your explanations. Not your advice, however wrong or right you might be." She shoved her way through people to distance herself from Freesia. She needed a timeout. Nothing she did or said was right. In fact, she despised this version of herself—petty, selfish, and immature. Why, she could be a female clone of Noah. A bitter laugh escaped. "Good one, Cam. So appropriate."

"I won't stop until you hear me out." Freesia skirted around to stand in her path. Her finger wagged. "Hey, here's a piece of advice. See that guy over there? You know, the one you claim to love and trust?" She scowled. "I overheard him talking with Trina. They are up to something. I feel it in my gut. So, if you were having doubts about the two of them, that tidbit should seal the deal."

"Seriously, when will you stop? I can't take anymore." Camellia's voice quaked more from anger than anything. "I do love Noah, and I trust him. When will you accept the fact?"

Freesia shook her head, her red curls bouncing. "Never."

"Let me by, Sia. I'm not arguing with you. People are staring." She spoke under her breath and shifted her glance from side to side.

Without another word, Freesia took several steps to one side, clearing a wide path, and waved her arm.

"Thank you." Camellia spoke in a breathy tone. Before she managed to escape, Camellia spotted Trina blocking her way. "Oh for...now it's your turn, I take it?"

"Cammie, sweetheart, I hoped to find you and apologize for the other night. I was drunk and in a foul mood. Forgive me? Of course you do." Trina smoothed the sleeve of Camellia's dress. "Is this one of yours? How cute. Anyway, what I wanted to tell you was how proud I am of your new accomplishment. Such a—ah—cute little shop you have."

Camellia counted to ten but the effort didn't help. "Shove it, Trina. Your apology and your *cute* compliments." She pushed her out of the way and stepped forward, keeping her gaze leveled on the ground to avoid those watching. Rather than steering toward the table and Noah, she aimed for the back door.

"Hey! Cam, where are you going? You can't leave," Noah shouted.

"I sure can, and I will." She tromped up the stairs and into the house. Who did Freesia think she was, butting into her business like that? She grabbed a bottle of wine out of the fridge and a glass out of the cupboard. Why wouldn't everyone let her choose who she wanted to be with? "Noah, of course." She nodded firmly then moaned, picturing Weston's kind face. Once upstairs and in her bedroom, she locked the door. No more thoughts of Noah and Weston tonight. She was having a meltdown.

Chapter 16

Camellia dug her knuckles into her eyes and rubbed away the itchy dryness. This running away and drowning her problems in wine had to stop. At the shrill ring of her cell phone, she groaned. Her head pounded and both ears reverberated. Digging out from underneath the covers, she patted the nightstand with her hand. "Hello?" Her raspy voice sounded more irritable than her stinky mood.

"Hey, boss. It's me."

Silence.

"You know, Remy? Anyway, you sound like crap. You okay?"

She took a swig of the only beverage in the room. Warm wine. At least it soothed her dry throat. "Yeah, super. What's up?"

"Ah, well, since you're not at the shop, I was wondering when you plan on coming in?"

She opened one eye, then the other, and squinted to view the clock. She gasped. "Holy—" She popped out of bed then grabbed the post to keep from falling. Once her balance returned, she put the phone back to her ear. "Give me twenty minutes, and I'll be there. If anyone shows up, stall."

"Yeah, but what if I can't—"

"No time. See you in a few." She disconnected and hopped from one leg to the other, pulling on her jeans, and then slipped her arms through the sleeves of a yellow silk blouse. After splashing water on her face and running a brush through her hair, she bolted downstairs. Cupping one hand over her mouth, she sniffed her breath. "Gross."

Despite the sharp, stabbing pain in her eyes, like the pounding force of a thunderstorm in her head, bits and pieces of last night's events returned to memory. She didn't want them to, but they appeared like bright neon flashes, popping up in her brain. She thought of Noah calling after her when she left the party and winced. She'd abandoned him. Nice. Great girlfriend she was. Without warning, she pictured Weston and his smile, and his touch. *Smooth, real smooth, Cam.* She was such a loser.

"Stop. Stop thinking, right now." She shook her head as she entered the kitchen.

"Stop what?" Dahlia peeked around the pantry door.

"Oh, my." Camellia clutched her throat. "You scared me. Not good." She moaned and snatched the bottle of pain reliever off the shelf then popped three pills into her mouth. Taking several sips of water, she sat and moaned again.

Dahlia stacked several cans of vegetables on the counter before she walked to the table. "You want to talk about whatever happened last night?"

"I don't know what you mean." Feigning ignorance seemed like the best choice at the moment.

She pursed her lips. "Oh, I think you do. I might not have been an eyewitness, but I got the full report from Mom and Sia *and* Zinnie. They can't all be wrong."

"You're being ridiculous." Camellia shook her head with a force her present health didn't handle well.

"How about Noah? He caused such a scene, that anyone around would've gotten an earful. Can't deny that messy detail, can you?"

Deep creases of concern furrowed Dahlia's brow. Camellia scooted out of her chair and clutched the bottle of pain reliever. She shoved it into her bag. "I can't talk. I'm late opening the shop. You have a great day, Dahlia. When I get home, I'll be sure to help clean up the mess. Okay?" She spewed out her excuses as she burned a path to the front door.

"Coward." She grumbled under her breath, shoved on her sunglasses then threw open the car door. Old habits were too hard to ditch. How could she claim she was starting over? All the successes in life meant nothing if her weak and faulty behaviors didn't change along with them. Denial and avoidance were biggies. She needed a strong dose of courage, especially if she wanted to stand up to people like Trina Averaux. The name made her smile. She'd told her to shove it. Maybe not the mature thing to do, but, in some ways, Trina deserved a dose of truth. Not because of what had happened between them. That part was old news.

Right now, Remy concerned her. The more she dwelled on him, the more she was certain something wasn't right in the Averaux household.

She pulled into the alley next to Camellia's Cave but not before noticing a familiar car parked across the street. Her headache faded. However, her stomach exercised a series of flips and turns. Now was not a good time. Of all days, he picked this one. She smacked her forehead then groaned with renewed pain. The call.

They'd played cat and mouse leaving messages, but she dropped the ball. Now, she had a personal visit from Detective Hulsey.

Camellia opened the shop door and, with concentrated effort, smiled. "Good morning, Detective." She glanced sideways at Remy and was met with a shoulder shrug. He'd tried to warn her, but she'd cut him off. "What brings you here?"

Detective Hulsey stood and extended a hand. "Good to see you, Miss Holiday."

"Please, call me Camellia. I think you've earned it." She motioned for him to sit then grabbed another chair, facing away from the window glare. "Remy, could you run next door and get coffee? Detective, would you like some?"

"Thanks. Make mine black." Hulsey leaned back in his chair and stretched his legs.

"Sure. Three coffees coming right up." Remy nodded.

"So, where were we? Oh, right, why you're here." Camellia stretched her lips into a stiff smile.

Hulsey plucked an envelope from the inside pocket of his jacket and laid it on his lap. "Some new developments have popped up."

"Really?" Camellia fixated on the envelope.

"NYPD called the other day. Seems Miss Volteri's personal assistant had a few confessions to make."

Camellia jerked to attention. "Oh?" Maybe the day wouldn't be a total ruin after all.

"Authorities received an anonymous tip. Stephanie Tumler hid stolen goods in her apartment. Anyway, one lead led to another. Finally, Detective Braum obtained a search warrant." He crossed his arms over his chest and grinned. "When he and his men searched her place, they found the stolen dresses. You remember the ones I told you about? All of them were stashed in her closet."

"Well, what do you know?" Camellia laughed despite the pain it caused. Stephanie duped them all, but being Gloria's personal assistant gave her an easy opportunity to steal.

"There's more." He tapped the envelope against his thigh.

Remy hurried through the front door. He handed Camellia one coffee and another to Hulsey. "I'm gonna unpack some boxes, okay?"

Camellia loved how Remy read her mind. "Sure, Remy. Our talk shouldn't take much longer. Right, Detective?"

"Not long at all." He held out the envelope. "Anyway, you'll want to read this after I tell you the rest."

She closed her fingers around the envelope but didn't make a move to open it. She waited while Hulsey slowly sipped his coffee.

"Good coffee. Thanks. Anyway, Miss Tumler also had a stack of envelopes addressed to various people, all with return labels from Gloria Volteri." He leaned forward and nodded. "And, get this deal. All of them were opened."

Camellia choked on her coffee and coughed for several seconds. "You mean she…" She glanced at the envelope. Indeed, it was addressed to her, along with a return address from Gloria. "She never sent any of those envelopes police found? But why?"

"Exactly what I asked. Detective Braum claims Miss Tumler shut up like a clam right after saying she wanted a lawyer, which worked until she was cuffed and put in the back of a squad car. Then she caved, blubbering and singing like the proverbial canary with one confession after another. Of course, all of them were accompanied with multiple excuses." Hulsey set his cup on a nearby empty box crate.

"I can imagine what sort of excuses they were." Camellia snorted.

"Oh, she has plenty. Like how Gloria stiffed her out of more than two months' pay but kept ordering her around as if nothing had changed. According to Braum, she wanted compensation. From what some of those envelopes contained, she had plenty of ammo to get more than enough payback."

"For instance?" Camellia knew how much Stephanie disliked her, but, after hearing Hulsey's story, she realized she wasn't the only target of the assistant's wrath. She should feel better but didn't. Instead, she resented how Stephanie blamed everyone for her actions.

"Buyer account numbers, checks for returns, and the biggest one was Volteri's stock info. Those envelopes were loaded." Detective Hulsey stood. "Funny how most accused say the same thing. Miss Tumler only regrets getting caught and not having enough time to collect all her newly-gained loot and leave town."

"Costa Rica or maybe the Bahamas?"

"Monte Carlo." Hulsey nodded. "Real nice this time of year, she claims."

Stephanie was more disgusting than imaginable. Self-centered and bitter, and those flaws were the tiny tip of a huge iceberg. Camellia lowered her gaze to study the envelope and the opening torn across the top. What were the odds she left anything of value to see?

"I don't think you'll find what you expect," Hulsey said. "However, according to Braum, you might get some answers." He shrugged. "Can't say since I haven't read it myself. Wouldn't be polite. Besides, this investigation isn't mine. Just me, the messenger, doing the right thing."

Camellia had to smile. His use of the word polite made her picture a British gentleman who sat sipping tea and eating a crumpet, with a napkin tucked neatly under his collar. Hulsey, on the other hand, fit into the more rustic type who shouted at football games, with a beer in one hand and a burger in the other.

Inserting her thumb and forefinger into the envelope, she removed a letter. The message was brief and in Gloria's handwriting. Two paragraphs quickly offered her apology and explained how she wanted to make amends with a gift, which she'd like to deliver in person. Camellia chewed on her lip for a moment. Finally, she relayed the information to Hulsey. He deserved as much.

"It's too bad you'll probably never learn what the gift was." Hulsey rubbed the sides of his jaw.

"True. You know, her gesture is hard to imagine. The Gloria I knew never apologized to anyone. She offered no regrets for her actions and not one hint of feeling guilty." Camellia refolded the letter and stuffed it back into the envelope. "Well, whatever the gift was, it couldn't erase all the misery I've experienced. So, the loss really doesn't matter."

"You sure?" Hulsey curled his lips into a smile.

Camellia gave her shoulders a casual shrug. "I've

learned money and success don't necessarily go hand in hand. I mean, success is not the same for everyone. Sure, I want the American dream, one that might not include a husband and a family or a house in the suburbs. Not even the get-rich-from-my-career fantasy." Without warning, a notion occurred. "I don't think I know yet what my dream is." Pouring out her heart to someone who was practically a stranger made her flush with heat.

"Don't feel bad. I'm nearly twice your age, and I haven't figured it all out, yet. Not by a mile." He chuckled. "In fact, I'd bet some folks don't get the message until they're standing at the pearly white gates. Too late then, right?"

"Let's hope neither of us have to wait that long." Camellia held out her hand to shake his.

"Say, if you ever figure out what she planned to give you, let me know, will you? Curious, is all. Comes with the job." Hulsey tipped his hat.

"Certainly. You have a great day, Detective. Thank you for the letter. At least it clears up why she was coming to see me."

"There is that much." He called out a good-bye to Remy and then left by the front entrance.

Remy appeared in the doorway with his arms full of office supplies. "Another delivery from the city supplier. You want me to stock the shelf or store them in your desk?"

"Shelf is fine." Camellia slipped the envelope into her bag. She needed time to think, which meant having time alone whenever she found it. At lunch she planned to stop by Noah's and deliver his favorite sandwich with a huge apology. He'd overreacted about her leaving him at the party, but in truth her behavior was pathetic and inconsiderate. An apology was in order, and that should come from her. "Talk about people who can't say they're sorry," she mumbled, more upset with herself about losing control and ending up with a major hangover.

Remy wiped his dust-covered hands on a rag and sat next to her. "All done. You have a good visit with the man?"

She chuckled. "Cute. The man. You watch a lot of cop shows, don't you? Detective Hulsey, the *man*, he's a decent guy. So, yeah, the visit was good."

"I watch cop shows. Tons of them. Even met some cops in real life, and not in a good way. Back home, not much to do when you're a kid with no wheels to get around. My life in Goose Creek—TV and fishing." He laughed.

Camellia studied Remy's face. He'd lived a whole other life, in Goose Creek no less. To think she didn't know much about him, other than the sordid details delivered by Noah, bothered her. She wanted to learn more because it somehow seemed important. "Bluegill?"

"Yep. Catfish and brown trout, too. Plenty of fish at supper." He tapped his heel against the chair leg.

"Maybe when you're free, you can teach me how to fish." Camellia waited until Remy grunted what sounded like yes. She sighed. Getting to know Remy? One small step at a time. She headed toward the front door and flipped the open sign to face outside. "Well, let's see if we get any customers this morning, or at least what's left of it." Making this shop a success could be the turn-around in her life.

****

"I brought you lunch." As she entered Noah's house, Camellia shifted the bags in her hands. "Your favorite. Crab cakes and hush puppies with plenty of Salty Sam's special sauce." She rushed to the kitchen. Maybe the aroma of food would sooth his grumpiness which probably festered and built overnight. She'd do anything to avoid the complaints he might shoot at her. As she rounded the corner, she noted his scowl and rigid posture, destroying all her optimistic thoughts. "Before you start, let me say I have no excuse. My behavior was horrible, and I'm sorry." She leaned a hand on the counter, her lungs deflating.

Noah's shoulders relaxed, but the scowl lingered. "Well, I should certainly hope you are. You left me. You embarrassed me in front of our friends and family." He wheeled around the table and closer to Camellia. "I was so upset, I couldn't sleep. You hurt my feelings, Cam. I can't believe how selfish you acted."

Camellia scratched her forehead and frowned. Immature and over emotional might describe her behavior last night, but selfish? "Wait. You're calling me selfish? Me. The one who's been breaking her back and running on empty juggling and caring for two jobs, two lives, yours and mine, taking what little is left of the day to help care for you, while you do nothing but complain." Her face warmed. Rage built and crested to the point of exploding. When was her effort ever enough?

He clenched his jaw. "I think you're overreacting. I wasn't the one who ran out, traipsing off with your mother to have some sort of girl talk. You promised to stick by me. You knew how worried I was about attending this party. To make things worse, I hear when Trina Averaux offered an apology, you insulted her. And don't think I hadn't noticed you talking to Weston Murphy. We had an agreement about you staying away from him, or did you conveniently forget?"

Camellia slammed the lunch bag on the table. "*I'm* selfish? I could rattle off the list of all your selfish moments, but something tells me you'd come up with an excuse for each and every one. You know, we loved each other once. Where did our love go, Noah? I'll admit, I thought we had a chance to give us another try, but now?" She threw up her arms. "Our relationship is becoming too hard. I struggle, you struggle. Love shouldn't be so much work. I feel like I constantly have to prove myself worthy and how much I love you." She turned away. Her heart hammered against her chest.

Noah touched her arm. "Cam, I—don't say that. I do love you, and I know you love me. Since the accident, I can't think straight. When you aren't around, I go crazy. I think once you move in with me, things will be better."

As her chest tightened, Camellia drew a deep breath. She shook her head. "No. I can't. I don't know anymore. I have to figure out what it is between you and me, but I can't do it by living here, Noah." She gently removed his hand. "I'm not sure if what we have between us is love." She let the words fall from her lips, though saying them hurt, and admitting them felt worse. In the past several weeks, he'd made her miserable many times. Yet, she didn't want to end it, not this way. "I'll call you later," she whispered and steered toward the hall.

"Wait. The doctor called."

She stopped but didn't turn to face him.

"He says I might get out of the wheelchair sooner than expected. He's referred me to a physical therapist, but I'll need to do these exercises every day. I could use some help, you know. Cam, I don't think I can manage without you."

She nodded. His voice trembled, and the sound nearly persuaded her to go back, but she didn't. She remembered those clever words and the smooth manipulation he'd used too often. Only now, it sickened and humiliated her to clearly hear and understand them for what they are. Why had she allowed him to get away with that behavior? "I'll call you." The sound of her steps down the hall echoed with the pounding in her chest.

In the car, she rested her head against the steering wheel and cried until her throat ached. Grabbing her phone, she texted Remy to close the shop. The day was ruined, after all. She'd go home and wallow in her grief, eat a tub of ice cream, or maybe binge on Zinnie's fudge brownies but drink no wine. Definitely not wine. Tomorrow, she'd pull herself together and figure out if what she had with Noah was over or not. Giving up on them would be another failure. She pictured being alone, and her heart sank.

Chapter 17

Early morning sunlight streamed through the kitchen window. Camellia squinted then faced the other direction. At least the weather was having a wonderful day. The clock chimed eight. After nearly ten hours of sleep, she remained groggy but with a coffee-induced, irritable edge. She shoved her mug to the side.

"You've been sitting in that chair for over a half hour, brooding, sulking, or whatever you're feeling. What gives?" Freesia leaned closer.

"What gives won't be the topic of this morning's breakfast conversation," Camellia grumbled. "Pick another one."

"All right, how about your blowout the other night? That one's good for a few laughs. Lord knows I could use something to make me smile."

Camellia raised her eyebrows. "Why? What's your problem?"

"I don't want to talk about it." Freesia lifted her chin and stared at the ceiling. "Although, I do believe men are not in my future. Maybe I'll switch to women. Seems less complicated."

Camellia dismissed her comment with a wave. "Oh, please. You of all people? Men will always be who stirs your heart, and you know it."

Releasing a howl, Freesia smacked the table with both palms. "I do know. Why do relationships have to be so hard? You like a guy. He likes you back, and then, *pow*! The happily-ever-after moment that should follow never happens."

Camellia didn't want to ask, since she might not like the answer, but she was weak. "You're talking about Weston, right?"

Freesia lowered her arm and glared. "Not Weston. I have feelings for Jaime Steele. You know, from high school? I hoped after seeing me at the party he'd—never mind."

"I just thought…" Camellia's words trailed to silence. She said not Weston. "Jaime Steele, huh?"

"I knew it. You assumed this thing between me and Weston was staged to make you jealous." Freesia threw up her arms and snorted. "Boy. Sometimes you are so clueless. No wonder you have relationship problems."

"Hold on a minute. Weren't we talking about your broken heart? Leave mine out of it." Camellia scowled and stood. She marched out of the kitchen, leaving Freesia with her jaw dropped. What did she care? Weston wasn't her problem. Noah was. At least Freesia got one thing straight. Love was plenty complicated.

"Oh, good. I hoped I'd find you this morning." Gwen appeared from the study. Her face glowed along with her smile. She traveled with a spring in her step.

Despite the discouraging start to her day, seeing Gwen and her mood helped ease the tension a bit. "Hi, Mom."

"Oh, dear. You don't seem well. Is everything okay?" A frown replaced her smile.

"Hmm. If by okay you mean, is my life in order? All my little ducks in a row? Satisfied in life and love? Then, no. Not okay. In fact, I'm as far from okay as a person can get. Sorry." She shrugged.

"Come with me. I'll fix you one of my herbal teas. I won't take no for an answer this time. Lemon balm will do wonders to lift your spirits, with a touch of chamomile to calm the nerves." Her eyebrows puckered while she studied her daughter for a minute. Her hands massaged Camellia's shoulders. "Maybe I should add a pinch of skullcap to release all that tension."

"I'm not going back into the kitchen." Camellia shook her head. "My remedy is to find peace in the sanctity of my bedroom and go back to sleep."

Gwen placed an arm around her and led her to the study. "Sleep is not a solution. Besides, I have everything in my bag, right here in the study with a hot plate sitting on the desk. I always come prepared. Trust me, Camellia."

The determination in her voice and face left no room for argument. Camellia relaxed. Sometimes Mom did know best. "Fine. Tea it is."

For the next hour, they sat drinking Gwen's special brew. Camellia had to admit, her body didn't feel as tense, and she almost forgot why she'd been upset. Almost.

"Now, why don't you share?" Gwen set her cup on the table and curled her feet underneath her thighs.

"Share?" Camellia peeked over the edge of her cup.

"Share details. We started the conversation the other night, but my intuition is telling me there's more."

Camellia squirmed in her seat. No child wanted to disappoint her parent. Yet, here she was, spilling her guts about all her failures. "I've already told you about the Gloria debacle, losing my job, and coming home for a do-over."

"Oh, I'm sure there's more. So, spill. You'll feel better. Cleansing your soul and freeing your mind of all those worries might help." Gwen leaned forward with elbows resting on her thighs and chin in her palms. "Please."

"Well," Camellia started but didn't know where to take the conversation. Skirting around the uncomfortable stuff was her knee-jerk reaction. She didn't think for a second Gwen would buy her excuses. They'd argue until Camellia caved. She might as well save time and energy. "Um, well, business with the shop is stressful." Her shoulders sagged. Epic fail. Gwen's scrutinizing stare told her as much. She skirted the issue, but for the time being, Gwen allowed her to do so.

"Are sales not good?"

"What I expected at this point. Turning a profit will take time. My friends from New York brought several of their designs for me to sell, which helps." Her foot tapped the floor in a staccato tempo.

"I'm sure it does. What else?" Gwen stared at Camellia, unblinking.

"Hmm. Detective Hulsey stopped by the shop yesterday. He had news." She explained the letter and the questions still left unanswered. "I guess I'll never learn what Gloria intended to give me, which seems strange, you know? Almost like she realized what fate had in mind, so then she scrambled to make good on all her wrongs before time ran out. Silly, right?" She shrugged.

"Not silly. Let's say imaginative to some, but reasonable to those who believe in a higher power and have faith." Gwen.

Camellia shrugged. "She was so mean, at times. Believing anything spiritual applied to her is hard to accept."

Gwen lifted her brow. "Why? Because she was mean? All sorts of people have faith, Camellia. Good and evil."

"I'm saying she came across as mean. She was such a pragmatist and never sugarcoated anything for anyone, meaning she never used a filter to soften the truth—or at least her definition of truth." She clipped her words as she recalled the unpleasant Gloria moments. "Everything required a rational explanation, scientific proof that it existed. If not, she'd call it hogwash. Her words. Bottom line, she was hardly the person to believe in faith."

"Faith doesn't have to be rational or scientifically proven for one to believe. Or at least that's been my experience. No matter, everyone has their own take on it." Gwen smiled and nodded. "Go on, what else?"

"Else?" Camellia frowned. "Nothing else." Gwen pursed her lips as if to say let the battle begin. She tensed, bracing for what was to come.

Gwen leaned back and frowned. "What about Noah? How are things with him?"

"Yes. Noah." She pressed a hand to her stomach as queasiness rippled through it. "To be honest, I'm still figuring out things." She left it short and not so sweet.

"Figuring out *him*, you mean?"

Camellia groaned. Gwen would pluck each detail out of her head. Every one of her follicles hurt imagining it. Pure torture. "No, figuring out what I want from—oh, hell…from love…romance…all of it." She waved a hand in the air.

"Ah, I see." She traced one finger along her bottom lip.

"You do?" Camellia's voice squeaked. "Then please share, because I sure don't have a clue."

"You want love and romance to come in a tidy box wrapped with a pretty bow and labeled 'Camellia's Life as It Should Be'? Gwen shook her head. "Love is messy, sweetie. Never neat and tidy. Love comes with bumps and bruises as well as the glorious parts."

She blinked. "So, you're saying I should stay with Noah?"

"Not at all. What I'm saying, if what you're looking for is a perfect fairytale romance with a happily-ever-after ending, you might not find it. Don't settle but don't be unrealistic either."

Camellia puffed her cheeks and blew out air. "If this behavior is you acting helpful, it's not working. I'm more confused than ever."

Gwen threw back her head and laughed. "Now you're getting it. Love is confusing, complicated, and sometimes painful. However, it's also exciting, wonderful, and the best feeling you can have. Don't give up because the quest is difficult or feels like an uphill battle." She squeezed her daughter's hand. "The real thing will come your way. Be patient."

Camellia bounced out of her seat and leaned over Gwen, embracing her with an affectionate hug. "Says the woman who has it all. Seriously though, you are a wonder of wisdom. Thank you for the tea. I feel lots better."

"Good." She patted Camellia on the back. "See? No sleep required. You can get on with your day."

"I certainly can. I should open the shop before the morning gets away from me. I have a mountain of tasks to finish."

"Maybe you should add a call to Emily to your list," Gwen said.

She snapped up her head. "What?"

"Emily. Maybe she received a similar apology letter from Gloria?" Gwen raised her brows.

"Oh, of course. Emily. She'd know what Gloria had in mind to give me, if she received the same thing. You should be the detective. Thanks." Camellia gave Gwen a smooch on the cheek and hurried from the study. She leaped up the stairs and speed-dialed Emily. After several rings, the receiver clicked. "Hey, Em. How's Paris?"

"Great, I'd imagine, though I can't say personally since I'm not there. Good to hear from you, Cam."

Emily's voice was flat. Camellia scowled. "Why? Where are you? You said Paris was a done deal. Unless, it's—is the magazine having you travel to explore fashion culture? That's so exciting. Why don't you sound excited?" She sat on her bed and leaned against the headboard.

"I still have my job in Paris. Mom had a stroke two weeks ago. I flew home to help my dad. She's getting better, but I'm exhausted. Go figure. I thought Gloria was demanding. My parents beat her by a mile."

Camellia slouched her shoulders. "Oh, I'm sorry, Emily. I had no idea. You should've called. I'd have taken the next flight north to be with you and offer my support, you know." She gripped the phone tighter.

"I do, but you have your own troubles. A new business takes full-time attention. Besides, in the past

247

few days, family members have been popping in every day. I'm discovering cousins I can't recall ever meeting. Family dynamics are insane, but everyone's pitching in and giving me and Dad some relief."

She brought an arm to rest behind her head and smiled. "Good. Give your mom a hug and kiss from me."

"Now that we've covered my problems, I don't suppose you called just to chat, did you?"

"Maybe we can talk about it later. You've got enough going on, and I don't want to add to your plate," Camellia said.

"Ah, not so fast. This conversation doesn't happen to involve Gloria, does it?"

Her mouth hung open. "How did you guess?"

"I planned to call you this week. A few days ago, I received a letter from Gloria, addressed to my place in Paris. Being rerouted to the states took a while. I bet a carrier pigeon works faster. Anyway, I guess you received one, too?"

"I did, but mine traveled by way of Detective Hulsey and the NYPD." Camellia brought Emily up to speed about the latest with Stephanie and her criminal acts. She stood and smoothed the crumpled bed cover.

"What a crook. Who'd guess her IQ made her capable of conjuring up anything more than vicious gossip and jealousy?"

"Can't say I'm surprised, though. Jealousy will drive people mad. She's a caricature of the green-eyed monster. So, what about your letter? Did Gloria write you an apology?"

"Yes, and she mentioned tossing me an olive branch in the form of a gift. I must say, I wasn't expecting much. Maybe some leftover unopened bevy of toiletries I'd never touch."

Camellia's heart skipped and hopped several beats. "Did she include the gift with your letter?"

"Actually, it arrived a day or two later. Same route. New York to Paris and back to the States. No toiletries, thank goodness."

As her heartbeat quickened, she paced the room. "Well? Don't make me beg. Tell me, what's the gift?" Camellia asked.

"You mean you don't know? I assumed—Oh my. I bet she planned to deliver yours in person, but then, yeah... Sorry, Cam. The gift is stock shares in her business."

Camellia choked on her laughter. After a minute of coughing, she cleared her throat. "Boy, a gift of stock shares. How ironic. What are they worth? I'd say about one cent each?"

"Wrong. I assumed as much until I did a bit of research. This stock has nothing to do with the fashion business. This stock is from a company called Silver Care which manufactures products for the elderly lifestyle. Who'd have guessed Ms. V was such a savvy entrepreneur? She hit the right market. Big money, Cam. She gifted one hundred shares, which at the moment are worth ten grand."

"One hundred dollars a share?" Camellia gasped. The joke and irony were entirely on her.

"I'm only guessing, but if Gloria planned to give you the same, wouldn't the stock certificate have been with her at the time she, ah, you know? And if the case is closed, Charleston authorities would've sent her possessions to relatives by now, I imagine."

"I don't know, but I plan to find out." If a tidy sum in stock shares bearing her name existed, it would go a long way toward building her business. She recalled her words to Detective Hulsey. Maybe nothing made up for the harm Gloria caused. She sighed. An instant strike of conscience deflated her enthusiasm while the image of Remy clouded her thoughts. A local charity, perhaps for orphaned children, always needed cash. Her business would do fine without it.

"I should go. Mom's ringing her bell like there's no tomorrow. Guess it's my turn to answer the call." Emily chuckled.

"Oh, sure. Thanks, Em. At least your news clears another mystery. Take care and best of luck with your family, unfamiliar relatives included." Emily's laugh echoed through the phone. Camellia ended the call, and then stepped toward the window and took in the view of the backyard.

Gwen squatted in the middle of the herb garden with a basket in one hand. Atop her head sat a floppy straw hat.

Immediately, Camellia thought of another time, when she was eight or maybe nine, and the memory filled her with comforting warmth. She stood next to Gwen, holding the same basket, and listened to her mother prattle on about the benefits of herbs and the history of local tribes. Cherokee, Chickasaw, Creek, Shawnee, the list went on. She had a litany of facts for each one.

"Knock, knock." Zinnia peeked around the door. "Do you plan on being here for supper this evening? Dahlia wants to have an informal business meeting about the mayor's gala."

Camellia nodded while slipping into her dress. "I've tons of stuff to do, but I'll be back by five." She grabbed her bag and sweater and took swift strides to the door. She refused to act out another scenario of this morning's conversation with Freesia. No doubt, the details traveled through the household. The puzzled but cautious expression on Zinnia's face said as much. "You have a wonderful day, Zinnie." She leaned over to plant a kiss on her cheek. No sour mood lingering, here.

Zinnia's face relaxed. "You, too?"

Once Camellia was on the road, she composed her agenda for the day. First stop, the post office. She patted the oversized shipping envelope lying on the seat. Five completed designs rested inside, ready to send to Barbara, her favorite couture. She'd have them sewn in no time. Arranging a fashion show in New York was part of the plan. Adelaide and Monique offered to find models. Of course, such a huge event was something she never imagined arranging on her own. The idea popped in her head while talking to Noah. He mentioned the flash mob concept worked for him when advertising. Everyone wore shirts with the Burke logo. The crowd surged through the huge mall in Charleston. Business spiked twenty percent in one month.

"Hey, dear friend and designer extraordinaire. How are things lining up for the flash mob?" Camellia spoke to Adelaide on the car speaker.

"Great. How are things in Sleepy Town, USA?"

"Sleepy, and oh so peaceful. Don't knock it. You've found enough models, I take it?"

"More than enough. I sure hope Barb can complete

the job. Oh, and I ordered the shirts printed with your name, shop name, number, and website. Two hundred should be enough, don't you think?"

Camellia's stomach grew queasy. "Watch me get dozens of dirty phone calls."

"I suggested you get a business phone line and not use your personal number. Remember?"

As a car swerved in front of her, she laid on the horn. "At the moment, I can't afford it."

"Suit yourself. Anyway, in one month, Saturday at one pm, the masses will flood the courtyard in their shirts while goddess-like models, personally selected by fabulous me, will walk across the stage in your gorgeous designs. Perfect, right?"

"I certainly hope so." Camellia gasped. "Ooo, where's my mind? Two of your dresses sold this week, and you have requests for more. I emailed you contact info, in case you're interested."

"You're a Georgia peach, even though you live in South Carolina," Adelaide quipped.

"You're such a cornball. Gotta go. Talk later." Camellia pressed the end call button and swung into the post office parking lot. A familiar vehicle sat near the entrance. She groaned. Her mood had been so happy. She grabbed the envelope and stepped inside.

Trina stood at the counter.

"Thanks, Rita. Let me know when you'd like me to start your dress. Only a couple weeks until the event, you know." Trina turned. The upward curve of her mouth dipped south. "You." She gave her head a shake and steered to the exit when suddenly, she stopped and swiveled to face Camellia.

The smile was back in place, but not genuinely

pleasant. "Trina." Camellia spoke, hesitation in her voice.

Trina twisted her neck toward the counter. "Rita, did I remember to purchase that delivery notice thing you do? You know, so I'll be sure the folks at the fashion show received my entry?"

"Yes, ma'am, two days ago. You should receive notice anytime."

"Oh, good. Such a relief to hear." Trina faced Camellia again and nodded. "The Charleston Southern Ladies Group and the fashion show event, you know."

"What are you talking about?" As her words tumbled out, Camellia's voice hitched.

"Oh, I'm sorry. I guess you weren't aware. Your name's probably not on their mailing list. Anyway, fliers were posted in town. Maybe you've been too busy to notice, taking care of Noah and turning your little enterprise into something worthwhile. Poor thing." Trina removed a lipstick case and mirror from her bag. After touching up, she turned and smiled. "To catch you up to speed, the Ladies sponsor a fashion show in Charleston with national coverage. Such a great opportunity for struggling designers, wouldn't you say?"

A snarl curled her lip. "Silly me. I forgot to mention the best part. Of course, you've missed the entry deadline. So sad. Anyway, the judges chose five finalists out of those designs entered. You're looking at one of the five." She clasped one hand to her throat. "Isn't it wonderful? I sent in my dress the other day. Sewn by the fabulous Paulo, a local master of the arts residing here in South Carolina. You can't imagine my excitement. Maybe I'll even win first prize. I can't wait for Friday. Well, toodle-loo. Have a great day." Trina waved then clicked her heels to hurry out of the post office.

"Yeah, well, best of luck," Camellia called, swallowing the words she was tempted to say. When Trina was involved, suspicion of motive always crossed her mind. The memory returned with a vengeance—an instant replay of the Charleston Fashion Charity from years ago. Maybe not learning about the contest until it was too late to enter wasn't a coincidence. Trina would stoop that low. Could she despise her any less? She slammed her parcel on the counter and grimaced at Rita who stared back, wide-eyed and speechless. "Sorry. First class to New York, please." She fished out her wallet and counted bills while her mind reeled.

Patching up things, forgiving and forgetting, and all that turn-the-other-cheek nonsense stretched more and more out of reach. She was being petty and knew it. A huge sigh escaped. Without warning, an idea struck. Attending the event wasn't a bad idea. Even without an entry, she'd have an opportunity to schmooze with the fashion moguls. Functions like this one drew a crowd of them, all wanting to snag the next fashion ingénue and make her their own. She'd ask her sisters to come along. They'd make a day of it—supper at Mama Mia's and drinks at the Choo Choo Club. A grin spread, squashing the scowl from a second ago. She'd make lemonade out of Trina's sour-lemon intentions.

Chapter 18

With so much to do running the shop and her sisters planning for their next event, the week passed in a whirlwind. Friday and the fashion show were a welcomed relief. Camellia sat in the front row of the Charleston Ladies' lodge with Freesia and Zinnia to her right.

Dahlia stayed home to hold an emergency meeting with Mayor Buell. He had a major meltdown because of Mrs. Buell. At this point, Dahlia played psychologist in addition to event planner. She was a superwoman who wore many hats.

The Ladies decorated the hall in bright colors. Melon, fuchsia, and canary yellow for the flower displays and wall paintings, while the background with colors of sand and eggshell provided a mellow touch. Music streamed through the speakers—a selection of southern originals penned by native artists, mostly from pre-Civil War days.

"The Antebellum South at its most glorious," Freesia whispered.

"Of course. The Charleston Langfords won't have it any other way." Camellia grinned and pointed at Gladys Langford, president of the Charleston Southern Ladies, whose head bobbed enough to fall off and roll down the aisle.

She carried on a conversation with one of the

judges, pointing every so often at the end of the runway. After a few minutes, she marched toward the back and out of sight.

"The show will start soon." Zinnia tapped her watch. "I can't wait to see Trina's design."

Camellia scowled.

"I mean, it's got to be awful, right? Those judges won't know what hit them." Zinnia stammered and squirmed in her seat.

"I'm sure the dress looks great. Why else would the judges choose it?" She compressed her anxiety, which ballooned to near bursting. Nearly a week passed since she spoke to Noah, which made her an emotional mess, but as promised, she hadn't called. More surprising, he hadn't called her. Camellia didn't know what to make of his silence, or if she cared. Being unsure both aggravated and confused her.

"Ladies and gentlemen, it gives me great pleasure to introduce this year's fashion final entries." Mrs. Langford shouted into the microphone.

Camellia sat forward, resting her meandering gaze on center stage.

"To narrate our wonderfully creative designs, I give you Temperance Stanhall, a fashion icon in her own right and native to our dear city of Charleston. Please give her a hand."

The applause was mediocre, suggesting not many locals attending recognized the name, let alone what she'd accomplished. Being the cover of *Fashion Quarterly* five times wasn't something to scoff at if you were a part of the industry. Getting her endorsement assured a boost to her line of clothing, if only Camellia would have the chance to speak with her. Maybe after the show, she'd track her down. Freesia's voice interrupted her thoughts.

"Ha! Fashion icon practically no one knows. Fake flowers. I bet the wine is the five-dollar bargain variety from a local convenience store. Don't even get me started on the wall art. A three-year-old could paint better." Freesia bellowed a raucous laugh, which gained scowls from everyone around them.

"Seriously, Sia. Stop embarrassing yourself." Camellia frowned.

"You mean stop embarrassing you, right?" Freesia poked a finger at her.

"Cam's right. Hush yourself. This show is a classy event." Zinnia crossed her arms.

"Some kind of classy."

Camellia rolled her neck to work out the kinks. "Just because I didn't have a chance to enter doesn't mean you need to slam the program, Sia. Play nice."

"I call it like it is. Nothing more to it than me being honest." Freesia glowered at the stage.

Camellia's impatience reached its limit. "Uh huh. Okay. Well, I'd like to watch *and* listen, if you'll remain quiet for the next several minutes?"

Freesia shrugged then snuggled lower in her seat.

"Our first design is by Marsha Quinn. You'll notice Pasha is dressed in a full-length gown made of Charmeuse silk in peacock green."

Camellia leaned forward to study the design features. She admired the cut, the way it flattered and clung to the body yet remained elegant and not trashy. The next couple of designs were equally as attractive, but not one stood out above the others. Deciding would be tough for the judges.

"Our final design is by a former graduate of USC, Trina Averaux. This exquisite gown is something every woman should want. Watch Katrine as she walks the runway, how the combination of crepe de chine and taffeta embrace her figure, moving in such harmony."

When the model Katrine stepped from behind the curtain and onto the runway, Camellia studied the dress. With her heartbeat quickening, she leaned forward.

The model approached the end of the runway, closer than a dozen feet from the front row of seats, then paused for everyone to admire the design.

Camellia gasped. "Oh, no. No, it can't be." The words strangled from her throat.

"What? What can't be? Can't be a great design? I'd love to hear those words come out of your mouth." Freesia snorted. "Though truth be told, I can't tell what's great and what isn't. Give me a pair of tight blue jeans and a silk blouse and I'm thinking dressy." She twisted to face her and widened her eyes. "Lord, Cam. You're teetering like you're about to pass out."

Camellia clutched the sides of her chair and forced air into her lungs. Either faint or upchuck the entire contents of her stomach, she thought. Instead, she took one more breath. "We have to go," she whispered.

Freesia blinked. "Go? But the show isn't over. Aren't the judges doing their judging thing and picking the best entry? You're making no sense." She nudged Zinnia. "Something's wrong with Cam."

"What's wrong, Cam? You look pale as a ghost." Zinnia lifted an arm to fan Camellia's face with her program.

Camellia smacked it away. "I'm fine, but I'm leaving. Come with me or stay. It's up to you." She stood, her focus back on Katrine who now sauntered down the catwalk, away from the audience. She didn't want to see. To believe the scene was a bad dream was more comforting. However, she knew better.

She excused herself to pass by all the guests seated in her row. Freesia and Zinnia followed close with Freesia's hand resting on her shoulder. Camellia ignored the continuing monologue coming from Temperance Stanhall. If anybody mentioned Trina's name one more time, she'd scream.

"Leaving so soon?" Trina sat at the end of the row, grinning.

Her pulse racing, Camellia wanted to smack the grin right off Trina's face. "It's personal," she muttered.

"But you'll miss the final judging. Such a shame. I do think I have a good chance at winning, don't you?"

As her jaw worked back and forth, Camellia clenched her fists. "Excuse me, I need to get through."

Trina opened her mouth.

"Hey, either move out of the way or sit your keister in a chair." A woman directly behind them barked.

Trina leaned back in her seat while Camellia, Freesia, and Zinnia passed.

"Why is she gloating? She hasn't won yet. Seriously, will you tell us what's wrong? Got to be something, or you're having a breakdown. You aren't having a breakdown, are you?"

Zinnia rambled but kept her volume at a minimum. "I'm *not* having a breakdown, and after we get to the car, I'll tell you why I'm upset," Camellia snapped. She led them through the building exit and into the parking lot.

"Aren't we walking to Mama Mia's? What about

dinner?" Zinnie shot forward to edge closer. "What about the Choo Choo Club?"

"Would you shut up, Zinnie? You heard her. As soon as we get to the car, she'll tell us. We can walk from there to Mama Mia's." Freesia patted Camellia's shoulder as she flanked her other side. "Right, Cammie?"

"Oh, for—don't patronize me, Sia. We will go to Mama Mia's, but I'd like to drive there and not get drenched." She pointed above them where dark clouds hovered in the sky.

"Of course." Both Freesia and Zinnie chimed then spent the remainder of their walk in silence.

Camellia slipped into the driver's seat, her fingers wrapping tightly around the steering wheel, but she didn't speak. Convincing herself not to overreact was pointless. She wanted to throw things or punch them. Heat invaded her cheeks and kept her from thinking clearly. One thought remained, planting itself like a bad seed inside her head. "Trina's design isn't hers," she stated without emotion. The challenge was real.

"What do you mean? How can you be sure? Even though I'd love for Trina to be outed as a fraud, I think lots of designs look similar." Freesia gripped the car seat.

"I know because the design is, well, it's not mine, but it's close, too close." The design was one of her best and part of the collection she planned to make for the New York show. Her voice continued in a flat monotone. Maybe she was going into shock like Zinnia suggested. Maybe she was delusional and only imagined the intricate details—the tiny silver leaf epaulets on either shoulder strap and the puckered seam sewn in a zig-zagged pattern on one side as the dress's model stood close enough for her to see. Camellia clenched her jaw. That unique puckered seam was *her* signature. No one she knew in fashion design had used it. Of course, Trina changed the neckline to no back slit, and the waistline wasn't cinched, but everything else was the same as her design. Her chest tightening, she gulped air. *Her design* ripped off by Trina. What else could she think?

"I can't believe she'd stoop so low." Camellia slammed on the steering wheel and accidently beeped the horn. "What am I supposed to do?" Of course, she had a couple ideas, and neither of them were legal.

"You should go back inside and tell the judges. Trina can't get away with stealing your design," Freesia said.

"Which is the problem." Camellia moaned and eased her hand off the steering wheel. "I can't tell anyone because not one person would believe me. Don't you get it?" She shifted in her seat to face them. "After the Gloria scandal, my credibility was flushed down the crapper. Ironic, isn't it? How the infamous Ms. V keeps haunting and ruining my life, even beyond the grave."

"Well, we have to find some way to prove it. How did she steal your idea anyway? You keep your work locked in the shop," Zinnia said.

Camellia shook her head and stabbed at the car ignition. "I wish I knew." She maneuvered out of the parking space and exited north to find Mama Mia's. In her mood, she'd rather skip dinner and go straight to the Choo Choo Club. Drowning her misery was an attractive idea, even if it wasn't practical, and she'd vowed not to drink any more. Tomorrow, she'd figure out a plan. She sighed. Her typical response. Always tomorrow.

****

Of all the nightspots in Charleston, Trina and her entourage chose the Choo Choo to celebrate.

Camellia clenched her jaw as she turned away from the unwelcomed sight.

"She won. Oh, my lord, she won first prize. Now you have to figure out a way to catch her, Cam." Freesia slurped her margarita through a straw until she drained the glass.

"Maybe we should leave." Zinnia shifted her head back and forth from Camellia to Trina's table.

Camellia shrugged. "I'm not leaving. She'd expect and probably hope for me to, which is why I'm sitting here until closing."

Freesia glanced at her watch and scowled. "Two more hours? I can't stay that long. I have an early shift at Chico's tomorrow morning."

"Fine. I'm expecting a delivery at eight am, anyway. But let's at least stay another thirty minutes." Camellia willed herself not to glance at Trina. Instead, she threw back her head and laughed.

"What's so funny?" Zinnia wrinkled her brow.

"Nothing. Pretend like there is, though."

"Oh, I get it. Yeah, you're a real hoot." She smacked the table with her hand and howled.

"Easy, sister. We're going for happy, not insane," Freesia said.

"Would one of you fine ladies care to take a whirl around the dance floor?"

Camellia glanced up and was surprised to find

Weston. She shook her head. "I'll pass." The way his smile dropped made her chuckle. Out of the corner of her eye, she caught the exaggerated wave of Trina's arm.

She called out Weston's name, but he didn't turn to answer.

Too hard to resist, Camellia smiled and extended an arm. "You know what? I will take that offer." Fair or not, she chose her own brand of war, with casualties being a necessity, ends justifying the means, and all that stuff. She soared with a venom-induced level of despicable.

Grasping Weston's hand, she led the way onto the dance floor, and within a minute, the song changed to a slow dance. Camellia stiffened. Her impulses were never her wisest ideas. Getting this close to Weston was one. Before she could pull away, he wrapped his arms around her waist. She went on the defensive, anything to distance her mind from what her body couldn't. "Why are you here?"

"Meaning?"

"Meaning, are you following me? What game are you playing, Weston Murphy?" Why did she always need to be suspicious of people?

"I'm with some colleagues. We history geeks love to explore cities like Charleston. So, we perused the many sights before stopping at this fine establishment to unwind and have a few beers." He curled his lips into a smile. "Why are *you* here?"

Camellia shrugged. "A fashion show put on by the Charleston Southern Ladies group."

"You don't act excited about it. You thrive on fashion."

"I do. Can't you see the joy beaming on my face?" She stretched her lips wide.

"You're scaring me. Don't do that—ever." He shuddered. "So, what ruined it?"

"Nothing."

"You're lying."

"A behavior you should know well." Her voice dripped pure sarcasm.

Weston sighed. "Change of subject. I do want to thank you." He leaned closer.

His forehead nearly touched hers. "For what?" Her voice weakened and her heart pounded, ramming beat after beat against her chest. Getting closer was definitely not wise.

"Forgiving me. Giving me a second chance."

"Oh, I'm not forgiving you. We're sharing a dance and nothing more." Regret grew inside her for making the decision to use him in her battle against Trina. Out of guilt or because it became uncomfortable, she wasn't sure, but the regret stayed. She straightened her back and refused to relax.

"Aw, come on. I know you love Noah." He sighed. "You never really answered me before. We can be friends. Right?" Every muscle in his face tightened.

"Friends? Yeah, I guess."

"Good. Now, relax, would you? And enjoy a dance with a friend."

"Uh, hum." Though hard to admit, she was comforted by the warmth of his body. She closed her eyes, nearly lulled into a quiet, peaceful state. For a moment, she forgot about Trina and Gloria and her problems with Noah. Here in his arms, she completely unwound, though her sense of reason argued with her emotions. The little voice in her head spoke. Why lean on any man for emotional support? She needed to stand on her own.

In the next instant, the song ended and the mood vanished. "Thanks." Camellia broke the embrace and stepped away.

"Please, Cam. Wait." Weston clutched her wrist.

She stood for a moment, studying his face, the deep blueish green of his eyes and the softness of his lips. "I have to go, Weston." She forced herself to keep from looking at him any longer. Discomfort flooded in and became too much to handle. He didn't try to stop her, and she hurried back to the table.

Zinnia talked to a woman seated nearby, while Freesia tipped her head back as she drained another glass.

Camellia remained standing. "You two ready to leave?"

Zinnia swiveled back to face her. "Yep. We have a long drive, and I do need my beauty sleep."

"Are you sure you don't want another dance with Weston?" Freesia quipped.

Camellia detected the frosty mood and suddenly understood why. A familiar throaty laugh carried through the air. She scanned the room.

Jaime Steele sat cozied up to a cute blonde.

Poor Freesia. She didn't need this torture. "Nope. I'm ready to go. Come on, then."

"Don't mind me. I'm over him. Really." She stood and slung her bag strap over a shoulder. "Although I must say, one thing good came out of this evening. Weston Murphy has eyes for only one lady." She pointed an unsteady finger. "That guy has it bad for

265

you."

"Oh, stop. He wants to be friends is all." Camellia lifted her chin.

"Uh, huh. Friends with benefits."

Camellia snorted and marched toward the exit. "Friends. Just friends."

"You keep on denying the truth, sister. It's what you do."

Camellia ignored the retort and gave Trina a final glance. She was deep in conversation with the model Katrine who still wore her design. Camellia's design. Her shoulders sagged along with her confidence. Life steered in directions she'd never anticipated. How many more surprises could she take? Several hours passed since the contest and witnessing the Trina knockoff of *her* design on the runway. By this point, she had time to connect and form an image she didn't like and a conclusion she didn't want to believe. Yet, how else could copying her design have happened? Only one answer came to mind, and it started with Remy.

Chapter 19

Anyone who lived in or around Serenity knew traffic along Divinity Boulevard at seven am should be sparse unless a holiday weekend occurred. Of course, today was one of those rare exceptions. For the tenth time in as many minutes, Cam checked her watch. She'd be late to the shop and miss the delivery truck. She stretched her neck out of the window to view around the cars ahead to see the hold up. She sniffed. The stinky odor told her even more.

A truck overturned and spilled the entire contents of its bed. Hundreds of fish scattered across the road while a crew of men hurried to clear the mess.

Ten minutes later, she was on the move again. A quick call to the coffee shop and a word with Anita relieved her anxiety.

Anita promised to send over one of her employees to wait for the delivery.

Sure enough, upon entering the alley, she found the delivery man and Trudy sitting on a couple of box crates, chatting.

"Thanks a bunch, Trudy. I owe you." Camellia exited her vehicle.

Trudy shrugged. "It was nothing. I enjoyed talking with Mr. Shelley. You take care, all."

"You, too. When I'm done here, I'll stop by for that cup of coffee," Mr. Shelley said.

Trudy blushed and skipped across the alley.

Camellia smiled and raised her nose to take a sniff. "What do I smell? Why I believe the bloom of romance is in the air. What do you think, Norm?"

Norm Shelley scoffed. "Nonsense. Minor flirtation, is all. She's miles too young."

"Only a few years. I hear she's single and looking." Camellia wiggled her brows.

"Stop, now." Norm lifted the cab door of his truck. "Got your order, or what looks like most of the items, according to this invoice." He handed over the paper.

Camellia studied the list of goods and nodded. "I see most of them here. One item backordered. Okay. Let's take these boxes inside."

An hour later, Camellia sat at her desk. She stared at the bill of lading. Everything was unpacked and checked off, but she couldn't motivate herself to move on. She stared at the paper and sipped cold coffee. After a few more mindless minutes of doing nothing, she rearranged items on her desk, stacking papers and notes in one corner, and her calendar and other items nearer the center. A note scribbled on the calendar caught her eye.

"Shoot. How did I forget?" Camellia grabbed hold of her phone and punched buttons. "Hi. May I speak to Detective Hulsey if he's available?" Elevator music filled her ear to ease the dragged-out wait.

"Hulsey."

"Hi, Detective. This is Camellia Holiday. You told me to call if I had news." She explained her conversation with Emily about the stock certificate and to ask her questions about Gloria's belongings.

"I can check, but I do believe everything went to

the closest relative. Let me see."

Camellia chewed on her thumbnail and waited while listening to the shuffling of paper on Hulsey's end of the phone.

"Ah, here we go. Cleo Lioni, son of Gloria's deceased sister. He lives in San Francisco. Married with children, thirty-five, and works for a local business, a print shop called Progressive Designs."

"Much more than I needed and not really helpful, I guess." Camellia sank in her chair. What was she supposed to do? Track down the man and demand her stock shares, which should've gone to her in the first place? The more she considered it, the more ridiculous the idea sounded.

"Give me time to follow up. I can check with this guy and find out what he has to say. Don't worry. I get results."

Camellia laughed. "I'm sure you do. Seriously, thank you. I appreciate all your help."

"I only offer to the deserving ones. You have a good day." Hulsey ended the call.

Camellia stared some more at her desk and snatched a marker to check off the note to call Hulsey. At once, the stomping of feet and slamming of the service door grabbed her attention. She shifted in her seat and found Remy standing in the doorway. "Wow. I didn't realize the time was so late." She frowned. "Why are you wet?"

"Rain is pouring. Wind's blowing everything everywhere. I'd swear a hurricane hit the coast." Remy shook out his jacket and hung it on the coat rack.

"Hmm. The storm will pass, soon enough." Camellia let her mind race with all the things she wanted to say. She found no easy way to bring up the dress, but she had to know. "So, what did you do for fun last night?"

"Went down to the pier to meet up with some friends. We hung out most of the evening. Anything to get away from my crazy family."

"You've made friends. Good." Camellia nodded, her nerve wires sparking with tension. "I had an interesting evening."

"Oh?" Remy shoved his stool over toward the corner and rested his back against the wall, arms crossed tightly over his chest.

"Yeah, my sisters and I traveled to Charleston for a fashion show. Figured the event might be fun."

"Was it?"

"Not exactly." Her heart pounded.

"Why not?" Remy leaned forward.

She detected no guilt in his expression. Maybe he was innocent. She tried looking indifferent. "Oh, well, one thing happened, which surprised me. I mean, such a huge shocker." She paused, letting him take the bait.

Remy squirmed in his seat, but then he stood to walk over to one of the racks. He faced the front while straightening dresses. "A shocker, huh?"

"Yep. All these models walked the runway for a local fashion contest, and one caught me off guard. I mean the dress with that design looked so familiar."

Remy dropped one of the hangers. He quickly picked up the jacket and returned it to the rack.

"In fact, the dress is a match for one of my designs. A few minor changes, but so much like mine. I kept thinking how impossible the idea was because I never entered any contest. So, I'm wondering how my dress, *my* design, could end up on the runway. You know?" Camellia leaned forward in her seat and kept her gaze on him.

Remy's hands shook as he rearranged the dresses.

"So here comes the real kicker and the biggest surprise of all. That dress with the design similar to mine belonged to your cousin, Trina. Weird, right?"

Remy gave a slight nod. "Yeah, I guess."

"Very weird." Camellia stood and took casual steps to reach Remy's side. She helped rearrange the dresses. "Of course, my mind is reeling by this point. How could Trina design a dress that looks almost identical to one of mine? Unless…" She tapped a finger against her bottom lip, and then pointed it at Remy. "Unless she got a peek at my portfolio. You don't happen to know anything about how she could have done so, do you, Remy?" Subtlety just flew out the window.

A half dozen hangers and dresses clattered on the floor. Remy's face blushed to vivid red. His fists clenched. "Are you accusing me of something?"

Camellia shook her head. "I'm only asking a question, Remy. I want to know if you know anything. You see Trina every day. She's your cousin. Maybe she said something or did something odd."

"No." He wagged his head and backed away. "I think you're accusing me of stealing. I didn't steal anything. You're like everyone else. You see me as some loser who can't do anything good." He stabbed a finger into the air. "I thought you were different."

Camellia wanted to say more but remained silent as Remy stormed out of the shop. Maybe he told the truth, but she doubted it. The way he'd been acting the past several weeks and how Trina behaved that night at the club raised suspicion. She had a hold over him, but only now did Cam suspect what it could be. She shuddered. Trina would stop at nothing to get what she wanted and destroy her competition, and even worse, she'd stooped to manipulating her own cousin.

****

Camellia waited out the rest of the morning and early afternoon, but Remy didn't return. She'd certainly upset him. He might never speak to her again. Too late for regrets. The clock hands read three, and she gathered her bag and raincoat to leave. Remy's jacket still hung from the rack. She sighed. Why couldn't the situation have gone in another direction?

Her emotions bottled up inside like the contents of a soda shaken and ready to explode. While speaking with Hulsey, she nearly spilled the story of her woes about Trina. Freesia, Zinnia, and by now, Dahlia and Gwen, knew the story. She struggled to dampen her emotional overload and find something more positive to do. Getting in her vehicle, she traveled the familiar path to Noah's place. "You're a pathetic optimist, Camellia Holiday." She let herself inside and found Noah in the study poring over his business ledger and computer. "Hey. How are you?" She hung back near the doorway for a moment.

Noah raised his head and smiled. "There she is. I wanted to call you, but I had the feeling you needed some space and time." He rolled the chair closer. With eager fingers, he squeezed her hand. "I'm glad you're here. I missed you."

Camellia swallowed to dissolve the lump in her throat. She leaned over to give him a brief hug. "I-I missed you, too." The words stumbled from her lips.

She rolled her tongue as if to wipe the strange aftertaste from her mouth.

"Hold on." His smile widened. He spun around and wheeled back to the desk. "I have something for you." He pulled open a drawer and removed a small box, clutching it in his hand as he returned to her side.

A ring box? Camellia gasped, her chest tightening, and her stomach filled with sour apprehension. She readied herself to bolt toward the study doorway. A scream of protest would carry her the rest of the way to her car. She wasn't ready. Not at all. Didn't he listen to her comments and those words explaining she needed more time?

He opened the box, and a silver trinket of a star lay inside. "I thought you'd appreciate a charm for your bracelet to commend your work accomplishments. Rising star fits the occasion, right? And there's more." He slipped an envelope from his vest pocket and held it out.

As she took both the box and envelope, Camellia gulped, her hand trembling. "Noah, you're very kind, but I can't."

"Please, Cam. Open the envelope before you say anything else."

Inside was a plane ticket. "New York?" Her voice cracked. "But why?"

"I figured you deserve a bit of a break. So, I called my travel agent who's a dream at finding the best deals." He leaned forward and cupped his hands. "You work so hard all the time. Why not have some fun? Visit old friends and places and do stuff you want to do."

"Noah." With her chest tightening, she set the box

and envelope on the coffee table.

"I'm sorry, Camellia. I truly am. I keep screwing things, and I know my behavior hurts you and our relationship. I don't mean to. I want us to be together like we were in the past. Don't you?" His eyes filled and glistened.

His voice was unsteady and trembled with emotion. She nodded. "I can't say. I-I can't give you an answer, yet. I'm here for another reason. I—oh, Noah." She dropped into the nearest chair and bit her tongue to keep from sobbing while the tears fought to escape.

"Hey." He grabbed her hands and squeezed. "What's wrong? What can I do?"

"Okay." She sucked in air to calm herself. She gently eased her hands out of his grip. "I had a horrible evening. Totally horrible, and I wanted to vent. Can you believe it? After all my efforts to push you away and put distance between us? And I turn to you. Ironic, right?" She laughed and hiccupped at once. What was she thinking? He had history with Trina. Sketchy, but their time together existed. Was telling him what happened wise? "You know. Forget what I said. I shouldn't bother you. Besides, you can't do anything about my problem. Let's just enjoy our visit. I don't want to spoil the time with whining."

"Eh, eh. Nope. I'm here to support you, whining and all. Now, spill." He nodded.

Against her better judgment, she did. She told him about the fashion show, about the contest, and about Trina's entry. "I'm not sure. I mean, I have no proof. I'm suspicious, but my hunch might be mere coincidence." Saying the words aloud made them harder to believe.

"I don't know much about fashion and design, obviously. However, I do know Trina enough to say stealing your ideas is not beneath her." He frowned. "But you don't have much to go on. Be hard to press charges."

Camellia sighed. "I know. The whole situation is frustrating and discouraging. I couldn't despise her more. She's proven again and again how much of a conniving cheat she is. Some people never change."

"Camellia." He cupped her hand in his once more. "She doesn't matter. You don't need to go through this struggle, time after time. You have me." He smiled.

She scrunched her brow. "What do you mean?"

"I'm talking about you and me. I can support you. Heck, with the family business exploding in sales, I can support you and our children without your income. You don't have to work. Let me take care of that role. Why put yourself through such grief?"

Our children? She hadn't accepted the idea of marriage, yet. "So, what you're saying is I don't have to work? I can stay home, be the picture-perfect wife and mom, and take care of the house and our children, and you'd be totally content. Hmm. Well, I have no words." As the heat of anger spread, she clenched her jaw. Oh, she had words all right. Instead of any retort, she flipped her wrist to glance at her watch. "Wow. I didn't realize how late the time was. I have to get back to the shop. This working girl needs some sales to keep the business going. Nothing like yours, of course. I can only imagine that explosion of sales must make you dizzy."

She popped out of her seat and tipped her chin at the box and envelope. "Thanks for the gifts, but you shouldn't have." Noah called her name as Camellia hurried toward the door. She didn't turn or stop.

"Are you okay? Did I say something wrong?"

"Nope. All good. Talk to you later, Noah." Once she cleared the house, got inside her car and closed the door, she screamed to release her frustration. The unbelievable part was how she came back, thinking he'd change. What was the saying about a person doing the same thing over and over and expecting a different outcome? Did this behavior make her insane or stupid? She felt stupid and maybe a little insane. She definitely wasn't using common sense or seeing things for what or who they were. Her unabashed level of neediness left her nauseous. How was that for standing on her own two feet?

Instead of returning to the shop, she decided to crash at home. Only a couple hours remained until supper time. She'd take a relaxing bath and drink a glass of wine. By then, she'd be back to normal. The picture of sitting around the table with her family made her smile.

Pulling into the drive, she stiffened, her breath hitching. Weston's blue Volvo was parked behind Freesia's car. Why was he here? She touched her cheek, reminded of the dance last night and the way he'd held her close. No matter how hard she tried, she failed to dismiss the moment as trivial. Score one for the heart and a fat zero for her common sense.

Camellia threw open the car door and got out. She straightened her skirt and raked fingers through her hair. He wanted to be friends. Easier said than done. Who knew what direction a friendship with Weston might take her? A cool, keep-your-distance approach seemed wiser and more practical. "Yeah, let's go with that idea." She mumbled while marching toward the front porch. She forced open the door and collided with Dahlia who was on her way out. "Oh my. Dahlia." She stepped aside.

"What's the big hurry? You late coming from or going to somewhere?" Dahlia smiled with a shake of her head. "Either way, you look a wreck."

"I do not." Camellia reared back her head. "I mean, you really think so?" She smoothed her hair and then straightened the bottom hem of her blouse.

Dahlia laughed. "You're fine. The expression on your face tells me enough. Your mouth is set like you want to kill someone."

"Seriously, Dahlia." Camellia skirted her way inside. "When I opened the door, you nearly gave me a heart attack. That's all."

"Uh huh. Okay. Well, if you're looking for Freesia or Weston, they are in the kitchen." After glancing at her watch, she groaned. "I'm late to meet with the flower arranger. I can't believe the mayor's gala is little more than three weeks away."

"Yeah, I know." Camellia pressed together her lips while thinking. She shifted her head from the stairs to the kitchen doorway but remained planted in her spot. Right now, the idea of a face-to-face meeting with Weston threatened her emotional state. She returned her gaze to Dahlia. "Well, have a productive meeting. See you at supper?"

"I should be back well before then." Dahlia closed the door behind her.

Left alone in the foyer, Camellia wiggled her shoulders to relax. Procrastination wasn't healthy. With a firm nod of her chin, she took lengthy strides to the kitchen. She'd grab a bottled water and toss a quick hello and good-bye to Weston and Freesia. She could manage without a hitch. Piece of cake.

Camellia stepped into the kitchen. A shuddering tremor whipped through her body. Her knees weakened, and she avoided looking at Weston. "Hey, you two," she said in a breathy tone as she passed the table and reached the fridge. She opened the door and leaned forward, breathing in huge gulps of cold air until she relaxed. She clamped her lips, determined to avoid asking questions, like why Weston was here, sitting at the table in her family kitchen.

"Hi, Cammie. Weston stopped by to drop off Zinnie's wallet. I'm surprised she didn't notice it missing, but you know Zinnie. Anyway, Weston and I were just talking about you."

The inward groan shivered through her. "Oh?" Her voice squeaked. She cleared her throat. "About what?" She kept her head stuck inside the fridge, pretending to search for some food or drink item.

"Oh, the Trina thing, for one. Her troublemaking action still fumes me. I'd like to rip the head off that fat neck of hers," Freesia said.

"Easy. Don't let your flaming red hair get the best of you." Weston laughed.

Camellia lifted a bottle of water from the back and closed the fridge before turning to face them. "Well, I'd just as soon forget the whole nightmare. Days of Trina sabotaging my life and letting her get to me are over." She walked toward the doorway.

"Now wait one minute, you. Honestly, you aren't fighting her about stealing your design?" Freesia raised her voice. "Stealing is criminal. She can't get away with it, Cam."

Camellia sighed. "What do you propose I do? Go to the police? With what evidence? I've got nothing but my word against hers."

Weston cleared his throat.

Both Camellia and Freesia stared at him.

"You have something to say?" Freesia spoke first.

"I do." He shifted his jaw muscles as he leveled his gaze on Camellia. "I'm usually good at figuring out people, and you're no quitter. But I can see by the expression on your face, you want to give up. You can't throw away what you're passionate about, right?" Weston circled around the table until he stood close. "Don't quit. Fight back. Fight her. Otherwise, she wins, which is exactly what she wants."

"I can't." Camellia's voice choked. The lump hardened and lodged in her throat.

"You can." His fingers wrapped around her arms and squeezed. "You have to want that success more than her. Fight her."

Camellia blinked to clear the blurriness clouding her vision. His words stung, but in a good way, as if they sparked her emotions and stirred the complacency which settled inside after her visit with Noah. She struggled not to but recalled his words, telling her he'd take care of her and how she didn't need to worry about working any longer. To find comfort in such a sheltered life was tempting. She'd leave behind all her problems—no more competition, no more struggle to be better or the best, and no more worries about whether her shop failed or succeeded.

She took a deep breath, her shoulders quaking. She

studied Weston's face, the determination in his cheerful smile then nodded. "All right. I will. At least I'll try. Any suggestions?" She turned a hopeful gaze on Freesia.

"I do have one, sort of, but I'm working out the details." Freesia stood and paced the floor. "We have another fashion contest. Locals only."

Camellia frowned. "How will another contest help?"

"Simple. Or maybe not so simple because we need Remy's help. Did you speak with him, by the way? I mean, the answer is a no brainer. He slipped Trina your design. Who else had the opportunity to get into your files? Creepy, little skunk." Freesia scowled.

"We talked." Camellia sat in a chair and dropped her head into the palms of her hands. "The conversation was an epic failure because I scared him away, but good. He screamed, saying I accused him of stealing, but I didn't. He's not a creepy, little skunk, Sia." Oddly enough, she needed to defend the poor boy. Who else was in his corner? Certainly not Trina or Laverne.

"You have to admit he's the most likely person to have done the deed." Freesia pulled the iced tea pitcher from the fridge and poured a glassful.

"Let me try. A man-to-man conversation might work." Weston nodded.

Camellia shrugged. "Then what? How can Remy help?"

"We get him to tell Trina about the fashion show and dangle the bait." After emptying the glass of tea, she snapped her fingers. "I got it. You draw some fake design, horrible, but not too horrible. We don't want the idea to be obvious. Then, Remy can deliver the goods.

She designs the dress for the contest and *bam*! We got her—accused, tried, and found guilty. She'll look great in orange, don't you think?"

"I think you have a devious mind, sister." Camellia tapped her fingers on the table. "I also think she won't fall for the scheme. Getting away with stealing one of my designs worked once. A second time? She's not that stupid or foolish."

Freesia raked fingers through her hair. "No, but she's that greedy and competitive. I swear she'll take the bait."

"I don't know. Quite a bit of this plan is banking on Remy's participation." Plenty of doubt weighed heavily on Camellia. "Besides, I don't like the idea of involving him. The plan is too risky." She played back the scene of Trina's cat fight with Freesia's and Laverne's strong-armed intervention. Getting them angry could be dangerous.

"He's already involved, Cam." Freesia planted both fists on her hips. "I know the perfect time and place. We'll use the mayor's gala as a venue. We can put an ad in the Charleston newspaper and make sure Remy gives Trina a copy while he talks up the event. Then we reel her in like fish on a hook. Please say yes." She held her hands together and pressed them to one cheek while batting her eyelashes.

"Oh, for heaven's sake." Camellia swatted her arm. "Stop. Okay, I give. I still don't think we can fool her." She pointed at Weston. "As for Remy, I doubt he'll open up to you. He's stronger than you might imagine."

"Oh, I have my ways of persuasion. Trust me." Weston grinned ear to ear. "Some adventure, right? Could be loads of fun, you know?"

"Yeah, a barrel full of hysterical monkeys." Camellia sighed, but when Weston squeezed her hand, a tingling sensation resonated through her body.

"Another idea just hit me. Wow, I am good." Freesia beamed.

Camellia chuckled. "Go ahead."

"How about we call Mom and see if Robert will offer to do an article about the contest winner in *Fashion Quarterly*? Can you imagine? Trina will be salivating over that kind of publicity with her name and story in a national magazine." Freesia laughed.

"Got to admit, you might have hit on the perfect way to lure Trina." She lifted her chin. "The one thing she loves more than winning is being in the spotlight and furthering her career at the same time." Confidence replaced Camellia's doubt. This plan had possibilities, if Remy agreed to go along. She smiled at Weston. His looks and charm worked on the ladies. She'd bet he could just as easily persuade Remy to admit the truth and convince him to help. "Yeah, this plan just might work," she whispered. Otherwise, her business and career might tank while Trina's soared.

Chapter 20

Camellia awoke tired and edgy. She'd tossed around in her bed like a fish flopping on dry land. Too many thoughts about everyone and everything in her life worried her. Would her problems ever get easier to handle? At the moment, she doubted they could.

She finished ironing out the details of the plan for the fashion contest with Weston and how to make the event a success then suggested he should drop by the shop the next morning. While Camellia stepped out for coffee, Weston and Remy would talk. If Remy showed up for work, that is. Camellia feared he'd stay away out of guilt. She tossed her bag on the car seat and drove to the shop. None of those details mattered because the plan was set in motion.

At half past ten, the service door opened and shut. Steps shuffled across the storage room floor and stopped at the doorway. Camellia spun and smiled. "Good morning, Remy. I'm glad you came in today."

Remy shrugged. "Why wouldn't I? Unless I'm fired or something." His brow creased as he steadied a narrowed gaze on her.

"Don't be silly. Of course, you still work here. You do want to work here, don't you?" Now was her turn to frown.

"Yeah. I need the money." He grabbed a box from the stack of the morning's delivery and tore open the lid. He held up the cache of designer scarves in his hands. "You want these on the front table?"

"I do. Thank you." Camellia glanced at the clock. Ten minutes until Weston arrived.

"Okay. When I'm done, I'll go back in the storage room and rearrange those office supplies like you asked." He studied the box of scarves.

A heavy weight of guilt pressed on her chest over the sullen mood she'd created. Camellia found no words and nothing encouraging to say, not even to apologize.

As the entrance door opened, the dangling wind chime tinkled. Weston stepped into the shop.

He was early, and Camellia was grateful. "Hey…there. What brings you here?" The rehearsed dialogue dribbled from her lips, but she doubted Remy noticed.

His head popped up for a second, and then he was back to his task of folding scarves and laying them on the table.

"I dropped by to see what you've done to the shop in the past few weeks. I must say the place looks great." He nodded.

Camellia pressed two fingers to her lips to keep from laughing. His voice couldn't lack more emotion if he tried. Now, she felt less guilty about her own performance. "Nice of you to say. How's your work going? I hear you found a new historical site to explore and right here on the island."

"Yeah, things are going well." Nodding, he dug both hands into his pockets as he tilted his head toward Remy.

"Ah, Remy? You remember meeting Weston

Murphy?"

Remy grunted hello and nodded once.

"Well." Camellia stood, rubbing her hands down the sides of her thighs. "I'm making a quick run to the hardware store for those hooks we need. Then I'll stop for coffee. You can watch the shop, Remy. Either of you want anything?"

Remy raised an arm without looking up. "I'll take a large coffee."

"Same for me, if you don't mind." Weston gave a thumbs-up sign.

After one more nervous glance at Remy, she was out the door. She'd give them about twenty minutes or so. Beyond that point, her absence might look suspicious. If Weston's skills were as great as he claimed, twenty should be enough.

The stop at Browne's Hardware took five minutes. A sign on the front announced Browne closed due to a personal emergency. Now, she had plenty of time left to stop for coffee and a chat with Anita.

"Good morning. What a surprise. Where's Remy?" Anita greeted.

Camellia smiled. Anita was always cheerful, especially when talking about Remy. "Oh, he's in the shop chatting with a friend of mine. I'll be sure to send him next time, though. Three large coffees, two with cream, and one with sugar."

"Sure thing." Anita worked the machine to fill three cups then poured the creamer. "I must say, I was surprised to see Trina Averaux come to your shop. A couple weeks ago, I think. You two aren't exactly best buds, are you? Least ways that's the story I hear from Remy." Anita set the cups in a carrier. In the next second, she frowned. "Where was I headed with this conversation? Oh, right. Trina coming to your shop. Well, then I remembered Remy saying how they were cousins. Can you believe that news? Night and day, those two. Guess same blood doesn't mean much." She snapped lids on all three cups and rang up numbers on the cash register. "Comes to seven fifty."

Camellia fumbled through her bag while she puzzled over Anita's information. She laid money on the counter. "I don't recall Trina stopping by. I must've been out at the time."

"Uh huh, you were. You drove out to Noah's that morning. Remember? You stopped in for some breakfast egg croissants and coffee because you wanted to do something nice for him. Don't think you were gone more than an hour. A few minutes after you left, Trina showed up. Funny how timing can work." She shrugged and placed the change in Camellia's hand.

"Yeah, funny." Camellia glanced up at the clock. A half hour passed. She lifted the coffee carrier and hurried back to the shop. She hashed over the possibilities filling her head. Trina visiting the shop at the exact moment she left? Far from coincidence. What if Remy called her and let her know she was safe to come? Did he help her steal one of Camellia's designs? She jingled the store keys in her hand. Maybe the incident was harmless. Trina wanted to deliver a message from Laverne and tell Remy something, anything that had nothing to do with stealing.

She groaned. An impending headache forged its way inside. Lack of caffeine and sleep left her vulnerable to its force. She used the service door entrance instead of the front. Maybe she'd get the chance to overhear part of Remy's and Weston's conversation. However, when she stepped inside, total silence welcomed her, which worried her even more.

After a second's hesitation, she took pronounced long strides to the front. Good thing she had such a grip on the coffee carrier. At the sight of Weston's arm wrapped around Remy's shoulder while the boy sobbed, she grounded to a halt. She stepped behind the doorway, out of sight, then cleared her throat. "I'm back." She retraced her path to see Remy squirm out of Weston's hold and hop up from his seat.

"Coffee sure is the best part of waking up." Weston grabbed the carrier from Camellia's hands and set it on the desk. He removed two cups and handed one marked cream to Remy and the black with sugar to Camellia. As he wrapped hands around his own cup and sipped, he winked. He released a sigh. "Thank you."

"You're welcome." She stole a glimpse of Remy who faced the window as he adjusted the display. "You two getting along?" She returned her attention to Weston as she whispered.

"Swimmingly."

"Talk much?"

"A bit much." He grinned.

"Hmm. Good to hear." Camellia rolled her neck. As the caffeine kicked in, she felt her tension eased. "Maybe you'll share sometime."

"Depends."

"Depends?" Irritation replaced her fatigue.

"Depends on how interested you are in teen romance and the hot barista who works next door. Or baseball. Or grunge and punk music. Or…need I go on?" As he whispered his comment, his mouth nearly

287

touched her ear.

"Oh." Disappointment, sprinkled with a heavy dose of titillating arousal, left her uncomfortable. She backed away several steps and fanned her face.

"Too hot?" He smiled.

"Excuse me?" Her voice elevated, almost becoming shrill. When Remy turned with a puzzled frown, she smiled and nodded. After setting down her cup, she grabbed the coffee house menu from her desk. She fanned her face harder, glaring at Weston.

"The coffee." He pointed. "Is it too hot? Maybe you should remove the lid and give it time to cool a bit." The smile on his face spread wider.

Camellia had the urge to slap the amused expression off his face. She spoke to Remy but kept her glaring eye on Weston. "Remy, I need to speak with Mr. Murphy about supper plans. We'll be right outside the service door. Only for a minute. Okay?"

Remy nodded without comment.

"You. Come with me." Grabbing Weston's sleeve, she tugged him toward the back. Once outside, she found her voice. "What were you doing back there?" The loud and forceful sound of her words resonated. "If you think any of this situation is funny, well, I don't. Got it?" She poked his chest with her finger.

Weston held out both arms, palms up. "I wasn't being funny. How were any of my comments funny? Those subjects are the ones we talked about—girls, baseball, and music. I never cared for grunge, but I must say his comments make me want to check out one of those groups. Maybe we can go to a concert together. Explore new things. As for girls? We totally agree on that topic."

"Oh, for—you're impossible, you know?" She clenched her jaw. "Did he admit to stealing my design or not?"

Weston nodded. "He did. Well after all the other talk about girls, baseball, and music. He took a photo of one design and gave it to Trina."

"But why?" How could such a sweet boy, one she believed in, consider doing such a thing?

"Trina. She threatened to send him packing and put him in foster care, if he didn't do what she asked, or more like ordered him to do." He frowned and shook his head. "Lousy way to treat a kid."

"Sure is. Trina's despicable. She'll stop at nothing to get what she wants." Camellia sat on a bench situated next to the building. "Poor Remy."

Weston sat alongside her. "Good news is he wants to redeem his bad deed by helping us."

"He does?" Camellia scooted a few inches to the right, away from Weston.

"Yep. He'll be a willing participant in our scheme to undermine the infamous Trina." He slid closer.

As she glanced at the very edge of the bench, Camellia frowned. She was stuck. The warmth of his body elevated the temperature of hers. She flushed with heat. She clenched the menu she'd brought with her. In the next moment, she fanned herself, again.

"Well, now I know the coffee isn't what makes you hot." He chuckled, and then stood to take several steps toward his car. "Have a good day, Camellia."

She glared as he drove away. Her irritation was probably more from embarrassment than anger. He played with her emotions as if he enjoyed the effort. She couldn't be that easy to read, could she? He hardly knew her. They'd met only a few weeks ago. For most of those, she'd barely spoken to him. Yet, here she was, thinking all these things when she shouldn't be bothered. "I don't have time for playing games with you, Weston." She muttered to herself and stomped off toward the door. She had tons of work to do. The first task was to make amends with Remy.

****

Afternoon dipped into early evening. Camellia and Remy smoothed out the wrinkles in their relationship. She was relieved. "Okay, I think we're good. I'll draw up a design or two. You take the photos and give them to Trina. If she asks for them, that is." Camellia refused to guess who was more nervous. Although, Remy's troubled expression mirrored her own.

"She'll take the bait. She's too lazy to make her own designs."

Camellia scrunched her nose and shrugged.

"Have you seen her work? If a date of mine showed up wearing one of those ugly dresses, I'd turn and run the other way." Remy shook his head.

Camellia snorted with laughter. "Enough said. Tomorrow, I'll have the designs ready and the mock-up for the event flier. You can make copies at the print shop, right?"

"Sure. Then, evening is show time. Hey, I got this. Stop worrying." Remy puffed out his chest.

"Me? I'm not worried. Nope. Not at all." Camellia shrugged with a face of wide-eyed innocence.

"You can stop, and don't ever try acting. You stink at it." He scoffed with a shake of his head.

Camellia huffed and smacked his arm playfully with her hand. "Funny guy. Now, I say it's time to close up. You can go on ahead. I'll finish."

"Ah, Cam?" He scratched the side of his neck then heaved a sigh.

Camellia paused to wait.

"Thanks."

"For what?"

"Forgiving me. I did a rotten thing. She kept on pushing me, and I couldn't fight her, you know." He let out a sigh.

"Don't worry. We all make mistakes and learn from most of them. How else could we turn out so awesome in the end?" Smiling, she ruffled his hair and then returned to the storage room. "When you leave, flip the sign on the door. Okay?"

"Will do, awesome boss lady. See you tomorrow." He waved before shutting the door.

Camellia spent several minutes going over the books and closing out the register. After putting the day's profits in the safe, she made her way back to the front of the shop. She bolt-locked the door. While turning out the window display lights, she peered outside. A car sat in the public beach parking lot across the road. A blue Volvo. Camellia frowned. "What are you up to, Weston Murphy?" she whispered.

Rather than acknowledge his presence, she returned to the storage room, grabbed her jacket and bag then left. Getting in her car, she glanced toward the alley. No sign of anyone. No sign of Weston.

A light drizzle misted the windshield. She flipped the switch on the wipers to intermittent and exited the lot. Traveling down the boulevard, she discovered no sign of the Volvo, which puzzled her. Why return to the shop if he didn't plan to speak with her? Was he a creepy stalker or watchful protector? Or maybe he'd wanted to talk, really intended to but wimped out.

When Camellia arrived at the corner, she stopped. A right turn took her home. Left led to Noah's. She drummed her fingers on the steering wheel. Slowly, she aimed right. When she'd checked during the afternoon, a half-dozen phone messages lit her screen. All from Noah. She avoided answering. No words came to mind. None he'd want to hear.

She navigated into the driveway. All the windows were dark, except for one in the study. Dahlia doing some evening work on the mayor's gala, she guessed. "Glad someone is productive." The thought of staying up until the midnight hour to create designs, ones guaranteed to make her cringe with disgust, exhausted her. So little time, but she had to finish, despite her reluctance.

"Hey, sister o' mine. How'd things go today with Remy?" Freesia greeted Camellia at the door, bouncing on elevated toes and clasping her hands.

"Well, he admitted to helping Trina, and he also agreed to give us a hand with our plan." Camellia dropped her bag on the floor and tossed her jacket onto the coat rack.

Freesia tilted her head. "Why so glum then? You should be over-the-top excited."

"Like you?" Camellia eyed her sister's continued toe-flexing and the foolish grin on her face.

She stilled her body and frowned. "Remaining upbeat can't hurt."

"I guess maybe I should be happier." For whatever reason, she wasn't. She couldn't force her mood to lift, either. Another thought surfaced. "Did Weston happen by earlier this evening?"

Freesia shrugged. "Not sure. I was at the club most of the time. Why?"

"Nothing important. Okay, well, I am going upstairs to take a bath and then probe my brain for crappy design ideas. See you in the morning." She stepped around Freesia to climb the stairs. No more dwelling over Weston this evening. Besides, she didn't care, did she? As Camellia entered her bedroom, she groaned. Of course she cared. Why did life have to be messy?

Chapter 21

Morning sunlight filtered through the windows and warmed the shop. "Here you go. Take photos of whichever you want. Guess I shouldn't be surprised how creating such crap is so easy. I finished in less than an hour." Camellia handed Remy the folder and the event flier. She walked to one of the racks and rearranged dresses. "You know, you could go early this afternoon to pitch the event to Trina. Then come back here to finish out the day." Impatience grew inside like ugly weeds, squeezing off every breath she took. She wanted to be done with this underhanded mess and move on with her life.

Remy studied her in a moment of silence. "You don't like going along with this plan, do you?"

"I don't know what you mean." Camellia picked at her frayed sleeve and sat at her desk.

"Getting even with Trina makes you feel like crap, and like, well, nothing like you expected. Right? I feel the same. I so wanted to get back at her for treating me like I'm nobody." Remy crossed the room to grab his jacket. "Now, I feel like I'm no better than her."

"I'm sorry, Remy." Camellia heard the strain in her voice. The aching inside swelled like a pus-filled sore ready to burst. "Maybe we should can the whole scheme."

Remy shook his head. "Can't. I read the ad this

morning in the Charleston newspaper. She's probably seen it. I'd bet people are entering by now."

"Great." Camellia settled into her chair. "Yeah, well, we're marching forward and all that stuff." Her smile was weak, and the encouraging nod she offered him was probably pathetic.

"After I make copies of the flier, I'll swing by Trina's shop to see if she's there. Either way, I should be back within a half hour. Might as well leave these designs with you. Until...you know." Remy slid the folder across the desk. He gave her a hand salute and traveled out the door, the flier tucked inside his jacket.

A half hour passed and no sign of Remy. Camellia busied herself with straightening and reorganizing merchandise, opening emails, replying to emails, and filling up on coffee. By the time he returned two hours later, she was wired, frazzled, and ready to explode with energy. "Did she take the bait? What did she say? How did she react? Was she suspicious? What took you so long?" Camellia paused to breathe.

"Wow." Remy glanced at the dozen or so empty sugar packets strewn across the desk and the half dozen empty cups. "I leave you alone for a couple of hours, and what do you do? Overdose on caffeine." He clucked his tongue and wagged his head before bursting with a huge laugh. "Yeah, she took the bait, but I had to wait until she got her pedicure, manicure, and hair done. Not much of an improvement, if you ask me. Anyway, she wasn't the least bit suspicious. I don't know whether to be disappointed or glad. Accepting I'm in that gene pool isn't easy, you know?"

Camellia grinned and pushed away from her desk. "You are nowhere near that gene pool. In fact, I'd say you are in an entirely different ocean. I guess you'll need these designs, now?" She shoved the folder toward him.

He sighed. "You should've been there. She read the flier then bounced around the room like she was in a pinball machine, bumping into furniture, and jumping up and down. When she calmed enough to talk, the first words out of her mouth were to get more shots of your designs."

"Same threats?" She clenched her teeth.

"Word for word. You should've seen my reaction. I even managed a few tears, begging her not to send me away. Now, that's acting." He curled his lips into a sly smile.

Camellia smirked. "Whatever works, I guess." She expected to feel better—hearing how Trina behaved and having the proof she was a thief and a cheat. She ought to feel encouraged but didn't. "I'm gonna leave the shop for a bit. Maybe take a stroll past Trina's place, stop at the post office, the grocer's, and chat with people. Think it'll convince her you had time to sneak into my files and take photos?"

"Yep. But you don't have to." He smacked his thigh with the folder. "She's too busy dreaming about the win and her name in national headlines to get suspicious."

"Well, I do need to run some errands. If any customers stop by…"

Remy groaned.

Camellia pressed together her lips to keep from finishing her instructions. "You know the drill." She headed west on Divinity to pass by Trina's boutique. She lingered, as if searching through her bag, only for a few seconds, then continued on. First stop, the grocers.

Stepping to the door, she sensed someone approach her side. With a sideways glance, she smiled. "Good morning, Mr. Murphy. What brings you to Greco's? Run out of coffee?"

Weston chuckled. "As a matter of fact, coffee is on my uncle's list, plus a few other items. You?"

At this point, she turned to face him. Along with the greenish-blue color of his eyes, tiny specs of gold in them glinted from the sunlight. She'd never noticed before. Sandy blond wisps of hair fell across his forehead. He swiped them back as if they were a nuisance. "Coffee, filters, and creamer for the shop. Our supply is low." She grimaced, recalling her coffee binge from earlier this afternoon. Caffeine overdose was her explanation for all the fluttering twitches in her stomach at the moment. An inward groan vibrated through her.

"I hope our little plan is percolating." Weston cocked his head and chuckled. "Did you catch what I said? I used a coffee metaphor." He dropped the smile and cleared his throat. "Come on. I aimed for funny and clever."

Camellia lifted her head to stare at the ceiling. Then she lowered her gaze to face him. He made her smile inside and out. However, with a deliberate cough, she hid the grin forcibly stretching her lips. "Coffee humor. Corny clichés, which are so like you."

"I beg to differ. Clichés are the backbone of America's history, the life's blood of our culture, and the very definition of who we are as a people." With his chin tipped upward and one hand over his chest, he sang out. "God bless America."

Camellia erupted with a throaty laugh. "You are

such a cornball but very entertaining. The plan is, eh hem, percolating. Remy says Trina salivated with anticipation after his pitch. At this very moment, he's taking photographs of my not-so-fantastic designs. He'll deliver them this evening. I should be happy, beaming with joy, right?" She shrugged and rubbed her fingertips across her lips. "Then why is my stomach churning and my mood flat?"

Weston lifted two baskets from the stack and handed one to Camellia. "Guilt, maybe? I can't relate. I'm positively perky." He wiggled his shoulders and batted his eyes.

"You *are* a cornball. So, you're okay with our plan of entrapment? Not one ounce of regret?" She stepped around the display of canned soups in the center of the aisle.

"Nope. In fact, let's think of our mission as cathartic. Your ongoing rivalry, which has undoubtedly made you bitter and totally miserable, will be cleansed from your soul and leave you refreshed." He placed a can of decaf in his basket.

Circling him, she grabbed two containers of the fully caffeinated grind. "Whoa there, Dr. Phil. I see where you're going with this line, but your logic ends up hitting a brick wall. I'm fine. No bitterness. Not miserable. I'm ready to move on and leave behind the ghost of Trina Past. Got it?" The ruffle of indignation stirred, but she flattened that emotion.

"You know best." He shrugged.

After collecting a few other items, Camellia stepped up to the checkout counter and alongside Weston. On impulse, she nudged him. "Thank you."

"For what?" His brow wrinkled.

"For encouraging me and for believing what I do is important enough to fight for, I guess." A frown knitted her brows together. Noah's words haunted her more than Trina's actions. She knew him or thought she did. Truth be told, she let him bother her because his suggestions had some appeal. She couldn't shake loose of his argument about marriage, family, and the promise to shelter her from all things scary and threatening. Who wouldn't be tempted?

"You deserve encouragement and more. Giving up is a coward's way. You're not a coward." Weston set his basket on the counter. His gaze, however, remained on her.

Camellia tightened her grip on the basket of groceries. The queasiness, the elation, the pure joy of his presence, and his words filled her in ways she never experienced. "Why don't you stop by this evening for supper? My way of saying thank you." She blurted the invitation, surprising herself, and her jaw dropped, along with items from her basket. Oranges rolled across the floor while she and Weston scrambled to retrieve them. When reaching for the same orange, she bumped his shoulder.

"I accept your gracious invitation, Miss Holiday."

With a sweet and sensual tone, the words hung in the air. "Role-playing southern gentleman again?" She drew in a deep breath, and another as her heartbeat sped like a reckless hammering against her chest.

"Of course, you bring out my charming style." His hand gently touched her cheek. "Southern gentleman meets southern lady is an essential part in the script."

"Only we're not in a play," she whispered and pulled back to straighten her knees and stand. In a second, the spell was broken. This life was her reality—confused, torn, and broken. She needed to heal but without a man's help. Dismissing the haunting images of Noah's face, she stumbled over her words. "I should hurry. I'll see you this evening." She shoved money at the cashier and grabbed the coffee, creamer, and filters but left the oranges behind. She didn't need the vitamin C.

"You're silly and stupid and immature, Camellia Holiday." As she wove in and out of the pedestrians walking in the other direction, she mumbled under her breath. Clouds gathered and knitted together to cover the sky while a strong gust of wind whipped strands of hair in her face. "Why do you act like such a fool around him? You freeze, clam up, and then run." She shook her head. No reason to act that way. They were friends, which is what she wanted. Right? "Yeah, let's go with that explanation."

Forgetting about the other errands, she directed her path to the shop. Lucky for her, she found no sign of Trina as she passed her store. She touched her cheek and felt the heat. At once, she fanned her face. After rounding the last corner, she entered the shop through the back.

Remy stood at the door. He puckered his brow. "That trip was quick. What did you do? Run all the way?"

"What do you mean?" She draped the strap of her bag on the chair and set the groceries on the shelf. She swiped at the unruly strands of hair sticking to her forehead.

"Your face is red and sweaty. Never mind. I took the photos and sent them to my laptop. When I get home, I'll show Trina." He leaned closer and touched her arm. "You sure you're okay?"

"Yeah. Super." She sniffed. "Awfully windy and muggy out there. I think a storm is building. You should leave before the rain comes."

He raised a brow. "But it's only three."

"I think I'll close early." *Again.* "Did we get any customers while I was gone?"

"A couple. I put a dress and two blouses on hold. They'll be back tomorrow." He scratched behind one ear. "I can stay, you know."

"No need. I'm exhausted for some reason. Maybe I need to rest. I'll keep the shop open longer tomorrow to make up for the time lost. You go on home." Camellia kept her voice even. "Text me if you run into a problem with Trina, but I'm sure you won't."

"Got it. See you tomorrow morning." Remy pulled on his jacket and jogged out of the building.

Camellia waited until Remy crossed the parking lot then closed the door. She clenched her hands to steady the shaking. A headache pounded with intensity. She'd lied about going home. Right now, she wanted to be alone and sulk. At the front of the shop, she switched off the window display and slid shut the bolt lock. She studied the stack of fliers lying on the desk.

Fashion show and contest at Mayor Buell's Gala, Saturday evening, August third. Local designers welcome to enter. A cash prize and full article in Fashion Quarterly goes to the winner.

"You're absolutely right, Remy. We can't turn back now." Camellia lifted her chin and took hurried strides to the storage room. She slid a box from one of the top shelves to the side and stretched her arm to feel the shelf surface. She touched the bottle, grabbed hold, and then set it on the table. She didn't bother with a glass. Plopping in a chair, she twisted off the lid and tipped the bottle of whiskey. The sting of liquor touched her lips. After a few swigs, she sighed, her blood warming and pulsing through her body, and she finally relaxed. She set aside the bottle before pulling out her phone. She pressed a number on speed dial and waited.

"Em. I'm so glad to hear your voice. Do you have time to chat?" She recognized the tremor in her tone and cursed under her breath. She licked at the salty taste of tears trailing into her mouth and hiccupped. "I need someone to listen."

Within an hour, the whiskey and Emily did their job. Camellia eased back in her chair, legs propped up on a crate, and enjoyed the moment of familiarity. Taking a few more sips, she then capped and reshelved the bottle. After that night of the reunion party, she learned her lesson.

"You feel better?" Emily asked.

"Of course. Maybe not totally, but this booze and your pep talk will carry me through the next few days. Seriously, thank you, Em. Next to Gwen, you are the wisest and most honest person I know."

"Some might disagree, but I'll take the complement. He sounds wonderful, Cam. Don't blow it."

"I'm damaged goods, which is probably why I'm such a mess." Camellia frowned.

"We all are, sweetie. Messy moments are what make life entertaining and exciting and a real adventure, not knowing what we'll find around the next turn. Take your time. He'll stick around. Trust me. He's not going anywhere. I'd bet my Gucci bag and sunglasses on my words." She laughed.

"Well, if that's the case…" Camellia laughed with her. "I should go. It's late."

"Anytime you need me, you call. Got it?"

"Will do. Hey, I'm glad your mom is better. She's a rock." Camellia stood and stretched her legs.

"She is indeed. Dad, too. You have a great evening with your Weston. Serve up some dessert. A dose of sweetness always does the trick."

"Thanks, again. Night." Camellia ended the call and set her phone on the table. "I wonder if Zinnie planned on dessert." Dozens of recipes that Weston might enjoy shuffled through her mind. She shifted her thoughts to sounds and images of his face, his smile, his peculiar way of talking, his warm laugh, and so much more. She needed to call Zinnie and let her know to expect a guest at supper. Once more she sank into her seat. As she closed her eyes, pleasant images of Weston filled her head and made her smile.

A sudden, loud thud against the outside wall startled her awake. In mere seconds, the realization hit her. "Oh, no." A groan followed her glance at the clock. She jerked her head to face the window and the darkness outside. "No, no, no, no." She sprang out of the chair, and her phone clattered to the floor. She snatched the device and pressed the home number. Silence met her ear. She scowled at the empty gray square on her screen and stabbed the power button, but the phone didn't come to life. Of course, she took the cheap route with no land line. "Great." The one time she failed to be punctual had to be this evening with her supper invitation to Weston.

"I'm only a half hour late. Easy to forgive, right?" As she slid arms into her jacket and shouldered her bag, she mumbled words and excuses. She'd be home in ten minutes, if she hurried. The lights flickered for a second as she stepped toward the rear door. A howling wind hit the building, and the far corner window shimmied and strained at the edges. "Oh boy. That's not good."

She lifted one hand to open the door, but a gust of wind slammed it inward with a force strong enough to knock her down. She managed a quick hop in reverse and to the side before regaining her balance. Wind ripped through the opening and scattered papers across the floor—some plastered to the walls and ceiling, some escaped outside. She gripped the frame with both hands and battled the door, inch by inch, until it closed.

Camellia dropped her bag and settled into the chair once more, her head buried in the palms of her hands. A tingling sensation spread across her chest. Struggling to breathe, she sprang up to pace the floor. No phone. No way to escape. She was trapped.

Chapter 22

For someone whose name meant perfection, gratitude, and reasoning, Camellia added up to a pathetic zero out of three. She was never perfect, acted out of emotion rather than reason, and when was she grateful for anything or anyone lately? All she did was complain. No more than a half hour passed, but the wind intensified, and the rain pummeled the windows like the firing of bullets. With a long groan, she caved and let go of the tears. Between hiccupping and sobbing, she peered at the bottle through blurry eyes. "Oh, what the hell," she muttered and got up to snatch the whiskey from the shelf. This time she grabbed a glass and poured.

With her glass of fortitude in hand, Camellia ambled around the storage room and eventually made her way to the front. She scrutinized each detail. If nothing else worked in her life, Camellia's Cave was something. She was proud, and nothing would take away that feeling. She finished her drink and sat on the window display ledge. "Not Noah and his negativity. Negative Noah. Ha! I like that name." She smacked a thigh and laughed. "Well, Negative Noah, I won't let you get to me. You or your floosy, Trina. Yeah. Shove that one up your patootie." She stabbed a finger at the window then leaned back against the wall. She drew her knees into her chest as she clasped them with her arms.

The sobs generated through her but no tears fell. She was completely cried out, dried up and had no more to give.

A pounding on the window jarred her back, and she stiffened. Slowly leaning closer, she peered through the glass at a face smashed against the window with its ugly and distorted image. She screamed and barely heard a voice shout for her to open the door. Why should she open the door for some scary-looking face? Who goes outside in this weather? A crazy person is who. She shook her head.

"Come on, Cam. Let me in. It's me, Weston."

The words came through loud enough to understand this time. "Weston? Are you insane?" She hurried to open the bolt lock and door.

Wind, rain, sea oat grass fronds, and Weston blew their way inside.

Camellia closed the door then stood back. On unsteady legs she planted her feet, crossed her arms, and glared. "Whatever are you doing? Don't you know a storm's going on?"

Weston lifted his brows and shook his head. "I'm here because of you. When you didn't show up for supper, your family and I worried. I called your cell."

"But the service is out. I know."

Weston leaned closer. "Have you been crying? It's only a storm. No hurricane sighted. Should be gone by morning."

Camellia stuck up her chin. "I can take care of myself. You didn't need to come running like you're some knight rescuing me." *Stop being so defensive.* The sound of Emily's scolding words interrupted.

"You're welcome. Though I think I'll stick around,

if you don't mind. Nasty weather brewing." He grinned.

"Ha. Funny. Sure, take a seat." She glanced around at the one desk chair. "Maybe in the back?" After a few seconds, she twisted away. She forced herself to breathe evenly and concentrated on taking a straight path to the storage room, not the unsteady, wavering trail her legs wanted to go. How much did she drink?

"You okay? Need me to help you walk?"

The snickering of sarcasm was in his voice. "Nope. I'm good. Just a bit tired. We can sit here, if you like." She pointed at the bench straddling the wall and the one chair situated across from it. When she spotted the bottle of whiskey, she pressed fingers against her lips to cover a nervous twitch. No way to hide it now, though. Of course, he noticed, and his arched eyebrows told her he wanted an explanation. She sighed. "I got cold and bored. Maybe a bit frustrated. My southern friend with a kick helped."

"I'm sure it did. You mind?" He pointed toward the bottle.

Camellia shook her head. "Have at it." She quickly took the chair. Benches, she recalled, invited trouble. "I want you to know, I usually don't drink this much."

"I'm not judging." He smiled.

"It's just too much has happened this summer giving up my New York dream, coming home and feeling like a failure, and, now, dealing with that pain in my rear, Trina." She heaved her chest then let go of a sharp laugh. "I'm not handling it well."

"Join me?" He held up the bottle.

Once more, she shook her head. Emily's words echoed in her mind. *Don't blow it.* She bit down on her lip. Should she take her time or seize the moment? *He's not going anywhere.* Somehow, she spoke. "Maybe just a little one. I already have a glass, but you'll find another behind you on the shelf." She stood and was surprised how she'd regained her equilibrium. Quick, determined strides took her up front to find her empty glass. What was the harm? Maybe fate played her hand. With the storm and being stranded, maybe some unworldly force orchestrated the whole scene to give them an opportunity to talk, really talk.

Camellia returned and found her chair gone. As she searched the room, she wrinkled her brow. However, the impish grin on Weston's face told her something. "Where is it?"

"Where's what?" He flattened his grin and, with a head tilt, blinked.

"You know what. I want my chair." She crossed her arms and tapped her foot, driven by impatience.

"Tell you what. You answer one question truthfully." He sat in his chair and tipped his glass. "Then I'll give you back the chair. Deal?"

She chewed the inside of her cheek. "How can I trust you?"

"Camellia, I'm talking about a simple Q and A exchange. I can even sweeten the deal. You answer my question, and I'll answer one for you."

She held out her glass and contemplated the terms while he poured. "Stop." She covered the glass with her hand. "Okay. Deal. Ask me."

Weston tapped a finger against his mouth and lifted his head to stare at the ceiling. A few seconds later, he pointed at her. "Do you love Noah? And remember, your answer has to be the truth. I'll know if you're lying. I have a gift."

Camellia laughed with a snort. "A gift, huh?" She took a generous swig from her glass and let the liquid slowly drain down her throat, burning her insides as it settled in her stomach. "I do love him." Not exactly a lie, was it? She loved him for many things but hated him for others. For the hurt he'd caused. For the selfishness. She didn't voice those thoughts aloud because he didn't ask that question.

"How do you love him?"

"Eh, eh. Asking two questions breaks the rules. I answered. Now, give me back my chair." She tapped her foot once more, impatiently driven.

Weston reached behind a stack of boxes and slid the chair toward her. "Your turn."

"Hmm?"

"You want to ask me a question?"

"Oh. Right." None came to mind. Certainly not one she dared to ask. She settled for option two. "Do you love Sia?" *Touché, Weston Murphy.*

He blinked. "Not what I expected from you. No. I like her. She's fun to be around, but no, I don't love her. I need much more in a woman. Something deep and soulful."

His gaze burned with intensity. Camellia wanted to crawl underneath a table or anywhere out of his sight and that gaze. *Don't blow it.* She hitched her breath and grabbed the chair to sit. "Good because she loves Jaime Steele. Has she told you about Jaime?" She wagged her head. "Poor Sia. Jaime doesn't love her back. He toyed with her emotions and now she's—I tell you, somebody should warn him. She's not the kind you can play with. You can't tease her emotions. Trust me. She'll destroy your manhood."

Weston laughed. "Good to know. We're friends, Cam, only friends."

Camellia puffed up her cheeks and blew out air. Somehow, his admission relieved her. "The truth is Freesia hoped that being with you would make Jaime jealous. I hope that news doesn't hurt your feelings."

He crossed his arms and tipped back the chair. "I already knew, and I agreed to play along. What a shame. I think the guy's a fool. Sia is a great catch."

"Women aren't fish, Weston. You don't catch us." She scowled.

"I apologize and retract my phrasing. Sia is an outstanding woman. Any man would be lucky to date her."

"Huh. Much better." She lifted her lips into a smug grin.

He finished his drink and poured more into the glass. "Since we're stuck here for a spell, why not continue the game?"

"You mean like Truth or Dare?" Her heart raced. She couldn't take back the suggestion, right? She stared at the whiskey bottle. Then she glanced at her empty glass. "Refill?"

"Camellia Holiday, I was unaware you have a dangerous side." He poured the rest of the whiskey into her glass. "You wouldn't be hiding another bottle somewhere, would you?"

Camellia nodded at the cabinet. "No more whiskey. But behind the left door you'll find my welcome home present from Zinnie. She's an expert in picking out wine. The good stuff is all she ever buys."

"Bless your sister. She's got excellent taste." Weston eyed the bottle but then turned to study her.

"You sure you want to play Truth or Dare? I can be a ruthless competitor."

She gulped to dissolve the lump in her throat. "Ha. Game on, mister. I got this."

Weston sat on the bench and patted the seat next to him. "The rules require body proximity."

"Oh really? Why?" Her voice weakened while her heartbeat raced fast enough to make her dizzy. Or maybe the sheer amount of alcohol and lack of food in her belly caused her response.

"In case a question involves a dare with physical contact, which I do have in mind." He smiled.

She shoved a stray lock of hair behind her ear. A dose of courage dared her, and she couldn't resist. "All right. Let's play." She lifted from her seat and managed several steps toward him, feeling like she floated in a strangely induced trance. Approaching the bench, she then took a seat, inches from him. "You first," she whispered. She wiggled her fingers until she rested both hands in her lap.

"Any question is fair game, you understand. Here's mine." He stroked his chin. "Why do you keep some folks at a distance?"

"I don't." Her mind raced for a better answer. "I'm only cautious. I take my time to know people and to trust them. Isn't that approach wise?" Camellia got up to search through a utility drawer then handed Weston a corkscrew.

"To a certain point, I guess. Sounds pretty calculating and not much fun. Tell me. Haven't you ever let go and take a chance on your gut feeling?" Weston popped the cork on the wine and poured some into both their glasses.

"Gut feelings and impulsive behavior can have some ugly repercussions. My turn." She took the glass and swallowed a few sips, and then scratched her chin. She plucked a question from her thoughts. "Have you ever been in a serious relationship? I mean the kind that seems like your love will last forever?"

He closed his eyes for a few seconds and pressed his lips together.

She waited while he shifted in his seat and drew up one leg under his chin. "Care to make this round a dare instead?" A crooked smile formed; the woozy, medicated effects of the whiskey and blackberry wine worked their way through her. She stared at the empty glass in her hand. So much for correcting bad habits.

"No. I'll answer. Hard to pick out one of many lovely ladies in my past." He winked.

"Ha. I said the forever-lasting kind. Not some one-night stand or week-long fling." She scrunched her nose and stuck a finger in her mouth to gag.

"I know what you meant. Me trying for humor again, which always seems to be lost on you." He clucked his tongue and pointed. "Anyway, as far as true love goes, I've not been blessed with such a relationship. Yet."

"Hmm. Would've never guessed. Okay. Your turn." She extended her glass for a refill. This game put her on dangerous ground, but the time to retract passed.

"I do have a question I want to ask." He shifted to face her. "What are your feelings about me? Am I the forever kind?"

She downed the wine in less than a minute and squeezed her eyes. A dizzy sensation left her queasy. When she opened them, she was certain Weston sat inches closer. "I'll take the dare."

"Big mistake," he whispered and leaned forward, close and then closer. "I dare you to kiss me."

She opened her mouth but found no words. Not a one. His breath was sweet and warmed her face. So, now what? Freeze. Clam up. Maybe run. Or…she was spurred on by too much liquid courage. She stilled, her breath held, and she closed her eyes once more. Warmth from his lips touched hers as they kissed. Soft and gentle caresses overpowered her, like an aphrodisiac, better than the whiskey or blackberry wine.

His arms embraced her and his lips pressed harder as the kiss lingered.

She opened her mouth and moaned. He explored her face with his lips; each kiss sparked her emotions like tiny fireworks. She hitched her breath as he backed away. She wanted to protest, but the numbing effect of his touch left her unable to speak.

"You want to go on with the game?" he whispered the words into her ear.

"No. I'm good." She murmured then leaned into the hollow of his arm. "I think I need to close my eyes for a bit. I feel awfully tired."

"Yeah, me too." Weston cradled her.

A tiny hint of guilt tickled her conscience, but Noah was the one who caused their relationship problems, right? In a way, he drove her to this moment. She snuggled deeper into Weston's arms. Guilt could take a flying leap to someplace else.

****

"Well, aren't you two comfy-cozy?"

Camellia popped open her eyes and bolted out of Weston's embrace. "What?" She winced, kneading her

313

forehead, as she shifted to spot Freesia in the doorway. Sunlight fanned brightly behind her, and she grinned like a Cheshire cat with its self-satisfied smirk. Her arms crossed and head bobbed like a miss know-it-all. Camellia raised one eyebrow and gave her a sour stare. "What are you doing out so early?" Of course, she had no idea how early that time was. She remembered falling asleep, right after... She twisted her neck too fast to glance sideways at the warm body sitting close and knuckled the sore spot. "Weston."

He smiled lazily. "Hey there, sweetheart."

Camellia scrunched her nose and slid to the end of the bench. She turned her attention to Freesia. "This situation is not how it looks."

"Oh, I'm sure it is, but your affairs are none of my business." She grinned ear to ear and chuckled. "At least, you've told me, many times. No, I only came to see if you survived the storm. Obviously, you did, and then some. Hi, Weston. How's it going?"

"Well..." Weston started.

Camellia wiped both hands down her face then eye-daggered him a warning.

He rubbed behind one ear. "I'm great, and you?"

"Better and better." Freesia laughed.

"Stop with the innuendos, will you? Nothing went on." She stabbed a finger at each of them. "You're both wrong. I don't need everyone checking up on me like I'm some helpless child. Got it?" She stood, and her stomach lurched. How much *did* she have to drink? She dared another glimpse at Weston and blushed. Maybe not enough to forget that kiss.

"In that case, I'll leave you two. I've got tons of errands this morning before I head to the club. *Ciao.*"

She wiggled her fingers and pivoted on her heel.

"Wait," Camellia blurted. "You can't leave." She struggled against the inner voice telling her to run. "I mean, maybe you could wait until I make sure my car isn't flooded. I might need a ride home."

"Oh, I'd say your knight-to-the-rescue can take care of your needs." She winked. "Can't you, Weston?"

"Of course." Weston rose and stepped closer to Camellia then squeezed her shoulder.

Camellia pushed away his hand and glared at the sly grin teasing the corners of his lips. "But I have no reason to keep him waiting. I'll grab my jacket and keys. Won't take more than a second." As she pleaded with Freesia, she tapped her foot.

Freesia's gaze shifted back and forth between her sister and Weston. All at once she sighed and shrugged. "Fine, but hurry. I do have lots of busy work this morning."

"Cam." Weston touched her arm. "Maybe we should talk about…you know?"

"I don't think we have anything to talk about. Nothing happened." Camellia flushed. She picked at her blouse. Sweat dampened her underarms. She grabbed her jacket, bag, and keys. "Thanks, though, for stopping by and everything." She tensed at the sight of those two empty bottles on the shelf. The lump in her throat refused to dissolve, no matter how many times she swallowed. "We can do the supper date some other time. I promise."

She stepped to the doorway then turned to wait for him to follow. She chewed on her lower lip.

He remained still with hands shoved in his pockets. After a few seconds, in a slow pace, he passed by her to reach the parking lot.

"Have a nice day, Weston," Freesia called as he got into his car. In a split second, she spun to scowl at Camellia. "Well, aren't you the rude one?"

"Rude?" She drew back. "Listen. I won't argue with you about him. What I do and who I do it with is my business. We've covered that ground, right?" Nerves prickled and left her agitated.

"Totally agree. I'm talking about not showing up for supper on time. Why, you didn't even call Zinnie to let her know you'd invited Weston."

"Oh, yeah. I was a bit distracted. Crazy storm and all." Camellia silently replayed her conversation with Emily. Way to follow a friend's advice. Instead, once again, she ran away.

"One more thing. You need to shit or get off the pot."

Camellia knitted her brow. Her head pounded, causing Freesia's words to echo in her ear. "Meaning?"

"Don't be so sure he won't give up eventually. Guys have little patience, even the ones like him." Freesia stood next to Camellia's car. "I know I promised to stop interfering, but you have to make a claim and stick with your choice. Weston or Noah—you decide which one's best."

"Oh, hush." Camellia climbed inside her vehicle. The engine sputtered at first but finally turned over. "Okay, guess I'm good. I'll see you at home." She closed the door before Freesia could give her anymore sisterly advice. She was ashamed enough about the truth, her faults, and her fears. She was in worse shape than she imagined. Snapping her fingers and saying she'd change was a fool's wish. At best, the effort would take hard work and maybe a long time. Freesia or Emily. Which one was right? How long would Weston wait? Or Noah? Forever? She doubted it. Even if she wanted to be with one of them, she might end up with no one.

She mumbled as she exited the parking lot and onto Divinity. "Such happy endings you write, Camellia Holiday."

Chapter 23

Time ran out. She resigned herself to face the unpleasant moment with no other way to handle the problem. Dive in and get wet. Sink or swim. Shit or get off the pot, as Freesia said. Camellia sighed and slammed the steering wheel, accidentally setting off the horn. As the driver in front of her returned the sound, she winced. She stuck her head out the window. "Sorry!" The past several days, each morning and evening, she passed by Noah's road. Each time, she lost her courage but not this morning. This time would be different. Besides, avoiding him hardly seemed fair. Not to him, at least. He'd called and left messages. The least she could do was acknowledge his efforts.

She steered her car into his driveway. This undertaking needn't be difficult. She'd spend the morning with him and let her feelings guide her to make a decision. "If only." She gripped the handle and shoved open the door. With each step, she hesitated, her legs growing heavier. "You can do this." She raised a hand to ring the bell but then shoved her key into the lock.

"Noah?" She searched through the house, front rooms to rear, and found him tucked away in his office. She cleared her throat, which got his attention. When he faced her, a gasp caught in her throat. Ashy black circles underneath his eyes contrasted with his pale skin.

He shifted in his chair and let out a groan. "Camellia. You came." He winced then turned his mouth into a quivering smile.

She swallowed hard and slid a chair closer to his. "It's—I've had a busy week. I meant to stop by, but...how are you?"

"I've been worse. These exercises are a challenge. That physical therapist of mine is brutal." He chuckled. "I'm glad to see you."

Camellia sensed he meant what he said. His smile warmed and his face glowed, causing her heart to flutter. The impulse to wrap her arms around him and care for him challenged her decision to reject what they'd built on for such a long time. Her decision wasn't easy. "I'm proud of you, Noah. Those exercises must be hard."

He wheeled closer. "I missed you. You know I'm miserable without you. You can see I am, can't you?"

"I don't know." She sucked in her breath. "I don't think I can give you what you want. Not now." Okay. She got wet, dove in, and barely treaded water, but at least she wasn't sinking.

He leaned back in his chair and studied her in silence. His nod was curt. "I see. I guess your comment explains why you've avoided my calls and messages, which, if I'm not mistaken, had nothing to do with your busy agenda." He bit his lip and gripped the wheelchair arms. "Look, I have been patient, Camellia, because I love you."

"I know you have, but..." She braced her shoulders for what she had to say.

"Let me finish. I can wait as long as it takes." He

touched her cheek. "As long as you need, Camellia. You are the only woman in my life. We belong together. In time, I'm sure you'll see."

"Noah, please." Camellia shook her head but then stopped. He caught her off guard and went in another direction than expected. Confusion muddled her thinking. What else could she say? *We're done, Noah,* or *I can't love you that way*? In her head, Freesia scolded her. *Shit or get off the pot.* She had to say something to let him know. She clenched her hands.

"Why don't we table the discussion for now?" He smiled. "Change of subject. How are plans for the mayor's gala coming along?"

"Good." Camellia's mind raced. What just happened? Where was her decisive attitude? It disappeared and fell into that pot she got off of…that's where.

"According to my mother's gossip grapevine, Trina and you are in some competition. Another Trina escapade? I'm surprised."

He smiled, making his eyes twinkle, as if he enjoyed the idea. Camellia skirted the topic, leaving out the details of their scheme. "Yeah, well. This fashion contest fell into my lap. I couldn't resist. Maybe this opportunity is my chance to redeem confidence in my skills."

"Well, whatever makes you happy. Why don't you stay for lunch?"

Camellia hesitated. A miserable weight settled like a led balloon in her gut. She drew in several breaths, as if she suffocated from the way things shifted. Somehow, the train of her mission left the tracks. Was this act her being wishy-washy again, or was she duped by Noah's smooth talk?

"I have to run errands for Dahlia and Zinnie, and then open the shop. You understand." She stood and backed to the doorway. At once, she recognized the disappointment on his face. "Maybe some other time." She spun and nearly collided with the person coming into the room. "Oh. Sorry."

"Don't apologize. Barging in the way I did is my fault." A brilliant smile covered her face. "I'm Noah's PT. Angie Donovan." She extended a hand to shake.

Camellia took her hand and the time to study Angie who was blonde, shapely, and perky. "Glad to meet you. I'm Noah's, that is, my name is Camellia Holiday."

"Of course. Camellia. Noah's spoken of you quite a bit. We meet for his therapy every day, sometimes twice a day."

Her laugh contrasted with the grim tightness in her jaw muscles. "Every day, twice a day, huh?" Camellia gave Noah a questioning gaze. A blush reddened his face. "That's *quite a bit* of therapy."

"True, but he needs it. He's such a brave boy. I'm proud of my Noah." She lifted her chin and narrowed her lips.

"Well, I should let you two get started. Have a great day, Noah. Sweetie." Camellia let the words practically drip like syrup from her mouth. She hurried out of the room, leaving him speechless.

Moments later, she threw open the car door. All those doubts and suspicions crept back inside her. Despite the ridiculous nature of her thinking, the idea stuck in her head. Angie and Noah were more than therapist and patient. Okay, so maybe he didn't feel the same way. Maybe the attraction was all one-sided—Angie's side. After all, Noah and the family business were a prize catch. If she was that kind of woman, she'd notice. Camellia sniffed. A series of hiccups erupted as she blubbered. "Stop acting immature, will you? He deserves happiness as much as you do. Right?"

She'd prepared to come here and end things. Now, some convoluted jealousy triggered her desire to keep him. Why? She slammed one hand against the steering wheel. No way. Hadn't she despised guys who acted so fickle? Ones who love only when faced with the chance of losing that person? The pathetic behavior was such bull and not her way of handling people. She'd base her decision on how she truly felt about him. A queasiness rippled through her stomach. Staying on the fence became too comfortable. Somehow, she needed to find the courage to move forward and break off her relationship with Noah before it destroyed her.

****

"You look like crap." Freesia stood alongside Zinnia wrapping cookie dough in wax paper and shoving the packages into the fridge.

"No crappier than usual." Camellia poured coffee into a mug and snapped on the lid. Two days passed since her encounter with Nurse Perky, and her emotions still churned like a tornado in her stomach, whipping and tearing until she wanted to hurl or roll over and die. She despised herself for all those emotions growing like weeds and taking over her soul.

"Cam, please. This behavior has got to stop." Zinnia dunked her doughy hands in water to rinse.

"What? You mean the pathetic triangle I've become a miserable participant of, or maybe you're talking about this crazy contest scheme I let all of you convince me to undertake. Either way, I'm a living version of The Perils of Pauline."

"You can be the Calamities of Camellia. Right? Damn, I'm clever." Freesia pinched a gob of dough and popped it in her mouth.

"Stop." Zinnia smacked Freesia's hand. "You'll make yourself sick, not to mention we need twenty dozen cookies for the gala. Not two."

"Oh, please. I've hardly touched the stuff." Freesia shrugged then turned to Camellia and winked. "But Zinnie's right. I've told you before you…"

"Need to shit or get off the pot. Lord love a duck. How many times do I have to hear that lame expression? I'm trying, but my life keeps getting more complicated." Camellia waved her arms.

"Enough. Has Remy mentioned anything about what Trina is up to? Is she using your design?" Freesia asked.

"He hasn't been in this week yet. I gave him a couple days off to visit colleges." Camellia sipped at her coffee while reaching for her bag.

"Colleges? Can he afford to attend? Of course, he can apply for grant money or a student loan." Freesia frowned. "It's not easy. Trust me. After six months of saving, I still need a loan to cover half of my tuition."

"Hmm. I imagine something will work out, and he'll be fine." Camellia smiled. "Gotta run. See you at supper."

"Can you stick around a little longer?" Zinnia lifted her shoulders and smiled. "I have some appetizers coming out of the oven in a few minutes. You can help me decide which are better."

"Why not stay? Then you won't have to worry about lunch," Freesia added.

Camellia stared at them. "I better not. If I'm stopping by the post office for those gala programs before opening the shop, I need to leave right away." She stepped into the hallway just as the doorbell rang. Hurrying the remaining distance to the door, she opened it to find Weston. Her breath stilled.

"Hi, Cam. Good to see you." Weston hesitated only a second then stepped inside. "Sia wanted me to stop by and taste-test Zinnie's appetizers. When it comes to food, I'm always on board." He grinned.

Camellia nodded without speaking. She shouldn't be surprised. Freesia schemed, and she coerced Zinnia to help. She clutched her bag and skirted around him. "Wish I could stay and chat, but I have to open the shop." She avoided looking at him.

"Cam, we need to talk about that night."

They hadn't seen each other or spoken in over a week. "I know. I've been thinking and, well, I know you're right, but I can't. I need a little more time. Okay?" Her voice strained as she pleaded with him. How could she make any decision about him before figuring out her relationship with Noah? The Calamities of Camellia. Nothing could be truer.

"I'll wait but not too long. Have a wonderful day." Weston held open the door.

Camellia glanced over her shoulder. "Thank you." After the door closed, she released her breath. "Making progress." While walking out to her car, she grinned. "No running, no freezing, or clamming up. Progress."

The mayor's gala was two weeks away. While the Holiday household drowned in chaos, Dahlia and

Zinnia beamed with energy. They thrived on the pandemonium while Camellia and Freesia remained on the sidelines and did their best to help.

Dahlia sent out the order for two hundred programs. The same business printed the invitations. Camellia planned to pick them up at the post office. Afterward she retraced her route. Heading for the shop, she caught sight of Remy.

His hands dug into his pockets while he shuffled down the sidewalk.

Judging by his glum expression, he wasn't having a great day. She pulled over to the side of the road and lowered the passenger window. "Need a lift?"

Remy's head whipped around, his stare wide-eyed and unfocused. All of a sudden, his face softened. He approached the car, opened the door, and climbed inside. "Thanks."

Camellia tapped on the steering wheel, keeping rhythm to the song playing on her stereo. She hummed along without attempting the lyrics.

After a moment, Remy extended an arm to punch the off button.

"Hey there. I guess you don't care for classic rock? Van Morrison is sublime." She tried for small talk.

"Van Morrison is, *was*, a marshmallow. A sellout to the music market." Remy hunched in his seat and stared out the window.

Camellia drove behind the shop and parked. "You want to grab those packages from the back seat? Not the smallest one. That one belongs to Dahlia." She walked to the back exit and unlocked the door. Teens can be moody. She remembered well. Freesia was the worst, though she, Dahlia, and Zinnia weren't much better. Thing was, girls talked, they cried, and they confided all their problems. Boys clammed up and remained sullen, sometimes using unproductive actions to vent.

Reaching the storage room, Remy dropped the packages on the floor and hung up his jacket.

Camellia chewed on a fingernail and scrambled to think of something wise to say. "You watch sports?" Not so wise, more like lame. She groaned.

"A little football. Not much, though. Whenever they're at home, Laverne and Trina don't allow those programs." Remy took a path to the front.

"Speaking of Trina…" She paused, wondering how to go from there.

"I saw the dress. She had her friend, Tiffany, try it on. God, does it look awful. I mean the ugliest dress I've ever seen." He shook his head. "You want to know the sad part? I so hoped she'd decide to can the idea out of guilt or something. But there she was with that dress, all happy and proud. Showing off like the dress is the best thing she's ever done. Can you believe that crap?" Remy raked fingers through his hair until it spiked in all directions.

"No morals. No taste. Her behavior goes back to our college days. Sorry, Remy." Camellia gave him a hug.

"Yeah, still has me worried. Who says she'll stick to her promise? When she has no more use for me, she'll kick me to the curb. You watch." Remy sank in the chair and buried his face in both hands. "I'm screwed."

"No, you aren't." Her words and voice were assertive. She squatted to eye level and lifted his chin.

"No curbs. Got it?"

He jerked his head.

She grabbed his chin to pull him back. "You are one brave young man, Remy Averaux. I couldn't have survived all you've gone through. You're honest, so honest, I'm jealous. You won't go anywhere near a foster home. I have a plan. Besides, if no other way is possible, you'll come live with me and my sisters."

"Cam, you can't." He protested with a firm shake of his head.

"Yes, I can. This decision is one I can make without any doubts. I promise, Remy. I truly promise." Her voice caught at the edge of tears. She blinked them away, hiccupped, and gave him another hug.

He nodded before wiping his eyes with one hand. "We've got a pile of boxes in back. I'm gonna start unpacking, okay?"

"Sure thing. I'll be up front, working on the books and taking care of the customers. Holler if you need me." Her plan, if it worked, was mostly all she thought about in the past twenty-four hours, other than those about Noah and Nurse Pretty-Perky. At least this plan, unlike Freesia's to take down Trina, was a healthier sort of accomplishment and the kind to make her hopeful for redemption. Rather than satisfying her own needs, she'd take care of Remy's. If only the plan worked. A lot of details must fall into place or, like a row of dominos, they'd topple with a touch of one finger.

Morning marched into afternoon, which melted into evening. Exhausted, Camellia sat in the chair with her head resting on the desktop. Throughout the day, shop activity buzzed with customers and sales, mostly women who needed formal attire. The mayor's gala.

Every lady on the invitation list drove herself into an anxious frenzy knowing the event was days away. Dresses were ordered weeks before, and now they waited on racks for their owners to retrieve them. Next, customers would flock to the shoe store for matching accessories, and a day or two before the big event would be a trip to the hairdresser.

By the time six o'clock rolled around, she turned off the lights, locked the door, and staggered to her chair.

Remy found her in that spot after he returned from the post office to drop off packages. "You should go home." He nudged her shoulder.

"Yeah, I'm going." Camellia mumbled her words without lifting her head.

"Don't you have supper plans?"

"Hmm? What?"

"Weston Murphy and the make-up date? Or whatever you call it."

"Oh wow." Camellia popped up her head, and she rubbed both cheeks until they tingled. "Supper at seven. I had my phone alarm set. Or I thought I did." She scowled at her phone.

"Well, it's after six. I can close out the register and lock up if you like." Remy lifted his brows.

"Been taken care of. Let's scoot." She grabbed for the keys and her bag. As she exited the rear, Camellia replayed this afternoon's phone conversation with Weston. The encounter she had earlier at the house must have given her a jolt of courage. On impulse, she called to invite him, apologized for the short notice, but he didn't seem to care.

He agreed to come and bring a bottle of blackberry

wine.

She shuddered at the reminder. At least her bold action prompted the plan for another one. Turning onto her street, she sorted through possible solutions. She'd visit Noah, first thing tomorrow. She'd use plain words, no skirting around the issue, no innuendos, and no hints, just a straightforward confession. "I don't want to marry you, Noah. In fact, I realize I have feelings for someone else." Sure. Those words could work. A lengthy moan resonated from her throat. She passed the house and cursed under her breath then reversed to pull into the drive.

Camellia killed the engine. Glancing in the rearview mirror, she smiled as Weston steered into the spot behind her and exited the car. Her heart fluttered at the sight of him. This feeling was right. No more evading the obvious. She'd made her choice. "Glad you came."

Weston approached. "Truth is, I had no plans for the evening." He held up the bottle. "Wine, as promised."

Camellia entered the house and stood in the foyer, waiting for Weston to follow. "Sorry." She pointed at herself. "I didn't have time to freshen up. Why don't you go on back to the kitchen and chat with Zinnic? I'll be down in a few minutes."

In no time, she rushed downstairs to find Weston and Zinnia huddled in quiet conversation. "Did I miss anything?" Zinnia was easy enough to read. Her face blushed, and her mouth worked without speaking.

Weston, on the other hand, stood casually and shrugged at her question. "Not really. We were discussing the best way to roast a turkey. I prefer using a crockpot. I add carrots, celery, and mushrooms for flavor. The bird turns out juicy and tender. Isn't that right, Zinnie?"

"Ah, absolutely." Zinnia's head bobbed while she tapped her spatula on the counter.

Camellia scratched behind one ear. "Turkey roasting. Hmm. I'll have to remember that tip." She neared the stove, dipped a ladle into the gravy, and tasted. "Zinnie, you make the best gravy. How about yours, Weston? Did you share your recipe with Zinnie?"

"Okay, enough talk about turkey and gravy. Before you came, we were discussing the gala and how it will go. All right?" Zinnia slapped the spatula on the counter.

"You cave too fast. I think we had her." Weston winked at Camellia.

"You didn't. However, I don't care if you were talking about the gala and more likely about Trina. Doesn't matter to me." She took another sip of gravy.

"You don't care? I'm surprised. Trina's been so mean to you." Zinnia slid a tray of rolls into the oven.

"She does care, but she won't admit it." Freesia entered the kitchen. "You must get at least the tiniest bit of satisfaction, Cam. Otherwise, you're not normal."

"Okay, I'm not normal. However, I *am* done with Trina." The ladle dropped into the sink with a loud clunk. "And I *am* angry at how she used Remy. The boy is a true sweetheart. She threatened him with blackmail to get what she wanted, not once but twice. She's a disgusting fool." Camellia set out plates and silverware.

"You should be happy to get some sort of justice.

People like her never learn. The only way is to catch them in the act, teach them a lesson, and make them pay." She clenched her jaw muscles.

"Down, girl, before you explode." Camellia laughed. "I'll admit, I'm not sad she'll get her comeuppance, but I won't gloat. I have another idea."

"What's that? If the plan involves tar and feathers, I'm in," Freesia said.

"Tar and feathers, burning at the stake, scorned with a red letter across her chest—none of those are what I have in mind."

"Then what? Come on. You can't tease with those words and leave us hanging in the air." Freesia stuck out her lip.

"When she's ready, I'm sure Cam will tell us." Zinnia turned from the oven to smile.

"I will." She kept her focus on Weston. For a second, she was startled. The reaction lasted only in that second, but she'd read his look. He understood. She couldn't explain why or how she knew if someone asked, but she was certain. Somehow, he understood the reason behind her thinking and her decisions. Embarrassed to be caught staring, she snapped her head to face Zinnia. "Is supper ready? Should I go find Dahlia?"

"I'm right here." Dahlia entered the kitchen and handed Camellia a folded piece of paper. "Here's a message from Detective Hulsey. Since he couldn't reach you on your cell, he called the house. Anyway, I wrote down everything he told me."

"Yeah, my phone's been acting up since the storm." She bit her bottom lip and glanced at Weston then back at the paper in her hand. She unfolded it and read.

"Well?" Freesia asked.

"He has news about a stock certificate from Gloria." She reread the message. "Gloria's nephew found the document inside a box of her belongings."

"Why didn't this nephew send it to you?" Freesia circled behind Camellia to peer over her shoulder.

"I wonder the same thing." Camellia frowned. She didn't know what to think. Sure, having money to fund her business would be great, but right now, raising her hopes was premature.

"Well, you should call Hulsey and find out." Freesia crossed both arms and nodded.

"Maybe the nephew didn't find the certificate until recently." Dahlia said.

Camellia refolded the message. "Maybe. Freesia's right. I need to call Hulsey, if I want more answers." She glanced at Zinnia and the turkey platter. "But it can wait until after supper. Let's eat before everything gets cold." She settled into her chair.

Weston pulled out the one nearby and sat. He extended an arm underneath the table to find her hand.

The tingling sensation from his touch sparked her nerves while queasy discomfort settled in her stomach as she thought of Noah. First thing tomorrow, she'd tell him then.

****

"What did the detective say?" Dahlia asked.

Camellia worked alongside her to empty the dishwasher. Zinnia went up to bed and Freesia had a late-night gig at the club. Weston lingered for a bit longer until Camellia shooed him out of the house. With a quick peck on the lips, she promised to see him at the gala and not any sooner. She had too much to do.

"The nephew claims the certificate doesn't have a recipient's name, which would explain why he hadn't contacted me or the police." Camellia shrugged. "Anyway, whether the nephew is telling the truth or not, I don't care. I told Hulsey not to bother looking into the matter any further. Let the nephew have the stock."

Dahlia's eyebrows arched. "I thought you wanted what is rightfully yours. Isn't that the reason you asked Detective Hulsey to help?"

"But what if Gloria meant to give the stock to someone else? Maybe this news is some sort of sign and fate didn't intend for me to have the certificate." Camellia widened her eyes and pivoted on her heel. "In fact, Gloria's nephew can put the money to good use. I don't need it because I have all I want to make me happy."

"You sound like Mom." Dahlia smiled.

"If I am, being like Mom is a good thing, right?" Camellia draped the dishtowel over the oven handle.

Dahlia hugged her. "I'm proud of you, Cam. You've grown up quite a bit since you've come home."

"*Humph*. Says you. What I see is me tripping, bungling, and crashing along the way. When it comes to men, I've been indecisive, noncommittal, and a total wimp."

"You picked yourself off the floor after the Gloria scandal. You started a business. Whenever your family needed help, you've stepped in, and you've made new friends. I'd say the score reads—success a perfect ten and failure a zero."

Camellia warmed inside and her heart swelled.

"You have to see things that way. You're my sister. Surrogate Mom when Gwen is away. I do wish she and Robert would stay longer." She frowned.

"They're returning for the gala. Mom called this morning to let us know. In all the commotion over Hulsey's message, I totally forgot. Sorry." Dahlia gave her another hug.

"Great. I can't wait to tell her about…hmm, maybe not. No point in jinxing it." Camellia blushed.

"You mean Weston? He's such a good guy. I'm happy for you." Dahlia finished returning dishes to the cupboard.

"Please don't say anything. I'm not sure how we will work out."

"I think you should be the one to announce your news. I'm heading for bed. You coming?"

Camellia hesitated then glanced at the back door. "I think I'll sit on the porch for a spell."

"You want company?"

"Thanks, but I'd like to spend some time alone with my thoughts." Camellia waited until Dahlia disappeared down the hall. She grabbed a bottled water from the fridge and then directed her steps outside. She did have tons to think about, like what she planned to say to Noah tomorrow morning. She chose the best way to handle matters or hoped she did. The niggling of doubt and that need for perfection plagued her.

"Nothing is perfect. Get used to it." She grumbled and then settled into the chair. Frogs croaked in the distance while fireflies winked in the darkness. *Sometimes the heart knows what's best.* Gwen's words of wisdom resonated all through her. Maybe she'd lead with her heart and hope for the best.

****

Sunlight streamed through the soft haze of clouds, and the morning chirp of birds announced the start of a perfect day. If only her disposition and agenda matched. Camellia steered her car onto the street and headed west. In ten minutes, she'd pull into Noah's drive. In ten minutes, she had to prepare, get her act together, and know what to say. She groaned for the umpteenth time this morning but arrived at a decision and made a practical, reasonable choice about the romance in her life. At the same time, all she wanted was to wimp out, run away, or hide under a rug. She stopped at the corner and closed her eyes. The image of Weston's smile gave her courage and positive reinforcement.

When she arrived at Noah's, the jabbering in her head clamored so loudly she wanted to scream. How many ways existed to tell him their relationship was over? "Pick one and stick with your decision." As she approached the front porch, she lectured herself. Taking a deep breath, she unlocked the door.

"Noah? Are you awake?" She entered the foyer and made a path to his office. He spent most mornings in there, going over his business agenda. Getting closer to the doorway, she pulled to a stop at the sound of his voice. If he had company, she needed to wait and deliver the news later. She swallowed the sour taste rising in her throat. She couldn't delay any longer. Keeping the words bottled inside for even another minute was too much to handle.

She stepped into the kitchen and found Noah talking on the phone.

He nodded at her and raised one finger. "I have to go. I'll talk to you tomorrow, and thank you for such great news." He put the phone in his lap. A wide smile erupted, stretching ear to ear.

"You seem positively joyful. What's up?" Camellia set her bag on the kitchen counter.

"The best news ever." He bobbed his head then wheeled in circles before steering over. "Burke's Bathroom Fixtures is branching out and venturing north to open a store in Chicago. Isn't it great? We can make the expansion work. Profits are up, and the capital is there." He rubbed both hands across his face. "Dad will be so proud. I can't wait to tell him."

"How wonderful. I'm happy for you." She forced at least a hint of enthusiasm into her voice.

"Happy for us, Cam. You and me." He laughed.

With no more shadowy, under-eye circles and the return of color to his skin, he'd transformed into someone much healthier than he'd been the last time, which should make what she had to say easier. "Noah, I—"

"Wait, now. I have a wonderful idea. I need to be on site by the middle of November when they start construction."

"What? You're going to Chicago? How can you? Don't you think the time is too soon? I mean, your condition and all." Camellia ranted while clenching her fists. Why should she care? She forced air into her lungs. "Of course, you know what's best. You and Nurse Per—ah, you and your PT."

"I've got the doctor's okay. Besides, I'll have everything set up to stay there for a year or however long opening the store and training a manager and staff will take. No worries."

"A year?" Bracing one hand on the table for

support, she lowered into the chair.

"Or more." He nodded. "Now, here's where my idea comes into play." He wheeled over to where she sat and grasped her hands. "We can get married, planning for a simple wedding sometime in October. After we tie up things here, we'll move to Chicago. Maybe we'll decide we love the place and stay. If we can stand the cold weather, right?"

His laugh was a nervous twitter. She had no words, other than names to call him. Audacious? The word certainly fit. Stubborn? More than ever. Self-centered and oblivious? Got that right. He never once considered what she wanted. Her sacrifices meant nothing—not leaving family and her home nor giving up her career and business. She'd told him. Marriage wasn't in her immediate future. She wasn't even sure about their relationship. She'd told him, but she hadn't yet said the words she planned to today.

"I know telling you is sudden, and you're most likely in shock. Heck, I'm in shock. This news is life-altering." He patted her hands and then let go. "Give it some time, Cam. I want you to come with me. I love you."

Giving her head a hardy shake, she stood. She walked to the kitchen counter and picked up her bag. Clutching it under her arm, she glared at Noah. The anger built, flooding her insides from head to toe. Add chauvinistic to the list of naming calling. All her thoughts of the thousand and one ways to tell him they were over vanished. The anger gobbled them up, and now she had one thought left. "I should go. I'll see you at the gala, I suppose." She dug her fingernails into the leather of her bag, leaving pitted marks.

"But—aren't we going together?" Noah's mouth hung open.

Seriously? She sighed. "Maybe you can get your PT, Nurse Pretty-Perky, to take you. I don't have the time. Bye, Noah." She reached her car and struggled to keep her knees from buckling before sliding into the seat. She'd failed again. Her moment came and went. She wanted closure, but he stole the scene. Sad to admit, he wouldn't have listened. He never did. Only one way would work. She didn't like the idea, but after all, weren't he and Trina alike? *Teach them a lesson.* Exactly what Freesia said. "Guess this event will be an evening for lessons."

Chapter 24

"One Mississippi. Two Mississippi. Three—" Freesia teased and poked a finger at Dahlia's arm. "Will you stop? Checking your watch every five seconds won't make them magically appear. The band is coming. Trust me." She tipped her head and scowled. "Besides, panicking is not like you. What gives?"

"Nothing. Everything. I want this event to be perfect. Our business is riding on the success of the mayor's gala. We can't fail." Dahlia straightened the centerpiece on one of the tables.

Camellia scanned the hall to admire their work. Blue, red, and white confetti sprinkled around mini replicas of the state capital building with miniature flags perched on top. Crescent moons with a palmetto design set against a blue background to represent South Carolina were scattered across the walls. Mrs. Buell insisted on all of those details, and Dahlia complied.

"I think I see them coming." Camellia pointed to the far-left entrance of the town hall. Since last week when she'd paid her visit to Noah, she lived with her own sort of pins and needles. Needless to say, anticipating the arrival of Weston didn't help calm her. How did the saying go? Absence makes the heart grow fonder and certainly did in her case. With each minute of waiting, her longing to see him increased. This feeling was right in every way. How she arrived here after all her emotional vacillating and sheer fright of anything to do with commitment to relationships, she hadn't a clue. Yet, now, her heart swelled with love, and not one ounce of doubt remained.

"Are those balloons in the corner drooping? I ordered them filled with plenty of helium. What is the matter with people? I can't seem to cut a break." Dahlia carried on her gripes and groans as she marched across the floor.

Once again, Camellia studied the room and all its decorative details. Streamers with sparkling glitter attached to red, white, and blue balloons. They swayed to and fro, as if waving to the guests. Colors carried the theme of patriotism. Mrs. Buell would be pleased. She searched the crowd looking for Weston and spotted Trina. Her smug expression of confidence turned Camellia's stomach.

Camellia felt a tap on her shoulder and turned to find Remy and a young woman holding his hand. "Hey. You made it." She squeezed his arm.

"I want you to meet Trudy. She works for Anita. Trudy, this is—"

"I know who she is, Remy." Trudy nudged him in the arm then smiled. "Hi, Miss Holiday."

"Hi Trudy. I'm glad you came." Camellia eyed Remy whose complexion flushed bright red. So, this petite blonde with the shiny smile and blue eyes was the reason for doing the coffee runs every morning. Not Anita, who was too old for Remy anyway. Trudy was the one who captured his eye.

"Can I speak to you for a minute? Trudy, the restroom is near the back." Remy nodded and waited until she reached the far side of the room.

"What's going on?" Camellia frowned.

"I wanted you to know Trina is really fired up. She thinks she's got this contest won. When she doesn't hear her name called as the winner, I'm not sure how she'll react."

"Let me worry about Trina." She patted his arm. "You go have fun with your date, who happens to be a beautiful and kind young lady. And she serves up a great cup of coffee."

"Oh, I know. She's the best." Remy grinned then went in search of Trudy.

"Ladies and gentlemen, may I have your attention, please."

Like everyone else, Camellia shifted her attention to the stage.

Mayor Buell hugged the microphone with one hand while waving with the other. "First, let me say how grateful I am for y'all attending this event. The love and support of our community is what makes this job so enjoyable. Besides the beautiful South Carolina weather, right?"

Applause echoed throughout the room along with a few whistles.

At that moment, Camellia spotted Weston. He was deep in conversation with the town pastor and his wife. She trembled, and her heartbeat skipped out of rhythm.

"You okay?" Freesia leaned closer and, all at once, her smile widened. "Ah, I see. Weston, my sister's conquest."

"He's hardly a conquest." Camellia scowled.. "Shouldn't you be back stage changing? I'm pretty sure the mayor is about to announce the contest."

Freesia gave a salute. "Yes, ma'am. I'm on my

way, though your dress being last on the list gives me plenty of time."

Camellia narrowed her eyes to scowl.

"All right. I'm going." She wiggled a finger in Weston's direction. "Don't mess up your chance with him. I swear, if you do, I'm snatching him away."

"Oh, hush." Camellia gave her arm a playful swat. "Hey, thanks for filling in."

"Good thing I'm a perfect fit. How about your model getting the chickenpox? Bizarre, right? See you after the show." Freesia skipped through the crowd toward the stage door.

"Well, ladies and gentlemen, before I ramble on too long—I see my wife running a finger across her throat to signal the time—let me turn the mic over to Mr. Hench, owner and manager of *Fashion Quarterly*."

"Isn't he the handsomest man?" Gwen whispered over Camellia's shoulder.

Camellia laughed. "You sure are one lucky woman. Hi, Mom. I'm glad you could attend." She wrapped an arm around her shoulders and squeezed.

"Wouldn't miss this occasion for the world. Besides, with the magazine offering the prize and feature article, let's just say Robert insisted."

"You know, by legal rights with me being your daughter, I shouldn't be allowed to participate."

"True, but since Robert altered the rules and removed that particular clause, you're fine, sweetie," Gwen said.

"Mom, I have something to tell you." Camellia eyed Weston getting closer to where they stood. "It's about Noah."

"Oh? I imagined you'd talk about Weston." Gwen

smiled.

"Okay. Noah and Weston." She nodded. Loud applause drowned out her voice.

"*Fashion Quarterly* is proud to sponsor and present its first Coastal South Carolina fashion designer contest." Robert waved to the commentator sitting to the right of the stage. "Christine Farnell, ladies and gentlemen, will announce our models and describe the designs. Please see her after the show, if you have any questions about purchasing."

"You were saying?" Gwen stood closer.

"Later. It can wait." Camellia had to see what the local competition looked like. A dozen entries filled the agenda and more than she'd expected on such short notice. Two were from Charleston, several from the Lowcountry, including one from a small burg named Bluffton. Though she'd lived in this state nearly all her life, the name of the town was unfamiliar.

Unlike Trina, she took the competition seriously, with all its ups and downs. Somebody would always be better. If not today, then sometime in the future. Knowing and accepting that reality gave her an edge, kept her on her toes, and always progressing toward better.

Model after model strutted across the stage while Christine narrated. A couple of the outfits truly impressed Camellia. However, when number six strolled into view, her heart lurched with both excitement and envy.

"Misty is wearing a chic yet classic design by Susan Delaney from Bluffton. The black silk contrasts with…"

"How gorgeous." Gwen gasped.

"I'd say Ms. Delaney has a shot at first prize. Don't you think?" Camellia chewed on a fingernail and glanced at Gwen.

"Oh, I don't know. Call me biased, but yours is sure to be a winner."

"You're right. You are biased." Camellia grinned. "One of the many reasons I love you." She squeezed her shoulder and gave her a peck on the cheek.

Number eight was Trina's. Unlike with the other entries, an awkward silence followed this one, with a straggling of applause from a few polite folks.

Trina glued a smile on her face as if she didn't notice the lack of enthusiasm. Camellia winced as the model sashayed across the stage. The dress was worse than Remy described. In fact, the changes Trina chose made it uglier, if that instance were possible.

Within a half hour, the final entry emerged from behind the curtain. Camellia puffed out her chest with pride as she fixed her gaze on her sister. Freesia walked with complete grace like she'd modeled all her life. She orchestrated lengthy strides across the stage, interspersed with pivots from side to side when she paused. Her flaming red hair contrasted strikingly with the bright green taffeta.

"Ah, sweetie. There's no bias when I say that dress is pure heaven," Gwen whispered.

"Only because one of your other daughters is modeling." Camellia squeezed her hand. "I still love you for the compliment."

"You do?"

"Uh huh, I do."

Within five minutes, the panel of judges made a decision.

Once more, Robert climbed the stage. "We have a winner who will of course receive a five-thousand-dollar prize along with a cover article in our fall edition."

Camellia glanced across the room to watch Trina. Her complacent smile remained. Her hands braced on the chair as if she was ready to pounce at the announcement and claim her prize. Remy was right. She wouldn't take defeat well.

"Susan Delaney. For her exquisite black and tan classic dress. Susan, please join me on stage."

Everyone applauded while the winning designer wove in and around tables to reach the front.

"I'm sorry, sweetie. I know you'd like to have won." Gwen patted her back.

"Winning wasn't important, and never a part of my plan." Camellia smiled.

"Seriously? There must be a mistake. Susan who?" Trina stomped toward the stage while two volunteers sidestepped to block her way. "And where the hell is Bluffton? Is it even in South Carolina? I demand a recount."

"And there she blows." Camellia shook her head and mumbled.

"Why don't you sit back down and shut your pie hole?"

Camellia strained her neck to see who spoke. The voice sounded familiar, but she couldn't place it.

"You shut yours, missy. I don't pay you to have an opinion." Trina shouted while shaking a finger.

"Well, it's about time everyone heard my opinion, so don't you dare try to stop me." The other woman stood and waved her arms. "See these hands? These are the hands that save this despicable woman's lousy creations. Yep. You hear me. Though I certainly won't take credit or blame for that piece of garbage."

Camellia recognized the petite figure as the assistant, Selena Martez, who helped out in Trina's shop. Remy mentioned a thing or two about her, stating how mean Trina treated the poor woman.

"I told you to pipe down." Trina shoved her way back to the table. Her finger poked at Selena's chest.

"Not this time," Selena hissed and poked back. "You hear me everybody? Trina Averaux is a fake. She couldn't design her way out of a paper bag. I have to fix all of those hideous creations. She pays me next to nothing to do all her work. Do you hear me, Miss Trina Averaux? You're a fake, a cheapskate, and ugly to boot."

A few chuckles echoed throughout the crowd of guests, but when Selena added in the ugly comment, raucous laughter erupted. Enough to send Trina storming out of the room.

"Well, that scene was certainly entertaining." Gwen chuckled.

"Better than we expected." Camellia nodded as relief washed over her. "If you'll excuse me, I need to carry out my plan."

"What plan?" Gwen asked.

Freesia returned to the table, out of breath. "Did you see that showdown? Wasn't it awesome? Now, you've got your proof, Cam. You can take her." She glowed with excitement.

"I told you. I have another idea in mind." Camellia stepped around Freesia who blocked her way.

"But the timing is perfect. You can't let her go."

Freesia stuck out her bottom lip.

"Would somebody tell me what's going on?" Gwen interjected with more than her usual force.

"Not now, Mom. As for you, Freesia, I'm taking care of Trina my way. So, move." Camellia waved an arm.

"Fine. Ruin the best opportunity ever. I don't know what the plan is, but I say it stinks." Freesia called.

Camellia worked her way across the room to find Trina. She had a fairly good idea where she'd gone. In fact, she only needed to follow the screechy caterwauling emanating from the foyer where the judges congregated for a coffee break.

"I'm telling you. You made a mistake. My design is the best." Trina smacked the palm of her hand on the arm of one judge's chair. "The best."

"Miss Averaux, we've made our decision, and it stands."

Camellia narrowed her eyes as she recognized the person who spoke. The grim face of the elderly Flo Haverstraum confirmed she'd refuse to bow down to the demands of Trina Averaux.

She shook a wrinkly finger at Trina. "You listen to me. I know your mother. I know you think everyone should give in to whatever you say. Laverne spoiled you. You're a selfish brat. Better go away before I get really mad."

Trina opened her mouth to say more.

But Camellia grabbed her arm. "Trina, I need a word."

"I'm not through here." Trina wiggled and pulled.

"Oh, yes you are." Camellia grimaced and tugged harder, leading Trina around the corner until they were out of sight and earshot from the judges.

"I don't have to listen, especially to the likes of you." Trina snapped her words.

"I think you'd better. Your future depends on listening to me." Camellia spoke in a calm tone.

Trina's jaw muscles relaxed as she stared. "Go on, but whatever you have to say better be good."

"I know you stole my designs. Twice. I have the proof." Camellia lifted her chin.

"Don't be ridiculous." Trina threw back her head and laughed. "Your behavior is so pathetic. Can't accept the fact you aren't any good, can you? Why, you didn't win tonight. Isn't that proof?"

Camellia refused to let her provoke anger. "Neither did you, but I know the reason why. Remy confessed everything, Trina. We know you blackmailed him and used my design, altered it a bit, and entered it in the Charleston contest."

"You haven't any proof. That boy is a sniveling little liar. When I get a hold of him..." She frowned. "He'll be on the next train to Charleston, straight to the orphanage."

This time, Camellia let her anger explode. She grabbed Trina's arms and shook her. "You won't do anything to hurt Remy. You understand? I have enough proof to take to the authorities. If you don't listen, you'll be spending the next several years behind bars. Besides, your reputation as a designer will be over, if it isn't already after your little outburst everyone witnessed a few minutes ago." Camellia stopped to let her words sink in and wait for Trina to weigh her options. The transformation was almost theatrical. Trina's expression changed from angry to confused then to frightened, all within seconds. "Are you ready to listen?"

"To what?" Trina sniffed and blinked away the tears. "You've clearly stated what you plan to do. Aren't you satisfied?" She clenched her jaw then lifted her chin. "You are such a bitch, you know. Always have been and obviously always will be."

For a brief moment, Camellia considered being that bitch. However, she refused to let Trina anger her any longer. "I have another idea in mind, and my way doesn't include visiting the authorities or seeing you behind bars. Though I'm picturing you in an orange jumpsuit and it looks quite becoming, almost a perfect fit."

Trina opened her mouth.

But Camellia held up her finger.

"You go home with what little dignity you have left and act as if nothing happened to upset that huge ego of yours. Then, you apologize to Remy for forcing him into your despicable scheming. Afterward and from this day forward, you'll treat him with respect." Camellia leaned forward, millimeters from touching nose to nose. "And I do mean respect. No more talk about foster care or kicking him out of your house. You'll love him and treat him like you were his mother, if you actually possess a motherly bone."

Trina opened her mouth once again but no sound came out.

"Oh, and one more thing." Camellia held up a brochure she'd kept in her bag. "You see what's in my hand? A brochure from USC, the school with excellent programs, remember? I think Remy would like enrolling there."

Trina snorted. "Unless he sprouts genius brain cells and lands a scholarship, he can't afford to go."

Camellia widened her eyes and caught her breath. "Oh, but he can because of you." Camellia poked Trina in the chest. "You'll pay his way through college."

"But…" Trina's lips flapped.

"Oh, don't worry. You have a year to save the tuition. My deal stands. Take it or leave it." Camellia smiled with confidence. The feeling she had for that effort of giving back to someone she cared for and grown to love was better than anything she believed possible. Remy deserved every bit of happiness.

"I guess I really don't have a choice." She pursed her lips and folded the college brochure in one hand. "Then we're even, right? I'm seriously done crossing paths with you. You go your way, and I'll go mine."

"Not quite. I will be checking in from time to time to see how Remy is doing. I'm not going away, Trina. You better not cheat him out of this opportunity, like you do everything and everyone else. Understood?" She narrowed her eyes and tilted her head.

"Understood. Are we done?" Trina waved the brochure at Camellia. "Or do you have more threats to torture me with?"

Camellia shook her head. "Aren't those enough? Yeah, go. Spending time with you isn't my idea of fun either." She waited until Trina disappeared out the front door. Heading back into the hall, she found Freesia waiting. "Hey, Squirt. You looking for me?"

"Actually, I eavesdropped. Got to admit, your plan was better…lots better." Freesia wrapped an arm around Camellia's waist and squeezed. "Way to go, Cammie."

"Yeah, way to go. Now, let's get back to our table. I smell food, and I'm starving."

"You're always starving." Freesia laughed and took her hand, leading them around the people and tables.

Camellia shifted her head side to side. "Have you seen Weston?"

"Not since the fashion show started. I tried my best, by the way. Sorry you didn't win."

"No matter. The only thing important to me was that Trina lose."

"Ha! With that dress? Lord, it can't be uglier. Got to give you credit." Freesia stopped to wait for Miss Haverstraum to shuffle across their path.

"I tried my worst." Camellia shrugged. As she neared their table, her breath caught and then released with heart-throbbing blows against her chest. She stepped backward and alongside Freesia to distance herself. "Noah, you came."

"I did." He adjusted his tie and straightened the cuffs of his shirt.

His mother stood behind him, her face tense.

Camellia wondered why Nurse Pretty-Perky hadn't come along. "How nice to see you, Mrs. Burke." The greeting was received with a prim smile.

"I have something to show you," Noah said.

At once, Mrs. Burke placed her hands on the back of the wheelchair to steady it.

Noah gripped the arms of the chair and pushed. His stance wavered somewhat, but within a few seconds, he stood.

Mrs. Burke placed crutches in his hands.

Hesitating for a moment, he then took several steps

toward Camellia.

"Oh, my." A wave of heated emotion rushed through Camellia as she covered her throat with one hand.

"I wanted to show you the other day, but you rushed out of the house. I figured this event was a perfect time." Noah gripped the crutches and stood taller.

"How wonderful. I'm so happy for you, Noah." Camellia's voice trailed in a breathy whisper.

"I'm not through." He waited until his mother placed a small box in one hand. "When I told you I won't give up, I meant it." He opened the box.

Camellia covered her cheeks and gasped. "Noah."

Freesia peered over her shoulder. "Lord love a duck. Will you look at the size of that rock? Must be two or three carats."

"Please, Sia," Camellia murmured in her ear.

"Sorry. Your moment." Freesia stepped away.

"Camellia Holiday, will you do me the honor of becoming my wife?" He held out the ring. "Sorry I can't bend down on my knee."

Camellia swallowed. "I—" She glanced at each of her sisters and Gwen who drew closer.

At that moment, Weston appeared. His forehead wrinkled while his mouth turned down at the corners.

What was she thinking? *Tell him. Tell him, now.* The words screamed inside her brain. She turned her attention to Noah. "I'm sorry, Noah. I can't marry you. You'll find someone else, someone who'll make you happy and be the perfect soulmate, but that person isn't me." The silence was awkward as he trailed his tongue over his lips. Enveloped in their own little bubble, the chatter and clattering of dishes continued on around them.

"I see." He glanced over her head. "You're saying those things because of him, aren't you? He's put ideas in your head." He shook his head and stepped back. "You know, you used to be such a sweet girl."

She bit her tongue while the calm, but somewhat nervous, mood shifted. The anger grew, and defensive words exploded. "You're right. I'm not that girl. I'm a woman who's making my own choices and not letting you or anyone make them for me. Not any longer."

Noah's mouth formed a rigid line. "You're making a huge mistake, but I guess you two deserve each other," he snarled. "You know, Trina was right. She warned me years ago. You never loved me." His legs wobbled as he stepped farther back until he sat in his chair.

Weston stepped forward and grabbed a tight hold of her hand. "I think you've got that ass backwards, bud. *You* never loved her. Not the way you should have." He turned to Camellia and smiled. "Not the way I do."

He pulled her away from the family and Noah before anyone spoke and led her onto the dance floor.

The band played an up-tempo song, and Camellia tapped her foot to the beat.

"Care to dance, Miss Holiday? I do believe they're playing our song."

"Ours?" Camellia laughed. "We have a song?" She leaned closer at the touch of his arm around her waist. They twirled onto the dance floor. As she rested her head on his shoulder, a sense of belonging warmed her insides. Finally, she listened to the truth in her heart and found the courage to tell Noah how she felt.

"Listen. You hear the words?"

She concentrated for several seconds and then smiled. "Blackberry wine. You really want our friendship based on that song?"

He cocked his head. "Friendship? I was thinking more like a couple who see each other in a romantic sort of way."

"Hmm. A couple, huh? I don't know." She tilted her head toward the ceiling as if deep in thought. The tingle and spark of romance lingered and aroused her playful side. She wanted him, and the realization made her giddy.

He trailed the back of his hand across her cheek. "Please say we can at least see each other once or twice a week. Nothing serious, just two like-minded people getting to know each other better."

"Well, I am a busy working gal, you know. I hardly have time for much else other than building my career and running the shop." She pressed her lips together to keep the laugh from bursting.

"Give it some thought?" He gently nudged her chin.

"Of course. You free for supper one day next week?" Camellia lifted her shoulders and finally smiled. Her heartbeat soared, leaving her breathless. She wanted to give him and whatever this was between them a chance. *Give it time. He's not going anywhere.*

A word about the author...

Kathryn Long is a retired teacher and novel-reading addict who loves weaving intricate details together into stories readers can't help but enjoy. When writing and the creative muse take a break, this author loves to travel, especially to warm, sunny beaches, and to watch heart-wrenching movies with happy endings.

Kathryn lives in the City of Green located in northeast Ohio with her husband and little pooch Max. She is a member of Sisters in Crime and International Thriller Writers. Kathryn has several other published works.

To read more about this author, visit her website:
www.kathrynlongauthor.com

Another title by the author
A Deadly Deed Grows

Thank you for purchasing
this publication of The Wild Rose Press, Inc.

For questions or more information
contact us at
info@thewildrosepress.com.

The Wild Rose Press, Inc.
www.thewildrosepress.com